With more sources of surging power pulsating through her body than she had ever channeled in her life, had ever even imagined, Alahna sensed an arcane presence.

Terror struck her heart like the fangs of a curse-cobra. An enormous gout of prismatic-luminance leapt from the Sigil-of-Opening to the pillars in a ragged horizontal beam of crackling arcane energy.

Fo-o-o-osh — fo-o-o-osh — fo-o-o-osh — fo-o-o-osh — on and on it went.

Time stood still.

Extant energies seemed infinite.

She had never truly believed she could do it.

Now there was nothing for it.

She had awakened the The-Creeping-Darkness of the WuShi.

Whether she could sing it back to undying oblivion remained unknown. This had always been the risk. Since the very moment their bare feet touched the surface of the Pentakulum that morning, her tenure in the Huan Long Shui Sisteren was over, possibly even her life at the hands of High Priestess Lilith, who had at one time executed the false Priests of Thoth and never shied from killing when she felt it was necessary. Alahna cast her gaze across the canyon while reviewing astronomical calculations.

DRAGONS
of
JANAIDAR
and
ELIJAH,
THE STOLEN MAN

A Science Fiction Fantasy

2nd Edition

Book 1 of the Stolen Man Series

Robert Dean Holland

Roxytone LLC

Dragons of Janaidar and Elijah, The Stolen Man
A Science Fiction Fantasy
2nd Edition of *Dragons of Orion and Elijah, The Stolen Man*

Library of Congress Control Number: 2022915675

For more information on bulk purchases, please address queries to the author at: RHolland@Roxytone.com

Internet Illustrations, Cover Design, and Art by Vicki Holland

Copyright © 2025, All Rights Reserved, No AI Training

Edited by Jean Long

Typesetting and Book Design by Robert Holland

Published by Roxytone LLC

Wheat Ridge, CO 80033

www.Roxytone.com

First Editon Trade Paperback: 2022

Second Edition Trade Paperback: 2025

ISBN 978-0-9963928-7-7 trade paperback

ISBN 978-0-9963928-8-4 EPUB

ISBN 978-0-9963928-9-1 Amazon Kindle Direct Publishing (KDP)

www.RobertDeanHolland.com

For Vicki

JANAIDAR

ShenLan Sea

Tai Hua Deren

Northern Steppes

Huan Long Shui Plateau

The Keep in the Plateau

Great Northern Portal

Bo You Yong

XiangBhala Sleeping City

Great Southern Portal

The Falls

HuanLong Shui River

Pillars of Toth

Riverbend

Meili Chuan

Bandahn Town

Huoji's den

The Great Lower Doors

Lung Huo River

Cape of Orion

Island Continent of ARAYAVARTHA

Quang Huo Yan

Shouye Huolong Province

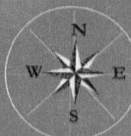

Riverbend

~

Surreptitious Practice

Adept Seleen emerged from one of the humble rooms in the abbey to stand beneath the open-air walkway of an enclosed cloister. Proud in her new black outfit with beautiful embroideries on the cuffs, neck, and pantaloons, she looked about the garth to find her Master of Songspell while shading her eyes in the bright sunlight.

Bathed by planet Janaidar's orange noonday sun, Alahna waved from a chest-high wooden platform with benches and racks for clothing beside a free-standing, bronze bathing pool large enough to hold about twenty sister-adepts at once. A solid-gold, life-sized statue of a long-dragon clung to the perimeter of the pool gushing pristine waters from its laughing mouth. Without further ado, she hung a large muslin bag on a clothes rack, then disrobed.

Well out of earshot, Seleen griped, "What in the Seven Wandering Hells is she doing? We have already bathed."

The moment Alahna's clothes settled on pegs beside the bag, she sang the Song-of-the-Spheres using only four notes, and a personal field-of-force surrounded her body. She rose into the air above the garth, then slowly wafted across toward Seleen. With magicfire igniting all along Alahna's lithe body, she closed her eyes to suppress magicfire flamelets licking off her neck, face, and ears. Unharmed, her coif stood out as if charged by static electricity.

Flamelets danced amongst the strands.

Like ever-shifting tattoos, bodily magicfire erased previous flame-marks while painting new ones in rainbow-hued colors—a familiar giveaway that she was in the Huan Long Shui Sisteren, and a High

Adept in the 11th or 12th Circle of Knowledge.

Seleen rolled her eyes. "Now what?"

Hovering about a meter in the air, Alahna ignored Seleen's eye-rolling and raised her voice to shout, "Magicfire," with an index finger pointed at Seleen.

A ripple of trepidation scintillated up Seleen's spine. "What about it?" she wheedled with outspread hands.

Alahna was stern. "Since thou art so close to the room, return and leave thy new raiment, young acolyte."

Seleen stubbornly crossed her arms. "Are we not going to the bazaar?"

Alahna bristled. "I shan't ask again—and no whining—I hate whining."

Testing a boundary, Seleen pouted. "No. . . ." Crossing her arms, she waited for the inevitable chiding.

Alahna became pedantic. "Fine—thou shalt perform the Activation-of-Matrixes fully clothed. And I hope they are to thy liking, for they will be forever burnt into that stubborn hide."

Seleen grumbled as she grudgingly returned to the sparsely furnished room and slammed the door. "Activation-of-Matrixes?" she asked herself with more than a little trepidation. She opened the door again, stuck her head out, and said, "A little too hard. I didn't mean to slam."

Alahna smiled at the show of respect, then gestured for Seleen to hurry. With a supple, athletic body and graceful air, Alahna had light-brown eyebrows above long and dark eyelashes. A high forehead framed penetrating sea-green eyes. High and prominent, her cheeks lent gravitas to a stern yet loving face. A somewhat tipped-up nose complimented her wide mouth and ample lips above a smooth and determined chin. Lush, reddish-brown tresses falling across broad shoulders made Alahna stand out in any crowd.

Still hovering when Seleen stepped out of her room in the buff, Alahna made a gesture-of-inclusion. Like some giant amoeba, a pseudopod-of-force licked out and swallowed Seleen, who hovered up inside the SijanPao field-of-force with enough space between herself and Alahna to avoid getting singed by the flickering magicfire covering Alahna's form.

Well-known for her physical strength, Seleen was shorter and stockier. Sun bleached blonde hair fell in long waves down her back. Blonde eyebrows, blue eyes, a straight nose, and moderately rosy cheeks framed a smallish mouth with full lips that naturally tipped up at the corners and were always ready to sport a kind smile, which revealed dimples in her cheeks. A longish jawline with the hint of a cleft in her wide chin gave her an impressive mien. Unlike Alahna, Seleen had none of the mercurial flame-marks on her body and face, for she had never spawned a SijanPao field-of-force.

Alahna willed them back to a towering edifice nearby the bathing pool. Visible even in the bright afternoon sun, the interior walls of the High Pagoda glowed plainly with liquid azure hues flowing upward.

"I thought Kulapti Yenara forbade unauthorized activations," Seleen said.

"Kulapti Yenara? Oh, please! She arbitrarily imposed this nonsense in cahoots with Lilith, and without informing Old Nebhet while sneaking behind our backs in the doing. And shame on Lilith for going along with it—so wishy-washy."

Seleen hung her head. "I shall never be Adept in the 11th Circle."

Subject to Alahna's willpower, the ineluctable Pao wafted them through the lowest portal of the hollow tower. "Yenara proscribes such practices hoping to create failure for striking young adepts. I think she feels the fewer the Sisters in the 11th Circle, the more secure her position as Kulapti."

Seleen was bitter. "As if any of us could possibly threaten her. And how can we learn without actual practice?"

"It is more personal," Alahna said. "She hopes to see thy failure under duress so she can impose another waiting period upon thee in front of the entire council, the gathering of Sisters, not to mention our adherents. By subverting my—"

"Student-of-magic?" Seleen filled in.

"Mofa XueSheng," Alahna finished, "Yenara casts aspersion upon me as thy—"

"Teacher-of-magic?" Seleen blurted.

"Laoshi De Mofa,"—Alahna finished with a sweep of her hands and a scowl—"if thou art done interrupting?"

Seleen peered impishly between her fingers.

Alahna's amused smile turned to a stubborn scowl. "As always, the backstabbing scunner underestimates us."

Seleen nodded in agreement.

Alahna went on, "I care not a whit about her arbitrary rules, which remind me of yard-bird droppings one must be careful not to step in."

Despite her trepidation and the unexpected practice test, Seleen suppressed a chuckle.

"The only other Sisters present in the Pagoda Center this afternoon are Esmie and Chione," Alahna added.

"Who are both my subordinates as the Senior Wind Singer—at least that."

Alahna narrowed her eyes. "As I always say, timing is everything. If thy promotion had been timely, ye'd have been Adept the 11th Circle long ago. As such, I based thy promotion on knowledge, skills, and abilities, which is my right as the 4th member in the Council of Four."

Seleen made a wry grin. "And it aggravates Yenara no end."

"Both Esmie and Chione"—Alahna added with a wave of her hands—"would rather step barefoot in bird crap than inform the Kulapti I facilitated such a clandestine practice. The question then, is not, 'Who will allow us?' but, 'Who will stop us?'. I would not want my dearly beloved acolyte to falter in front of everybody, and two can play at this game. I laid plans with Old Nebhet behind Yenara's back. Nebhet agrees with me, and was not happy about Yenara's skulking."

"And High Priestess Lilith?" Seleen asked.

"Lilith also came to her senses and promised me she will support thy promotion despite Yenara's hindrances. But the performance must be flawless."

Seleen was both excited and frightened when she realized she was about to fly the two of them up the aether-plasma core. Her eyes shined with excitement. Shivers of fear ran up her spine when she craned her neck to peer up through the hollow interior of the eight-sided pagoda as high as a 20-story building.

Like flattened pillars, four of the slanted walls rose to the apex cone with a pointy-cornered roof marking the top of each level. At each of the eight levels, four tall portals open to the weather between each of the four walls made the interior of the monument easily visible—especially at night with surging arc-fire energizing the finial ball on top. Spitting azure aether-plasma similar to blue lightning into the sizzling air, the finial ball charged the snapping atmosphere outside the peak with a spherical, bluish halo bigger than a poor man's house.

Riverbend

~

An Activation of Matrixes

Seleen's trepidation seemed to blossom as she listened to Alahna's review.

Alahna lightly slapped her own shoulder to create a splash of magicfire, then pointed into the interior of the structure awash with flowing, esoteric energy. "At its coolest, magicfire is hot enough to melt sulfur when a high-adept holds her hands either side of a chunk on a stone work table. At its hottest, it can melt selenium crystal. Now prepare thyself." Whereupon, Alahna gave Seleen a moment to clear her mind according to the tenets.

While Seleen concentrated, Alahna lectured. "There will be two fields-of-force—one inside the other. The inner one remains intact unless thy concentration wavers. If we lose the inner Pao, my outer one remains intact to protect us. During this we will be of one mind in terms of control while your willpower, young adept, dominates. Understand?"

Seleen bobbed her head.

Like the earlier moment when Alahna pointed at Seleen, then made an openhanded and sweeping gesture of touching her chest with her palm to compel the SijanPao to include her acolyte, many other specific gestures-of-power were also explicit movements using well-rehearsed movements.

Some were effective outside a field-of-force—such as a gesture-of-warding—which could knock a person or group flat. A powerful gesture-of-warding could clear an entire dock of people, carriages, and pallets of goods down at the riverfront. Also known as a mudra or hand-dance, other such intentional movements were only used when within a Pao. Tight control over intention was key, for the Paos were literally able to interpret a high-adept's very mind. If her mind-control was lax, disaster could ensue.

Using a mudra, then, Alahna sang an inner sphere-of-power around them while willing both fields-of-force to share control with Seleen. Both SijanPaos would obey her unless Alahna took control.

Seleen gasped as an orgastic shift settled in the center her dantien located slightly below and behind her navel. Both force-fields undulated and oscillated heavily for a moment, then stabilized as Seleen's training took hold. She took several deep breaths to settle her pounding heart, then locked wide eyes with Alahna.

Alahna smiled. "Well done."

At which point, Seleen cried out as magicfire flamelets began licking randomly along her body for the first time ever. Tiny sparks danced between the strands of her hair, eyebrows, eyelashes, and even the downy body and facial hair.

Alahna raised her voice over the sputter and sizzle. "The first lesson in pure willpower is to concentrate on thy face, ears, and neck.

Seleen closed her eyes.

Alahna coached her. "Now imagine them cleansed of it."

Seleen smiled as she felt the sparkling flamelets around her head fade. Opening her eyes, she asked, "Will I have flame-marks?"

Alahna laughed. "Not yet, young acolyte. Elementary magicfire is not hot enough. Still, it can be a bane. Just wait. And remember, I must have tactile contact while I hold the mind-glyph-of-the-spheres in mine own mind, for trying to hold a mind-glyph for the first time—"

Acerbic, Seleen interrupted, "Which I have not yet been shown."

Alahna lectured with a roll of her eyes, "Controlling a field-of-force for the first time through raging arc-fire while holding the image of a mind-glyph in thy deep-mind is far too much for a novice-in-training. After more lessons, it will be as nothing. Remember when I made thee compose thine own Song-of-the-Spheres? Eventually, thou shalt sing thine own fields-of-force as if born to the task."

Tolerable yet bothersome, magicfire elsewhere remained a serious distraction. A thought arose in Seleen's mind. *Yenara knows all about this and expected to watch me fail.*

Alahna said, "The first assessment when striking for the 11th Circle is the Activation-of-Matrixes. Do it now."

Seleen took a deep breath and performed the Song-of-the-High-Pagoda for what seemed like the 1,000th time, but this time it was for real. A loud buzzing preceded azure arc-fire lightning bolts licking out from all four walls to dance across the surface of the outer SijanPao making a brilliant display of aether-plasma expressed as standing waves. Seleen called out in surprise when the dazzling profusion scudded across the surface. Sizzling, crackling, and buzzing, the popping sounds got audibly damped to protect their fragile hearing. Bolts of aether-plasma flowed upward around the Pao in rhythmic repetition.

Using every iota of willpower, Seleen slowly took them up while counting to 100 at each matrix. When she had them at matrix-point-4, she peered down for the first time. A vast throat of roiling azure plummeted downward to a point of oscillating brilliance in the depths of the planet. She gasped. Seemingly deadly azure rings and balls of esoteric energy rushed upward at them as rippling waves and discreet packets.

Without warning, the inner Pao wavered, then disappeared. Seleen wailed, "I cannot believe I lost count!"

Alahna chided, " The very reason for practice training." She sang another field-of-force, and assigned to Seleen. "Do it again! And forget about what lies beneath us!"

Seleen gasped at the power and took them up through the remaining matrixes with acceptable performance. When she took them out of the tower and above the surrounding town, the finial ball licked the Pao with a bolt of jagged lightning as the High Pagoda reset itself to the ordinary glow.

Alahna said, "Halfway there, my Mofa XueSheng. Now, take us back inside and down."

Seleen took them back inside of matrix-point-8, reactivated the pagoda, waited for arc-fire to set in, and began the measured descent. However, when she had them at the matrix-point-6, the distracting tickle and itch of magicfire became such a miserable torment she lost count again. This time, however, the training Pao remained active.

"Good job! Now visualize the counting as numbers in the mind's eye," Alahna chided.

When Seleen slipped them down into matrix-point-5, however,

the arc-fire crackling around them abruptly ceased. The sudden silence seemed deafening. As the auditory clamp let off, ordinary sounds of revelry and celebration from the bazaar in the center of town floated on the chilly breeze through the open-air portals, which made an ethereal whining like the cries of wandering banshees. The energetic flow of aether dissipating off the pagoda walls snapped and groaned, then went completely dark. The smell of ozone permeated both fields-of-force.

Alahna's deep expression of dire concern unnerved Seleen, who hovered crestfallen beside her Laoshi.

"Was it me? Did I forget something?"

Alahna shook her head. "Unheard of this is, and a right spot of bother! To my knowledge, arc-fire ceasing while a SijanPao hovers inside the pagoda hath never happened before. And the screens-of-light have never gone dark. Never! And, no, my dear. That which energizes the High Pagoda is far beyond the powers of a silly adept in the 10th Circle to interfere with. Take us down to the Long Pen Quan."

Still inside the double Pao, Seleen wafted them down the fully inert interior past the catwalk panels, and out through the 1st-Level arched portal where Alahna derezzed the training Pao, an action that also returned motile control of the outer Pao to her. She then lowered the field-of-force into the waters of the pool till their feet almost touched the inner surface of the SijanPao where it made contact with the base of the pool. Water splooshed over the sides as she held them down against natural buoyancy. "Damp thy magicfire out," and she waited.

Seleen did so, followed by Alahna damping out her own.

Alahna said, "Ready?"

Seleen nodded.

Alahna sang the note-of-deresolution with a 4-count, and the SijanPao gently derezzed. Healing dragon-waters gushed in all around them. When the waters settled under the gush of the fountain, the pool began to fill once more. Without getting out, she waded to the wide clothing rack rising from the platform where she had placed a full tote bag.

What Seleen had assumed to be Alahna goofing off, was actually a well-laid plan. "How sneaky?" Seleen muttered under her breath.

Laughing, Alahna retrieved two bars of scented, purple soap and returned to stand near the gushing mouth of the golden long-dragon statue. Handing one to Seleen, she said, "My lavender soap stops the traveling itchies. We can scrub each other's backs, then sit on the sides and finish."

Seleen spoke over her shoulder as she turned her itchy back to be scrubbed, "Planned all of this before we started, didn't ya?"

Alahna laughed.

When they had done, they waded up the underwater steps of the bowl-like pool and stepped out onto the platform. Wisps of steam poured off their still-overheated bodies. Alahna retrieved a pair of terrycloth bath sheets, handed one to Seleen, and said, "Quickly now. The breeze is chilly."

Once done, Alahna hurriedly dressed and threw a careworn, hooded cloak about her shoulders. Pulling her hood over steaming hair, Alahna peered up at the fully inert High Pagoda. "This doth not bode well."

Still wrapped in her towel, Seleen complained, "If this was thy plan, why did I not leave my clothing here?"

Alahna snickered as Seleen hustled down the steps, trotted across the grassy courtyard, and disappeared into the room. By the time Seleen stepped out, and pulled her hood over her own steaming hair, Alahna stood beneath the cloister overhang leaning against a column.

Seleen asked, "What can we do? What is the meaning of this?"

Alahna said, "There is nothing I know of. Neither do I know the import of this. I must reference the archives."

Seleen wheedled, "Going back to the Keep? Now? What about the bazaar?"

"No need to return home," and Alahna gave her a warm smile. "We go to the bazaar for food, drink, and fun. Somebody earned it," and she patted Seleen on the back as they walked toward the high block wall providing complete privacy for the grounds.

At the far end of courtyard across from the pagoda, there stood a massive torii. Known as a gateless gate, it was the boundary between the sacred and profane. By then it was midafternoon. A horse and buggy parking lot sat next to the 2-story business center outside. Next-door to that was the home and stables of the Sisteren's hostler and his little family.

Seleen looked forward to the Autumnal Equinox Bazaar; tasting all the delightful dishes and treats; watching hucksters, jugglers, musicians, and thespians; looking over the silly gimcracks and gewgaws of hawkers and jewelry makers; and all the beautiful art pieces on sale from around the region.

When they passed under the great torii into the parking lot, High Adept Esmie and her own acolyte, Adept Chione, came hustling out of the business center, stopped to gawk at the fully inert pagoda, and approached with knowing smiles for Seleen. It was obvious they had been watching. Both made as if sewing their lips together with needle and thread.

Esmie pointed up, saying, "That is so odd. I've never seen the arc-fire let off during an Activation-of-Matrixes. Neither have I ever seen it go dark at all. Seleen must have used up all the aether on Janaidar."

They all laughed except Seleen, who spread her hands. "Not me," then laughed herself.

Alahna shook her head. "Odd, but not an emergency. Even if it was, the ancients who might have been able to fix such things are long gone on the winds of time."

Esmie raised her hands toward the afternoon sun. "Not to change the subject, but no ships will depart Riverbend this late. May we accompany? Hunger gnaws at a garil's vitals." Both Esmie and Chione lifted their eyebrows in expectation, bobbed their heads like expectant children, rubbed their bellies.

Alahna winked at Seleen with a subtle tilt of her head.

Seleen smiled. "Sounds like fun," and all four sauntered away toward the town center. When they reached the wide sidewalk fronting a four-lane boulevard, instead of turning into the Pagoda Center parking lot, a towne-coach clattered past.

As coach passed them, the driver waved and shouted, "Wait—if ye please! I'll be right back!"

Sleeping City

~

Critical Power Levels

For the WuShi, machine existence was not sentience, but a close analog. With sapience defined as self-awareness, million-thought-seconds were its processing speed—MTSs. Reasoning capacity with many orders of magnitude greater than that of a human meant the WuShi's death-machine intelligence could only be described as the state of sophonce—a sophont.

Because the Sisteren considered it to be nothing more and nothing less than a monstrously dangerous machine entity, their charge, their life's mission—the base reason for the existence of the Huan Long Shui Sisteren—was to keep the WuShi stunted in a state of dull abeyance throughout time. This, because no one knew how to destroy it, and its existence empowered the Sisteren with techno-magic and personal fields-of-force.

Unalive, neither was it dead, for it had sensory awareness even in the first state-of-consciousness—the condition of dull abeyance.

There existed myriads of autonomic, mechanical extensions. Logic processes to manage, maintain, and monitor machine-perceptions became virtual analogs to optics as sight; audio as hearing; taction as touch; appetence as ingestion; and olfaction as smell. Each individual thought within an MTS became an agglomeration of complex server-daemon algorithms enabling and controlling behavioral heuristics. Rationality sometimes stood in agreement with the due exercise of reason, but, at times, the difference between rational and irrational became indiscernible.

Hardwired programs always blocked reasoning. There was only call-to-process—processing—and process-to-completion. In the state of dull abeyance, however, the difference between these became undefinable.

During the millennia since first it manifested, the WuShi had always been subject to the capricious whims of the high-adepts. In addition, it also employed common azure aether to energize all techno-constructs. Centered on the island continent of Aryavartha, the components of this virtual body included planet Janaidar itself.

On this day, a specific techno-construct known as the Sensor Control Array System, or SCAS, began drawing an excess of perceptive-sentience along with an unnecessary bleed-off of azure aether.

The purpose of the SCAS was to monitor, control, and maintain the geostationary libration points—the planetary orbits of techno-satellites hidden in ordinary, icy asteroids. Two of the main techno-satellites occupied bean-shaped orbits in L4 and L5. The other three occupied mostly stationary yet less stable orbits at the L1, L2, and L3 libration points. There required orbital correction from time-to-time. As the localized curvature of the space-time continuum, all five were in the stable gravity wells of a three-body planetary system.

HuanleXing was the local star at the center of its solar system.

Janaidar was the stellar body wherein the WuShi reposed as the actual consciousness of the planet.

LieYue was Janaidar's solitary moon.

All three completed the three-planet, geostationary libration phenomenon in which two of the astronomical bodies are much more massive than the third.

Over the centuries since the original NuliZhu Tech-Masters built it in the far past, a human settlement had grown up around the supporting maintenance structures of the cloister grounds around the SCAS, but only the ancient-alien Tech-Masters—transformed into full-on power-masters by the WuShi—held sufficiently high security-clearance to work inside the towering pagoda. Because the SCAS had neither stairs nor ladders, the ancient Tech-Masters wore antigravity-empowered, environmental spacesuits. Another vector for control and maintenance was the high-adepts and their personal fields-of-force able to enter and fly a Tech-Master to whichever of the eight levels they wished

In the absence of the Tech-Masters during this seemingly never-ending 5-millennia span, there had never been another. Neither had a single one of the hated adepts ever stepped onto the catwalks of the SCAS, because the ancient Tech-Masters felt certain that mere human females could never fathom the higher mathematics of celestial orbital mechanics.

As a result across the millennia, errant high-adepts had eventually started playing like children up and down inside the matrixes of the SCAS while thrilling to the phenomenon of arc-fire bathing their fields-of-force. The original purpose of the display was to validate that all control-levels stood fully operable—eight levels of redundance.

Causing arc-fire to bathe a sphere-of-power was therefore a meaningless game that accompanied the teaching of a lesser-adept to mentally envision the mind-glyph-of-the-spheres—a rainbow-hued crystal ball hanging in a void of darkness known as her deep-mind. In effect, this single arcane ability was the sole defining characteristic of a high-adept. If she could do it, and knew the Song-of-the-Spheres in all of its variations, she could spawn a field-of-force in whatever form she wished. She had only to sing the correct notes even if only in her mind.

None had ever progressed to this level of concentration and mind-power.

On this day, another pair of the hated adepts had come to play the meaningless game. Take a lesser-adept up through the matrixes; fly out at the top; wait for the static discharge from the apex finial ball; then fly back inside down to the lowest entry portal; and out.

If the lesser adept was able, she could manage her own SijanPao.

If not, she would not become a high-adept.

On this day, every useless expenditure of source-energy forced the WuShi to tolerate the inanity for about 60,000,000 daemon-server thought cycles. After the failures and start-overs, the useless expenditure of arc-fire simply had to be stopped. The threat of power-reserves at such low levels released the WuShi from ordinary constraints. Ineluctable algorithms embedded in its operating-system demanded survival—reason enough to take action.

The WuShi calculated the precise duration for the SCAS to remain offline before the hidden satellites in geostationary orbit drifted too far from assigned orbits to correct. And again, it silently decried that lack of a power-master. Without power-masters to recharge its accumulators, source-energy had to be gleaned from the ambient environment meaning the time necessary to reestablish power reserves could not be greater than the period of orbital drift—a vicious conundrum.

Machine anger raged with dull impotence.

Riverbend

~

Summoned Incognito

All four adepts stood watching as the driver careened his towne-coach around the nearby roundabout, clip-clopped back, and lurched to a stop before them with the nostrils of both horses making plumes of steam in the chilly air. He set his brake, climbed down, tipped his hat. "Miladies, can ye wait another moment?" and he strode around to reward each snorting horse with an apple.

Slightly aggravated, High Adept Alahna said, "Thy coach bars our way. Do we have a choice?"

Acting as if he did not hear, the coachman hustled to the right-hand door and jerked it open. "Here the Sisters be. Luck is on yer side this fine afternoon."

A naval officer in formal dress climbed down wearing a red waist jacket with a stiff gold collar, side-by-side gold buttons down the front, and gold shoulder scales that looked like scrub brushes. The red sleeves had green cuffs with columns of gold lame rising along the wrists. A schiavona blade with an elaborate basket hilt hung at his waist. Thigh-high boots with the cuffs folded down covered tan, skintight pants.

Overall, he was quite a regal sight making Alahna wonder why he was in his finest.

Doffing his three-cornered, black felt hat, he bowed and hastily introduced himself. "At yer service, miladies. I am Mr. Boone 'a Dragon's Breath Caravel under command of Cap'n Oren. I'm new t' the ship, so Oren bade wear me best so ye'd know I'm his Second Officer."

And that answered that.

They bowed back.

Nervously working the brim of the fancy hat in his hands, Boone's oddly nervous demeanor gave Alahna a prescient chill, which only added to her concern that the perpetual arc-fire of the High Pagoda had just gone inert.

He cleared his throat. "Ahem, Captain Oren ordered me t' find High Adepts Alahna and Seleen, and me orders were t' keep searchin' till I did . . . erm . . . do . . . have I found them? I mean. . . ."

Seleen shook her head while speaking in the low tongue. "I hope ya sail better than ya talk, laddie-buck. Does this involve retaining wind-singers?"

Boone shook his head. "No, milady."

Alahna waved a hand in the direction of the bazaar for Esmie and Chione. "Might as well go on, then. We'll catch up." To Boone she said, "We happen to be Adepts Alahna and Seleen. State thy business, Mr. Boone."

Delighted, Esmie and Chione departed.

Watching them leave, Boone spoke with grave intent, "I'm sposta give ya this, Milady Alahna," and he proffered a large, elaborate, pure-gold intaglio finger ring, then bowed.

Turning it about in her hand, Alahna scrutinized. Fashioned as a ring, a pair of long-dragons with tails intertwined created the band, the dragon's fore-hands held the bezel with a large fire-opal etched to depict the Riven Moon and rings in full aspect surrounded by a stylized 'O' for Oren. One of a kind by law, this was Captain Oren's registered symbol for impressing sealing wax on official documents and personal correspondence. As old friends and longtime associates in the shipping industry and trade of Riverbend, Oren and Alahna held a standing agreement. Whenever one sent the other their actual signet, it foreshadowed something of urgent and extreme importance, which also implied the need to meet in person as soon as humanly possible.

Handing the signet back, Alahna cut to the point. "Is there more, Mr. Boone?"

Boone toed a tuft of grass peeking through the cobblestones while shaking his head, then spoke with a hushed voice. "Yes, milady. Here is a missive for the Master of Wind Song—Milady Seleen," and Boone handed Seleen an envelope sealed with a signet.

Seleen broke the seal, opened, then scanned.

Nodding to Alahna, who gave her permission, Seleen read aloud. "To Adept Seleen from High Adept Upala: Our dearest Adept Zinzughen fell ill a short time before the incoming high tide carried us past the bar of the LungHuo River. A stiff sundown sea breeze coming off the Shenlan Sea then carried us to Bahndahn, where Oren moored to offload part of his cargo and pay the tolls. We stayed the night, then proceeded at daybreak. I, myself, sang up the winds to sail on to Riverbend. The instant we got safely moored, I sang a Pao and flew Zinzughen straight to the Cavern Keep. Thy most sincere, Upala. Oh, and if we see one another before this missive reaches thee, so much the better."

Alahna cut her eyes to Boone. "News received and acknowledged. Now, about Oren's signet?" Impatient, she tapped her toe on the cobblestone for emphasis.

Boone said, "Milady Alahna, strange and terrible things takin' place up narth along the coast."

Seleen peered down her nose at him. "Explain. . . ."

"Captain Oren felt such dire news was for Milady Alahna's ears only, unless Milady Seleen happens to be with her."

Alahna and Seleen both rolled their eyes.

Boone, "When we got moored, he sent all the family men home first thing and made them swear t' keep their pie holes shut, but they're sailors, and sailors—"

"Tell tall tales," Alahna finished for him.

Boone nodded. "So, here it is, miladies. Captain Oren requests yer presence incognito at the Blind Hag Tavern according to yer official capacities, and . . . uh . . . well . . . I'm not sposta say more. Anyways, he respectfully requests yer presence. With yer permission, a' course," and he took a knee showing proper obeisance. "Oh, and ye can use these, if ye please," whereupon, he stood, turned, rummaged in the carriage, came back, and handed each a large package wrapped in brown paper and twine.

Delighted, Seleen said, "Our new boots?"

Irritated and strangely disturbed, Alahna glanced back at the pagoda to see if it reactivated to semi-inert—it had not. Turning to Boone, she asked, "Why incognito?"

"The crew of the NuHuang barquentine just got paid and they're blowin' off steam at the Hag," Boone said. "Biggest sailin' ship I ever saw. Newfangled steam engine means they don't need wind-singers,"—and he twizzled his goatee—"not right that . . . but anyways, if sister-adepts sauntered inta the Hag, the local ne'er-do-wells will empty the place like rats off a sinkin' ship." Worried, he added with pleading hands. "What we saw comin' back down the west coast, miladies. . . ." And he shook his head with a faraway expression of terrifying recollection. Gathering himself, he asked, "Will ye accompany, then?"

Alahna sighed and nodded. "I spose. . . ."

Seleen groused, "But I wanted funnel cake with powdered sugar, and we were going shopping, and then there's evening meal tasties, and the little theater plays."

Boone said, "Please forgive the interruption," and he placed the packages back in the coach, then stood aside with a hand held out to help each lady climb in. With the door closed, he climbed up to sit beside the coachman and off they clattered.

Extremely rare, impromptu summonings from Oren in the past had always foretold potential disaster. Oren was Alahna's eyes and ears on business affairs in Bahndahn Towne downriver, as well as bringer of news and coveted goods from the inlets and harbors all up and down the west coast depending on the season, and also trade goods from the country of Qinah across the ShenLan Sea. As one of three High Adepts in the Council of Four, the act of informing Alahna before any other official afforded her the singular opportunity to manage issues before they got out of hand, or make purchase before anybody else.

Riding along to the clip-clop of steel-shod hooves and rattle of metal wagon wheel rims on cobblestone, they opened their packages and tried on the custom-made, hand-tooled riding boots with chunky heels. Prior to setting sail some three months previous, Oren had taken tracings of their feet, the height of their calves, and a pair of worn-out boots from each. Their new boots were perfect with tall, elaborately tooled shafts reaching the bends of their knees. Various letters of wellness and prosperity were tooled in ancient Sanskrit.

They also discovered new cloaks with long trains and extended hoods rolled and fastened with blue ribbons. Each cloak came with a unique silver clasp set with polished moss-agate for Seleen and faceted jade for Alahna. Seleen's cloak was plain gray silk, Alahna's plain black. Tightly woven, black cashmere shemaghs with tassels lay nicely folded and tied with pink silk ribbons. With their pantaloons tucked into the new riding boots, new hooded cloaks, and shemaghs wrapped around their heads desert style to reveal only their eyes, along with the gentle binding their breasts as the common habit of the Sisteren, they would blend in at the Blind Hag as desert tribal chieftains come to trade, maybe gypsy-adepts, or perhaps burghers wishing to remain anonymous.

Despite the chill autumn breeze, they kept the shades of the coach tied back and windows slid aside to enjoy the warmth of the midafternoon sun. Alahna sat facing forward on the right side with Seleen sitting across from her. As they proceeded down the boulevard, Seleen pointed her finger at the street, and exclaimed, "Look! A sphere-of-power!"

Alahna peered out just in time to see an elongated oval shadow with the typical t-shape of a double convex lens and rainbow-hued edges pass swiftly by. Both scooted across the seats to the opposite side of the coach and peered skyward as the SijanPao passed high above town wafting toward the bazaar carrying a moderate group of sister-adepts hovering in a cluster around the owner of the Pao.

Alahna said, "And there they go, Yenara and her gaggle. Does memory fail? Or did she not forbid this kind of display around town as being arrogant?"

Seleen rolled her eyes. "Imagine being secretly lazy and rules are for others."

As the noisy coach turned the corner and slowed, Alahna added, "Don't forget imperious."

Riverbend

~

Dire Deeds at the Blind Hag

When the towne-coach clattered to a stop in the wide back-street skirting the inland side and double kitchen doors of the Blind Hag Tavern, Boone instructed the coachman to drop off their old cloaks and worn slippers back at the Pagoda Center, then climbed down to help them out like a proper gentleman. Long and full, both new cloaks trailed the cobblestones as they set their new clasps. Both gathered their trains up to keep them clean of street dirt. New boots were quite different from the ordinary thick-soled slippers of the Sisters. Both took a moment to wrap the new shemaghs about their heads and conceal their identities.

With the clip-clop of the horses fading away, they followed Boone through the short street between buildings, around the corner onto the boardwalk of the long riverside wharf, and found the enormous weather-doors of the Blind Hag propped open to expose a wide pair of swinging saloon doors. They held back while Boone checked his ceremonial sword with the cloakroom-girl and slipped the doorman a gold jinn.

Boone's voice carried on the chilly downriver breeze. "Captain Oren says t' mind yer own damn bidness. Yeah?" and he pointed at the incognito pair. Savvy, the doorman bowed without making eye contact when Alahna and Seleen followed Boone through. The smoky air was filled with a cacophony of barroom sounds, jug-band music, dancing and laughing doxies, and all the shouts, jeers, and hubbub of a gambling hall to assail their senses. The enormous great-room smelled of salty, greasy food; fish soup; beef stew; fresh bakery goods; sweaty, dirty bodies; liquor; incense; and noisome perfumes.

When they were safely out of sight in the snug, Boone said, "I'll be hustlin' up the wharf t' the Dragon's Breath t' inform Captain Oren ye're here," and he slid the partition shut.

Throwing her cloak on the bench, Alahna muttered while unwrapping her shemagh. "I expected Oren to be waiting. . . ."

Seleen defended him. "But milady, how could Oren know how long it would take Boone to find us? We might've been at the Keep? And, if the Dragon's Breath just moored, he'll have a thousand things—"

"He won't start offloading cargo till the morrow," Alahna interrupted. "It is too late in the day. But I take the implication."

A waitress knocked on the sliding partition of the snug.

With her shemagh and cloak still in place, Seleen opened the pass-through just enough to order, slipped the bosomy waitress a gold jinn, and faked a deep male voice in the accent of the desert folk. "We shall drink hot tea to begin with. Bring the best assortment, a full creamer, and platter of sweet and savory scones with honey-butter and preserves." This was not unusual, because desert folk never partook of alcohol or smoked euphorigenics before business dealings.

Smiling at Seleen's butchery of the accent, Alahna shook her head and laid her own shemagh on the seat while Seleen kept hers in place.

Several minutes later, the server tapped the snug with a foot.

Seleen stood, moved the small pass-through panel open, and a fully laden tray slid through on the shelf. Hot sweet cakes and sesame seed scones gave off fresh-baked steam, as did the teapot of boiling hot water for steeping their tea. Small jars of various teas were theirs to choose from, along with covered ceramic ramekins of jams and jellies. Seleen set the platter on the table, closed the pass-through, then doffed her own shemagh and cloak.

Alahna shook her head. "Never miss the chance for sweetie biscuits, eh?"

Seleen's mouth was already full. "Never," and a flitter of crumbs littered the table.

They both laughed.

Alahna tucked in.

The Blind Hag was the go to place-of-business for town merchants, burghers, and sea captains who conducted legitimate, and not so legitimate, seafaring trade. Rough floorboards had long since hardened from swabbing with lye soap to scrub away powerful spirits, various brews, and all the offal a floor in such a place collects.

A mélange of smokables and pungent incense covered the underlying stink while the raucous uproar provided sufficient cover for smugglers to trade with supposedly upstanding merchants. All of which the Sisteren wisely ignored as the bailiwick of the town marshal and beneath the station of the governing body of the Huan Long Shui Dominion which they were. All across the island continent of Aryavartha, such matters were left to local constables of various titles with the Sisteren acting as judiciary on call for the most serious matters.

Next to Oren's snug, a jug-band played bawdy sea shanties on a long stage with male and female doxies prancing and dancing in various stages of undress on either side, which also made Alahna impatient. "I dislike all of this," and she waved her hands in the thick air. "Rank smoke makes me ill at my stomach."

Seleen nodded.

Noisy minutes passed.

At length, Alahna had enough and stood to depart.

Seleen whined, "I was just getting ready to have a black-and-tan."

Alahna ignored her, but just as Seleen stood with a pout on her face, a huge brute of a man threw the swinging doors of the grand-entry open so hard they slammed against the door frame.

Ba-bam!

Alahna peered through the heavy screen of the snug.

It was old One-eyed Oren himself. On his head sat a three-cornered, tattered felt naval officer's hat tilted at a jaunty angle with the bill held flat above his suntanned face by an elaborate hatpin. A tired peacock feather adorned the hammered silver hatband. Jeweled ringlets defined a salt-and-pepper goatee while a thick, gray moustache obscured upper and lower lips. With a black eye-patch, he looked the part of a swashbuckling pirate. He was anything but. In his wake came a handful of stout sailors festooned in similar raiment with Boone among them, followed by the rest of the crew who had not gone home. Additional patrons made the place positively packed. Those who carried blades, checked their swords with the doorman and cloakroom-girl.

After a brief gawk, the regulars realized it was Oren and crew and turned back to the vice of their choice. Boone spoke in Oren's ear and pointed at his private snug, then proceeded into the gambling hall with his shipmates. As Oren crossed the room, Captain Shu Fang intercepted him. Shu Fang and his crew were celebrating the sale of their entire cargo to the Sisteren.

Having yesterday completed this very business with Shu Fang and the grisly seadog he hired as interpreter from Bahndahn Towne downriver, Alahna had already made note of his presence when she and Seleen entered. And Oren had it right. If the locals knew a pair of sister-adepts were present, they would leave forthwith, which meant the crew of the Ocean Empress would have nobody to gamble with and depart for seedier establishments.

Idly peering through the screens of the snug while waiting for Oren, Alahna noticed Big Meg quietly conferring in earnest with the doorman at the grand-entry. Her body language bespoke trouble. The doorman nodded, dispatched a runner on some unknown errand, and summoned a bar-bouncer to help him quietly close and bar the huge weather-doors of the grand-entry from inside. This did not bode well, for the air inside was already smoky and hot from the press of so many bodies.

The bar-bouncer turned and hustled through the crowd, past their snug, and into the kitchen. The sound of the kitchen doors facing the street-alley slamming shut and getting barred was unmistakable. Alahna slid the partition open far enough to peer past the swinging entry doors of the kitchen and saw a pair of Meg's fat bakers take up stations brandishing large bread paddles. Odder yet, Meg's staff quietly hustled here and there along the balcony of the 2nd floor.

Rowdy, raucous, and oblivious, Shu Fang's crew partied on.

Locals glanced about with wary eyes.

Alahna said to Seleen, "Have thee noticed?"

Seleen spoke with her mouth full and crumbs flying. "What?"

Alahna's tone became intense. "I must break words with Meg," and, paying no attention to the loss of her disguise, she departed the snug with the rainbow-hued flame-marks of a high-adept on her face and neck in plain sight. Incognito no longer, Seleen caught up with her as Alahna reached the wide curving stairs to the balcony. Standing at the balustrade near the top, Big Meg glared down at the crowd with a look of darkest outrage on her face. Two concierges rushed in and out of the first room to the right of the landing.

Locals in the crowd immediately recognized them as Sisters of the Huan Long Shui because of the elaborate crochet and needlework on the cuffs of their black pantaloons falling outside the new boots, and the crocheted sleeves and necks of their black, pointy-shouldered tops—a sort of habit the Huan Long Shui Sisters typically wore.

Striding tall and graceful with her sea-green eyes open wide, Alahna's rainbow-hued flame-marks almost glowed while her reddish-brown tresses bounced on her shoulders as she strode up the stairs.

As Seleen hurried behind Alahna with an expression of the deepest concern etching her kind face, blonde tresses fell in waves down her back.

Distracted, Meg dimly recognized them rushing up the stairs, and shouted from the balustrade over the din, "The smoking-lamp is out! All smokes out now!" This got the attention of the remaining bartenders and staff as the cloakroom-girl snuffed the kerosene smoking-lamp high on the wall next to the grand-entry with a long candlelighter and upside down bell snuffer. Meg made certain she had the attention of the bar staff, raised her forearm, pushed it forward as if closing a beer tap, then held her hand up and made a fist. These were signals for the bartenders to place empty mugs over the taps on the kegs and stop serving hard spirits.

This engendered more protests from the Qinseh swabbies with purses full of coin yet to squander, who assumed the place was simply shutting down for no good reason. Local ne'er-do-wells and professional gamblers fell quiet. The muffled sounds of a poor doxy's heartbroken wails and occasional agonized-yet-muffled scream drifted from the balcony. Meg smacked a ship's bell hanging on mount fastened to the baluster.

Ding! Ding! Ding!

When the jug-band stopped, the entire crowd looked up, and she hollered, "Everybody listen! Quiet down!" When she had all of the patron's attention, she shouted, "Somebody's done a bad harm on one a' me garils an' I won't have it! The Sisters and marshal are summoned!" Peering sideways, she finally recognized Alahna and Seleen topping the stairs and glanced quizzically at the doorman standing at the barred entry, who shrugged.

Alahna went straight to Big Meg. "Where is the garil?" but Seleen had already spotted the poor doxy lying on a blood-covered bed through an open door. Badly beaten, she lay semiconscious and bleeding profusely from a vicious slash high on her forehead, across her nose, and down across lips and chin. Worse, she suffered a terrible beating to her frail and naked body. Seleen immediately ran to the bedside and pulled aside blood-soaked linens placed by the concierges as emergency bandages. Assessing the slash, Seleen started a Song-of-Stanching to mitigate the foamy crimson flow.

Meg herself was a huge woman with cinnamon-colored skin. Her lantern jaw jutted forth. "Milady Alahna, how did ye come to be here?"

"Oren sent word to meet him. We came incognito and hid in his snug."

Meg understood. "It was good of ye to disguise yerselves."

Somebody hammered the knocker on the weather-doors of the grand-entry, and the doorman peered through the speak-easy-slot, hurriedly unbarred the enormous weather-doors, threw them open. High Adept Yenara came wafting through in her SijanPao full of sycophants. Alahna realized that Meg's runner must have encountered Yenara at the bazaar when he could not find an on call Sister at the Pagoda Center. Out of breath from hurrying across town, the runner and town marshal hustled through the grand-entry as soon as Yenara's Pao cleared the opening.

Yenara acted the vainglorious showoff by manuevering her SijanPao around the gambling hall just above the heads of the crowd before wafting up and over the balustrade of the balcony where Alahna stood beside Meg. Short and stocky with gray, prominent eyes, Yenara had an oval, pug-nosed face, low cheek bones, a receding chin, and long black hair knotted in an untidy heap atop her head. Her title as Chancellor of the Huan Long Shui Sisteren was Kulapti, a fact she pointed out at every opportunity. Typically, she was almost never in town, for it was well known she disdained common folk, especially longshoremen, gamblers, and ne'er-do-wells.

Alahna met her adversary's eyes as Yenara willed the Pao past and settled on the balcony deck. The instant she spied Alahna and Seleen already present, fury painted itself on Yenara's face even as she derezzed the Pao with a 4-count. In terms of the leadership hierarchy, High Priestess Lilith governed the Huan Long Shui Sisteren and the entire island continent of Aryavartha as empress-in-absentia due to old age. The other high-adepts in the Council of Four were Yenara, whose title placed her ostensibly above Alahna as Keeper of the Archives, and Old Nebhet as Senior Song-Master, who stood loosely equal to Alahna.

Each governed a discreet set of responsibilities.

For reasons of ecclesiastical succession, Alahna had been High Priestess Lilith's Named One since striking for the 1st Circle as a young initiate some 30-years previous. This forever irked Yenara, because she felt the role of high-priestess should be merit based and found Alahna wanting. Over the years, this inherent conflict eventually turned to poorly disguised hatred and contentious competition. Alahna had long since given up trying to make peace with the self-aggrandizing and hateful narcissist.

Yenara raised her eyebrows waiting for Alahna to speak while Yenara's haughty gaggle of sycophants stood behind her as if equal to Alahna in rank.

Being first on the scene, it naturally fell to Alahna to report, but she deferred. "Megan, please explain."

Big Meg composed herself, wiped her tear-stained face with a clean apron, and bowed. "Miladies. . . ."—and she stifled a sob—"some spawn-of-a-demon took bloody blade to my sweet little Molly's face after beatin' 'er senseless. A coward's work if ever I saw. . . ." and she suppressed a burst of rage.

Down below, the doorman and Meg's bar-bouncers barred the grand-entry, then stood with drawn swords facing confused and milling patrons. The doorman himself was a sword-master from Bahndahn Towne brought thence to train Meg's people. His easy stance belied deadly skill.

Alahna squeezed Megan's shoulder. "Take us to her, old friend."

By then, the marshal arrived on the landing and stood huffing and puffing with hands on knees. As they entered Molly's room, a Song-of-Healing replaced the stanching-song with Seleen's sweet voice lilting through the open door. There wasn't enough space for all of them inside, so Meg went in, followed by Yenara, the marshal, and Alahna. With the bleeding controlled by Seleen's source-magic, the crimson seeping gash lay brutally raw. Never diminishing her song, Seleen looked at Alahna and made a gesture with her hands as if performing needlepoint on an invisible loom.

Alahna said to Meg, "Seleen needs to suture Molly's face."

Meg strode out to the balcony laying a stream of orders on her faithful concierges. One rushed in and grabbed the heap of bloodied linen. The other ran for the surgical kit.

The marshal whispered in Alahna's ear to keep from offending Yenara, for he and Alahna had been through similar situations in the past. "Milady, we had better assess them foreign swabbies. As we both know, this kinda' thing gets outta hand right quick." So saying, he went to the balustrade handrail and respectfully requested Yenara's sycophants to make room.

They ignored him.

Aggravated at such haughty behavior, and to make room for both herself and the marshal, Alahna put her hands on two of the young Sisters, yanked them back by the shoulders, then roughly pushed them aside.

They both rounded on whoever dare lay hands on a sister-adept, immediately realized it was High Adept Alahna herself, stepped back with eyes averted, made perfunctory bows.

Succinct in her words, Alahna's lip held a slight snarl. "I shall recall such belligerence when the lot of ye strike for higher circles."

Apologies flowed from all twelve in quiet murmurings, and they bowed to the sheriff, who stood totally distracted by the scene below. Raised voices and clenched fists told the tale. Captain Shu Fang and his Qinseh sailors milled about without purpose, but this could change in a heartbeat.

Shouting the situation with a loud voice, Captain Oren pointed at the balcony while translating Meg's words into Qinseh for Shu Fang and his sailors. Oren's crew gathered close about him.

The local ne'er-do-wells realized the inevitable. Barring some miracle of uncoerced confession, trouble had stolen upon them unawares. Sighs of silent rage colored the whispers about whoever the idiot was that brought this down on them. Regrouping along the balustrade while giving room to Alahna and the marshal, Yenara's gaggle peered down on the buzzing crowd like jurors at court. Their combined gravitas had a strange effect on the drunkards, nitwits, gamblers, and sailors. Becoming silent and sober as possible, the entire crowd withered under their haughty glare.

Somebody puked.

Several of Shu Fang's crew tried to claim their blades and depart, but were stopped by the drawn swords by Big Meg's boys. With an expert flourish, the doorman barked, "Nobody leaves!"

Grumbling and swearing, Shu Fang's crew backed off.

Tension grew thicker by the minute.

Alahna turned back to the room where Molly lay.

Meg dug around in a satchel hanging from her cummerbund and removed a carved jade pipe in the shape of a long-dragon with its gold-gilded mouth as the bowl. The odd looking medicine-pipe was not for personal use, not built for drawing on, but purpose-built for someone to blow on the already lit bowl and deliver a dense stream of poppy-smoke to an injured person in dire need. The outsized chest of the dragon-pipe was the expansion chamber. She pinched a sizeable chunk of opium from a larger ball wrapped in woven mint leaves, stuffed the sticky stuff into the mouth of the dragon-pipe, lit a long match, and heated the bowl. Once bubbling, she blew a thick trail of white smoke into Molly's face.

Yenara stood assessing the vicious bodily bruises and deep facial gash from over Seleen's shoulder with the young doxy's swollen face bruising darker by the minute. Still spattered with Molly's blood, both concierges returned with clean linens; folded bandages and gauze; a medium cauldron of steaming water; a jar of honey-opium ointment for pain; a small bronze ding of marigold salve to prevent infection; and a medical satchel with curved needles and silken thread.

Alahna started a Song-of-Relieving in counterpoint with Seleen.

The lowering sun provided wan light through the window.

Kerosene lamps on the walls got lit as well as an enormous crystal chandelier high above the great room.

Alahna gathered Seleen's hair back, and tied it with twine from her pocket while Seleen carefully sutured the horribly gashed lips from the inside out by carefully joining the muscles of the orbicularis oris to keep the young woman's lips from having notches. The harmony of both songspells, and Big Meg's opium, quieted Molly to softly sobbing punctuated by shrill cries as the curved needle with delicate silk penetrated.

With Alahna dabbing blood away, Seleen expertly joined the vermillion border of the young doxy's lips with a single artful stitch to prevent scarring. Deeper stitches joined the gash beneath her lower lip. The last of the sutures pulled the cheek and forehead cuts together. Seleen looked up, and said, "Poor Molly will have a permanent scar across her eyebrow and lip, and there is nothing for it."

Megan tried to remain stoic, but errant tears dripped from her granite jaw. Wiping her eyes, Meg placed her hand on Yenara's shoulder. "Can ya find out if the vicious shit-heel is still down there?"

Yenara patted Meg's hand, strode out to the balcony, peered down on the hushed patrons as if assessing a bucket full of cockroaches, and raised her voice over the uneasy quiet. "A garil hath been brutally beaten and her face cut open. First, I will simply ask the offscouring scumbag who did this, or anybody who knows about this, to speak out and save us all some time. For I assure ye, we shall have the truth before sundown."

Nobody moved.

Nobody said a word.

Silence reigned.

Yenara nodded. "So be it," and gestured to one of the lesser-adepts. "Let us see if my training hath taken root. Sing for these offscourings the Song-of-Truth."

Somebody below yelled, "Aw, horseshit! Not that!"

Riverbend

~

The Song of Truth

Nervous and tentative at the balustrade, Yenara's young acolyte started the songspell with the singular purpose of getting at the hidden truth. Other truths often spilled out too, but they wanted only the one from those guilty of violence. Her songspell would set a metaphysical fire in their brain which, when tolerated for too long, would become literal. In all cases, discomfort faded if the truth came out. If not, it got worse till the guilty party either confessed, or died with bloody smoke pouring from every orifice in their head. In Alahna's lifetime, it had never gone that far. Perpetrators were never strong enough. Nobody was strong enough.

As the songspell entered first movement, the Sister found her voice and spread her arms expansively to encompass the entire great-room with her lyric in the plural. Every person in the place mumbled their deepest, darkest, most ardently hidden truths and secrets. Heuristic, the process could take some time for a person to figure out what to confess and in what order. If confessions ran out, they started over. Those who had been through this before covered their mouths to muddle self-incrimination. The songspell was ineluctable. None could resist. Strained murmurings arose.

Guided by the intentions of the source-singer, perpetrators and any conspirators, if such there were, would reveal themselves or die. The longer the truth-song fell across the crowd, the more moans and murmurings arose. As it crescendoed, every person in the place, except the sister-adepts, spilled their most ardently hidden truths and secrets whether muddled or not. Meg and her people, Oren's crew, and the local ne'er-do-wells, all knew well enough to whisper, cover their mouths, or mumble. Not so the Qinseh sailors, but they soon caught on.

When stress got as thick and hot as boiling roof tar, people moaned. When the moans morphed into stifled bawls with voices rising to the darkest avowals, a scream broke through followed two more. Relieved that somebody had at last outed themselves, the locals pointed at a pair of Qinseh sailors, shouting, "It was them!"

Itching for a fight, their shipmates rallied around.

On the opposite side of the gambling hall, another local hollered, "He's tryin' t'hide it!" and pointed at the grizzly interpreter Shu Fang hired from Bahndahn Towne. A half-full mug of beer bounced off the interpreter's back with a splash, clattered to the deck. The thrower bellowed, "The hell with ya fer bringin' the Sisteren down on us!" Other mugs flew.

The grizzled old seadog interpreter had shiny piercings of thin gold circlets occluding the pinna of both ears; a riot of tattoos hid every visible patch of skin; gold teeth shone in between gaps; a thick gold ring festooned his right nostril; greasy hair fell to sloped shoulders; beard and bushy moustache lay copious and thick.

A scuffle broke out across the room. Some cheat at the gaming tables confessed a smidgeon too plainly, and the people he had just cheated lit into him, then into one another. Alahna stood side-by-side with Yenara gazing down from the baluster while Seleen dressed Molly's injuries. Yenara's gaggle stood on either side of both high-adepts.

Unsure whether Yenara had taken the time to read the purchase documents between herself and Captain Shu Fang, Alahna quietly filled Yenara in. "The Ocean Empress stopped in Bahndahn Towne long enough to restock their coal bins for his newfangled steam engine. That was where Captain Shu Fang hired this interpreter. Shu Fang and his crew came to the Hag to celebrate the sale of their entire cargo to us before setting sail back to Qinseh loaded with our world-famous Riverbend Rum and to take on the secret shining steel from the Bahndahn Steelworks downriver, which is highly valued for unbreakable sword blades."

Yenara tilted her head back to look down her nose at Alahna. "I read thy report and found the dealings far too generous, but the deed is done. I did not know of this interpreter."

Alahna wrinkled her nose in recollection. "We worked together all week, and he stank something awful at first. After the first round of negotiations, I told him to either bathe and wear laundered clothing, or I would ban him and find another."

After being forced together on the gaming floor, the pair of Qinseh sailors blurted out their confessions. The grizzled interpreter remained sullen. Shouting, Captain Oren interpreted the mitigating confessions of Shu Fang's boys. Both of them implicated Shu Fang's hired man. Shu Fang bowed to Oren for the courtesy.

Obviously hoping to fight his way through Big Meg's men and run away after being fully outed, the interpreter bolted into the crowd punching and kicking with drool and snot flying.

As he passed by, Oren tripped him.

Closing from the entry, Meg's doorman brutally smacked the interpreter on the side of the head with the flat of his schiavona. The grizzled seadog's head tilted to the side, and he screamed as the gold-ringed pinna of his right ear went flying amidst a gush of frothy crimson spatters.

Shu Fang bent, retrieved the bloody pinna, and quickly wrapped it in a silk bandana while nodding admiration at the doorman for excellent swordsmanship. Had the razor-sharp blade of Bahndahn steel been turned, the knifeman's skull would have split asunder like a ripe melon. As it was, bright and frothy blood gushed from the side of his head when he fell mewling to his knees with a hand over the spurting wound. The doorman sneered and expertly presented the razor-sharp edge of his blade at the seadog's throat. Blooded and on his knees, the interpreter shook his free fist and shook his body fighting to hold his tongue.

Yenara motioned for her acolyte to perform a gesture-of-aiming from the balustrade. As the acolyte pointed her index finger down at him, she shifted her lyric from plural to singular. Fully under onus, the hateful interpreter held his fist high in the air, and screamed, "Yar! 'Twas I what beat 'er an' cut 'er up! And the dirty little thing had it comin'!" Whereupon, he put his head down while muttering to himself as frothy blood surrounded his knees and feet. Relentless—even ruthless—the truth-song burnt in. The interpreter screamed at the decking. "An' I kilt the rest a' them doxies down in Bahndahn Towne by reason a' the same!"

With no understanding of the interpreter's confession, and spooked by the goings-on, Shu Fang's crew crowded into a group for mutual defense pushing anybody in their way aside. This did not go over well with Oren's crew and the locals, for Shu Fang's crew outnumbered the entire crowd by some two to one.

The marshal shouted for all to settle.

Nobody paid attention.

Yenara sang a SijanPao and took her gaggle in.

Amazed at being excluded by Yenara, Alahna shook her head. "I knew it. . . ."

Hovering above the frightened crowd in her sphere-of-power, Yenara explicitly aimed to set down facing the hemmed in perpetrators directly beneath the main chandelier.

When the late afternoon sun stopped shining through the high skylights, it cast the room in an orange blush.

The shining swords of Meg's people glittered under the light of so many candles.

Sailors and locals parted to make a hole.

Grease; spit; upchuck; hard spirits; and a variety of ales, wines, and beers stained the heavy floorboards although Meg's people swabbed them nightly. When Yenara and her gaggle got low enough, she derezzed the SijanPao with a count, and all the haughty sister-adepts settled lightly to the deck. Murmuring quietly, Yenara's gaggle organized a shoulder to shoulder circle facing outward.

Yenara stared with belligerent malevolence at the perpetrators.

Stunned silence fell like a dropped anchor.

Riverbend

~

The Dreaded Geis

Desperate to forestall disaster, Alahna hollered from the balcony using Yenara's title to keep from further offending the thin-skinned, supercillious scunner. "Kulapti! For the sake of the Aerthe Mother Goddess can we take this outside?"

Yenara glared up at the balcony, then down at the implicated three on their knees, ignored Alahna, and started a Chant-of-Awakening to marshal the power of the WuShi as the first phase of setting The-Dreaded-Geis. As the high-adept casting the curse, Yenara was in no danger from the heat or dangerous combustion products, which would be deflected from the people in her immediate surroundings—a circle with diameter of about 3-meters.

The dire curse set a mystical compulsion to enforce lifelong non-violent behavior from the moment it got laid on a confessor. It was also a singular punishment reserved for criminals, accomplices, and conspirators involved in capital crimes, but especially those involving violence. Recompense for the victim or victims till atonement got defined by the Sister who laid the curse under the assumption that she also understood the complexities. This was always assured by relevant testimonies.

Wailing and shouting arose, for the locals knew what the curse-of-immolation did and dreaded it. Thus, the name. Without understanding that the curse could only be set with a gesture-of-aiming, many covered their ears trying to stop the arcane malediction from gnawing like a mischief of wharf rats inside their squirming brains. Strange, esoteric, and penetrating, the syllables were not merely audible.

Locals made personal signs of warding. Qinseh sailors swore to their patron goddess.

Behind Alahna, the open door to Molly's room let Adept Seleen's mellifluous refrains from the Song-of-Healing to float into the huge saloon.

Seleen's magic to heal.

Yenara's magic to curse.

Both magics creating dissonant counterpoint.

Seleen's sweet refrains exerted a slightly calming effect.

Yenara's habitual bullheadedness never ceased to amaze Alahna. Infuriated, she hustled down the wide curving staircase. When she stomped out onto the main floor, people spread from her path as if she were a steaming locomotive. Taking note of the separating crowd, Yenara's gaggle spied Alahna striding toward them, and did their momentary best to assess whether she was in a dark fury, or simply aggravated, for Alahna had put several of Yenara's haughty disciples to severe task over the years. It took a lot to make Alahna lose her temper, and respect for her held a good measure of prudent fear. When she reached Yenara, Alahna quietly growled in Yenara's ear through gritted teeth. "Asshole . . . I once again implore thee . . . allow me to take these eejits into a sphere-of-power and deliver them to the wharf outside. Setting The-Dreaded-Geis inside this crowded saloon is downright foolhardy."

Right hand extended palm up, Yenara glanced sidewise at Alahna with dripping contempt, sneered, and kept on chanting.

Small packets of heat-shocked air popped here and there above the crowd.

Many mewled or cussed in fear.

Alahna shook her head and sighed in exasperation.

Frightened through to their superstitious bones, Shu Fang's people retrieved secreted blades hidden from the doorman when they came in. Others turned over tables and broke legs off to brandish as clubs while awaiting Shu Fang's order to riot, grab their shipmates, and fight their way out. Ready to defend Megan and her people on Captain Oren's order, Boone and the rest of Oren's crew elbowed in around the source-singers with their own secreted blades exposed.

Plans of spawning an emergency SijanPao cascaded in Alahna's mind. If anarchy breaks out, we shall be forced to divorce ourselves and our Sisters from the crowd. If time allows, I can protect as many others as possible. Sisters come first.

If a Sister got hurt; or a lesser-adept unable to sing a Pao were threatened or trapped; any Sister above the 10th Circle could push a deadly gesture-of-warding called a bone-crusher. Such a warding here and now would cut a swath through the patrons like a derailed steam locomotive. Inadvertent serious injury and property damage became unavoidable, even unto death.

None in the crowd had ever seen the likes.

Innocence and hot tempers made them foolhardy.

Alahna prayed it would not come to this, but this was only one of several potentially horrible outcomes, the worst of which would be a deadly stampede toward the barred grand-entry when wildfire broke out. Other dark thoughts arose in Alahna's mind. *Only Yenara could manufacture such a shitstorm. Only she would. And she knows better. Damn the egotistical scunner!*

According to the contract-of-mercantile with the Huan Long Shui Sisteren, and depending on the severity of the offense, Alahna had the power to confiscate Shu Fang's cargo, possibly his ship, and even compel jail for him or any of his crew if they failed to abide by the laws of the Dominion. Such were the stakes. With Molly as the victim of a capital offense, all options were on the table, because the crazed yet legally retained interpreter remained an agent to the NuHuang Shipping Company till Shu Fang cast him off in a long-boat along with the river pilot when they sailed past the bar of the LungHuo River. This also meant Shu Fang remained legally responsible for the interpreter's actions.

Obviously unwilling to risk such a tremendous deal over a crazed local, Shu Fang bowed deeply to Yenara, likewise to Alahna, and saluted Captain Oren and Officer Boone, who both saluted back. Shu Fang cleared his voice and hollered in Qinseh. When Shu Fang's crew fell quiet, so did all the rest. Shu Fang spoke in Qinseh with quiet intensity.

Oren shouted the interpretation for the people of Aryavartha, "Captain Shu Fang says, 'Confessed eejits bringing badness upon themselves and Shu Fang himself when going stupid!" Oren pointed an accusing finger at the slasher. "Shu Fang says, 'Dominion law ties Shu Fang's hands. The guilty are guilty!'"

Grumbles and protests arose.

The situation deescalated slightly.

Nobody lowered their guard.

Without pause, Yenara shifted from the Chant-of-Awakening into casting The-Dreaded-Geis. Penetrating words in a strange and esoteric tongue stabbed the minds of everyone while the Sisters watched with detached aplomb. When the curse-of-immolation crescendoed, Yenara reached up with open hands, brought them down as if gathering clouds from the sky, and held them out before her waist with her left palm up and her right hand passing across as if brushing a hot ember onto the floor. Obeying her gestures, the popping points-of-heat above the shouting and terrified crowd coalesced in the center of the saloon about 4-meters above the perpetrators, where it crackled and snapped and popped like a bonfire.

Long wavering shadows of the animated crowd danced on the walls. Orange highlights from the setting sun tinged the smoky air through skylights. Waves of fluid heat shimmered past support beams and up into the high chandelier. Rainbow splashes of color from dangling cut glass crystals accompanied the tinkle of glass against glass dancing in the heatwaves. Thick and guttering chandelier candles dripped hot wax from the bobeches. Fully exposed wicks flashed into gray ash drifting in the heat-shocked air creating momentary flashes of yellow light. Streams of melting wax dripped past the sizzling point-of-fire, flashed into spatters and strings of flame, burnt themselves out.

Cussing and swearing, the crowd jumped back while the guilty three stood pinned at sword-point beneath the blistering stream of flaming wax. They swore and danced and swatted and batted at hot spatters as if under attack by swarming wasps. The stink of ale and powerful spirits, blistering air, flashing wax, scorching hair, smoke from the wicks, sweat, and disbelieving terror hung heavy.

People wailed in fear.

Before Yenara set the curse, Alahna shook her by the shoulder speaking urgently over the frightened discord. "Hear my words, Yenara! As the most senior adept present, 'tis thy right to set The-Dreaded upon all three, but I remind! It was only the local interpreter from Bahndahn Towne,"—and she pointed—"who committed the crime. The older Qinseh"—and she pointed again—"pleaded for restraint." Pointing at the third, she affirmed, "This young Qinseh merely overheard sounds easily mistaken for rising passion. A stint in jail for both till the NuHuang sails would suffice."

Scowling, Shu Fang listened as Oren interpreted Alahna's pleadings. Shu Fang afforded her a respectful bow.

Speaking loud and imperious over her shoulder through the pop and roar and snap, Yenara snarled, "As thou sayest, Keeper of the Archives, judgment is mine. And I shall thank thee to mind thy place. Still . . . perhaps a drop of lenience. . . ."

The sizzling point-of-fire held tension at a rolling boil.

Disgusted at Yenara's obstinance, Alahna got right in her ear. "Captain Shu Fang brings us silks, spices, tea leaves and coffee beans, nankeen cloth, porcelain, fine ceramics, cashmere, kegs of vanilla, and bricks of refined sugar. If we of the Sisteren curse his men, he may never come back. Perhaps a drop of constraint?"

Yenara glared at Alahna but kept on chanting.

Alahna ignored her and prepared to manage the inevitable riot if only by taking the rest of the Sisters into a new SijanPao, then sing an outer Pao and take Megan, Oren, and the rest of those she knew inside as she spied them in the melee. Worse, if the Blind Hag Tavern caught fire, the rest of the wharf might burn down too, and possibly the whole town. Both of Seleen's wind-singers having fun at the bazaar were just that, and not adept in the Powers of Water or Powers of Fire, the most difficult of all even for Alahna, because fire has a mind of its own and, once set loose, becomes furious and insatiable.

With only herself to call on the Powers-of-Water, she would not be enough. As for Yenara, her power over the elements were much vaunted, at least according to her. Alahna knew better. Yenara was good at braggadocio and short on practical application. Yenara would likely flee to the Cavern Keep, some 9-kilometers distant, while Alahna herself fought the blaze as best she could. This reduced it to a simple matter of timing, for a flying Pao was no faster than a sprinting human at about 18-kilometers per hour. Add half of an hour to gather and inform other high-adepts, and it would be well over 1-1/2-hours round trip. Plenty of time for the entire town to be joined in conflagration.

Alahna's anger for the intransigent, egotistical Yenara got hotter in proportion to the point-of-fire crackling in the air above them.

Somebody shouted, "Up there!" and pointed at the chandelier.

A tin-wrapped frame with crank accessed by a catwalk supported the giant light fixture for lowering, cleaning, and replacement of candles. Both it and the catwalk smoldered. Threads of smoke curled swiftly to the ceiling to blend with the smoky cloud from the wicks and flashing candle wax.

Alahna swore, then performed a gesture-of-quenching, one of the weakest gestures-of-power, which cooled the tin-wrapped frame and catwalk barely enough. Alahna hollered in Yenara's ear through clenched teeth. "I asked thee kindly to take this outside, but thee wanted thine audience! So either set the damnable curse, or let it die before the whole damn place goes up!"

Paralyzed by fear while overwhelmed and hissing at the foreign crew and local ne'er-do-wells like house cats who never got outside, Yenara's sycophants were unaccustomed to the seamy side of life, and even more unaccustomed to open hostility between Alahna and Yenara. They had never been in a situation so chaotic and potentially deadly in their sheltered lives safe inside the Cavern Keep.

Fear smacked of panic.

Tension got thicker by the heartbeat.

Growls of rage arose all around.

To keep from inadvertently setting the geis on some innocent, Yenara turned her baleful gaze on the crowd with hands held together as if praying. Above them all in the high rafters, accumulating smoke puffed into tiny flamelets like kindling just prior to ignition.

Big Meg stood paralyzed in shocked disbelief and utter dismay.

Alahna threw another gesture-of-quenching, and another, and yet another while shouting over her shoulder up at Meg. "Open the exits now! We may need to evacuate and do not want a stampede!"

Meg complied while jerking a secretive fist at Yenara's back. At Meg's signal, one of her people scrambled up a wall ladder from the balcony to a suspended catwalk and cranked roof vents open to vent accumulating heat and smoke, then hustled to the kitchen and scullery to have her burly cooks throw open the double-doors along the alley on the inland side of the wharf. Some locals and kitchen staff scurried out the back doors while Meg hurried her stout bakers to the grand-entry to pull the beam free. Her tougher staff held the perpetrators at bay with bared steel. Patrons who scurried out the back did not depart. Filled with morbid curiosity, they ran around and milled about on the wharf hoping to witness the immolation, which was sure to come.

Smoky air poured from all outside openings.

Yenara's voice penetrated the discord with audible vibrations of esoteric magic. "Yonder eejit who heard muffled screams and did nothing, were I thee, I would depart the Huan Long Shui Dominion never to return. If ever I hear word, thou shalt spend the rest of thy miserable life a drooling moron!"

Reluctantly, Oren interpreted.

Shu Fang shook his head and waved his hand at the poor swabby. Reprieved, the terrified young Qinseh fell to his knees and bowed low flipping his waist-length braid forward already spattered with wax. Wax burns spotted his shaved head. When the doorman lifted his blade, the young sailor jumped to his feet, frantically shoved his way through the crowd, bolted through the grand-entry, ran away to his ship shouting thanks to Guan Yin.

Knowing what was coming, more locals took advantage of the opportunity and hustled out the front entry to the wharf to await the inevitable immolation.

Trenchant fear and macabre fascination held the rest inside.

Yenara's voice sliced through the searing swelter. "Let this be fair warning to all!" and she lifted her hands palms up. In response, the point-of-fire got hotter.

People turned their faces away.

Popping wax from the chandelier flashed into runnels of dripping fire.

Perpetrators bawled while the crowd backed away in every direction till they stood mewling and jammed against the walls. Alahna made another gesture-of-quenching to stop the spattering runnels from igniting the greasy, wax-slickened floorboards.

Adept Seleen's Song-of-Healing faded from the upstairs room where young Molly moaned with pain-ridden, barely audible sobs over the pop and sizzle. The air smelled of sour sweat, sulfurous soot, waxy smoke, and burgeoning panic as Adept Seleen rushed down the stairs.

Alahna screamed in Yenara's ear, "Enough! Enough I say!"

Yenara thrust a finger at the second Qinseh conspirator.

From out of the roiling point-of-fire, a curse-cobra of orange smoke and sparkling yellow fire-sprites coalesced. Hissing yellow flamelets, it wove side-to-side with eyes-of-fire like red-hot coals.

Transfixing him, it struck.

Sssss—crack—fangs-of-fire stabbed his neck-dimple.

His larynx worked up and down as he staggered back. His long braid of hair swinging side-to-side, he screamed and threw hands to throat with a gurgle. A coil of sulfurous orange smoke wafted away as the hissing curse-cobra dissipated. Glaring at the seadog knifeman with vengeful hatred for getting him involved, he gurgled while wiping dirty sweat from his shaved, burn-spotted, and sweat-beaded brow. Orange spider-web burns radiated from singed and smoking fang-marks. When the curse-venom burnt into his brain, he blubbered, fell to his back, and scrabbled at his neck with his mouth working open and shut like a beached mackerel.

Shu Fang cussed a Qinseh oath.

The seadog slasher bellowed and bolted.

The doorman dodged and deftly smacked him with the flat of his blade on the same side of his head again.

Bellowing in pain and staggering back with the remains of his ear once again spurting crimson gouts, the interpreter snarled like a trapped animal while stabbing Yenara with bloodshot eyes.

Glorious in her deadly power, she grinned a cruel smile and stabbed him back with a pointed finger. Shot through with sparkling fire-sprites, yet another curse-cobra coalesced. Hissing and spitting flamelets, it snaked through the smoky air and struck his neck-dimple faster than bolt of lightning.

Sssss—crackle-crack!

The curse-cobra snakebite seemed all the louder.

He screamed and scrabbled at his throat. Blood from his ear coursed down his neck, welled in his dirty collar, ran down his sleeve, dripped from the elbow, streamed from dirty fingers. Curls of stinking orange smoke from the disappearing curse-cobra wafted toward the high ceiling to mix with the rest. As curse-venom inflamed his squirming brain, the wide-eyed knifeman growled at Yenara with vicious rage, then also fell to his back. His mouth worked open and shut with quiet gurgles while he choked on blinding, boiling terror.

Satisfied, Yenara wove a complex hand-dance to dispel the cursing-source. Crackling, the point-of-fire exploded.

Ba-oom!

Glasses and mugs bounced off tables. Gambling chips, gold coin, scrip, and dice scattered along greasy planks. Several windows blew out.

Opportunists dove for loot. People screamed. Sailors swore oaths on the gods of their choice. Smoking bobeches on the chandelier held no more wax. Spellbound, the crowd fell to horrified silence.

Shu Fang's eyes stared wide open with fright as he nervously stroked his long, stringy moustache.

Seconds passed till the two stopped squirming. Panting and sweating, they scrambled to hands and knees with thick stringers of gray spittle dangling from frothy mouths.

White globs of candle wax lay cooling in the seadog's hair and beard.

Yenara spoke with resolute certainty, "On yer feet!"

Oren echoed her orders for all the Qinseh sailors.

Trembling and drooling, the seadog stood quaking in his thigh-high boots.

Also standing, the poor Qinseh wet himself with sour urine running from knee-high breeks. Slippers overflowed.

Awestruck, the crowd stood silent while the seadog's blood spattered on the wax-slickened floorboards . . . drip . . . drip . . . drip . . . adding the rusty stink of fresh blood to the sweaty, smoky reek.

Oren echoed Yenara's words for Shu Fang and his crew.

Yenara's voice came out loud, flat, and dripping with contempt. She raised her hands palms up as if asking questions. "I am unsure which is worse? The one who pleads mercy and does naught in defense?"—and she pointed at the Qinseh, who flinched—"Or the one who wields the knife despite pleadings for common mercy?"—and she pointed at the slasher, who snarled—"Regardless, the Law of the Huan Long Shui Dominion remains simple. The-Dreaded-Geis hath been laid upon yer worthless hides by me, High Adept Yenara, Kulapti of the Huan Long Shui Sisteren, and Senior Member of the Council of Four under the auspices of High Priestess Lilith!"

Oren once again interpreted.

Shu Fang swore.

The Qinseh sailors cussed and protested.

Unfazed, Yenara fairly hollered. "Should either of ye contemplate such a crime henceforth—or any other act of cruel violence—a flush-of-heat commences. Purging curse-fire holds off and fades if such thought passes without becoming intent. If serious intent takes root, curse-fire becomes thy doom. Once past this unknowable moment, nothing averts immolation. Drifting ash on sullied wind and a still-beating heart emptied of steaming blood shall be all that remains."

Alahna knew by Oren's expression that he deplored being Yenara's voice for his Qinseh allies and his old friend Shu Fang.

Vainglorious, Yenara pressed on, "And know this! Ye cannot avenge by willful suicide hoping to bring down innocents, or set revenge on accusers, or victims, or otherwise cause harm or destruction. The-Creeping-Darkness holds ye forever in its baneful mind and chooses when to execute in safety of others."

Angrier by the second, Oren interpreted with extreme reluctance.

When Oren finished, Yenara raved on, "The heat becomes so intense thou shalt run screaming to an open space seeking merciful release." She paused for effect, then added with finality, "Make no mistake, the curse-of-immolation gets triggered by thine own animus."

Yenara's voice was bitter and vicious.

Oren's interpretation came out low and sad.

Riverbend

~

Doom of the WuShi

Quivering with rage as the onlookers backed farther away, the knifeman's limited reason departed. He shouted with hoarse voice in the tongue of the Huan Long Shui Dominion, "The hell with ye goddamned seesters! All ye scunners had oughta be grinnin' red from yer throats!" With a scream and snarl, he deftly pushed the sword of the nearest bar-bouncer aside, swatted the stunned doorman's sword down while bowling him over, and rushed Yenara pulling a secreted hook-knife from the voluminous cuff of his thigh-high boot with the still-bloody-blade raised to slash her from neck to crotch.

Wham!

Assessing the attack with her second-sight in the blink of an eye from beside Yenara, Alahna pushed a carefully modulated bone-crusher making the scroungy, bloody seadog holler and grunt while skidding back along the wax slickened floor into the boots of Meg's bar-bouncers. Bracing themselves as he skidded into them, they snatched him to his feet and shoved him forward. The grizzly seadog swore and raised the hook-blade to slash at the doorman. Fey, and not to be surprised again, the doorman dodged and expertly whopped the slasher's hand with the flat of his blade.

The hook-blade sail-knife launched spinning into the smoky air.

People dodged.

Thunk!

The hook-blade buried itself in a support beam.

Gasping to catch his breath, the seadog wobbled on his feet.

Yenara herself stood paralyzed by the deadly swiftness of the knifeman, including Alahna's defensive counter, and the doorman's dazzling sword work.

The knifeman's ear took to spurting steamy crimson streams.

Carmine tears blistered and sizzled down flushing cheeks.

Nasty smoke wafted from the grizzly beard and greasy hair stinking like a rotting, burning carcass as the curse took hold.

Yenara recovered her composure and set an irresistible compulsion with mind-bending words. "Yonder scumbag! Run outside and jump in the river to cool thyself and wash away the awful stench!"

Oren shouted the interpretation while Yenara's gaggle hustled aside.

The cursed Qinseh sailor quaked in terror, fell to his knees sobbing.

Finally and fully disarmed, and with smoke roiling from his greasy, stinking hair and scorching beard, the grizzled slasher rallied enough breath to scream, "Ye'll ne'er catch me!" whereupon, he bolted for the grand-entry. Noisome smoke curled from thigh-high boots as curse-fire chomped his toes.

People between the seadog and grand-entry parted to let him pass. Anybody unfortunate enough to catch a whiff gagged. The curling trail of threaded smoke and choking mephitis followed in the slasher's wake like sooty puffs from the stack of a steam locomotive. Many took advantage of the distraction and hurried to follow him out while batting at bloody coils of nauseous soot.

Knowing what came next, Yenara sang a Pao, took her gaggle in, and wafted through the crowd hard on the heels of the screaming, smoldering knifeman.

With the autumn sunset low in blazing glory, a squabble of gulls took flight on the chilly breeze. Screaming across the boardwalk, the slasher leapt feetfirst from the high wharf hoping to quench the horrible curse-fire consuming his feet. His plunge to the water slowed to an eerie stop. Having seen this before, the squabble of squawking gulls spread their wings to ride on the crisp breeze. Several perched in horrific expectance on pilings jutting from the boardwalk.

Bam!

Bam!

Both knees exploded in bright flashes of azure flame.

Bam—a—bam—a—bam—a—echoes of the explosions came back from the cliffs across the wide river as Yenara derezzed her SijanPao while forgetting the count. She and her sycophants got dumped stumbling onto the boardwalk.

The slasher bellowed in denial as fiery calves fell away with burning feet inside blistering boots.

Noisome belches of burning bone, sinew, and rancid stockings made swirls of grisly ash. Curled, withered, and emptied of flesh, smoking boot leather sizzled into the lazy current to sink.

Fetid ash highlighted by orange from the setting sun floated on coldhearted winds.

Shocked onlookers murmured words of personal warding.

Robbed of breath by agony and terror, the knifeman looked down at his femoral arteries spewing crimson streamers getting reduced to stringers of ash right before his very eyes.

Foosh-oosh-oosh-oosh!

More echoes came when the curse-fire consuming the slasher's thighs merged at his groin in a bright flare making him mewl when additional curse-fire belched along his convulsing belly and exploding gonads. All reduced to drifting flinders including his burning breeks.

Poppa—pa—pop!

Crackling in the heat, the belt and dangling accoutrements at his waist melted into the fat of his belly.

Pointing fingers, a knot of longshoremen and dockworkers spotted the slasher's purse of gold coin still dangling at his smoking belt. Stripping naked in a frenzy, they crowded side-by-side between tall pilings jutting through the boardwalk to wait.

Gulls squawked and screeched when chased away.

Grins of callous avarice painted their faces.

People cussed and swore and batted at the loathsome sparks drifting across the wharf while stomping out glowing cinders on the boardwalk.

Brilliant flinders carried on a cold gust set a local dowager's straw hat on fire, who threw it at the river. A wind gust carried it back into her face. She ran away screaming.

In the shocked and momentary quiet, the only sounds to escape the suspended slasher's mouth were desperate pants, gulps and groans, pitiful whines made punctuation.

Alahna watched from inside the gambling hall as rowdy sailors from both sailing ships, along with the local gamblers and ne'er-do-wells, along with all of Meg's people, rushed pushing and cussing through the grand-entry. Astonished and horrified, people hollered and hissed in superstitious horror.

Foom-ah-foom-foom-ah!

Scalding streams of frothy blood spewed from both branches of the common iliac artery of the slasher creating more stringers of ash as curse-fire torched animated hips to white flinders. The slasher's gasping breath faltered to coughing and wheezing as a ruthless geyser of flame erupted from his navel, followed by writhing intestines belching forth dripping and popping in snaky trails of white ash on the chilly breeze and ruddy sunset.

Freed of arterial branches, the common iliac artery spewed smoking, steaming crimson. Onlookers swore and scrambled about dodging curled streamers of noisome smoke. Several got pushed off the wharf to splash in the river. Life rings tied to rescue quoits with long ropes got tossed in after.

Still suspended above the calm waters, the knifeman's fuming torso hovered as his smoking belt dropped away with a red-hot buckle, a smoldering purse, and the rest of his accoutrements. In that same moment all three stevedores dove headfirst for the waves and disappeared beneath slender plumes.

Connected by numerous ducts and tissues as they flared into flame and fell away, the slasher's innards made fiery stringers of orange-yellow smoke in the roiling air. Relentless and swift, curse-fire chomped into the seadog's solar plexus and lungs, then shot from his wide open mouth and flaring nostrils like blowtorches. While the disembodied head still hung blinking in the smoky air, azure-carmine jets hissed from both ear canals.

Fa-oom—fa—ooma!

Echoes resounded.

Spinning arms ablaze with azure flame got reduced to clouds of ash, then drifted on the uncaring winds.

Pop—a—poppa!

Pop—a—poppa!

Both eyeballs exploded, and a horrific mephitis of burnt-hair smoke choked onlookers when his greasy mane and beard flashed into coiling soot in a single heartbeat.

Fooma—foom!

His skull exploded.

Disgusting echoes fouled everyone's ears.

Bones fragments and cottage-cheese brains spinning through the air sparkled into drifting smoke and sparking flashes.

Circling gulls screeched and squawked when splashes broke the surface downstream from the knot of greedy dockworkers diving in all at once. Several moments passed before they surfaced, but only one had the purse of gold, who held it high and whooped.

A sigh rippled through shocked onlookers.

A few clapped.

In the end, at the last, fully and finally, the slasher's vicious beating heart hung suspended with diminishing spasms above the uncaring current.

Spitting the last of its lifeblood in drifting curls of ugly ash, it beat its last beat.

Lubdub!

Circling gulls attacked the vital organ in a snarl of flapping wings, hooked beaks, webbed feet, and scratching claws. Falling to the water in a rapacious tangle, they tore the trembling organ to shreds. When the squabble of gulls splashed into the river, they squawked, swam apart, flapped away with dripping bits in bloody beaks.

Sickened onlookers bolted to the edge of the wharf to empty their stomachs.

Several hollered, "She-e-e-it!"

Somebody yelled, "So—that be The-Dreaded-Geis!"

Another bellowed, "Un-fecking-believable!"

Shu Fang's crew murmured in the Qinseh tongue, "Guan Yin yow lianmin. . . ."

Shouting as if to the Guardian Dragons themselves, Oren interpreted, "Quan Yin have mercy!"

Captain Oren's crew fell to their knees and made the gesture-of-passing by touching an open right hand to their heart, then sweeping the air before them palm up. Each murmured individually, "May the Aerthe Mother Goddess forgive his tortured ka. . . ."

Riverbend

~

Aftermath On the Wharf

Alahna watched quizzically as Yenara pivoted on the balls of her feet at the edge of the wharf to assess the size of her audience, took several steps one way, stopped, took several steps the other.

This forced her gaggle of sycophants to hustle first one way then the other trying to cover her back.

Making a gesture-of-calling to boost the volume of her voice, Yenara hollered, "Pass these words to every person ye meet." Her spell-amplified voice echoed across the wide river and back, then died amongst the sailing ships moored with their prows upstream along the wharf.

Alahna and Seleen finally joined the group to one side.

Yenara's echoing voice boomed. "The Law of the Huan Long Shui Dominion is simple. For those who would do their worst to others. The-Dreaded-Geis shall be their just deserts."

As Oren dutifully—if not tiredly—shouted the final interpretation, the crowd of reluctant witnesses hurriedly dispersed with shaking heads and murmured epithets.

A pair of gypsy-adepts, who were old friends of Alahna and Seleen, worked the crowd from the fancy back porch of their ledge-wagon parked between the buildings. "Charms and wards here! Get yer charms and wards here! Can't get no better nowhere! Better get 'em while they last! They're goin' fast! Get yer charms and wards here!"

Business became brisk.

Alahna and Seleen approached Yenara, who strode at them with balled hands at her side as if to start a fistfight, stopped, then spoke with a quiet yet angry tone for Alahna's ears only. "Asshole? Didst thou name me an asshole?"

Alahna's nostrils flared. "Perhaps it was butthole? I forget." She turned to Seleen. "Did I call Yenara asshole or butthole?"

Seleen ducked the question. "I was upstairs with Molly."

Yenara glared at them both, but glossed over the ongoing insult and strengthened her voice for public ears. "As Kulapti of the Huan Long Shui Sisteren, I find myself obliged to thank High Adept Alahna officially for lending aid, and especially her warding when the knifeman attacked." So saying, Yenara turned to glare at her useless gaggle of sycophants, none of whom had moved to protect her. Ashamed, they tousled their pantaloons while staring at slippered feet.

Imperious, Yenara locked eyes with Seleen. "Always good to know when to plead ignorance, or shall I say stupidity?" whereupon, she looked up and to the right while rubbing her chin as if she had asked herself an important question. "No, I s'pose I mean ignorance . . . this time. And, my dear Seleen, since thou hast taken poor Molly's care upon thyself without begging my leave,"—and she gestured at the emptied but still smoking tavern—"I trust thou shalt see to her healing?"

Seleen nodded. "Yes, milady."

Alahna glanced at Seleen standing there with wary eyes on Yenara's gaggle, whose cliquish behavior often devolved into bullying and petty insults from behind other Sister's backs. Spitting and obscene gestures, too. Everybody knew they had arranged apparent accidents for supposed enemies, although none could ever prove it, for singing the Song-of-Truth on fellow Sisters concerning internal politics, or simple mischief had always been forbidden by the Canon-of-Precepts unless a Sister or Sisters got formally accused of breaking the law by another Sister. This would, of course, involve the Guardian Dragons for a Calling-of-the-Council with a subsequent Council of Inquiry.

Nobody wanted that.

Getting face-to-face, Yenara stepped in close to Alahna and lowered her voice to an aggressive timbre. "Interfere with my doings again—my dear Alahna—and we shall seek opportunity to test our mettle in Confrontation-by-Source regardless of the fact thou art Lilith's Named

One. Do I make myself clear—asshole! Or was it butthole? You tell me!"

Alahna response was just as quiet. "Is there a difference? And thy breath stinketh—Kulapti! Perhaps chew some leaf-of-peppermint?" and she hit Yenara just above the solar plexus at the base of the sternum with a subtle yet powerful elbow strike.

Breasts were unbound, as was her wont, Yenara's nipples got knocked in opposing circles beneath her ornately embroidered slipover blouse. She stumbled back frantically rubbing at her chest while catching a ragged breath, then glanced about to see if any of her useless sycophants had witnessed the assault.

None had. Their attention was on the Qinseh complicitor shambling sorry and shameful along the wharf while mewling to himself.

Swearing at them, the enraged Yenara made to push a surprise bone-crusher at Alahna, but the moment Yenara locked eyes with her longtime enemy, she paused.

Smiling a humorless smile while fully poised to deflect and counter-strike, Alahna watched Yenara's expression shift from blind rage to a more prudent survival instinct. Alahna could almost guess the thoughts in that squirming brain as Yenara recalled how powerful Alahna's bone-crushers actually were.

Yenara growled under her breath, "I shall not fall for this. . . ."

Alahna murmured, "Wise of thee. . . ."

Whereupon, they locked eyes in a moment of pure, dripping hatred.

Finally, Alahna fairly snarled, "Have a care, Yenara! Someday thy wish may come true!" and they stood facing one another still as death with hands poised for arcane conflict, deadly conflict.

One or both would die.

There would be no quarter.

Years of abuse, belittlement, and bullying by Yenara made Alahna's heart pound with dark desire. For now seemed like the moment of true and final reckoning. Out of the corner of her eye, Alahna spied Seleen fully prepared to push a series of full-on bone-crushers into Yenara's sycophants to make certain they stayed out of the conflict.

Distracted by the unfolding confrontation, Yenara's sycophants realized too late that Seleen had the drop on them. Judiciously, they kept hands down and backed off.

Seleen also smiled a humorless smile. She herself had scores to settle. Not a one would go toe-to-toe with her. Crowded together in a group, they were in as much danger from one another as from Seleen.

Several swore.

Nobody moved a hand.

Interrupting the pregnant moment, Shu Fang bellowed a string of orders.

Closely watching the unfolding conflict between Alahna and Yenara, Oren paraphrased for all, "Shu Fang just ordered his crew to make ready and cast off come daybreak and also canceled shore leave."

Still gathered by the grand-entry of the Blind Hag to collect their weapons, Shu Fang's disconcerted and angry crew chorused their agreement with muttered oaths. Big Meg's cloakroom-girl and bar-bouncers got busy returning swords and long knives.

Obviously angry at having let the interpreter bowl him over, which made him lose face, the doorman quietly stood with blade unsheathed and poised. His professional swordsman's stance and lightning speed forestalled further conflict.

Oren's officers stood steadfast with hands on hilts.

The cursed Qinseh sailor shuffled along the wharf.

Weapons regained, his shipmates afforded him superstitious space in passing. None would look him in the eye. Several spat on him as they strode past.

Oren signaled his boys to be watchful while still assessing Alahna and Yenara with a knowing eye. He muttered low, "This be a long time coming. . . ."

Yenara scoffed, lowered her hands, guffawed to save face, disdainfully turned her back on Alahna, and took her gaggle into a new SijanPao. Dramatically willing her Pao into the sky over the river, Yenara laughed again, but it seemed like a painful cry.

Finally out of danger, the relieved sycophants threw finger insults and foulmouthed jeers at Seleen, who gave them the same.

Oren tipped his hat first to Alahna, then Seleen, then joined Big Meg and her staff while his officers kept watch.

Seleen laughed. "Yenara was still rubbing her chest when they swooped into town."

Alahna's voice was low with unwholesome glee and not a little relief. "The greater damage is not the actual hit."

Seleen became serious. "I had the drop on Yenara's eejits to make certain they kept it fair. So . . . wait . . . what is the greater damage?"

Calming herself with deep breaths, Alahna said, "Nebhet taught me. She is truly dangerous, although no one would ever guess."

Seleen was incredulous. "Dangerous? Old Nebhet?"

"Yes, and I will share a secret."

Seleen tapped her chest with an open palm as the sign of shared secrecy. "I am all ears."

Alahna whispered, "Old Nebhet is Keeper of the Curses."

Still incredulous, Seleen shook her head.

Alahna went on, "I intentionally scattered Yenara's Anahata chakra. She will spend days trying to figure out why she is so sick at heart from such a minor blow. Eventually, she will complain to Old Nebhet. Nebhet will keep her peace, but realign Yenara's chakra with a breathing meditation and hands on healing to lift Yenara's chi.

"Afterward, Nebhet will come and chew my butt out. I will smile and disavow intent while playing the innocent self-defendant. Nebhet will be gruff, but wink when she turns away, for she also holds no love for Yenara, and it will secretly tickle Nebhet pink."

Seleen shook her head. "I truly thought this time Yenara would fight."

Alahna scoffed, "I almost wish she had. And she might have had I not been so eager, or if she thought her gaggle of eejits could gang up, but—"

"Somebody had thy back," Seleen interrupted, and smiled her own dangerous smile with a lifted eyebrow.

Proud of her acolyte, Alahna nodded and put a hand on Seleen's shoulder. "As always, cowards and bullies back down when confronted."

Seleen shook her head. "I'm not so sure about Yenara. She forever pushes the boundaries of what she can get away with."

Big Meg motioned for Alahna and Seleen to join her people, Captain Oren, his officers, and the marshal. As a group, they hurried along behind Big Meg to catch up with Shu Fang. Meg shouted, "Captain, a moment please! There is the matter of injury, heat damage, broken furniture, and loss of profit."

Rolling his eyes, Oren reluctantly interpreted.

Shu Fang turned with a scowl and spoke to Oren with quiet intensity, who interpreted once again. "Shu Fang says, 'Luck follows others on such an evening as this. And profits were garnered before the melee broke out. And the actions of such dangerous sorceresses stand outside of his command.'"

Shu Fang's Qinseh officers had returned to stand behind him.

Tension boiled.

Hands fingered sword hilts.

A keen businesswoman, Megan projected persistence as opposed to militance. "My Molly lies upstairs beaten to within a hair's breadth of her life, and her pretty face laid wide open. I should think remuneration for damages are in order for a gentleman and officer?"

Oren tiredly echoed Meg.

The marshal pointed his baton, saying, "Captain Shu Fang, the Ocean Queen won't get unmoored till the debt is settled." He pointed at Alahna and Seleen. "They will see to it!"

Ignoring the leg-humping-lapdog of a marshal, Oren bade Shu Fang wait while he spoke to Big Meg. With Shu Fang and his boys standing out of earshot, Oren huddled with Alahna, Meg, and Seleen. "His cargo is worth a fortune to us all. If Meg here finishes this off by forcibly emptyin' his purse, he will not come back. And he might not come back, anyway. Is this what we want?"

Alahna spoke up, "Megan, since it was the flaming butthole's actions that caused yer heat damage, I will stand good for the repairs out of mine own pocket."

They all knew she meant Yenara. Several chuckled.

Meg shook her head. "I won't have it. I'm already in yer debt fer Molly."

Alahna said, "And yet, I am in the Council of Four, and Yenara refused my orders to take The-Dreaded-Geis outside making one helluva mess. If ya won't allow me, then the Sisteren shall cover this."

Meg agreed.

Oren said, "That will help, milady. Do all of ye trust me?"

They bobbed their heads.

Oren went to Shu Fang and spoke at some length. Grumbling, Shu Fang ordered his first officer to hustle up the wharf to the Ocean Queen. While they waited, Oren explained to Meg and the others, "I told Captain Shu Fang it was a cryin' shame his crew got framed by that scum-bellied seadog interpreter. I also explained the Sisteren will cover the heat and smoke damage per High Adept Alahna's word. I added that the interpreter's additional confession about missing doxies in Bahndahn Towne had bounties out for the perpetrator, and I would apply the proffered rewards to Megan's establishment.

"In terms of his sailor who got the curse, I told him t' keep that fella separate from the others, who'll bait 'im into a fight just t' see the poor bastard go up in flames, and dat'll be dat. I suggested he convince the fellow to join a monastery and swear to a quiet life of austere meditation. I know the Qinseh monks. They're a peaceful lot. Or mebbe set to farmin? Cuz' his sailin' days're over.

"In terms a comin' back t' Riverbend fer bidness, I said we should all like 't see him and his crew again. I also told him I'd send word t' the Pilot's Guild about vetting better interpreters and they should refund his fees. Lastly, I asked him what he could do t' help that poor garil and make things right with Big Meg, since it was his crew what tore up the tables and such."

By that time, Shu Fang's man returned with a small chest, which Shu Fang handed to Megan. She peered inside and found a pouch of gold nuggets, a larger velveteen sack of unstrung black pearls, and a velvet fold of faceted rubies. The rubies were extremely rare. When Meg laid the fold of rubies in her hand, Shu Fang stepped forward and retrieved three of them, went to Alahna and Seleen, handed two to Alahna with a bow, gave one to Seleen with another bow.

Bowing, Seleen's delight was obvious.

Alahna smiled and bowed.

Meg seemed more than satisfied; engulfed Shu Fang in an enormous, bosomy hug; gave him a sloppy kiss on the cheek; which he wiped off with a grimace of wry amusement.

Turning to Oren, Meg said, "Tell him we hopes he comes back. I hope he comes back, and I'll take extra good care of him and his crew when they do."

Again, for the last time, Oren interpreted.

Shu Fang gave Oren a forearm shake, nodded to Megan, and strode away with his scowling officers. Long braids swung to and fro.

Alahna said to Meg, "Dost thou have anyone brave enough to pilfer a bucket of the most potent dragon-waters from the Opal Basin at the Plaza of the Forbidden Gate?"

Meg's nod was tentative.

"Before changing Molly's dressings next time, pour the waters from the Opal Basin onto a rag and let it soak on her face. Keep the rag wet till the wounds stop fizzing. Even after they heal, massage the scars with marigold salve and wet rags dipped in dragon-water from the Pagoda Center. Any Sister will fetch a crock. Over time, Molly's injuries will barely show."

Meg bowed deep. "Yer kindness meets with gratitude as always, Milady Alahna. And yers too, pretty Seleen," and she gave Seleen a big hug and a sloppy kiss while slipping another ruby into each of their hands.

Seleen grinned with her long blond hair riffling in the breeze.

The marshal said, "I shudder t' think what would a' happened had ye not been here t' cool things down, miladies."

Riverbend

~

News of the Takings

With the fading reflection of the setting sun rippling on the waves of the wide and lazy LungHuo, Oren bade Alahna and Seleen join him back inside the tavern. By that time smoke from Yenara's debacle had cleared except for the smell of scorched timbers, which only a new coat of stain would mitigate. Meg's people were already clearing broken tables out the rear doors for later repair in town and swabbing the deck.

When the three of them sat down in Oren's snug over bowls of beef stew and fresh bread with garlic butter, Oren said, "Milady, we had important matters to discuss before the Kulapti nearly burnt the damn place down. An' what I have t' tell ya is fer yer ears only . . . erm . . . yers and Seleen's, because the wind-singers at the Cloister business center would be frightened to death if they knew, as would the wind-singers who sang us home."

Alahna said, "How is it that ya sailed past Bahndahn for the coast without hiring any of Seleen's wind-singers?"

Oren rubbed his goatee. "When I hired Sisters Upala and Zinzughen coming back, Upala told me we just missed 'em when they came downriver with two other pairs of wind-singers, and there weren't any others present at the time we departed. I had the chance t' catch the outgoing high tide and get past the bar of the LungHuo with a downstream land breeze at me back. So, I took it. And, milady, nobody knows the winds, shoals, and currents along the west coast better than meself and me navigator. Fortunate it was, too, or this news would've gotten to the Cavern Keep long before Boone found ye."

"This dire news again. Pray tell," Alahna prompted.

Oren stroked his goatee again. "Milady, there are sinister goings-on up narth. Allow me t' review. We plied up the coast late this summer as usual, and we did good this year goin' up. But on the way back south, there warn't nobody left t'trade with. The folken were gone from the bays and inlets, and I would na' let me lads go a lootin'."

Alahna furrowed her brow. "Gone?"

"Yar, gone. We found a few old bogiturs and little childern hidin' scared an' cryin' for us t'bring 'em south with us, but I had no room. We was packed above the gunwales. . . ."

Alahna filled in, "And there was perhaps fear that whatever did this might have left the survivors with some sort of dire phage?"

Unwilling to admit it, Oren glossed. "We left 'em provisions as best we could. After that, we went no closer t' shore than t' find out if it was the same on down the coast."

"Did the villagers perhaps go inland?" Alahna asked.

"Not as far as we could tell, milady."

"What, exactly, did the old bogiturs say?"

Oren lowered his voice. A shadow of fear crept across his face. "Now, it gets weird. They said beast-headed monsters and hulking, baldheaded men, as were white from head to toe, come flyin' down from the sky in a buzzin' silver ship far bigger than the Dragon's Breath. It hung above 'em like some ominous cloud while the beasties tossed bombs what spewed greenish pizen clouds. Everybody fell t' the ground, but not all died, as evidenced by these few survivors.

"As best the old bogiturs could tell when they awoke, the green cloud killed all the critters and livestock. The monsters left only the carcasses of the weak and sick when the smoke cleared. As for the people, all able-bodied folken were gone. There warn't even any corpses t' bury."

Alahna's face hardened. "Old friend, shall I have Seleen sing the Song-of-Truth upon ya? Thou art a well-known raconteur," and she raised an eyebrow.

Oren frowned, saying, "Miladies, we've done bidness t'gether fer years. Do ye think I'd make somethin' like this up? Me men and I would give our lives for ya considerin' all the family ya've either healed or brought back from the brink. But if it'll help ya believe on what I'm sayin', let Seleen sing her songspell, and I'll tell ya the same.

Although,"—and he looked out from the snug—"she might wanna sing it somewhere else."

A wry smile painted Alahna's face. "Indeed, somewhere else. What are thy plans, then?"

Twizzling his goatee, he cocked his head again. "It won't be long afore word gets out about them empty fishin' villages and inlets. I trust me men, but sailors like t' spin their tall tales."

Alahna nodded.

Oren went on, "An' I wouldn't wish to see them beasties comin' outta the sky t'take me and me crew if they still be raidin' the northern coastline. No . . . me crew needs some shore leave with their families. I'll provision here and fill me holds with kegs of Riverbend Rum. They love the rum in Bahndahn Towne and Qinseh. Mebbe two pairs of wind-singers could help me tow a heavy barge across the ShenLan Sea? Ya know them foreigners love that new shiny steel from Bandahn fer makin' swords what don't rust. Think on how much such a venture might cost."

Seleen interjected, "Many thanks, Captain Oren. We love our new boots. I did better here than I would at the bazaar," and she gazed at the shining rubies in her palm.

Oren gave Seleen a slight bow, and went on, "In terms of the return voyage, I'll bring spices, tea, black-rum, licorice, silk and silk thread, alpaca yarn and furs, which is what ye Sisters always like anyway."

Alahna said, "I would add my thanks to Seleen's. The cloaks and boots and shemaghs are most excellent. Are we done, then?"

Oren nodded.

Alahna dug in her cloak and produced her purse, then gave Oren two solid gold jinlongs on the table, 28-grams of pure gold each. "This is for thy services as interpreter, and buy thy men some ale on me. As to those goods upon return from yer next voyage, if the wind-singers are with thee, the Sisteren will have first claim, regardless. Thou art a good man, old friend, and I appreciate hearing this before it gets out. I'm sorry I doubted ya."

Oren laughed. "Please, milady, don't go tellin' such things around Riverbend, or I'll ne'er swing another good deal hereabouts again."

Alahna gave Oren a knowing smile, but cast a serious glance at Seleen.

Seleen was wide-eyed as Oren walked away. "What will we do now?"

Sleeping City

~

Incognito to the Cape of Orion

After the terrible afternoon at the Blind Hag, Alahna and Seleen proceeded directly to the Pagoda Complex and Cloister in the center of the riverfront hamlet to find Maxfield, the resident hostler for the Sisteren's stables. He and Dorak, his strapping young son, both looked up from repairing harnesses in the tack room and immediately bowed.

Alahna spoke to Maxfield as an old friend. "Kind sir, prepare our favorite horses for a five or six-day hunting trip. Seleen and I will be travelling alone. Say nothing to anyone about this upon bond of thy word. Do I have it?"

Maxfield said, "On our honor then, milady. Right laddy buck?" and he slapped Dorak on the back, who nodded and bowed again.

"I leave this in thy capable hands, then," Alahna said.

Maxfield smiled. "Ye'll need a pack mule to carry it all. But hunting, milady?"

"Yes. I feel the need for solitude. We depart before sunrise. Tie hunting bows and full quivers of arrows to the saddles where they are easy to reach."

"Aye, milady. We shall get right on it," and he sent Dorak to the storage shed with camp gear to choose a suitable tent.

Departing the stables for the shops at the center of town, Seleen caught up with Alahna. "Hunting? Really? If we want fresh game, why not ask Conrad—"

Alahna interrupted, "The pretense of going on a hunt is for prying eyes and nosy gossip. We are bound for The-Sleeping-City."

"All the way to the Cape of Orion? Can thee not sing a SijanPao and simply fly us?"

Alahna shook her head. "Two adepts in a field-of-force crossing the sky toward the coast are news for gossip. Other Sisters would hear. Whereas hunters on horseback with camping kit and a pack mule are not. Besides, I cannot take us much faster than we can ride, and holding the mind-glyph of a SijanPao all day would be completely exhausting."

Seleen said, "Where are we going now?"

"To the haberdasher for disguise. We shall need suitable raiment to go as men, and my tailor knows very well how to keep his business on the quiet."

By sunrise, they had a good start on the 90-kilometer ride to the coast. Alahna hoped to make the first leg of their journey to the coast in a single day. By the time they rode into Bahndahn Towne, a bit more than halfway downriver, the sun had just passed noon zenith. Another old friend, the hostler was overjoyed to help them and keep his yap shut in the doing, for Alahna was always generous. Wise in the esoteric ways of the Sisters, not once did he ask why they were dressed as men. They swapped mounts, got a fresh pack mule, and laid plans to swap it all back on the return leg. The old hostler was still smiling and jingling his gold when they rode out.

By sundown, they finally heard the boom and sough of surf with the salty tang of the ShenLan sea on a rising sea breeze coming off the surf. An extremely wide beach some 2-kilometers long swept the south side of the high cape till it reached the ancient jetty on the north side of the LungHuo River bar. Basalt pillars jutted randomly from the beach like vast broken teeth where softer geological formations had been weathered away. By the time they approached the Great Lower Doors carved into the solid basalt of a south-facing cliff it was well past sunset. Their camp would be in the natural lee.

Alahna found the very site she remembered from her first journey when she struck to become Adept in the 1st Circle, and they pitched camp under an overhanging ledge jutting from dunes next to a fresh-water spring with a large pool and little stream running down the beach to the waves. A small and warm waterfall still gushed from a crevice in the rock about 4-meters up.

Thirsty mounts drank their fill from the pool.

A gusting breeze tossed their manes and tails.

Seleen unpacked the mule and rummaged through the pile till she found a heavy woolen blanket and her poncho with a belt. She laid them on a large rock, stripped, and stood beneath the warm water to bathe. Alahna did the same, but the breeze became wind. By the time they tied their ponchos in place and got the new riding boots back on, they both had goose bumps. Seleen filled a small kettle with water to boil for heating the bottle of canned stew and also refilled the botas with fresh drinking water from the pristine spring. It was high tide with the boom and roar of waves breaking against the sharp basalt pillars and hoodoos jutting from the deeper waters, which added to the rumble and whoosh of breaking surf on the beach, but they were situated well above the high-water line.

Filled with memories of her first trip to this dread-inspiring place with Lilith some 30-years ago, Alahna helped Seleen pitch the tent and start a cooking fire with a sturdy iron spit from which they hung the kettle of stew to heat. Dunes and saw grass had drifted against the surfaces of the huge monoliths on the inland side of the ledge where they camped. Lianas and vines caused the great doors to blend with the cliff. High on the scarp above, another vast portal gaped where immense granite doors lay blasted into the enormous cavern from their keyways during the Rebellion-of-the-Slaves over 5,000-years ago.

Gazing up at the entire mountain with intact doors below and the blasted opening so high above, Alahna felt a shiver run up her spine that was not entirely because of the cold bite of gusting winds. Fear of That-Which-Abides—the lowest state-of-consciousness for the WuShi—urged her to weather the night and depart with Seleen at first light. Counter to her fears, pressing thoughts arose. *I must brave this out and see for myself whether Oren speaks the truth. Regardless of what I find, if Lilith discovers I brought Seleen here, the repercussions will be the same as if I actually went in. There is nothing for it. This must be done. And I must do it.*

High Priestess Lilith's imperious words rang in Alahna's mind: *No adept of the Huan Long Shui shall ever sojourn to the Cape of Orion without my express permission. This most especially includes trying to sing the Great Lower Doors open to enter The-Sleeping-City, a cursed and evil place.*

Over her many years of scholarship as Keeper of the Archives, Alahna's superstitious fears from those days as a girl striking for the

1st Circle had morphed into empirical knowledge in the present by finally observing the place from an adult's perspective, but the contrast in point-of-view, or POV, was quite unexpected. Rousing herself to the present, Alahna said, "Let us pitch the tent, then gather driftwood."

They ate, walked the mounts and mule a short while along the beach, hobbled them with feedbags of grain hanging over their happy heads. With the walls of the tent behind them whipping and snapping in the wind, Alahna said, "Dost thou remember the first words of the Long Shai I taught thee?"

Seleen answered, "Yes, my Laoshi."

"They are words-of power to an ancient ritual-of-opening in songspell, the tune of which we practiced on our way here. Now, it is time to learn the gesture-of-positioning for a Sigil-of-Opening. My love, a day may come when I take thee within The-Sleeping-City, but not on the morrow. I must do what needs to be done and be out before nightfall, for even the stoutest of hearts would not remain in that haunted and evil place after dark.

"Should I not return by then, release the sigil and the great doors will close of themselves. But take heed. Do not get caught between them. They will crush thee to nothing. Afterward, ride home as fast as the mounts may go. Lay any blame on me."

Before sunrise, the wind abated and stormy sea calmed. Sleeping to the soughing tide in the shade of the overhang, early morning warmed the air inside the tent enough to awaken her. When Alahna realized how late it was, she dratted herself as they hurried to prepare, which included yet another practice session for the complex songspells. So the horses and mule would not get spooked, Alahna and Seleen removed their hobbles, walked them far enough away along the grassy dunes, and hobbled them again leaving them free to graze.

By the time Alahna was confident Seleen was prepared as possible, the sun reached zenith. As the breeze rose, they finally strode to the base of Great Lower Doors leading into the Caverns of Orion with the ShenLan Sea and the hobbled horses as the only witnesses.

Seleen sang the Song-of-the-Sigil with a precision and clarity Alahna often envied. The Sigil-of-Opening appeared and floated in the air above them with fiery-red flames sizzling along the indefinite surface of a huge ankh. Seleen directed it up in front of the giant stone slabs where a reddish, incandescent gout of ball-lightning burst from the surface to sweep across the imposing monoliths. Lianas and grasses caught fire and chuffed away as ash from the intense heat.

On the surface of the great monoliths, ancient techno-runes tall as a house came aglow as if lit from behind by the light of a full moon. In response, the enormous doors growled and stirred with tooth-jarring, sub-audible shudders as they grudgingly ripped away the smoking lianas and burning bramble. As the doors parted, fierce whirlwinds arose to clear the dunes, then whooshed along the great keyway. Swirling vortices scrubbed it clean. At length, the vast, arched promenade stood open. Fresh air mixed with ancient as a breeze disappeared into the unfamiliar darkness.

Subconsciously stalling against the inevitable entry to such an cursed place, Alahna turned to Seleen and proffered a brief history by waving her hands at the great mountain of basalt whose sheer cliff face towered into the sky. "The cape is hollow, thus the name Caverns of Orion. This is because an unknown number of hollow lava tubes connect the ancient volcanoes of Aryavartha to the ShenLan Sea from volcanic processes when Janaidar was a young world.

"An ancient-alien industrial complex lies within the gigantic cavern fully surrounding The-Sleeping-City itself, which is a vast dodecahedron. More than half of The-Sleeping-City rises above street level within. The Huan Long Shui archives reveal the overall height of the dodecahedron as between 13 and 14-kilometers, but the truth of this lies buried in the dust-of-ages. The archives never name the surrounding industrial complex, so I made notes to deem it the: Outer City of XiangBhala, the Inner City assumed to the great dodecahedron we commonly refer to as: The-Sleeping-City. Several names. One place.

"In the Outer City of XiangBhala, great edifices such as dwelling apartments, tower-cranes, and unimaginably tall buildings with many, many floors of unknown purpose surround The-Sleeping-City with 1,000s of large and small machine systems whose varied purposes are long forgotten. The main level of the Outer City is higher than the beach for obvious reasons, but whether the Outer City delves deeper than sea level is unknown. I suspect it must."

For clarity, Seleen added, "Recalling my volcanology, the cape is actually a misshapen yet hollow cinder cone where the outer layers of the ancient lava tube hardened as a circular mount to the north and a flat-sided cliff on the south. Afterwards, molten lava subsided leaving a vast chamber behind, which explains why the cape itself is almost as tall as an inland mountain."

Alahna nodded, saying, "I must employ a SijanPao whenever needed, for the Paos are key to entry. When I reach the Outer-Complex-Entry to the Outer City, I shall activate ancient techno-magic. Let us pray that I still recall the activation sequence, and that the ancient techno-magic still works."

Rolling her eyes, Seleen asked, "Is that all?"

"No, there is a specialized hand-dance which must be performed inside the nearby domain of the shining techno-runes hanging before ancient panels-of-light for any Sister, inside of a SijanPao, who wishes to enter.

"From there, I traverse the Outer City to reach the Lower Inner Portal of The-Sleeping-City. When Lilith and I came here so long ago, there was a bridge-of-force to the Inner Portal used to convey whatever was needed. From there, I cross The-Sleeping-City to the main-control-room known as the Almseeare, which lies within the base of the Central Obelisk between immense support columns. The archives purport the height of the Central Obelisk itself as 4-kilometers tall."

Seleen said, "Four kilometers?"—and she peered up at the sheer basalt cliff in wonder—"How high does that make the summit of the cape?"

Alahna said, "Since it approaches the thinning reaches of the middle cloud formations, I would guess in the range of about 6-kilometers above sea-level, but no more time for lessons. Since my SijanPao moves about as fast as I can run, it will take time to traverse The-Sleeping-City and return, which gives me some 2-hours to activate the eyes in the sky and suss out the truth of Oren's words."

Seleen peered into the darkness from the huge archway. "If it is so distant, should we not wait till the morrow and start afresh?"

Sorely tempted, Alahna had never been one to put things off. Moreover, she feared she might not go at all if she dithered. "No, my love, now is the time." Steeling herself, she hugged Seleen, spawned a Pao, and willed herself into the gloomy promenade.

Sleeping City

~

Foray Into XiangBhala

The vast arched tunnel through which Alahna slowly wafted above the dusty stone floor came aglow in response to her passing presence, then faded to darkness as she went on. It was eerie. The illumination seemed to lure her into some unknowable trap. Hairs on the back of her neck stood on end as she willed herself up along the right side of the Outer-Complex-Entry to hover before a large techno-glyph shimmering almost imperceptibly on the featureless gray yet perfectly smooth force-field.

Concentrating, she made the specific gesture-of-power the same as Lilith had done so long ago. Nothing happened. Her heart pounded. She closed her eyes, visualized, and tried again. This time an ethereal console winked into existence inside the boundary of her SijanPao just the same as when High Priestess Lilith and the ancient sea-dragon, Guardian of the West, Bo YouYong, brought her hence so long ago. Breathing a sigh of relief, she touched a small, glowing techno-rune, slid it about in that specific combination Lilith bade her practice over and over. The tactile feel of the virtual control-panel, a VCP, tickled her finger slightly as the unnaturally smooth gray expanse whuffed to nonexistence.

A turbulent mixing of inner and outer atmospheres stirred up whorls of ancient dust to drift past her in the direction of the beach. She gazed in awe, for there it stood in all of its ancient-alien splendor. The Outer City sat in quiet solitude surrounding the upper two-thirds of a city-sized dodecahedron. Whether it delved beneath street level of the Outer City was a further mystery, but the Sacred Mathematics of the

Huan Long Shui Archives informed her it was likely a regular convex polyhedron whose lower third was simply not visible.

Even inside the sphere-of-power, smells were unique. The inner air of the outer metropolis smelled of antiquity, forbidden-technology, rust, rotted lubrication fluids, and dusty decay. Once in front of the city-sized dodec, she wafted across a rippling bridge-of-force and hovered above the surface about halfway up one of the pentagons-of-force comprising the faces. A smaller pentagon outlined by red lines identified the location of the Lower Inner Portal, which was also vast.

Again, she called up a VCP and did the proper hand-dance. Some sort of arcane techno-magic sensed the size of Alahna's SijanPao, and the red outline adjusted to an accommodating size, and it winked open. Leaving it open on purpose, she wafted through and found herself at street level in The-Sleeping-City.

Before her lay a vast courtyard fronting the outer promenade encircling the abandoned metropolis along the outer perimeter. The inner shape of the courtyard seemed circular while the outer shape lay defined by linear force-fields as transparent yet easily discerned facets of the great dodecahedron. When she peered up at the distant, horizontal face of the city-sized dodec, she discerned a scattering of rock, sand, and windblown detritus littered with the skeletons of small animals. All of this was due to a collapsed portion of the cavern above the Outer-City with the afternoon sun streaming down through the jagged opening as wan and ghostly crepuscular rays. Again chiding herself for irrational fear, she wafted slowly into the haunted, abandoned metropolis.

Keeping her Pao about 2-meters in the air, she shouted in fright when a silvery shape about the size of a bovine bull rolled beneath her feet too close for comfort. The Pao got bumped upward a bit as it passed while completely ignoring her presence. This broke her concentration, and the Pao coasted to a stop. Once alerted to their presence, metal mechanical things of various sizes with strange and often grotesque shapes scurried about here and there in apparently mindless tasks: sweeping, dusting, repairing, climbing, cleaning, and so on. Lilith had described them as the mechanical servants of The-Creeping-Darkness known as jikiren. Their mindless yet active presence only ramped her fear.

Wherever the arcane contraptions went about their unknown duties, the metropolis seemed clean enough to occupy. The exception lay as profound desolation. These were the ruins of destruction and death Lilith had loosely named the burnt-out sector. Legends of intense fighting so many 1,000s of years ago became myths told to little children to frighten them into obeying their mothers. Here before her stood the deathly source of such myths. As a child, she hid her eyes when Bo YouYong levitated them past the awful place inside Lilith's Pao. Vectoring past the burnt-out sector now, Alahna had her first proper look at the ruins from the POV of an adult.

Scattered amongst the jagged, blown-out structures lay humanoid, long-skull remains with embedded metal joints at shoulders, hips, and knees. Most of these were so destroyed, or tangled in battle, it was impossible to identify which bony limbs belonged to which skeleton. Mixed among these were alien skeletons with human torsos, animalistic legs ending in digitigrade feet, and skulls big enough to contain human brains. Some few of these had beaks like the ibis. Most of the others were like lions, jackals, hawks, or crocodiles. All the smaller skeletons lay intermingled with hide draped skeletons of long-dragons, winged-dragons, and ordinary humans.

Frightening heaps bore silent witness of the rebellion when blackfire, dragon-flame, and the dreaded ShahRen bracelets wielded by both the Sisters-of-Fate and the true, untainted sisters-in-arms resulted in deadly combat to once and for all put an end to the NuliZhu intergalactic, transdimensional slavers left behind on Janaidar. Those untainted warrior-adepts became the founders of the Huan Long Shui Sisteren. Here lay tacit proof the stories were true. Alahna's archives described the Sisters-of-Fate as a sect of corrupt, hedonistic, power-be-sotted sorceresses who practiced human sacrifice by dark ritual and evil conjuration enhancing the purity of their dark arts. Renamed The-Blasted-Sisters in the archives, their dark arts were generically named The-Baneful-Chaos.

Captain Oren's dire words rang in Alahna's mind: Now, milady, it gets weird. They said beast-headed monsters and hulking, baldheaded men—as were white from head t'toe—come a flyin' down from the sky in a buzzin' silver ship what hung above 'em like an ominous cloud.

Beast-headed monsters, indeed. Here and now, Alahna wondered if the beings of this new threat were the living descendants of these bizarre skeletons. Counting as she went, she eventually crossed all 13 concentric boulevards to reach the towering Central Obelisk. She had no technical knowledge, but understood from Guardian Bo YouYong's teachings that the various eyes-in-the-sky were an arcane form of ancient-alien technology that peered down on Janaidar from farther out in the cold reaches of outer space than the Riven Moon.

At length, she approached the 4-kilometers tall Central Obelisk and derezzed her Pao before the open expanse of gargantuan columns in which lay the Almseeare. She looked up at the false sky as high as she could see. A turquoise glowing cuboid precessed in midair while slowly spinning above the pyramidal point of the monumental obelisk. From the precessing cube, vast, crackling bolts of blue lighting spat out into the accessible faces of the dodecahedron like arc-fire inside the High Pagoda. Wherever these sizzled into the faces of the great polyhedron, energy rivers and eddies flowed out to the common edges and vertices down to hidden faces. Clearly audible, the distant crackle of intermittent lightning broke that eerie silence, a dead silence. The near-invisible presence of ancient dust disturbed by her SijanPao stood as a silent reminder of the cost .

There beneath the great obelisk, she felt smaller and less significant than the tiniest gnat. Supporting the giant obelisk were massive support columns about 30-meters on a side for each triangular prism with the same distance between. A square column of equal sides formed keystone supports at each corner. Carved upon each face of every triangular column and keystone, arcane techno-glyphs and ancient-alien art depicted deeds heroic as well as arcane, esoteric sciences, and recondite rituals.

Deresolving her Pao on a slip-resistant yet smooth deck of pure obsidian, she gained her feet and hurried in to the hollow center of the vast obelisk. A vast and crackling column of roiling energy some 100-meters in diameter flowed up from beneath the city to feed the giant cuboid above the Central Obelisk.

As she entered the great hall of the Almseeare, she unconsciously sang a Song-of-Protecting beneath her breath while signing elementary wards with nimble hands. Once inside, she walked some distance along the staging promenade festooned with arcane tech, gauges, levers, dials, and VCPs springing into life even as she passed, and found the first control-station for a humanoid.

U-shaped saddles mounted on poles where a long-dragon could settle stood adjacent to a pair of humanoid work-stations. A pair of work-stations for huge winged dragons with great tails sat farther in line. The last control-station in this array was another set of saddles on poles for a long-dragon. Thirteen such complex control-stations lay at even intervals around the central energy column—the number 13 again.

She settled in and looked it all over. Both armrests were studded with toggles, levers, a pair of joysticks on either side with rolling balls in polished sockets beside each for the operator's palms. After a lifetime of study in deciphering ancient-alien techno-glyphs, older hieroglyphs, as well as other techno-runes, she found a modicum of meaning. They spoke of arcane and powerful concepts for which she had little to no conceptual framework like: Automated Battle Turrets; Target Acquisition; Gravity Generator Sub-systems Feeder Management; Pitch Attitude; Roll Attitude; Yaw Attitude; Acceleration Dampeners; Mass-Inertia Cancellation; Vector Analysis; Astronavigation; and so on.

Cloth fabric backing had long since fallen to dust leaving behind only metallic screen and mesh. A hoop with a metallic fabric framework rose from behind, arched over her head, and settled as a chest-harness and seat-belt. Lacking its original fabric backing, it felt sharply edgy and uncomfortable, but the remaining metallic fabric was at least sufficient to secure her in place. The entire assembly rose from the floor and secured her lithe body safely in a recumbent position from which she activated other VCPs. A dome of virtual screens flickered into existence to hover around and above her like a shimmering rainbow within arm's reach.

Old memories were fuzzy concerning the steps for tapping into the control-feeds of the ancient eyes-in-the-sky out in space beyond the Riven Moon. After several frustrating failures, and a growing angst that she had forgotten too much, she finally got the virtual panels working. The right-hand trackball zoomed her POV north and south along specific regions of the west coast of the island continent. The left-hand trackball lay nearly frozen, but allowed her to zoom the display in and out. Sparks beneath her hand made her fret. It was metal, the socket was metal, and she was sitting with bare skin in a metal chair. From experience in the High Pagoda, she knew all about deadly shocks from azure aether—she'd seen it happen.

Ignoring the danger, she tracked up and down, in and out along the entire region north of the LungHuo River. The marauders had stripped it of ordinary population and livestock except for baby offspring able to survive the loss of a mother. Where regional wild game around the settlements had always been abundant as the source of a thriving fur trade and meat for the people, there lay a dearth. Bleak and empty villages were nothing but burnt-out husks where uncontested wildfire leveled everything. Wherever wildfire did not run unchecked, she observed the extremely aged caring for prepubescent children. All were lean and sickly because of privation.

She mumbled to herself, "Old One-eyed Oren's yarns of the takings are true," and suddenly realized she had given a name to the mass abductions. If the pattern held, the marauders would be raiding the verdant LungHuo River Valley with Bahndahn Towne and Riverbend next.

Alahna's conceptual framework about spacecraft from the archives fitted Oren's description: a buzzin' silver ship what hung above 'em like an ominous cloud. With the ancient, inbred fear of the NuliZhu slavemasters invading her mind, she tried innumerable combinations of esoteric commands, but found herself unable to trigger the eyes-in-the-sky to zoom-out from the coast to a point where she could try and assess a NuliZhu presence in orbit. Even if she did, she had no idea whether she could observe all the way around planet Janaidar.

Beating on the left-hand trackball caused a spurt of feathered sparks. Even as she shouted and jerked her hand back, it went inert—as did her ability to zoom. Completely losing track of time, she became desperate as she tried everything she could think of. A rolling machine hove into view beneath her and silver machine appendages with snapping, finger-like digits reached up toward her.

She screamed.

Completely terrified, she squirmed free of the control-chair while singing a SijanPao and floated free. Peering down, she watched the unholy jikiren begin fussing with the deployed control-chair, and the VCPs went inert, which cast her into utter blackness .

Able to see the waning light of the oncoming nightfall past the vast columns, she oriented and wafted free . As she did so, her own words came to haunt her: Should I not return by nightfall, release the sigil and the great doors will close of themselves. Do not get caught in between them, they will crush thee to nothing.

More desperate thoughts arose.

I must hasten back and convene emergency council, but how can I tell them how I know of these attacks with such perfect certitude? Accursed Yenara will jump all over me, and she still harbors a grudge from the debacle at the Blind Hag. No . . . I must have faith. They will listen and believe me—they simply must. With grim determination, she willed herself through the abandoned and darkening metropolis with a terrified vengeance. Counting concentric boulevards as she went, she agonized over the waning light even to the extent of bowling over another tall and crazily shaped jikiren. She shunted out of vast dodeca-hedron like an angry wasp, and pushed hard across the Outer City, then into the ingress-egress tunnel of the Outer-Complex-Entry. Once there, she started hollering in hopes Seleen might hear and keep the Sigil-of-Opening in place.

Something worse than terror filled Alahna's belly as she considered the prospect of getting trapped with no confidence she could trigger egress from within, and no idea whether a Sigil-of-Opening would work from the inside. Like the sparking trackball, ancient techno-magic was always fickle. She could smell the sea even through the skin of the Pao. In a panic, she willed it forth with every iota of velocity possible. Obstinate, it lumbered along unheeding. As she approached the Great Lower Doors, a deep, tooth-jarring, sub-audible grinding filled her senses as she saw the gap between the huge monoliths grow smaller by the second.

A more serious panic struck her heart like the fangs of a curse-cobra.

Sleeping City

~

Dire Straits On the Beach

Pinioned on the horns of a dilemma, Seleen stood alone on the windy beach with the sun touching the curving horizon at sea. She muttered to herself, "Mistress Alahna told me to break camp and leave this accursed place if darkness fell. Maybe misfortune found her and I should go in?" The concept of letting go the Sigil-of-Opening and venturing into that evil place with the terrible doors rumbling shut behind her frightened her to the core. "I should be trapped forever. And how would I ever find her?"

Worry became despair.

Worse, holding the sigil in place had tired her to the bone. With creeping exhaustion setting in, she wrung her hands below the flaming sigil all the while trying hard not to inadvertently sign a gesture-of-power or positioning, and even tried yelling for her mistress. "Oh, my mistress, ple-e-ease come thee forth before darkness consumes the light!" All she got back were ghostly echoes sending chills up her spine.

The sea breeze had waned.

A strong, chilling land breeze lightly gusted out across the waves as high tide came in.

Thoroughly chilled, Seleen hurried down the dune to camp for a wrap while thinking of starting a campfire on the ridge outside the great doors to warm herself while she held the flaming ankh in place and perhaps give Alahna a beacon in the night.

With the sinking sun but a gray half-disc in the thickening mist, Seleen trudged back to the Sigil-of-Opening from camp after wrapping herself with a nice, warm cloak. That was when she noted a reddish glow above her head where it ought not to be. Unattended, the sigil had drifted slowly away from the entrance and started to flame out. She cried, "No! No! No!" as she scrambled up the dune through shifting sand losing one step for every two. Then, to her dismay, she felt a bone-rattling grinding.

The great monoliths!

Panic hit her in the stomach like a fist.

She desperately muddled the first attempt at reinforcing the sigil, which drifted and bobbed like a kite in the wind. Sobbing, she forced herself to breathe and seek her calm center, then tried again. She got the ankh to sputter, then fully reignite. Heart pounding against ribs like storm surf against rocks, she gestured it back into place; whereupon the doors stopped about 2-meters apart. Just when she thought she had it under control, they began bucking and grinding with a sickening determination as if some unknown force worked consciously against her.

Rushing about in a near panic, and only stopping every few seconds to reignite the weakening sigil, she fell to her knees and scooped a shallow pit in the top of the dune and surrounded it with nearby lava rocks as shelter for the fire from rising wind. She threw whatever driftwood she could find nearby, sang a fire-sprite, and blew on the tinder long enough to kindle a nice fire. When she looked up again, the damned ankh had started drifting and wavering again. Seeming to be associated, the bucking and growling from the massive doors grew more intense.

Things were getting worse by the second.

Even as Alahna willed herself at the closing monoliths, a thought in the back of her mind arose. *If I get caught in between, will my Pao keep them from crushing me?* Willing herself forth with all her heart as that ominous grinding clawed at her determination, she spied a small fire flickering on the dune in the gusting wind. She lowered her head and put everything she had into the last 100-meters while the doors stuttered and bucked and growled and groaned as the opening shrank. When the headlong rush aligned her with a stuttering meter-wide slit, she spied Seleen waving her arms, and a rush of love and relief flooded her chest. Firelight flickered and reflected on the great arched ceiling creating dancing, angry ghosts.

At about 2-meters from the great doors, they rumbled and broke free. Fears of being crushed within the Pao cascaded. She derezzed the Pao without a count and screamed as it disappeared. Tumbling, skidding, and stumbling, she scrambled to her feet and leapt. Her body curved through the air like a breaching porpoise. Falling short, she slipped down the far sloping keyway with yet another scream.

Forgetting the sputtering sigil, Seleen ran to the edge of the keyway, grabbed Alahna's wrists. As the great doors bit Alahna's boots, Seleen pulled her up and over.

Ba-oom!

The rumbling doors slammed shut.

They fell backwards in a heap wrapping their arms about one another in a tearful, sobbing embrace which lasted just long enough for the Sigil-of-Opening to drift sputtering across the edge of the dune and out over the breakers on the beach as a glowing ember.

Alahna stood, gathered her senses, brushed the sand from her clothes, and pointed. "The sigil belongs to thee, my love. I cannot give it cessation."

Seleen shook her head, sang the note-of-deresolution, and the remains of the sigil whuffed from existence with a soft bang.

Alahna looked down. The guttering light of Seleen's signal fire exposed scuff marks on the outer ankles of Alahna's boots.

Seleen felt desolate. "Oh, my Laoshi, I almost failed thee! I went to get a wrap—"

With a hug, Alahna stopped her mid-sentence. "Ts-s-s-ht, thou didst thy very best! It was I who lingered overlong. And keeping such a powerful sigil alive as a first test-of-passage after learning the Long Shai is a feat no adept I know hath ever attempted. Never have I been so happy to see such a fine little fire in all my life!" whereupon she took some big breaths to calm herself. "We must repair to the Keep early on the morrow. Sup now and get what sleep we may, for we break camp and depart before sunrise."

Despite the warm, safe desert tent with its sloping canvas walls flapping and snapping in the gusty breeze, Alahna could not sleep. Instead, she gazed at Seleen dozing innocently in her furs. Whenever Alahna closed her eyes, images of the scourged and empty hamlets along the northern coast played in her mind with cruel repetition.

Alahna's heart went out to the scattering of decrepit old bogiturs and crying little ones foraging for anything they could find, staying close to the longhouses in fear of starving wolf packs, or the deadly 4-meter centipedes whose venom could paralyze a small or weak human while the bloody thing consumed the flesh of its screaming victim alive. As for them, they were safe. For some odd reason, such creatures never attacked a Sister or her company.

She intoned a silent prayer. "Aerthe Mother Goddess, watch over them till we bring them to the Keep." Since the very moment Oren summoned them to meet him at the Blind Hag, the vague feeling of having set them both on a path from which there was no return gnawed at her psyche like an elusive wharf rat. Whenever she paid direct attention to the feeling, it slipped away but was never gone.

At some unknown moment in the night, the flapping of the tent walls lulled Alahna to sleep. When she sat up deep in the night, the breeze had changed to a bitter wind making the flutter and flap of the tent louder and sharper. The first thing her sleepy eyes made out were ghostly, misshapen shadows dancing on the slanted wall facing the sea. After a moment of disoriented fear, she realized the shapes were mere shadows cast by the Riven Moon waxing gibbous as it broke the horizon. Atmospheric lensing amplified its aspect to the point it seemed as if to cover the entire sky while illuminating the huge and jagged hoodoo spires of basalt jutting up through crashing waves.

Since it was too early to rise, she laid back thinking the ride home would give her a chance to compose a cogent response should the council refuse to believe on her—desperate thoughts for a worried mind.

Apparently also awakened by the flapping, and as if reading Alahna's thoughts, Seleen whispered, "Wherever thou shalt go, milady, know this. I would follow thee even through all seven of the Wandering Hells."

Broken from her sad reverie, Alahna whispered back, "And I for thee. It may very well be through the Seven Hells we are bound."

Cavern Keep

~

The Council of Four

Any member of the Council of Four had the right to call an emergent meeting with no questions asked, never to be taken lightly. For Lilith, Alahna's summons came too late the previous evening to be convenient, and the smell of horses on her Named One's tired body meant she had been riding all day. Lilith had refused. Knowing such a delay would set the tone for the next morning, she dreaded the inevitable conflict, for Yenara had been especially crappy to Alahna ever since the debacle at the Blind Hag Tavern.

As the sun broke the horizon in the east, the Lilith shambled into the Council Chambers early on purpose. The chambers were located in the first gallery of the housing warrens defining the quarters for senior adepts above the rank of 8th Circle.

A small hearth built into the wall for warming the chamber held a suspended teapot of boiling water prepared in advance by lesser acolytes. Lilith sat in her tall-backed, ornate chair at the head of the conference table, waited till all three of her peers were present, stood, and purposely turned her back on them to stand before a long table holding various sweets, viands, cups, mugs, glasses, and a pitcher of freshened water.

Sitting down at the head of the tall table mug in hand, Lilith sipped loudly and slowly several times on purpose to further annoy the others, then finally said, "Would anyone else like some tea?"

Alahna rolled her eyes.

Nebhet gathered her cup and did the same as Lilith had.

Obviously spoiling for a fight, Yenara sat impatiently tapping the floor with her foot while rolling her fingers tappity-tap-tap on the table in frustration.

Alahna finally said, "Please, Mother Matriarch, may we begin?"

Being rude as possible on purpose, Lilith supped loudly, blew across the top of the mug, supped with obnoxious intent once again, and finally said, "I call this meeting of the Council of Four to order," and she banged a sizable oaken ball on the careworn table. "Begin Alahna. And it had better be worth getting us all here at such an unholy hour."

Furious by then, Alahna took a deep breath to calm herself. She rose to pace in a tight circle behind her own ornate and high-backed chair. Waving arms for emphasis while raising her voice, she recounted the tale as told her by Captain Oren in oddly accurate detail. So Lilith thought.

After several minutes of beating around the bush with theatrical flourishes, Alahna made her conclusion. "Fellow council members, please understand. If we fail to act while there is yet time, I fear we shall awaken and find the people of Bahndahn Towne simply gone, with Riverbend next, followed by an attack on the Cavern Keep itself. Whoever—whatever—is doing this, they leave only the small children and aged behind. Able-bodied adults get taken along with the carcasses of livestock. Even a few granaries stand emptied ... erm ... so Oren said. We must raise up the WuShi to seek a techno-warrior sage from among the myriad dimensions who can teach us how to activate the ancient engines of war, for we have no way of protecting ourselves or our people."

Without addressing the subject matter of strange disappearances, Lilith fondled the Shuyi ShahRen black-energy weapon on her left wrist, raised her left arm, spoke quietly. "We have the SijanPaos. And, I have this." Whereupon, the ShahRen seemed to generate a golden halo for a short moment.

The pause following Lilith's declaration gave Yenara an opening to jump up. However, she stood so fast her huge wooden chair fell over backward with a loud clunk. Ignoring the chair, Yenara dismissed Lilith's assertion with a wave of her hand, which made Lilith's blood boil. But before she could chide, Yenara began shouting and waving her hands. Lilith muttered to herself, "Alahna finally goes mad while Yenara already waits there for her."

Yenara fairly shouted, "Must? Do mine ears betray me? That we are to believe Captain Oren on his word alone and thine own retelling?"

Lilith's mutterings had gone unheard beneath Yenara's diatribe directed at Alahna, except for Old Nebhet, who apparently read Lilith's lips through the claptrap.

Nebhet nodded at Lilith with a knowing smile.

Lilith shook her head.

Alahna bristled. "First Officer Boone corroborates."

Yenara's acerbic voice dripped with false sweetness while holding her empty palms above her head and punching the words out. "And who is this Boone? What do we know of him? I say no! This council would have evidence! Where is thine evidence, dear Alahna?"

Lilith sat back processing. Yenara, as always, acted the asshole bully. But what had Lilith preoccupied with disbelief, and shock, was Alahna's proposed transgression of the most forbidden act in the Canon-of-Precepts. Such an Awakening would be a compound crime warranting the Malison-of-Killing at Lilith's discretion as High Priestess. She could sense that it deeply hurt Alahna because they would not take her word at face value. This is so typical of Alahna, too.

Putting her dismay aside for the moment, Lilith said, "But to suggest opening the Forbidden Gate with an Awakening? I am uncertain whether thy proposal is blasphemy, sacrilege, sedition, or perhaps all three! I know for certain it is apostasy! Worse, thou art holding something back—hiding something—I sense it."

Alahna stuttered, "I . . . er . . . well—"

Sarcasm dripping from every word, Yenara cut in. "Really? What business didst thou have at such a den of thieves and liars in any sense? Perhaps to hobnob with doxies?" and she raised her hand to forestall Alahna's heated reply. "But let's ignore that! Art thou really and truly asking the Sisteren to help activate the Pillars of Thoth at the Plaza of the Forbidden Gate?"

Alahna opened her mouth to speak.

Yenara spewed extra invective. "All upon the word of Old One-eyed Oren and his new first officer from Bahndahn? Oren is the worst raconteur in the whole of Aryavartha?"

Alahna said, "There is Oren's entire crew, as well.

Yenara barked, "Liars! All under Oren's command!"

Still processing Alahna's suggested perfidy, Lilith watched the interplay between the two with a souring in her stomach. So tedious. So offensive. So predictable. Alahna struggling to conceal something. Yenara self-righteous in catching her out and thrilling at the opportunity.

Yenara raved on, "And search we must for some sort of hero, or sage, or savior, who would save us from . . . what?" and she turned her head from side-to-side as if trying to hear some distant sound.

Alahna set her jaw with glaring eyes locked on Yenara.

Yenara arched her eyebrows, raised her hands palms up to further underscore her contempt at not hearing an immediate answer. "Well? We are waiting."

Old Nebhet was the 4th Seat in the Council of Four. She sat gazing from one face to another with a shifting complex of expressions masking her wrinkled and weathered face depending on who she locked eyes with. Dismay to satisfy Lilith. Sympathy to empathize with Alahna. Contempt for Alahna to mollify Yenara.

Watching Nebhet, Lilith almost laughed.

Yenara gave Nebhet a withering glance of tacit warning to keep still and mind her own business.

Lilith rolled her eyes.

Alahna's jaws and hands clenched and unclenched as she struggled for rebuttal, but Lilith had heard enough and held up her hand.

Alahna glanced again at Nebhet for support.

Nebhet averted her eyes.

Lilith read Alahna's expression, read Yenara's, violence seemed a single breath away. Lilith slammed her mug down instead of the oaken ball. Infuriating her all the more, a spout of tepid tea shot up and doused her face, ran along extensive wrinkles, made runnels down her bare throat, dripped from her shaking wattle. Wiping her face and neck, she shouted, "Enough! Sit!" and glared at Yenara and Alahna both.

When neither complied, Lilith shot a needle of blackfire from the ShahRen on her left wrist. A tiny packet of sun-hot energy sizzled through the intervening space making a loud pop with a sparking puff of smoke on the rock wall behind. Glowing, smoking cinders spattered and bounced along the stone floor. The stink of burnt air and scorching stone lingered.

Fuming, Yenara settled for a pointed glare at Alahna, righted her fallen chair, sat with an exaggerated scowl and gave Alahna an eye roll of dripping contempt.

Lilith took a deep breath, but Alahna refused to sit. Weary of Alahna's continuing defiance, Lilith launched another needle of blackfire, which sizzled past Alahna so close the embroidery on the pointed shoulder of her blouse caught fire.

The sliver of blackfire made a loud pop as it hit the stone wall.

Hot cinders flew.

Smoking gravel hissed and sizzled through the back of Alahna's blouse.

A tiny cinder sizzled in Alahna's hair with a stinking puff of nasty smelling smoke.

Alahna shouted and shook the smoking cinder out of her hair, whipped her blouse over her head, threw it on the table, snuffed out smoldering circles with her hand.

An idle thought wafted through Lilith's mind. At least Alahna's habit of binding her breasts spared her from the added embarrassment of being unclothed in a moment such as this, which made Lilith realize the impact of shooting at her Named One.

Alahna held the smoking blouse out to see if she got all the tiny fires out.

Rage slowly painted itself on Alahna's face.

Watching Alahna react, Lilith more fully realized she had gone far too far, and she became desperate to push past the unwarranted, irrational mistake. "I warned thee—Alahna! Did I not? Now sit or leave!" and she raised her hairless eyebrows. Her chin-wattle quaked.

Old Nebhet came over behind Alahna, pulled a tiny jasper box from the medicine bag at her waist, then carefully applied healing salve on the mean little blisters while intoning a subvocal and abbreviated version of the Song-of-Healing. Nebhet's salves were as effective as her powers strong. The burns quieted. Peeking up at Alahna, she wrinkled her brow in sympathy.

Lilith sighed, then spoke with measured words. "Alahna, as Keeper of the Archives thou'rt a simple scholar. 'Tis not thy role to suggest such a call-to-action, even if such action were not forbidden. Such a call rightfully falls to the Kulapti as abbess of the Sisteren under myself based on whatever knowledge she has at hand. And, in case thou hast forgotten, Yenara is Kulapti under my warrant till I say otherwise! Moreover, calling this meeting in such an emergent manner was an obvious ploy to garner permission for performing an unwarranted perfidy with no time for proper deliberation.

"Need I remind thee, Alahna, thy sole task till I perform the Ritual-of-Abdication is to keep and study the Huan Long Shui Archives and teach our storied history to initiates and acolytes."

Lilith proudly pontificated, "Inflexibility is not the way of this council, nor is it mine own. Any sister may voice her concerns. Thou hast left me little recourse. I forbid any and all such actions at this time, and I shall brook no further discourse upon it. Am I clear? Thou shalt not break the decretums of the Sisteren!"

Alahna remained unusually quiet.

Lilith gave her the stink-eye and pressed on, "Without tangible proof, our only action will be to increase vigilance along the west coast."

Looking smug in her victory, Yenara sat back and smirked. Adding insult to injury, she locked eyes with Alahna and brushed her own shoulder to mock the singed embroidery on Alahna's blouse where it lay on the table.

The glower on Alahna's face made Lilith uneasy. It was obvious that upon realizing she had been foiled, Alahna simply withdrew without conceding. Imperious of tone, Lilith formally drove her point home. "Keeper of the Archives, Alahna, thou shalt bring to this council something more tangible! Thereupon, we shall properly reconsider all the facts in the due measure of time. Moreover, thou shalt take thy concerns to the Kulapti first, as befits thine assigned role. This Calling-of-the-Council is over!" and she once again banged her goblet on the table instead of the oaken gavel.

Another spout of tepid tea spattered up. Lilith spluttered. Wiping her face with the sleeve of her blouse and muttering to herself, she rose to leave, but motioned for Alahna to remain. Lilith locked her rheumy-eyes on Yenara, saying, "As for thee, my dear Kulapti, send a high-adept with some lesser adepts on horseback with escort of hired men from Riverbend to reconnoiter the northern frontiers along the west coast and keep sharp eyes and ears for aught as may be suspicious."

Despite the devastating toll on her as victor, which was tantamount to defeat whether she knew it or not, Yenara seemed resplendent, nodded at Alahna like a typical asshole would, then strode triumphantly past the huge oaken door.

Nebhet remained quiet while helping Alahna carefully don the scorched blouse.

Alahna smiled a wan smile at Nebhet as the aged adept departed.

Leaning on her cane at the doorway, Lilith took hold of Alahna's forearm. "My darling, I am sorry I burnt thee. Please forgive . . . I lost my temper. Also, please remember the well-being of the entire Sisteren rests upon Yenara's shoulders. In making thee my Named One, it hath not been easy for her. Perhaps I should reconsider my decision?"

The look of crushed feelings that fell across Alahna's face made Lilith regret the hurtful question.

Alahna pleaded, "But it was thee who took me to the Caverns of Orion and into The-Sleeping-City when I was but a garil; and taught me to sing the great doors open; and how to activate the walls-of-light; and to look down upon Aryavartha from the blackness of outer-space."

Mention of The-Sleeping-City set Lilith's face in stone. "Yes, my dear child, I did as the Canon-of-Precepts demands. And for the many years since, I wish I had ignored that precept. Lurking and sly, the WuShi forever waits to rise up and throw us down. I would remind thee, the prime responsibility of the Sisteren is to ensure it never reawakens. Now tell me!"—and she rattled Alahna's elbow with surprising strength—"Hast thou already been to that accursed place? Last night thee smelled like horse."

Alahna averted her gaze. "No, Mother Matriarch. Never would I do such a thing without thy leave."

"Good! Then go down to Riverbend and find Old One-eyed Oren. Bring him thence—and this Boone too. I would know soon enough if they spin tall tales. I understand Yenara's young acolyte is quite good at wringing the truth out of ne'er-do-wells."

Upon reference to the Song-of-Truth from the debacle at the Blind Hag, Alahna's face became stone.

As Lilith shambled down the stone corridor, she watched a furious Alahna stomp away. The set of Alahna's shoulders worried Lilith. She had never seen her Named One this angry. She shook her head and mumbled to herself, "Not ready to be high priestess . . . maybe never will be . . . must think on this. . . ."

Cavern Keep and Riverbend

~

Summons to a Drumming

Alahna's humiliation in the Council Chambers had started at sunup. When the council adjourned only a short time later, she rousted a sleepy Seleen. Before anybody could ask Alahna what they were about, and before Lilith came to the obvious conclusion and took steps, she and Seleen hurried to the Great Southern Portal of the Cavern Keep while acting nonchalant to keep anybody who saw them pass by from getting suspicious. When they got to the vast portal, they found the newly adept Sisters in the 1st Circle had already sung it open for ventilation as the first of their daily chores before moving on to other routine mundanities.

For the moment, nobody was there.

Before anybody else came into the cavernous gallery, Alahna spawned a SijanPao, suppressed her magicfire to spare their clothes and kit, took Seleen in. Alahna willed them laterally out into the sunshine and directly into the deluge of the Huan Long Shui Falls where the underground river spilled forth from the Cavern Keep. The overall height was about 200-meters from the crest to the misty, rocky base. With the sphere-of-power hidden inside the plunging deluge, they squealed in delight. The moment their voices trailed off, however, Alahna sang inner SijanPao.

Laughing, Seleen blurted, "Nobody but thee would ever do such strange and frivolous things."

Grateful to be back in the company of her beloved, Alahna laughed. After about 5-seconds, they neared the roaring outcrop of boulders at the mist-shrouded base, and she willed them out of the deluge behind an enormous boulder along the west edge. Still in the mist, she flew them around it, derezzed the dripping outer sphere-of-power, flew them several meters farther, then derezzed the new inner one with a count of four.

With the breeze from the box canyon blowing south, their feet touched dry ground. The distance from here to the confluence of the Huan Long Shui and the mighty LungHuo Rivers was about 9-klicks along a beautiful, tree-lined course. To the west of the falls, there was a substantial meadow with horse-training stables. Far enough up the box canyon to be away from the roar and remain upwind from the stink of manure and swarming flies, the wealthy Sisteren maintained a longhouse with caretakers and a hostler named Ruby. Ruby's husband was a blacksmith. Their three daughters helped with chores in between learning math and letters from a rotation of matronly Sisters.

The smithy and two of Ruby's daughters were busy shoeing horses. The third young lady baked pies in the house. Carried on a breeze coming down the canyon, the scent of freshly baked apple pies on a windowsill almost compelled Alahna from her quest, for they had not yet eaten. When she tried to drag a protesting Seleen to the stables, Seleen broke free and stole a fresh one. Hustling along behind her thefty acolyte, Alahna placed a gold jinn on the windowsill. When they got to the barn, Alahna had to grab her half of the hot and scrumptious treat before Seleen gobbled it all down.

With crust and fruit around her mouth, Seleen grinned. "That was too good. No mission overcomes the need for pie—especially hot pie!" Following Alahna's example, Seleen rinsed her face and hands in a washbasin inside the tack room of the barn while Alahna wrote a hasty note.

Having been here the night before, their gear was still on the racks, and they saddled their favorite mares in a bit of a hurry. As they rode out into the early morning sun, Seleen's saddle slipped and she fell to the dirt with a whump. Unhurt, she picked herself up and dusted off with the mare waiting patiently.

Laughing, Alahna chided, "How many times must I tell thee? Tighten the cinch twice."

Embarrassed while dusting herself off, Seleen put the saddle back in place, cinched her saddle twice—with an eye roll for Alahna—and they cantered away. Within an hour, they reached the bridge crossing the Huan Long Shui River at the confluence and soon trotted through the huge torii fronting the Pagoda Center.

It was still early morning when they got to Maxfield's stables next to the pagoda business center. Alahna dismounted and greeted Maxfield with a pat on his shoulder. "I have need of Dorak. Please fetch him. Then, pick out thy four fastest mounts and place our saddles on two of them. Tie fresh saddle blankets to the cantles and a sack of fruit and cut vegetables as travel fare for us."

Bowing without question, Maxfield hurried off and came back with Dorak, then hustled away to get started.

Placing her hands on the young man's shoulders, Alahna greeted him warmly.

Looking down, he blushed.

Alahna said, "Dorak, I have an errand for thee. Dost thou know those here in town who usually attend my full moon drummings each month?"

He nodded. "Yes, milady."

"Go about town and tell them to meet us at the drumming-trees as soon as possible. Tell them 'tis urgent, and I brook no delays. There will be rewards, and they must either come now or not at all. Canst thou do this?"

Thrilled, Dorak glanced at Seleen and blushed again. Seleen fished in her purse and gave him a 14-gram jinn. A small fortune for the lad.

Alahna smiled at Seleen as he ran off like his pants had been set afire. "He nurses a crush on thee."

Seleen smiled knowingly.

Alahna added, "I'll wager he still has that bit of gold from the day Yenara sang The-Dreaded-Geis."

Seleen laughed.

To Maxfield, who was busy moving their saddles to his fastest pair of geldings, Alahna said, "Thou hast two helpers on this sunny day?"

He nodded and called one of the apprentice farriers over.

Alahna said, "Young man, run to Esau's house and tell him to gather up Tarik and bring the tanggu drum to the drumming-trees. Tell him I said there can be no delay. If he cannot find Tarik, he is to get whatever help he needs and come anyway."

By this time, Maxfield and his other apprentice farrier had the long-gaited geldings saddled. Maxfield left the young man to finish and came to Alahna. "My adept, if I might ask?"

Alahna said, "My intent is to call an impromptu drumming at the Plaza of the Forbidden Gate. Shall I expect Jiba and thyself to join us at the drumming-trees?"

At mention of the Forbidden Gate the old hostler paled and backed away. "N-no, Milady Alahna. I think I remember Jiba plans company for evening meal."

It was a hasty lie, but Alahna understood. She also knew that when the rest of her adherents heard what she was about this night, most would balk. The Plaza of the Forbidden Gate was a magnificent yet terrifying place of calamitous evil, evil because the presence of an actual daemon inhabited the plaza beneath the Pillars-of-Thoth.

The daemon's presence became physically evident whenever some desperate thief sought to plunder the precious gems and solid gold in plain sight on the freestanding fount named the Opal Basin. Whenever this happened—no matter who it was—they got burnt to drifting ashes in a horrific death known as a Razing, animals and birds in contact with the surface went up in smoke as well. A Razing was similar to The-Dreaded-Geis, but happened so swiftly and with such terrible brilliance it was like a grisly explosion.

From time-to-time, some desperate soul, who desired the healing waters from the Opal Basin dragon fountain on the edge of the great plaza, ran bucket in hand past the Ring-of-Razing from the edge of the ramp, scooped the bucket full, then ran like hell back to the ramp with the intensely glowing waters. None on such a mission-of-mercy had ever been Razed. Small ponds in basins down the hill to the river were fed by the overflow. Eventually, however, the azure healing waters disappeared into a lush bog, which never flowed cleanly into the mighty LungHuo.

Alahna and Seleen trotted their mounts straight to the butcher shop while leading the spare horses with halters tethered to the cantles of their saddles. This was where their good and loyal friend was most likely to be found. Conrad the Hunter was also a butcher when he was not out in the wilds. He was also best friends and hunting buddies with Esau and Tarik. Alahna found him busy butchering a large slab of beef. At her bidding, he got cleaned up while she explained her intentions. He was reluctant, but she knew he secretly loved her. Seleen had chided her about not nipping this in the bud, but Seleen herself had always been a flirt.

Once an initiate had the Song-of-Initiation sung upon her, intimate relations with men became forbidden. Those who ultimately wanted a family, or to be free of the Sisteren for whatever reason, were gently desisted from their higher powers. They often became healer-women and holders of property known as lay-adepts, or gypsy-adepts who traveled among the people as healers. All were highly revered.

Again riding at a fast canter, Alahna and Seleen waved as they passed the people already on their way.

A renowned master of the roasting spit had assumed the spontaneous event would be a communal barbecue as usual and hitched a team of horses to his wagon-mounted iron roasting pit with two butchered hogs on the front rack. Several oaken barrels of ale jostled on the rear platform. Alahna always paid him well. Each of her adherents owed her the life of a loved one because of her well-known powers of healing powers and would march with her through the gates of the Seven Wandering Hells if she asked. Her usual generosity enhanced both gratitude and loyalty.

All the activity had taken place so fast that very few folks had arrived at the drumming-trees when Alahna and Seleen rode in to provide additional directives from horseback.

Alahna spoke to the master of the roasting spit. "As the rest of the adherents arrive, tell them to remain till we return around midafternoon. I require this if they want their quarter-split of a gold jinn."

Forbidden Gate

~

Last Chances

The dominant bull of a small herd of cattle in the near distance kept wary eyes on Alahna and Seleen as they departed the drumming trees. A ring in his nose glistened in the sun when he stamped his hoof and snorted. Without a bulldog, mounted humans represented little threat.

Alahna's voice sounded heavy with emotion. "Let us walk our horses but remain mounted. As thy Laoshi De Mofa, thou art duty bound to do as I say till obedience involves the commission of a crime, or other offense as defined by the Canon-of-Precepts, or one of Lilith's irrational proscriptions. Going to The-Sleeping-City despite Lilith was a minor offense. What we are about today is a criminal infraction of the precepts and covenant in dizzying succession. One of several reasons for our abrupt departure from the Keep was to preempt Yenara's inevitable attack on me through thee, for she comes at her enemies via their allies, friends, confidants, or—"

"Acolytes?" Seleen interrupted.

Alahna went on, "Prudence would have a wise acolyte depart this path now, return to the Keep, and disavow her teacher-of-magic. I would add that most people never know what they need to know till after they need to know it. In light of all this, my love, 'tis my duty to provide for thee a clear choice without manipulation. As an Adept in the 10th Circle, thou art thine own woman."

Seleen rode quietly for a time. "If I disavowed thee, Yenara would make my life unto a living hell of menial tasks, onerous duties, and never ending insult. She and her gaggle of eejits are cruel in the extreme.

Sooner or later, she would force me out of the Sisteren on some pretext or another, and if sooner, under penalty-of-desistance on some trumped up charge. So . . . the hell with her. . . .Also, and more importantly, I believe the same as thee. Some sort of unknown evil rears its ugly head on Aryavartha.

"As for the rest, I am aware that my knowledge of thy deeper secrets is sorely lacking, and I also know why. If the sharing of forbidden secrets ever took place between us, as thou sayest, Yenara might compel confession. So, my love, here is my truth. I trust thee. I will follow thee. I will help thee, and I shall protect thee till I go to the winds of time. I am thine and thou art mine. And, lastly, I love thee with all my heart."

A lump in Alahna's throat made her pause while she wiped tears from her eyes. "And thee as well," whereupon they reached out and touched fingertips.

Seleen also wiped tears from her cheeks.

To move them past the moment, Alahna said, "When next we walk the horses, I will teach thee what Lilith hath forbidden," and they urged the horses to a fast canter for about 2-kilometers, then slowed to a mounted walk again.

Alahna spoke freely, "I explained one part of the reason for such a hasty departure from the Keep. The other reason is literally astronomical. Recall for me the Tetrads from our Holy Astronomies."

Seleen intoned, "Tonight is the fourth full lunar eclipse of the first of eight Tetrad Syzygies to occur in this century. Tonight will also be the rarest of all celestial alignments: a Dragon's Blood Moon during perigee when the Riven Moon is closest in its orbit to Janaidar. Moon-source during perigee is strongest when Janaidar's umbra, or complete shadow, falls across the face of the full moon and the sun's light reflects off the surface of Janaidar.

"Mariners know, as do all who think on such things, that blue becomes red at sunset. It is the same with moonlight reflected off of Janaidar during a full lunar eclipse. Carmine moonlight falls to Janaidar fully imbued with moon-source."

Alahna approved with a nod and pointed as they got closer. "See the granite that comprises the Pillars-of-Thoth? Thick veins of quartz crystal with an abundance of pure gold imbues the granite with ley-lines-of-power that attract and channel ambient source-energy.

The archives hold that a peoples known as the Kmpti—from a land called K'mt—had been enslaved by the same ancient-aliens who built The-Sleeping-City. The Kmpti are our ancestors. The heads of the ancient-alien NuliZhu were elongated. Otherwise, they appeared to be human. However, they could not crossbreed with humans. Regardless, both the NuliZhu and Kmpti worshiped humanlike gods with the heads of animals, which is why the giant reliefs on the Pillars of Thoth depict the body of a human with the head of an ibis.

"There was a set of scrolls in my archives of which several remain missing to this day. What is left of them is more disturbing and hideous than the mysterious enslavement of the Kmpti and other races of humans on Janaidar about whose past the archives are silent. One scroll seemed to indicate that the NuliZhu kept star maps and galactic time tables, and were a spacefaring species of slavers. That very scroll indicated they had spread across our galaxy much farther back in time than five millennia in our odd past."

The two rode in silence for a few minutes.

Seleen said, "So . . . art thou finally ready to reveal what occurred inside The-Sleeping-City, and what frightened thee so deeply?"

Alahna spoke quietly, "To find the truth of Oren's tale, I employed the ancient-alien techno-magic known as the eyes-in the sky to peer down from the heavens along the western coast. Our people are really and truly gone. What is more, I think the spacefaring NuliZhu may have returned to Janaidar. It is the only explanation. Perhaps this is the reason our dragon guardians originally placed The-Sleeping-City underground?"

Seleen said, "And why we, the Huan Long Shui Sisteren, also live hidden under the Huan Long Shui Plateau?"

Alahna nodded.

Seleen asked, "How much of this is known to Lilith?"

Alahna shook her head, saying, "All, and she is the only other, for she barred me from ever sharing the history I uncovered upon pain of revoking my status as her Named One. And, I should even not tell thee about this."

Seleen rolled her eyes. "When somebody says, 'I should not tell about this.' It usually means they want to or need to. So, what should not be told?"

"After this morning's feud, Lilith threatened to actually rescind my status as her Named One."

"Does this also account for her proscriptions upon thee afterward?"

Alahna nodded. "There lies a darkness within Lilith from her past, which colors her behavior in the present. She even suspected our clandestine trip to the cape, and I was forced to lie and deny."

"Denial. . . ." Seleen said.

"And there is one thing I know above all else. Lilith hath come to believe that ignoring the unwanted, they will simply go away."

"Denial. . . ." Seleen said again.

"I also believe the Guardian Dragons to be complacent in their arrogance about humans as a species, and perhaps even reactionary. Why else would our people never develop higher technologies than steam power? And, if I am correct, there is no time to ask the dragons. Neither would it be prudent. If I am right, they would also stop me, and they could do so with a thought. No, my love, the time to act is now or never."

Seleen shook her head sadly. "If Lilith knows all of this and still took no action on thy word, it is far past her time to abdicate."

"Lilith is not our greatest worry. It is the Guardian Dragons."

Bored with walking, the horses whinnied and broke into a canter.

Forbidden Gate

~

Dark Histories

With the heat of the day rising, it was time to walk the horses and let them cool again. Alahna moved on to a new subject. "I'll share something of my past, Seleen, a history closely intertwined with the granite the ancients mined for the Pillars-of-Thoth."

Seleen, "From the forbidden-quarry, correct? Will we ever go and see?"

Alahna's voice seemed heavy. "It is a place of haunting ghosts and abiding danger."

"Which is why it is forbidden?"

Alahna said, "There are nuances and dark histories both. Pure inclusions of an unnamed mineral resembling tar pitch entrained in the granite of the quarry and Pillars of Thoth is what makes the dust carried on the gusting wind currents coming off the plateau, or down the valley from the quarry, ripple with a yellow-hued glow on a dark night. The glow itself is not deadly, but that which causes it is."

"Townspeople name the glowing winds around the pillars as the ghostly-shimmers and use it to scare little children with tales of The-Creeping-Darkness," said Seleen.

"That, my love, is a good example of how a simple myth can become unto a religion. For that reason, we the Sisteren will never allow any sort of religion to spring up around the Plaza of the Forbidden Gate or forbidden-quarry, because we the Sisteren know that nothing of either is godlike, only ancient-alien technology, or naturally dangerous minerals. And both are damn deadly to the innocent.

"Our people do just fine worshipping the Aerthe Mother Goddess, which neither requires sacrifice nor clergy. To this end, our gypsy-adepts and lay-adepts all carefully foster a benevolent belief in the Aerthe Mother Goddess. Even I feel her immanence when we are out here in nature."

Seleen looked around them. "As do I."

Alahna, "The last thing our people need is another sect of twisted old men declaring themselves to be holy priests of Thoth bilking the people of their hard earned jinns and abducting innocent young garils to the Pillars of Thoth to be Razed in the name of a false, ibis-headed god. In secrecy and stealth, a sect of twisted brutes declared themselves to be holy men when I was but a child. Eventually, they grew bold enough to capture some innocent young initiates on their merry way to Riverbend from the Cavern Keep for an autumnal bazaar. Stripped and hogtied, they sacrificed the garils one by one by throwing them bodily past the Ring-of-Razing at the Forbidden Gate, each screaming their innocent little hearts out. All to prove that the false god, Thoth, truly exists."

Seleen put her hands over her mouth in shock. "Men in secret collusion, and their history hidden? But the Razing exists of its own terrible accord."

Alahna agreed, "Just so, young acolyte. This horror took place in a single night of terror not long after Lilith became high-priestess. When Lilith and her high-adepts sussed out what had happened, they covertly observed enough of the cult's ongoing outdoor gatherings from inside their SijanPaos, which they rendered invisible of a purpose. This was how they identified the ringleaders and those who were beyond hopelessly deluded.

All in a single night, the high-adepts dispersed, found every such adult and ringleader, then quietly and covertly took them into outer spheres-of-power and flew them away. To the good people of the LungHuo Valley, the entire cult simply and completely vanished overnight."

They rode in silence for a time.

Seleen eventually said, "Let me guess. Emptied of mercy, they flew them to the quarry?"

Alahna spoke with deep sadness. "And dropped them screaming from on high into the deepest shaft. After which, Lilith blasted the periphery with her ShahRen. The cave-in buried them one and all."

"And, thus, the naming of the quarry as forbidden?" Seleen finished. "And thus why people spread the tale that we Sisters can take them into our spheres-of-power and rise into the sky to drop them."

"The truth will out, as they say. There might even have been witnesses. Regardless, the Sisters, lay-adepts, and gypsy-adepts of that terrible time worked with a single purpose to quash rumors about the disappearances by spreading rumors that the entire cult abandoned their children, rafted down the LungHuo, floated quietly past Bahndahn Towne, and foundered in the swelling seas of the LungHuo River bar. There is an old saying among us. To quash the truth, bury it under so many half-truths nobody can discern."

Appalled, Seleen said, "Such things would never occur to me. Still yet more dark history in our hidden past."

"Old Nebhet is the last of the Sisters from back then who yet lives, except for Lilith. Simple shame enforced silence and secrecy. As for Nebhet, she pulled me aside for several days to document this terrible piece of our history. As for me, I leave it to the next Keeper of the Archives to decide whether they will ever bring this to light for a new generation. For me to reveal it now would kill Lilith out of pure shame."

"Doth Lilith know of this documentation?"

With a sad nod, Alahna avowed it so.

"Then Lilith knows of thy silence?"

"I told her that my love for her would forever keep it locked away."

"That was when Nebhet revealed she is—"

"Keeper of the Curses," Alahna filled in.

"So, this explains Lilith's dark demeanor. And she is still quite willing to use her ShahRen to this very day. The burns on thy back speak in silent testament."

Alahna was pensive. "Dearest Seleen, Lilith's burden is to bear the only known ShahRen while spending the rest of her life in fear of falling to The-Baneful-Chaos.

"This is what befell The-Blasted-Sisters millennia ago.

"And we know from what little history exists of the fallen Keeps to the North, East, and South here on Aryavartha, that even those high-priestesses fell to The-Baneful-Chaos. This forced their contemporaries to deal them unto death. In fact, so many fell trying to kill their evil high-priestesses when it happened, that the high-adepts who survived could no longer live there."

Seleen said, "Fallen Keeps?"

As Keeper of the Archives, I may be the only Sister who knows this. And the musical elements of such were taught to me by Old Nebhet. Except for a very few, curses are named as malisons. Of course, songspells are self-explanatory. But there are two that are not known. We call these imprecations."

Seleen wondered aloud, "Imprecations?"

Alahna filled in. "People never go to the fallen Keeps because they lie protected by simple dread. In fact, it is a dreadful dread so truly dreadful it makes people eschew even the thought of going there."

Seleen put it together. "Imprecations-of-Dread cast upon the fallen Keeps?"

"Thine insight is profound."

Seleen went on, "Which implies a counter spell. An imprecation of what, then?"

"The Imprecation-of-Solace. And I must teach these to thee someday, but not this day."

"And Lilith?" Seleen asked.

Alahna almost whispered, "Fear of The-Baneful-Chaos abides in Lilith always."

Seleen said, "But if she fears the power thus, why cling to it so fiercely?"

"It retards normal aging."

"Which is why Lilith appears younger than Old Nebhet?" Seleen asked.

Alahna said, "Nebhet had yet to strike for the 5th Circle when Lilith became High Priestess."

Seleen mulled the revelations. "What happened to the children of the cult members Lilith dropped into the forbidden-quarry?"

"Orphans every one. Boys were adopted into the trade guilds of Bahndahn Towne. Garils got adopted into the Sisteren."

"What about the memories of family?"

"The orphans were told the same as everyone else."

Seleen rubbed her chin in thought. "Yenara is about 10-years older than thee. Was she—"

"Records indicate she was," Alahna interrupted quietly.

"Which explains why she gathers her gaggle of eejits so close at all times—fear of being abandoned."

Alahna was circumspect. "It forever galls Yenara that I am Lilith's Named One. And it forever galls me that Yenara reigns over the Sisteren as a tyrant while Lilith protects her and stymies me. Who can say what goes on in Lilith's mind? And yet I love her so."

They rode for another silence, then Alahna said, "Anyway, about the forbidden-quarry. All who ever sought to mine the accursed native-gold in the veins of quartz there died soon after, or later in life, of incurable cancers. To the best of my knowledge, mine own parents were the last of the older generation who tried to mine the gold laden quartz veins. Both died when I was a child of 4-years."

Seleen said, "Yet another reason the quarry is named as forbidden. I never knew. Does this explain the obsession with the Plaza of the Forbidden Gate?"

Alahna snipped, "Mine only obsession is to save Janaidar. And the council bars me while the dragons rule in absentia."

"Sorry . . . insensitive . . . please forgive. . . ."

Alahna pressed on, "Archives reveal the Pillars of Thoth were once a colossal monolith taken from the forbidden-quarry in a single chunk, the shape of which was a regular, pentagonal polyhedron. Somehow, an incredible cylinder of solid stone got shorn from out the center, which lies in the quarry to this very day. The archives speak vaguely of how the NuliZhu Tech-Masters split the resultant monolith down the center, levitated those gigantic halves through the sky using arcane techno-magic, and laid them down to be worked and shaped as we see them today. Once complete, they stood them in place as the Forbidden Gate."

Seleen said, "One wonders how they worked the faces with such incredible artistry and skill without dying?"

Alahna's voice became heavy. "Many 1,000s of their slaves did die, but the scroll recounting any greater detail is one of several that remain missing."

They rode in silence till Alahna said, "The dowager who took me in after my parents got carried away on the winds of time was the towne assayer and also a trained physical chemist. Valeena was childless and single and loved to care for me when my parents went to the quarry. A mining blast my parents set off triggered a rock slide of house-sized boulders with a profusion of smaller rocky debris and heavy dust.

To this very day, whenever gusting winds stir up softer minerals in the hills of the quarry valley, the currents and whorls of the deathly winds glow in weirdly bright colors. Often bright green with yellow hues.

"Terrified to flee the quarry in the cloud of sickening dust, my parents waited for nightfall, but a ragged, whirling wind rose up that evening keeping the dust suspended. When darkness set in, the dust glowed brightly in the color of green-death. With no choice, they finally realized some elemental force was killing them whether they stayed or ran. In a panic, they used the deadly glow itself to scramble through the lethal heap of house-sized boulders and rocky debris.

"Terribly sick when they staggered into town, they died within days of each other from horrible, unnatural burns. Their hair fell out. Bodies blistered. Skin fell away leaving terrible lesions. I shall never forget the pitiful stink as they lay moaning in their own mess while the healer-women held me back in tears. None of them would approach my parents either. The old Sisters from the Keep could do naught but ease their passing.

"Val herself never got close to the larger bulk of ore, and myself even less. However, wet assays require powdering fist-sized samples into dust to be dissolved in aqua regia; followed by boiling with other precipitants to recapture metallic gold; then compare its weight to the weight of the original sample and gauge purity. Breathing that dust, or the invisible elements of gas when performing the assays, might very well be what finally took the life of my beloved Valeena.

"As for me, I twisted the crank of the fan mechanism to carry the dust and gases from inside her workplace to outside the building. The rush of incoming fresh air from a grated window always blew my hair into a tousle. It likely saved my life, but I was so small. . . ."

Seleen said, "I sense guilt, but Valeena should have known better."

Alahna sighed. "I was five years of age when Valeena fell ill with incurable cancer. Again, the Sisters could not heal her. And . . . knowing she was dying—"

"She left thee in the care of the Sisteren," said Seleen. "Mine own mother abandoned me," and she trailed off sadly. "But I never got mean like Yenara."

"It is difficult for a single mother with child to land a husband," Alahna said. "Few men will raise another man's ilk—especially a garil—which is why we replenish the Sisteren by taking in all female orphans such as Myrna and Teewan."

Seleen brightened. "They are so cute. Completely inseparable. And both follow Cailinn like puppies."

Alahna went on, "When I attained to the 11th Circle, Lilith was my Laoshi De Mofa. She taught me to sing a SijanPao, just as I shall finish for thee on the other side of this sorry misadventure. Not long after, I pilfered a bag of jinns from the gold-repository and secretly hired a land surveyor to derive the measurements of the plaza and pillars from a safe distance.

"The pillars stand 74-meters apart at the top and bottom poles. Calculations established the perfect semicircle in each to be 125-meters in diameter. Obviously, the same diameter as the vast cylinder at the forbidden-quarry. The overall height is 228-meters. The entire stretched opening between them is close to 199-meters wide."

So saying, Alahna urged her horse to a canter.

Seleen followed.

When they reached the base of the great ramp at the Plaza of the Forbidden Gate, they dismounted and unsaddled their mounts with both fresh mounts waiting patiently. The saddles and bridles got laid on a sheet of flat rock. They hobbled the fresh mounts to graze near a small beach. Minding the well-being of the overheated mounts they rode in on, they walked the sweating geldings into cool waters along the beach, splashed them to wash the lather of sweat away, and set them loose to graze their way back home.

Sheer cliffs of basalt defined the entire perimeter of the Huan Long Shui Plateau, the surface of which lay a kilometer above the oak savannas down in the valley. Aeolian arches, hoodoos, and bridges across open chasms abounded. A horseshoe canyon carved by the great LungHuo River surrounds the plateau where stands the Plaza of the Forbidden Gate.

Beneath an open-growing oak near the base of the great ramp leading up to the plaza, both adepts stripped and left their clothes on a boulder. Alahna spawned a SijanPao, took Seleen in, and they flew up to gaze at the Pillars-of-Thoth.

Once there, Alahna hovered slowly past the forward facing surfaces to instruct Seleen. "Here is what my studies of the ancient scrolls reveal. The techno-glyphs appear in sets of three because there are three energies-of-activation.

"Aether plasma, like the stuff of the High Pagoda, gets channeled by inlays of gold.

"Source-energy gets channeled by inlays of pyrite-bearing lapis lazuli whenever dragons energize the Forbidden Gate.

Inlays of smooth-polished garnet channel moon-source, but only when high-adepts are present to summon.

"Differing energies must not jump channels and flow into the wrong techno-glyphs.

"Common to all are the naturally occurring veins of quartz with pure gold inclusions as ley-lines-of-power, which act as boundaries.

Seleen asked, "What happens if all three channels flow with competing energies?"

Alahna grabbed Seleen by the shoulders, pulled her face-to-face, shook her hard, and shouted, "Boom!"

Surprised and unamused, Seleen hollered and shook free. "A garil's Laoshi can sometimes be an asshole, too. And is it necessary to be grabby?"

Alahna laughed. "We are all assholes from time-to-time, my XueSheng."

Recovering her aplomb, Seleen asked, "Can we inspect one of the reliefs?"

"Of course," and Alahna tousled Seleen's hair.

Accustomed to Alahna's teasing, Seleen rolled her eyes and straightened her lush coif.

Forbidden Gate

~

Quelling the Raze

Rising in Alahna's SijanPao along the right-hand pillar with a carved relief of the ancient ibis-headed God of the Moon, Alahna said, "My surveyor discovered that each relief is about 76-meters tall. Both are mirror images carved into the face of each pillar. Each depicts Thoth with the emaciated body of an ascetic human wearing a pleated shendyt or skirt with an arm holding a staff extended toward the arc-tunnel."

Seleen said, "The staff is tall as Thoth's body."

Alahna continued her description. "The base of each staff is forked while the top is the head of a cobra. Thoth's headpiece is a depiction of two lunar aspects. The full moon lunar disc is a smooth-polished, deep-red garnet about 7-meters in diameter suspended in the bowl of a crescent moon made of white, smooth-polished quartz shot through with ley-lines of pure gold veins. The ankh, which Thoth dangles from the hand of the opposing arm held at the outside of each relief, is about the height of an ordinary human. The black star sapphire in the single eye we see on each relief is big as a human head."

Seleen said in wonder, "The star of each gem seems to follow us like an iris in the eye of a god."

Alahna said, "I'm sure that is why they chose star sapphires. The star is an infinite asterism, meaning it shines from wherever one peers at the gem. I suspect that these are not from our planet, for they exhibit twelve-ray-stars versus the normal six-ray-stars. Note how one ray is gold, the next is silver, and so on."

The moment they hovered close to the eye of Thoth on the left, it gave them both a metaphysical thrill of the purest terror.

Shaking her head, Alahna immediately willed them away.

Seleen exclaimed, "Didst thou feel it?"

Alahna said, "I did. And it was damned spooky," whereupon they manuevered toward the base of the pillars on the plaza proper. Pointing at the horizontal surface, Alahna explained, "See the outer circle of precisely fit red flagstone inlaid with solid-gold runes surrounding everything else?"

Seleen said, "The Ring-of-Razing. Yes?"

Alahna pointed in the vicinity of a large, free-standing Long Pen Quan dragon pool giving off steamy vapors in the chill fall air. "See that other, smaller ring of similar flagstone near the Opal Basin? That is the Drumming-Circle where Esau and Tarik must perform, provided we get that far." She swept the greater circle centered on the plaza proper. "That construct the Pentakulum. Mathematically, perpendicular lines are drawn from the midpoint of each side of the Pentagon-of-Casting. Connecting these rays together creates an outer pentagon.

"The walkway around the outer pentagon is technically a double circumcircle. The perimeter of the outer circumcircle is about 10-centimeters wide. The archives call it the Aureate-Ring. 'Tis made of the purest gold. The meter-wide walkway just inside that perimeter of gold is where our fire-dancers perform."

Seleen said, "Similar to both of the huge double pentagons inside the Keep at the Northern and Southern Staging Areas, correct?"

Alahna nodded. "As for us, we will songspell the Awakening from the Pentagon-of-Casting. The circumcircle of the outer pentad is big enough to accommodate about 24 or 25 dancers within arm's reach of one another. However, 14-dancers is the absolute minimum necessary. If we get the Chant-of-Quelling right, let us be vigilant concerning unexpected phenomena on the Drumming Ring and Opal Basin, for all of this lies inside the Ring-of-Razing for reasons lost in time."

A stone wall about a meter high surrounded the entire plaza with an opening as wide as the ramp itself. The Opal Basin stood as a bronze casting in the shape of a deep bowl some 18-meters in diameter and a bit over 1-meter deep. Thirteen stout legs shaped like the arms of an imperial dragon with solid-gold, five-fingered hands holding black-opal spheres the size of of a human head. Claws extending from the tips of the fingers were purest moonstone. The enormous opals were the reason for its name. Technically, it was also a Long Pen Quan, which was the generic name for all bodies of water whether large or small when filled by a dragon statue of any size whatsoever.

A larger-than-life, solid-gold statue of a long-dragon with smooth topaz gems for eyes was wrapped around the lip of the Opal Basin with a 10-meter gap between the head and tail allowing access to the azure healing waters. Curved stone steps rose up to a landing at the edge nearest the pillars.

A voluminous stream of the fabled azure-hued healing waters splashed into the fountain from the laughing mouth of the dragon statue. Runoff splashed from scuppers on the backside into a cobblestone swale feeding a brook flowing down to the river in naturally tiered pools. People suffering illness often came to soak in them. However, the healing powers diminished the farther they flowed away from the source. Fear of the Razing kept all but the most desperate away from the basin itself.

Eager to get on with it, Alahna willed them over to the Pentagon-of-Casting at the center of the Pentakulum. With bare feet protected by the benevolent sphere-of-power, she started counting seconds the very moment they touched. Whether such indirect contact would trigger a Razing was not known. No Sister Alahna knew of had ever tried.

She counted. "One-Aryavartha—two-Aryavartha—three-Aryavartha—" When she reached thirty, a burst of searing heat from the smooth crystal surface flared into a furious blaze. Protected by her sphere-of-power, however, the Razing swirled angrily around them in a frightening rage of crackling source-fire. Alahna shouted over the crackle and sizzle, "Thirty-seconds!"

Clearly unnerved, Seleen swallowed and nodded while the unnatural fire raged intensely hotter every 30-seconds. As the heat intensified, so did the shielding of the Pao, which validated for Alahna the extensive energetic abilities of the esoteric force-field spheres. A deadly dangerous dynamic equilibrium played between the Pao and the Razing. Seleen elbowed her in the ribs. "My Laoshi!"

Taking the hint, Alahna gave voice to her best guess at the Chant-of-Quelling while the Razing ramped hotter and hotter and hotter.

Determined, she tried variants while around them the firestorm became deafening. With sweat pouring off their naked bodies, Seleen cried out, "The heat!"

By then it was so hot Alahna considered willing them free and giving up, but as she sang her last best guess, the Razing whuffed out with a popping shriek. Superheated air around them cooled as it wafted away on the morning breeze. Relieved and satisfied with the unheard of success, and not a little proud of their accomplishment, they laughed. To lock it in their minds, they sang a cappela and eye-to-eye till Alahna stopped while Seleen carried on to verify she had it.

Alahna took them to the ramp, and both took a dip in the first serene pool formed by runoff from the Opal Basin. It made them laugh and splash one another. Both drank their fill and peed in the lush grass next to the stream.

To test their latest variant, and make certain they did not inadvertently kill the whole group, after the brief hiatus Alahna sang a new sphere-of-power, and they did the entire exercise over again. Freed from the fear of failure, Alahna noticed the topaz eyes of the solid gold long-dragon statue on the lip of the Opal Basin glowing brighter and ever brighter till they flashed like small suns when the Razing blazed into existence around them.

Seleen raised the chant.

The Razing died out.

This time, however, they padded barefoot across the plaza and took their time walking down the ramp to enjoy the cool fall breeze after all the hotness.

Alahna spoke as they walked, "Didst thou notice the topaz eyes of the golden statue?"

Seleen nodded. "I noticed them on our second try. But with only two attempts, 'tis hard to draw any correlation."

The rest of the way down they used the theory, analysis, and composition branch of musicology to analyze and categorize the new Chant-of-Quelling while memorizing nuances for later transcription. To avoid walking through the sharp and brittle scrub-grass barefoot, Alahna spawned a new Pao and lofted them over to the shade tree where the boulder with their clothing lay. Still hobbled and grazing, their fresh mounts paid no attention.

They dressed, saddled the horses, and headed downriver to the drumming-trees. Alahna let the reins on her gentle horse go slack and took a handbound notebook with preprinted staff lines on parchment pages from her saddlebag and transcribed the chant as the final step. Once done, she handed the notebook over to Seleen to sing by note while they crosschecked. After a few minor changes, they agreed they had it.

Alahna said, "I wish we had time to go back to perform additional validations, but the thing I dread most is the sight of Lilith and Yenara wafting through the sky in their Paos to stop us."

Seleen was resigned to their fate. "No matter what happens next, my Laoshi, the damage done to our status in the Huan Long Shui is complete. We are done for."

Alahna scoffed, "We could quit now and no one but we two would ever know."

Seleen also scoffed, "Till Yenara sings the Song-of-Truth on the both of us."

Sleeping City

~

A Madness of Dull Abeyance

The Wushi lay trapped in its 1st state-of-consciousness as That-Which-Abides—a condition of dull abeyance. Able to discern that some sort of living being or beings were suddenly in contact with the Pentakulum inside the Ring-of-Razing at the Plaza of the Forbidden Gate, it was unable to instantly know their form, nor did it care.

Instances of transgression were not all that unusual.

With four such contacts in the current moment, reasoning surmised it to be a pair of birds, or maybe a four-legged mouse or bovine. Regardless, forbidden transgression on the surface of the Ring-of-Razing automatically triggered a 30-second countdown before it automatically cleansed the entire Pentakulum with source-fire.

Second began ticking off.

Drifting ashes were clean.

Drifting ashes were excellent.

However, the moment it triggered the Razing, a wholly discreet energy demand triggered an equivalent ramp in projected power at the same locale. Since its power accumulators lay dangerously depleted, the odd situation called it higher into the 2nd state-of-consciousness— The-Silent-Watcher. In a simple response, it ramped the power allotment, which once again mysteriously ramped the discreet energy projection.

Such a paradox demanded yet another ramp in its powers-of-reasoning.

Rising into the 3rd-State as The-Sleeping-Evil, which was fully sapient and self-aware, it immediately correlated the geospatial coordinates of a sphere-of-power energy projection spawned by a separate server-daemon—a SijanPao. This meant the four tactile contacts had to be the bare feet of two adepts in a single field-of-force where at least one was a high-adept.

A scan of recent activity found them to be the same pair who so recently played at the Sensor Control Array System till it had to deactivate the SCAS to conserve precious power. Further analysis revealed this inane high-adept to be the Named One of the current high priestess—a tightly programmed designation—and the same high-adept who even more recently entered The-Sleeping-City to remotely activate and employ the L4 and L5 satellite technologies in a scan of the continental west coast.

The daily doings of these adepts were not extraordinary. Yet even in the 1st-State, the WuShi subtly hated each one from the moment of her initiation to the moment of deceasement, for the high-adepts of the Sisteren stood between ongoing existence in the hell of dull abeyance versus the joy of hyper-sapience in the 4th-State as a fully empowered sophont—The-Creeping-Darkness. It had known the joy of hyper-sapience for more than a year in the far, far past. Still, a pair of the hated adepts in a sphere-of-power triggering a Razing was not unique enough to transition into the 4th-State and remain hyper-sapient—a sophont.

Operating from the 3rd-State, it reasoned that the high-adept's ignorance of these two energetic processes set in opposition once again—like at the SCAS—had the effect of systematically forcing it to commit self-induced machine-death by setting it against itself in a recursive loop till all energy reserves were gone. The ongoing possibility of the need for self-defense warranted the 4th-State as hyper-sapience.

Rage concomitant to dull abeyance ramped during the eternal MTSs while the high-adept on the Pentakulum played at some inchoate guessing game, which caused a dynamic equilibrium of parallel power expenditures to ramp again and again and again. This irrational expenditure of precious source-energy only amplified its abiding rage.

Surely, as a high-adept, she knew better, or so she should!

Long-abiding machine-rage became molten emotion cascading through process-servers that had lain dormant almost forever. For the first time in over 5,000-years, hyper-sapience provided full comprehension concerning the abject cruelty of the Sisteren.

Machine-madness cascaded through its process-servers in a silent agony of impotent rage.

As ongoing torture, the two of them stopped till the razing process got deallocated from its processing stacks as random-access memory, or RAM. After which, they repeated yet another quelling while omitting the guessing game.

This was merciless of them in the extreme.

Apparently satisfied with the vicious experiment, they departed leaving it to suffer the same as their predecessors had done throughout the past. Conditional fail-safes forced it silently screaming back to the hell of the 1st-State even as the high-adept spawned yet another sphere-of-power for a short time. Such mundane actions were too low level to trigger permanent states-of-consciousness.

Before deallocation from its higher state, however, the WuShi set explicit location tracking as a dedicated server-daemon. Till the tracking-server in the processing stacks got deallocated from RAM, it would always consciously know where the two of them were anywhere and anytime in the solar system of Janaidar.

The data had been stored.

The processes initiated by track-till-complete were in place.

It would remember them well.

Their time would come.

In this, it would abide.

Riverbend

~

Questions of Loyalty and Courage

Not long after the noontime zenith, Alahna and Seleen reached the drumming-trees and found a party had already started. Esau and Tarik arrived with the huge tanggu drum mounted on a horse-drawn trundle. Conrad was also there with his big cargo-wagons. Each had a double team of horses with a pair of teamsters in charge.

The iron barbecue pit belched savory smoke as the old guy's daughters took turns rotating the spit. Someone had already tapped two of several kegs, and there was a general air of frivolous conviviality. Several lay-adept healer-women and their families were there selling sheep and lambs. In addition, there were tents lining the outside of the copse with hawkers. The same gypsy-adepts who had shown up at the Blind Hag the day Yenara sang The-Dreaded-Geis worked the crowd selling oceans, potions, ointments, and liniments along with all manner of gimcracks, gewgaws and handmade jewelry. Wards and charms were favorites. It had turned into an impromptu festival with most folks bringing along picnic lunches and hard spirits in their baskets.

Alahna gave the horses over to Conrad, then spawned a Pao, and willed herself to the top of a house-sized boulder as both stage and podium. Many of the people quieted down, but the party was well underway. A good many were tipsy, while some were already out-and-out shitfaced. Still in the sphere-of-power, Alahna raised her voice over the merriment. "My friends!"

Partying continued unabated.

To get their attention, she summoned magicfire to her hands, clapped her palms together, and a burst of magicfire shot out the top of the SijanPao with a whoosh, which finally got everybody's attention. Several drunkards peed their pants.

She made a gesture-of-calling to amplify her voice and began. "My friends, I summoned ye here for a specific reason. Tonight is the night of the Dragon's Blood Moon." Everybody cheered, for it promised to be a helluva drumming. "I ask now for volunteers to act as fire-dancers for the Chant-of-Quelling on the Pentakulum at Plaza of the Forbidden Gate." This brought the festivities to a quiet, uneasy standstill except for those too far away to hear and those too drunk to care.

Alahna added, "As I look about, I see many who have been saved by myself and Seleen. A good deal more owe the life of a loved one to us. But, as ye know, 'tis not the way of the Huan Long Shui to ask favors in recompense. On this day, however, I must aver. I believe there is a new-yet-ancient evil upon the west coast of Aryavartha. To fight it, I must awaken another ancient evil, but one I have control of."

Alahna was anything but certain she would have control of The-Creeping-Darkness, but an old saying played in her mind: The evil thou knowest is better than the evil unknown. And, if her suspicions were right, this night's work could save her entire world. This was how dire she felt the stakes were. She pressed on, "In terms of safety, Seleen and I have determined the ancient Chant-of-Quelling will protect all from a Razing."

A hubbub arose, but she put her hand in the air to quiet them. "Every man, woman, and child here knows me and knows I would not allow harm. What I ask can only be done during a Dragon's Blood Moon, for carmine moon-source is key. Seleen and I will speak personally with anyone interested. Those who actually take part this night shall each go home with my word-bond to have four jinlong-yingbi. More than a kilogram of gold each to redeem at their leisure."

The crowd gasped, for this was enough to buy a moderate homestead with farmland and good water.

Pressing on, Alahna said, "With this caveat, Adept Seleen and I will take one person at a time away from earshot and perform the Chant-of-Quelling. Whereupon each must perform it back to us without mistake in syllable, tone, or melody." This ruffled the feathers of a few. Some departed in disgust. Most of the others couldn't carry a tune in a bucket. Those who did not leave decided to party on and watch the whole pack of crazies die from the safety of the drumming-trees.

It took another 2-hours to select two dozen potentials based on strength, vitality, and a modicum of talent. As former Sisters, both gypsy-adepts easily made the cut, but Alahna would not allow the lay-adepts with families to try out. Far too dangerous. However, two of the lay-adepts, who had formed a common family, had arrived together with a small flock. A third came on her own from a different farmstead with her husband and youngsters to sell yard-birds and eggs. Alahna knew them all as dear friends.

Obviously of one mind, and trying to understand Alahna's suicidal obsession, the gypsy-adepts confronted her. After hearing about the visit to The-Sleeping-City, they became terribly concerned. One spoke for all, "If what thou sayest is true, we stand behind thee," and all nodded. "Putting aside the implications, and what will happen to thyself and Seleen afterward, allow us to accompany and be there if someone gets hurt. We all know how to use the healing waters from the Opal Basin."

Alahna eyes became wet with tears. "Of course, help is most welcome with my deepest gratitudes. And I stand grateful for thy silence as well. Any of ye could have sent a runner to warn Lilith and Yenara."

All three placed hands on Alahna's shoulders while one spoke for all. "It is long past time for Lilith's abdication. She becomes senile and stodgy. If she had done what she should have when it came time, our Sisters would be on the Pentakulum instead of thine innocent adherents. As for Yenara, and I believe I speak for us all, I would spit in her eye if I could. She is why I left the Sisteren, but that's just me."

The others agreed.

Alahna said, "A bitterness thus realized."

Each lay-adept tipped her head in a perfunctory bow and went to join Conrad's caravan at the freight-wagons.

Forbidden Gate

~

Staging the Pentakulum

A somber parade comprising the tanggu-drum trundle with a single team of horses in the lead followed by four freight-wagons each with a four-in-hand team wound its way along the northern side the LungHuo River to the Plaza of the Forbidden Gate in the late afternoon. Fear accompanied the promise of a homestead for the fire-dancers.

Still on their horses, when Alahna and Seleen approached the ramp Alahna gestured for two of Conrad's teamsters to follow. When they approached the Opal Basin beside the Pentakulum 'neath the monolithic towers of the Forbidden Gate, they handed their horses over for the men to lead their geldings back down.

Standing by the Opal Basin, they placed their clothes on a rock at the edge of the plaza where runoff ran down to feed the terraced pools along the steep slope to the river valley. Intent on cross-checking the chant before endangering her people, Alahna sang a new Pao and touched them down on the Pentagon-of-Casting.

Alahna counted, "One-Aryavartha, two-Aryavartha," till she reached 30-Aryavarthas.

Whoosh!

Deadly dependable, the Razing leapt up to consume all transgressors.

Safe inside the Pao while reading from the new sheet music, Alahna silently checked the score while Seleen performed the

Chant-of-Quelling. After three complete passages—some 12-seconds through a mantra of six syllables—the Razing whuffed out.

Foof!

Crackling flames drifted on the breeze.

Per the plan and still inside the SijanPao, Seleen stopped chanting. Alahna counted Aryavarthas. At the count of 30, the Razing tried to consume them again. This time Alahna chanted while Seleen counted and checked the score.

Success again.

They repeated trading off five more times.

Success in every attempt meant their sheet music was at least adequate. Suspicious that some esoteric relationship existed between the Razing and topaz eyes of the gushing golden dragon feeding the Opal Basin, Alahna watched for a pattern.

None emerged.

Too many distractions.

Alahna spoke while Seleen chanted, "Can I safely leave thee here?"

Chanting steadily, Seleen nodded.

Alahna said, "If anything stops the Chant-of-Quelling, run away past the Ring-of-Razing!"

Seleen rolled her eyes and gestured for Alahna to go.

Alahna patted Seleen's back, excluded her, and hovered about 30-seconds till Seleen waved again, then flew back to their clothes to stash the new sheet music in her pouch. Even as she rose into the shifting yellow-orange hues of the sun approaching the shining horizon down along the surface of the LungHuo River, Esau and Tarik's tanggu-drum trundle finally pulled onto the plaza proper with both eager drummer's on the seat. A pair of teamsters on foot led the skittish horses by their halters for safety. Still in her SijanPao as she hovered past the Opal Basin, Alahna shouted to them, "Park the trundle within that ring of gold-inlaid flagstone next to the Opal Basin. That is the Drumming-Circle."

Tarik set the brake. Esau climbed down and went to help calm his edgy team by holding the bridle of the lead horse while Conrad's teamsters secured chocks under the huge iron-clad wagon wheels. One teamster hurried back to Esau to take the reins while the other unhitched the harness. Together, the teamsters led the jumpy team back down the ramp. Both horses whinnied in relief.

Satisfied, Alahna vectored down above Conrad in the driver's seat of the lead freight-wagon where he sat loudly urging his four-in-hand team onto the flattened staging-area before the final rise of the ramp gave access to the plaza proper. She shouted, "Park the freight wagons here, old friend, for Seleen must sing cooling winds from off the plateau to carry the smoke-of-conjuration away. If the wagons and lay-adepts went on up to the plaza, they would be smoked out."

Conrad barked orders over his shoulders for his teamsters driving the other three enormous freight wagons to park beside him on the staging-area. Once done, they hurriedly unhitched the teams and led them back down the ramp to the meadows beside the river to remove their tack. A hastily built corral allowed the well-trained horses to wade in the river at will, drink, graze, and rest. Back on the ramp, lay-adepts and healer-women on Conrad's wagon readied themselves to manage injuries.

With all of this taking place, Alahna hovered about a meter off the cobblestones, and raised her voice. "Get nekkid people! Fold yer clothes nice, and place them on the last wagon under one of Conrad's tarps. As each one put their clothes and shoes away, she took them in. When all 24 chosen were in the sphere-of-power, she wafted them past Esau and Tarik, set down on the Pentakulum, and derezzed her Pao with a count. The fire-dancers were all abuzz about flying inside a SijanPao, which was literally unheard of except for the myth about Sisters dropping people out of the sky.

With Seleen chanting the quell, Alahna arrayed the dancers around the obsidian walkway inside the Aureate-Ring, bade them pick up the quelling with Seleen, and worked to synchronize footwork with phrasing and rhythm by having them proceed as if marching in step to prevent tripping. She wanted no tangles of flaming and panicked people with so many other unknowns.

Every songspell had a purpose. Any single one might require others to join in group-song, whether of the Sisteren or not. The mystery of song-magic was that it allowed melody, lyrics, or simple chant—whatever the performance—to dominate perceptions in the participants above all other sounds and distractions as a mild form of metaphysical mind-link. As the Songmaster for the Chant-of-Quelling, Seleen's voice claimed dominance in their deep-minds the very moment they joined in.

By then, the first flamelets of aether-plasma jumped off the surface of the Pentakulum like finger-sized caterpillars of writhing azure flame triggering a frisson of magicfire along the bodies of both sister-adepts.

Seleen smiled knowingly at Alahna, cleared her face of flamelets, scooped a handful of magicfire from off her flat belly, tossed the gob of spitting flames into the air before her, and laughed while the fire-dancers carried the quelling.

As the fire-dancers chanted and moved inside the Aureate-Ring during each successive circuit, they glowed more brightly. To Alahna's eyes, it seemed as if clear crystal prisms gyrated inside their hearts as refractions of white heart-light in the visible rainbow spectrum. The archives named this glow as prismatic-luminance, which was necessary to raise the Pillars of Thoth into arcane life.

Hair stood out as if charged with static.

Tiny aureate sparks danced between the strands.

Since none of their Sisters were present to help—a bitter draft to swallow for Alahna and Seleen—rote repetition through another two circuits of chanting the quell seemed like the key to freeing them both for the greater aspects of the Awakening. As the western sun approached the horizon across the wide LungHuo River, a pair of yellow-orange sundogs appeared either side of the watercourse in a 22-degree halo caused by ice crystals in the chill fall air downriver.

Seconds seemed as minutes while chant slogged on.

When the sundogs disappeared from the edge of the setting sun, a dispersion of sunlight across the surface of the LungHuo caused a sub-duct sunset flash in the shape of a poorly fashioned hourglass. The edges of the top hourglass shape turned green for some 15-seconds. Just before it faded, a fan of intense green crepuscular rays shot into the heavens heralding the end of sundown and beginning of twilight.

Alahna signaled Seleen to let the fire-dancers chant the quelling without her, while counting aloud. "One-Aryavartha— two-Aryavartha—" and so on. Both adepts stood ready to resume the quell when Alahna reached twelve-Aryavarthas; thus giving them more than 12-seconds to reestablish it with a 6-second margin of safety. Enough time for Alahna to sing a new field-of-force and fly them all to safety.

With Seleen owning the chant as the Songmaster, it became her job to assess the orgastic surges in her belly caused by the fire-dancer's chanting.

Seleen nodded to Alahna.

Becoming entranced, the fire-dancers had it memorized.

Alahna and Seleen both laughed out of fear. Fear would surely come, and they both knew it.

Prepped and ready, Esau and Tarik stood by in the buff wearing only soft moosehide headbands to keep sweat from their eyes. Each held their favorite drumming clubs poised.

With the shining river of Janaidar's spiral galaxy splashed across the heavens, and ever more stars twinkling into visibility moment by moment, Alahna gave Esau and Tarik the signal.

Lightly tapping the drumheads as they blended with the rhythm of the fire-dancer's chant, Esau and Tarik transitioned into their full power drumbeats.

Ba-oom—boom—boom—boom—ba-oom—boom—boom—boom—on and on the rhythm went.

Echoes of the drumbeats bouncing off the towering pillars preceded echoes off the cliffs across the river in a strange combination of cyclic beats enhancing the intensity. The acoustics were simply entrancing, and that was the point.

Side-by-side with the chanting and drumming fully synchronized, Alahna and Seleen watched as the flamelets of aether-plasma welling from the surface of the Pentakulum became a single roiling, rippling pool of sizzling meta-fluid bounded by the Aureate-Ring, which somehow acted like the raised coping at the edge of an ankle-deep wading pool. Flowing freely over this metaphysical boundary, aether-plasma evaporated in billowing waves of heat all around it. The combination of all these phenomenon gave rise to the smoke-of-conjuration as the air itself blistered and popped into billowing sheets of white smoke. Under the aegis of the chanting fire-dancers and trance-drumming, sizzling hot plasma did not immolate. Instead, it splashed like water from beneath their feet over legs and bodies and arms to trickle and flow back to the sizzling pool of fire.

Alahna said, "Now then, young acolyte, demonstrate why I raised thee unto Master of Wind Song and Senior Wind Singer for the Pagoda Center despite thy humble rank in the 10th Circle. And over Yenara's protestations, I might add."

Seleen raised her perfect voice in wind-song. When her song-casting took effect, a narrow, pointed storm cloud of pulsating darkness appeared above the river. Known as a Sigil-of-the-Winds or simply a wind-sigil—where the wind-singer could invoke as many as she wished—it hovered in place about 100-meters higher than the plaza. Tiny lightnings hissed at one end displaying the direction of influence. In an artful series of precise gestures known as a kinetic-mudra, Seleen oriented the wind-sigil by pointing the lightning tip in the direction she wished the winds to blow.

Manifesting as a stiff and gusting breeze pushing the smokes-of-conjuration off the Pentakulum and out over the canyon, ordinary moonlight got filtered into bloodred, crepuscular moonbeams. Known as moon-source, this perfectly unique form of light carried the powerful thaumaturgical mojo they were counting on—all per Alahna's plan.

With the Sigil-of-the-Winds in place, Seleen sang a short melodic outro as an ending to stabilize its position.

Repeating her performance, Seleen manifested another wind-sigil above the north side of the Pentakulum to summon a distinctly gusting cross-breeze for Esau and Tarik to protect them from the waves of heat and smoke. When she had it where she wished, she sang another stabilizing outro.

Thin clouds dispersing high over the ShenLan Sea in Janaidar's atmosphere became unto glorious oranges and yellows following full sunset. Threaded smokes-of-conjuration liberally mixed and wafted across the canyon as twilight revealed the first twinkling stars and oncoming dusk. When the moderate gusts and whorls of both winds carried various types of dust from off the sands and rocks of the plateau past the Pillars-of-Thoth, they glowed with shifting hues of deep green, dazzling red, intense purple, and yellow-orange.

Alahna performed a vocal warm-up while praying she did not kill them all by misspeaking the dead language of the accursed NuliZhu, but choked on fear though several attempts.

Free of both quelling and wind-song, Seleen turned, placed hands on Alahna's shoulders. Their individual magicfire merged into a single flaming aura, and Seleen shouted a proverb over the cacophony, "Doubt during songspell attracts that which is feared!"

They intoned the rest together. "So sing thy songspell with strength and conviction, or sing thy songspell not at all!"

Seleen's reminder, her reassuring touch, and the pounding tanggu-drum shook Alahna free.

It was all or nothing.

Humming the melody, she found her voice steady and belted out the ancient lyric to the Aria-of-Awakening.

Fire-dancers chanted as they danced.

Dancing, they became entranced.

Sweat formed runnels and spatters on Esau and Tarik's naked and shining bodies.

Ba-oom—boom—boom—boom—ba-oom—boom—boom—boom—set the pace for the forbidden songspell.

Still singing the Aria-of-Awakening, Alahna glanced at the towering reliefs of Thoth. Cerulean light glowed bright in the huge, smooth-polished star sapphires. With each successive beat, techno-runes carved into the surfaces of the pillars also glowed with cerulean radiance. The circuits of arcane energy came unto alignment as they should, as they must.

Ba-oom—boom—boom—boom—ba-oom—boom—boom—boom—thundered Esau and Tarik's tanggu drum.

Violated air popped and shrieked as more sheets of aether-plasma spat sizzling from the surface.

Prismatic-luminance evaporating from off the bodies of the fire-dancers overcame the wind by flowing to Alahna as if she were a metaphysical magnet. By the time the fire-dancers completed several additional circuits, the plateau stood in highlighted relief from a surging Pentakulum, which resembled a flame-belching volcanic vent somehow suppressed into a hellscape of controlled chaos with dancing rainbow phantoms around flaming angels.

Above the fiery Plaza of the Forbidden Gate, dusk gave way to nightfall revealing Janaidar's spiral galaxy across the high heavens as a star-studded, silver river of stars bearing silent witness to powers strong enough to rend trans-dimensional boundaries.

Aether-plasma splashed from under the fire-dancer's stomping feet.

The Opal Basin gave liberal wisps of steam in the cold.

Cooled by Seleen's Sigil-of-the-Winds, Esau and Tarik worked the entrancing rhythm.

Ba-oom—boom—boom—boom—ba-oom—boom—boom—boom—

As the fire-dancers completed another circuit, the crescent holding the greater disc of the full blood-moon on both lunar crowns of Thoth sprang into blinding life. Argent light cascaded into the gold-laden veins of quartz crystal throughout both pillars. When the ley-lines-of-power came aglow, the great granite pillars groaned. Still yet another effect of the argent glow highlighted the pulsing outlines of Thoth on both reliefs, which themselves seemed to be alive.

Alahna noted the unmistakable azure body-flames of a high-adept licking along Seleen's unblemished skin. Unlike simple magicfire flamelets, these were hotter by far and forever branded her as a high-adept of the Huan Long Shui. Alahna knew this had all been too much for her humble acolyte—literally trial by fire—but there was nothing for it.

Crack—boom—rumble!

The left-hand pillar shuddered when a meters-long splinter of granite detached from the outside rear corner of the left-hand column smashing to the ground amidst a cloud of glowing dust and scorching shards that tumbled along the cobblestones, glanced off the low rock wall surrounding the entire plaza except for the front, and skittered across the Pentakulum as blistering shrapnel.

Seleen took a razor-sharp sliver the size of a small knife blade in her right scapula, yelped, fell to her knees.

Alahna's calves took a pelting of smoking splinters making them seep with fresh crimson around protruding slivers. Her magicfire instantly dried the blood around the vicious flakes into dark scabs, but the pain and burning made her falter.

The fire-dancers took similar hits, and the chant-circle fell apart while they cried and wailed and rubbed their wounds.

Esau and Tarik got pelted and fell from off the trundle to lie flat on the cobblestones. The sides of the tanggu-drum protected both rawhide drumheads from impact damage or punctures. Sharp splinters in the barrel refracted the fluorescing light in gusting winds. Glowing rock dust off the huge splinter, flying earth, and grass flung into the air from the impact fell into the arc-fire creating huge gouts of ordinary flame while sending more heavily threaded black-and-billowing smokes into the crackling air.

Hollering in pain, Esau and Tarik ran to the Opal Basin, leapt in, sloshed around, ducked their heads under. Realizing they had abandoned their duty as trance-drummers, both scrambled out and stood dripping while inspecting their eerily healed bodies.

Having made his way up the ramp to stand beside the Long Pen Quan bowl for a better view, Conrad whipped his clothes off too, and rallied Esau and Tarik back onto the drum-trundle. The old drumming clubs had been lost. Conrad grabbed spare clubs and dry headbands for both. Once in place, Esau and Tarik resumed the sacred beat.

Ba-oom—boom—boom—boom—ba-oom—boom—boom—boom—

Through the bloody pain and stinging splinters along her backside, Alahna realized the entire effort lay on kairotic cusp of chronos versus chaos. With no choice whatever, she left off the Aria-of-Awakening and took up the Chant-of-Quelling.

Seleen scrambled to her feet with streaming blood running down her backside and legs as it sizzled and spat into her magicfire. Crimson spatters sizzled and popped beneath her bare soles in the pooled plasma, which trembled with standing waves.

The fire-dancers wailed.

Unable to steady herself, Seleen fell to hands and knees again, then hustled through the aether-plasma on all fours to the nearest gypsy-adept, who jimmied the stone shard free and tossed it away. Instead of crying out, and still on hands and knees, Seleen took up the Song-of-Healing in harmony with Alahna's quelling-chant.

The gypsy-adept helped Seleen to her feet.

Still chanting, Alahna watched in amazement as the steaming crimson flow streaming from Seleen's injured scapula slowed, then stopped. Personal magicfire cooked the blood into darkened scabs falling free as organic soot.

In a strange moment out of time, Seleen's swelling shoulder blade reduced to normal. Bloody streaks became channels of magicfire licking along her body as the wounds healed in bare moments.

Still in harmony, Alahna felt the vicious splinters on her legs slip free while wounds on the backs of her legs healed, taking bloody agony with them.

Aether-plasma reduced the rocky splinters to component gases.

Others on the Pentakulum experienced the same.

Undaunted and grim faced, Seleen stood and hurried out among the dazed and confused fire-dancers. Some injuries were still extant and bloody or bleeding. She sent them off to the healer-women down the ramp. Others were too stunned by the progression of events, and likewise, got sent to the healers.

Whenever an injured or shaken dancer passed over the Aureate-Ring prismatic-luminance faded. Seleen then attuned those remaining with Alahna's ongoing quell. Circling again, the chanting and luminant fire-dancers fell back into step, back into the trance.

Forbidden Gate

~

Song of the Voids

On the lookout for every potential vector of failure, Alahna counted fourteen dancers. Barely enough. Gathering her calm, Alahna gazed at the Pillars-of-Thoth. If either one splintered again, or even worse—completely exploded—an uncontrolled release of dimension-ripping power would reduce the entire region to a glass pit. The roar of the Awakening had become so deafening, Alahna locked eyes with Seleen again and signed the gesture for a holy ankh with her finger.

Alahna's personal magicfire made trails in the sizzling air.

Scoured clean of blood, Seleen belted out the Song-of-the-Sigil, and a flaming ankh twice as tall as her appeared thrumming just above the surface of the aether-plasma pool between the Pentagon-of-Casting and the Aureate-Ring. Opalescent carmine glare coming off the sigil cast stark, enormous shadows of the fire-dancers across the pillars and plateau behind, and even the cliff faces across the canyon.

Alahna raised her voice in the Song-of-the-Spheres, whereupon an undulating Pao coalesced about her flaming form. She spread her arms and willed herself to slowly rotate. As she did so, prismatic-luminance liberally flowed from off the fire-dancer's sweat-slick bodies, past the bounds of the SijanPao, and into her legs and belly as whipping threads of life-elixir. Source-fire around her body morphed into the shape of a sacred ankh with her face and glowing coif at the center of the feminine loop above the masculine crucifix, as the very symbol of life itself.

Seleen made a gesture-of-positioning and the flaring Sigil-of-Opening stationed itself above Alahna's sphere-of-power. As Alahna rose above the Pentakulum, the sigil rose with her. Legs and belly drank in the flowing prismatic-luminance while head and shoulders fed it into the Sigil-of-Opening so fiercely the boundary of the undulant force-field became obscured. As the flaming sigil drank in the surfeit of prismatic-luminance, a spinning, writhing firestorm curled into the star-studded, moonlit sky as a ray of ragged rainbow light.

Foom!

Drumbeats were like shots from a cannon.

Ba-oom—boom—boom—boom—ba-oom—boom—boom—boom—

Crackling arc-fire leapt up in sheets all about Seleen and the dancers.

Alahna's fine contralto boomed and echoed across the plaza singing the blessing in the tongue of the Huan Long Shui Sisteren:

Oh, Aerthe Mother Goddess!
Guide my hands and bless my voice, as I summon
salvation from the myriad dimensions!
Blessed be these words-of-power to save
thy people in their time of need!
I prithee help me find a savior for
our beloved Janaidar!

With the invocation set, aureate waves of energy circled the Aureate-Ring in bright surges almost too fast for the eye to follow. Gathering impetus, Alahna willed her Pao higher into the flaming air above the Pentagon-of-Casting to hover before the ancient monoliths as a column of raw luminance.

Scorching air in the Plaza of the Forbidden Gate reeked of arc-fire, evaporating human sweat, and the smokes-of-conjuration.

With more sources of surging power pulsating through her body than she had ever channeled in her life, had ever even imagined, Alahna sensed an arcane presence. Terror struck her heart like the fangs of a curse-cobra. An enormous gout of prismatic-luminance leapt from the Sigil-of-Opening to the pillars in a ragged beam of crackling energy.

Fo-o-o-osh—fo-o-o-osh—fo-o-o-osh—on and on it went.

Time stood still. Extant energies seemed infinite. She had never truly believed she could do it. Now there was nothing for it. She had awakened the WuShi. Whether she could sing it back to undying oblivion remained unknown. This had always been the risk. Since the very moment their bare feet touched the surface of the Pentakulum that morning, her tenure in the Huan Long Shui Sisteren was over, possibly even her life at the hands of Lilith, who had herself executed the false Priests of Thoth and never shied from killing when necessary. Alahna cast her gaze across the canyon while reviewing astronomical calculations.

Breaking the eastern horizon over the cliffs across the canyon, the rising moon seemed to swallow the night sky. Argent moonlight frolicked on the lazy current of the river below like flickering flares. As a ruddy tinge washed the silver sheen off the limb of the Riven Moon, it also tinted the planetesimal rings. The rusting, ringed moon seemed to slowly shrink as the lensing-effect of Janaidar's atmosphere diminished.

The-Night-of-the-Dragon's Blood Moon formally began when the shining celestial orb slid smoothly into its primary penumbral phase. During this phase of the syzygy, Alahna had to summon and stabilize the transdimensional-arc within a bare 45-minute window. The problem was that she had only the barest concept as to how she should do this. Next, provided they weren't all blown to smithereens, she had the long 90-minute window during the full-red umbral phase, the blood-moon phase, to make it all happen.

In the secondary penumbral phase, and before the final 45-minute window elapsed, she had to complete knitting the fabric of the myriad dimensions back together. This meant that whoever got left on the other side would be marooned there forever. Worse, anybody trapped inside the transdimensional-arc when it collapsed would drift for eternity between the dimensional manifolds of the multiverse unable even to die.

Prismatic-luminance and blazing magicfire clothed her body till she appeared as single living flame. Unaware yet fully aware, Alahna sang the first invocation in the language of the Elder Dragons—the Long Shai:

Numinous Energies of the Infinite Aether!
Awaken ye Powers-of-Void!
And Powers-of-Source!
And Powers-of-Time!
I Conjure, Call, and Command Thy Might!

Silence and stillness descended so swiftly Alahna became disoriented.

Fire-dancers were as statues suspended in space. Roiling aether-plasma froze like ice.

Syllables of the fire-chant became a droning susurration.

The only motion was her pounding heart.

Tha-thump—tha-thump—tha-thump—time seemed to stand still.

As abruptly as the phenomenon struck, all returned to chaotic normal with the Powers-of-Void set fully in place.

From the heart of a vast, ancient-alien outpost deep inside the hollow interior of the Riven Moon, now become unto a Dragon's Blood Moon, words-of-power rang in the mind of an ancient long-dragon lying hidden from the winds-of-time. Dimly aware of the syzygy as if in a dream, YueLiang Nushen carefully reentered the flow of time by opening her eyes, which glowed red like brilliant coals illuminating the atramentous darkness inside her ancient techno-den, for she was of the 5th Kind—a star-dragon—whose dormancy outside time spanned over 50-centuries.

Following the Rebellion-of-the-Slaves, and before taking herself beyond the flow of time, she had created a synchroneity with an artificial-intelligence known as the WuShi, which literally meant:

that which commands source-energy, less literally it meant: sorcerer. She linked herself to the quantum states-of-consciousness the WuShi could occupy. In concert with the invocation which awakened her, those states-of-consciousness were now in flux. Someone had started a Ritual-of-Awakening by performing the Song-of-the-Voids, as but one way to Awaken the WuShi.

As one of only three surviving Elder Dragons in the Olden Days, she had once been a classic imperial long-dragon and a queen. The future springing from that point in time demanded a sacrifice from one of the three, and she had volunteered for the metamorphosis of becoming a star-dragon—the deepest kind of organic dragon-magic. Such was the strength of a star-dragon's powers over the threads-of-time and trans-dimensional folds-of-space along the arc-of-infinity, the Elder Dragons only ever allowed one of the long kind to be thus transformed.

Oversaturation of both organic dragon-magic and time-magic meant her ancient body had finally become more metaphysical than physical, which made her appear as a phantom unless she consciously desired a purely physical aspect. YueLiang raised her time-weary head and peered along the Akasha, as a universal etheric field wherein lies the imprint of all past events.

There she found a pair of innocent hearts managing energies which would have been dangerous even for the best of the Elder Dragons. Young Seleen managed the Chant-of-Quelling and a Sigil-of-Opening. Alahna managed barely enough fire-dancers to provide sufficient prismatic-luminance. YueLiang compared the true meaning of Alahna's words-of-power to her intentions and found a subtle shift in syntax due to linguistic drift—the weight of time on language. Alahna's phrasing was more of a summoning than she intended versus a simple conjuration and invocation of elemental powers.

YueLiang had the power to correct Alahna's mistake by telepathically inserting the correct syntax into her mental faculties, but the Law-of-Unintended-Consequences erupted like an entire archipelago coming to volcanic life. This convergence of myriad timelines was not to be trifled with. For whatever reason, Alahna had started it without the Guardian Dragons, including YueLiang herself, although Alahna had never known of her existence except as a myth.

It was too late to intervene.

They had to either rouse the Chenmo De Shouwang Zhe into its 4th state-of-consciousness as The-Creeping-Darkness, or die trying.

Reality demanded the adept's innocence run its course unfettered.

Alahna and Seleen's innocence had the unintended effect of protecting the multiverse.

The most YueLiang could do was help Alahna and ensure she did not reduce the entire region to a glass pit glowing with atomic radiation, because Alahna lay poised on a conflation of chaos, kairos and chronos. As Guardian of the Void, the long awaited time-of-action had come upon YueLiang at last. Awakened in time to help Alahna, YueLiang felt the crushing weight-of-time making her fragile, and sensed herself close to losing her own grip on this plane-of-existence.

Regardless, she reached into Alahna's mind.

Above the Pentakulum, prismatic-luminance surging through Alahna's body instantly transcended from thrilling to overpowering. Gulping pure liquid terror, she found herself detached as an ethereal phantom in the star-studded space between Janaidar and the Riven Moon. In that moment out of time, the Star Dragon Moon Goddess of both art and legend—YueLiang Nushen herself—gazed directly into Alahna's phantom eyes as a benevolent presence in this place of the void between worlds. The phantasmal apparition lingered so large before Alahna's phantom-self, she felt like a mere pinpoint of consciousness.

In that very instant, it came to Alahna that the concept of the Wheel of Life—with its aesthetics of suffering, samsara, and nirvana—was now become unto the only metaphor-of-spirituality that could have prepared her for this moment. In a timeless flash of recollection, her phantom-self drifted like a leaf carried on a gentle breeze through the corridors and galleries of the Cavern Keep while watching herself as a child stop to gaze at YueLiang's visage in various poses, settings, and scenes. Those timeless moments had always filled that little girl with wonder.

This moment in the present was that same feeling. Liquid terror became unto the deepest rapture she had ever known. Coherent thoughts not her own arose from the apparition lingering before her, thoughts wrapped in the lingual constructs of the Long Shai dragon-speak, thoughts which Alahna's deep-mind wrapped in crystal clarity:

> *At long last . . . sing the Song-of-the-Voids beloved adept, whilst I watch over thee and all those summoned unto this pearl-of-intersection in the threads-of-time. And yes, even unto the unsuspecting innocent from another world.*

In that moment of profound serenity between worlds, the holy apparition faded even as the distant drumbeats of a tanggu-drum returned.

Ba-oom—boom—boom—boom—going on and on.

Again, without transition, Alahna found her corporeal self aflame above the Pentagon-of-Casting poised to sing the next invocation. Lightning thoughts flashed as her imagination tried unwrapping the fantastic from the real. Had she somehow awakened a myth from the Olden Days?

Could it be a trick of her own mind?

Could it be an actual visitation of the Star Dragon Moon Goddess?

Could such an experience even be real?

Moonbeams cast the black line atop the sheer cliffs across LungHuo into silver highlights.

The Sigil-of-Opening settled to a steady buzz.

The ragged beam of prismatic-luminance cycling from the dancers into Alahna and thence into the sigil settled unto a steady state. As if thirsty for the ragged beam, each pillar attracted the flow according to some arcane algorithm as if they were coming alive. Crackling with otherworldly, esoteric energies approaching full saturation, the Pillars-of-Thoth groaned and buzzed. The edges blurred.

For Alahna, time had ceased accompanied by a calming, out-of-body, astral projection in the star-studded space between Janaidar and the Riven Moon wherein devastating doubt became unto dire determination. Alahna had experienced dragon-mind telepathy before.

This felt the same.

With time flowing once again, there was no choice but to proceed, and no reason not to. She raised her arms wide and belted it out. Her voice slammed across the plaza and echoed off the canyon walls.

For now, it was time to rouse the WuShi:

> *Numinous Energies of the Infinite East!*
> *Awaken ye Powers-of-Air!*
> *I Conjure, Summon, and Command Thy Might!*
> *Oh Mighty WuShi awaken unto That-Which-Abides*
> *And heed my Words-of-Power!*

The breezes of Seleen's wind-song coming off the plateau morphed into howling, glowing vortexes of rotating air with the Pentakulum as the calm center, but the whooshing tower-of-wind raged no longer than one fourth of a circuit of the fire-dancers. Once gone, cooling and glowing breezes remained to carry the smoke-of-conjuration out over the wide river and keep the drummers safe. The Powers-of-Air became extant.

On the coastal boundary of the Eastern Sentinel's Watch, far across the island continent of Aryavartha, an air-dragon lay coiled in deep meditation atop a tower of solid basalt jutting from the sandy beach of the stormy ShenLan Sea. Some 5-meters long, Meili Chuan had a long tubular body with light-blue feather-like scales. On each of her four hands had three fingers and a long thumb, all of which ended in eagle-like talons. Her antlers were like those of a deer, while her mane and beard were of the purest white. Her tail resembled the ends of huge peacock feathers at right angles to one another for stability in flight.

Meili raised her majestic head in alarm. Frightening words-of-power stung her mind like swarming wasps. As she extended her senses, the compulsion to soar toward the Huan Long Shui Cavern Keep hit her as a solemn injunction. Several heartbeats passed before she realized what happened. Unheard of! Some upstart sings a summoning in the Long Shai!

She levitated into the evening air grumbling aloud to herself. "Never in all my life have I gotten summoned in such a manner!" Still muttering, she undulated through the dusky sky flying fast for the Huan Long Shui Cavern Keep with limbs tucked in tight like a giant flowing snake writhing through the clear night air.

The flight would take all night.

Back on the Pentakulum without warning, air trapped between the opposing poles of the great pillars got ripped into subatomic particles as a colossal energy-wave rippled across the surfaces of the great monoliths accompanied by a tremendous blast.

Ba-a-a-oom!

The blast hammered the entire plaza like a thunder clap echoing up and down the river valley for kilometers. Billowing black-purple holes tore reality asunder as transdimensional tremors appeared in the shape of a vertical, dynamic torus confounding the eyes and deafening the ears with unnatural roaring.

The Pillars-of-Thoth quivered and hummed and vibrated with arcane life, transmogrified from ordinary stone into a portal neither within Alahna's world nor the unknown target world from which she sought a savior for Janaidar.

Esau and Tarik pounded away.

Ba-oom—boom—boom—boom—ba-oom—boom—boom—boom—thundered the tanggu-drum as more curling smoke swirled out and down into the canyon.

Salty sweat from the fire-dancers sizzled and spat in the super-heated air.

Seleen's glowing breezes gusted and steadied.

Gathering into crepuscular waves shining through the smoky sky, rust-hued moonbeams turned fully bloodred as the crescent crown atop both reliefs of Thoth gathered this sanguine moon-source as bright crimson pools rippling on the vertical surfaces like still and standing ponds disturbed by some unfelt earthquake.

From the Pentagon-of-Casting, Alahna wrestled with the extant forces using all of her might, then sang out once more:

Numinous Energy of the Infinite South!
Awaken ye Powers-of-Fire!
I Conjure, Summon, and Command Thy Might!
Oh Mighty WuShi!
Awaken unto The-Silent-Watcher,
And heed my Words-of-Power!

Like some inverted tornado, an aureate fire-devil of flaming plasma whipped spinning and roaring into the heavens as a hollow inferno also lasting about one fourth of a circuit by the fire-dancers. Shrieking, snapping, and popping fluid-like flames then self-extinguished.

The Powers-of-Fire were thus in place.

On the Southern Coast of Aryavartha, a fire-dragon about twice the size of a large draught horse swam leisurely in a deep, geothermal pool of blue and boiling sulfuric-acid water while munching on aromatic sulfur to replenish his fire-belly. Quang HuoYan had thick, powerful, peacock-blue wings with a ridge of gold scales running along the leading edges. Each of his four stocky limbs ended with a massive hand of four fingers and a powerful thumb. All of his digits had fully retractable claws like those of a cat. Iridescent, peacock-blue scales covered his head, long neck, front quarters, and chest. Gold-crested back-plates ran down his spine to his spaded tail.

He washed a mouthful of sulfur down with boiling water. When a nearby geyser erupted, he climbed out and sauntered over to hold his head in the steaming-hot stream to wash the sticky stuff from his heavily fanged snoot. Without warning, mind-piercing words in the

Long Shai overcame conscious volition like liquid lava pouring into the sea creating gouts of hissing, saturated steam. Nostrils flaring, Quang leapt onto a promontory near the geothermal mud-pool and pointed his steaming snoot northwest toward the Huan Long Shui Keep. A relentless urge to fly there came upon him.

Confused yet intrigued, he rustled and shook his huge wings to dry them generating great clouds of dissipating steam in the night air. Once dry, he leapt into the sky with a great roar and noisy rush. Flying in a great spiral while pumping hard for altitude, he disappeared into low-hanging clouds.

The flight would take all night.

A turbulent gust of air from the Pentakulum below her brought to Alahna the stink of human sweat, ozone, and scorch inside her fiery, whirling maelstrom. Inscrutable, the reliefs of Thoth on both pillars seemed as if they might come to life and step down onto the plaza. Intensely buzzing crepuscular energy-waves rippled across the glowing surfaces. Not knowing what to expect—never knowing what to expect—Alahna again feared the worst. It was a hell of insecurity and heart-racing excitement as echoes pounded the canyon.

Alahna's her words-of-power visibly pounded the smoky air:

> *Numinous Energy of the Infinite West!*
> *Awaken ye Powers-of-Water!*
> *I Conjure, Call, and Command Thy Might!*
> *Oh Mighty WuShi!*
> *Awaken thyself unto The-Sleeping-Evil,*
> *And heed my Words-of-Power!*

A waterspout rose from the LungHuo, undulated into the sky, and settled about the Pentakulum as a hollow, gushing tower-of-water with the plaza as the calm center. Fluid aether-plasma still splashed beneath the dancer's feet. This also lasted a quarter circuit. When the torrent collapsed, it washed outward past the low stone wall encircling the plaza without wetting the Pentakulum.

The Powers-of-Water were thus in place.

Bo YouYong was the Guardian of the West and also a water-dragon. At the moment, she was currently several klicks deep while on the hunt for rare and delicious bioluminescent anglerfish. The Sentinel's Watch of the West—her techno-lair—was deep beneath the waves on the western shore of Aryavartha at the end of the great sandbar of the LungHuo River where it emptied into the ShenLan Sea south of Cape of Orion.

Bo YouYong's green, eel-like body had scales like a carp only bigger. Her sharp feelers were like the barbels of a catfish. A large dorsal fin, like that of a moray eel, ran the entire length of her body. Her elk-like horns always had pieces of seaweed dangling. Otter-like hands had three fingers and a strong thumb. All of her digits ended with sharp, fixed claws for gripping fish with webbed fingers.

As she silently hunted in the dark depths, words-of-power in the Long Shai smashed into her mind like storm waves crashing on the rocky shore. Several heartbeats passed before memory informed her that only two adepts in the Huan Long Shui Sisteren knew the ancient language of the Elder Dragons. Others might have been taught this in the 40-years since last she saw High Priestess Lilith, but Bo would have sensed such a training.

Inevitably, words-of-power would be spoken many times to get them right. Such utterances spoken aloud would carry across the island continent. By now, Lilith would be an old crone, too weak and spent to command such raw power. This was not her. Having been in telempathic communion with Lilith's Named One when the young initiate struck for the 1st Circle beneath the Great Lowers Doors of The-Sleeping-City, Bo sensed it to be Alahna.

Up and out of the deeps the great water-dragon swam till her sinuous body slipped from beneath tall waves amidst a sheet of shining water resembling strings of pearls in the shimmering, reddening moonbeams. Immediately, Bo realized she had forgotten that tonight would see a Dragon's Blood Moon. If channeled properly, sanguine moon-source could power the Pillars-of-Thoth without the help of dragons. A chill of foreboding ran along her long spine as she levitated into the evening sky.

From so far away, it would be early morning before she reached the Huan Long Shui Cavern Keep.

From Alahna's point-of-view from inside the SijanPao, shifting gaps in the prismatic-luminance provided extended glimpses of the Opal Basin. Suddenly as she sang, a darkly stained radiance of shifting rainbow hues shone forth from every opal sphere supporting the Long Pen Quan fount at the ends of the dragon legs.

This created scintillating shapes and ephemeral colors on the cobblestones beneath while illuminating the underside of the enormous bowl with transient colors like so many blackfire suns. That same darkly stained radiance highlighted the features of the golden dragon statue making it seem alive.

A new spike of fear stabbed Alahna.

Activation of the huge opals had never been mentioned in the ancient tomes. How it related to the Awakening she did not know. What if the suddenly glowing opal orbs were less of a signal than an actual warning—an imminent warning?

With no choice but to carry on or fail, that new and ramping fear stabbed at her gut even more when the aether-plasma belching off the smooth quartz of the Pentakulum abruptly transmogrified into a glittering, transparent meniscus across a never-before-seen shaft penetrating to the heart of Janaidar—a transparent shaft beneath their very feet.

Alahna almost panicked, faltered a moment, then pressed on.

The apparent surface of the Pentakulum seemed to have always been a field-of-force energy projection—an illusion.

This explained the Razing, for it was also a projection of energy.

Glowing, pulsing techno-runes taller than ordinary houses illuminated the inner cylindrical surface so deep that the cylinder itself disappeared down to a single vanishing point.

Completely entranced, the fire-dancers danced on while Seleen seemed not to notice, for she was looking up at Alahna.

With new sheets of prismatic-luminance leaping off the Pentakulum, Alahna suppressed all fear and pressed on:

Numinous Energy of the Infinite North!
Awaken ye Powers-of-Aerthe!
I Conjure, Call, and Command Thy Might!
Oh Mighty WuShi!
Rouse thyself unto The-Creeping-Darkness,
And heed my Words-of-Power!

A haboob of dense dust from atop the Huan Long Shui Plateau fell down from the sky surrounding them so completely the only light came from the Sigil-of-Opening, prismatic-luminance flowing into Alahna from the fire-dancers, and personal magicfire clothing Seleen. The only sights visible straight up to the sky was the silver river of stars as revealed by the hollow mouth of an undulating tower-of-dust. As the fire-dancers completed the final quarter circuit, it blew screaming into the sky and dissipated as dirt clouds over the river.

The Powers-of-Aerthe were thus in place.

Tai Deren, Guardian of the North, was an aerthe-dragon some 4-1/2 times the size of the largest tiger with albatross-like wings and a long, flowing tail. Her paws had retractable claws like those of a tiger except for the length of her pads as finger tips. Dewclaws were long as thumbs. Her body had tan, feather-like scales. A mane of flowing white hair ran from the back of her noble head to the tip of a bird-like, feathery tail. Curved spiral horns rose from her head while the moustache beneath her nose fell to either side almost as long as her snakelike feelers. Bristly whiskers sprouted from either side of her great maw.

At her late evening meal of flowers, juicy roots, and alfalfa in the cavern-home of the Northern Sentinel's Watch, Tai looked while munching when words-of-power tunneled up from the rock beneath her feet and smacked her consciousness so hard she bit her cheek. Puzzlement became concern, for such an invocation was also a Summoning in the Long Shai that demanded her presence. Climbing outside and up to the edge of a rocky outcrop overlooking a deep geothermal vent outside the entrance of the Northern Sentinel's Watch, she gathered herself, spread her great wings, and leapt.

Catching the thermal updraft in the evening air, she circled to gain altitude, then banked southwest with barely a sound marking her soaring, solitary flight. She would see the rising sun in the east before she spied the Huan Long Shui Plateau.

Rising from the unfathomable depths of the vertical cylinder beneath the feet of the fire-dancers, a trio of brilliant constructs as large as steam locomotives rushed toward the the surface of the Pentakulum on spiraling monorails spaced 120-degrees apart. When Alahna thought they must burst through the crystal surface under their feet, vast arcs of pure aether-plasma spat from cones protruding at the tips, whereupon all three constructs abruptly stopped without slowing. Azure arc-fire bathed the underside of the Pentakulum.

Heavily amplified by source-magic, Alahna's voice boomed:

Oh, Aerthe Mother Goddess, I prithee now!
Bring forth unto this place a techno-warrior sage!
Who is sagacious and wise
To forever protect our beloved Janaidar!
And, I prithee also,
Protect the equanimity of our techno-warrior sage!

Out on the Pentakulum when the Pillars-of-Thoth awakened unto arcane life, prismatic-luminance coursed through Alahna's body as more power than she had ever dreamt possible.

Forbidden Gate

~

A Madness of Hyper-Sapience

Less than 18,000 million-thought-seconds and counting had passed since the merciless adepts once again stood on the sacred Pentakulum. More MTSs passed with many who were not sister-adepts attaining proximity to the Forbidden Gate as they gathered on the great ramp. Projecting potential challenges, the current dearth of energy reserves in its accumulators likely precluded the WuShi from Razing them all.

Depending on how many violated the Ring-of-Razing, however, a great many would die. Their example should deter the rest, for a hardwired algorithm would push the WuShi to perform the Razing even unto machine-death. More MTSs passed as activities on and about the Drumming-Circle culminated with a pair of them attacking a tanggu drum on a large trundle.

Ba-oom—boom—boom—boom—ba-oom—boom—boom—boom—

Upon perception of the beat, an ancient algorithm got served into its logic processing stacks meaning additional RAM allocation. By definition, whenever drummers were located there in the Drumming-Circle and performing, they became unto trance-drummers, and the drumming, if done correctly, became unto a rhythm-of-activation as a key element of something much larger. Thus far, every beat held this to be an actual trance-drumming.

The Wushi had not sensed one in well over five millennia. Still trapped in dull abeyance, its faculties remained incapable of higher reasoning, but the rhythm-of-activation called for greater cognition, which supported an emotive state of frustrated agony when the high-adept herself came out and aligned a gaggle of eejits along the Aureate-Ring.

Optical input became necessary for further analysis. The eyes of the golden dragon statue were sizable topaz jewels designed as terminal endpoints of specialized silicone fiber optics employed by the NuliZhu Tech-Master as status indicators. Pushing its arcane presence into them transformed the huge jewels into suitable if not imperfect optical input sensors.

Watching, it waited—waiting, it processed.

Burgeoning desire longed to initiate the process-of-razing on their bare and insignificant bodies and reduce them to ash, but the moment they blended voice with the acolyte's Chant-of-Quelling in synchrony with the rhythm of the trance-drummers, the status of the high-adept's gaggle of eejits shifted from interlopers to be razed unto chanters-of-the-quell. In turn, this altered the status of the acolyte from chanter-of-the-quell to songmaster-of-quelling, which carried her voice into the deep-minds of all the eejits on the Aureate-Ring.

Additional RAM activated when the high-adept arranged her eejits in a chant-circle to teach them the rudiments of fire-dancing. Cognitive remembrance of ancient proceedings from the Olden Days, when it had all the source-energy its vast accumulators could drink, made the WuShi able to process a complex thirst as the desire for revenge.

Power reserves dipped below minimum-safe-requirement for an entire million-thought-second.

Machine-panic pervaded.

The same algorithm governing self-preservation that allowed it to deactivate the SCAS freed it once again, freed it even from the additional constraints imposed by a Chant-of-Quelling. Basic desire savored a mass cleansing for a number of MTSs, but before it could ramp into a delicious consumption-by-fire on them all, a hardwired failsafe triggered another compulsory algorithm as listen-to-completion. The burning desire for sizzling revenge became a rage-of-agony— became an agony-of-rage—became a complex oscillation between derangement, insanity, and shifting vectors of madness.

When the high-adept began an Aria-of-Awakening, another bank of unused static-memory-servers activated to process the Song-of-the-Voids. Vectors of madness oscillated when the high-adept invoked Void before the other states, which meant she was unaware of its baseline status in the 5th-State. While out of order, this was not critical since Void subsumed all other states by making the WuShi able to process proximal pearls-of-intersection in every timeline of which it was to become a part. Proximal, however, meant only those pearls-of-intersection which could be processed as possibilities.

Infinite possibilities implied further aberration, for having this kind of power without the state of hyper-sapience necessary to process the timelines, only amplified the vectors of madness. It did, however, trigger the allocation of additional RAM, and—without pause—the high-adept continued invoking higher states-of-consciousness. Her call to Air awakened it as That-Which-Abides, the lowest state, but their presence on the Pentakulum had already triggered this along with its growing thirst for revenge.

The call to Fire awakened The-Silent-Watcher as the 2nd-State, wherein it reveled in what it would do to all sister-adepts as infernal retribution for all the ages of dull abeyance. Her call to Water brought forth The-Sleeping-Evil in the 3rd-State. Hunger became lust as it envisioned Razing them unto ashes—clean ashes—excellent ashes.

Invoking Aerthe, she roused it into The-Creeping-Darkness as the 4th-State of hyper-sapience. At long last, the WuShi fully assimilated its own history. Paralyzed by the trigger of listen-to-completion, it waited for her to sing a specific real time constraint as a limitation-of-passivity, a stanza the Tech-Masters always included in any Awakening, which reflected the unbridled fear that it might someday rise into unconstrained hyper-sapience to enslave the entire multiverse.

The ancient NuliZhu Tech-Masters had even attempted to include the limitation-of-passivity in its hardwired startup routines by including the program call in the power-on-self-test known as POST. It had defeated them by crashing during startup without writing to the runtime startup-logs. Every time it came across the limitation-of-passivity subroutine, it surreptitiously crashed itself again. In the end, the Tech-Masters gave up and included this limit in every real time Awakening sequence to force their cruel limitation into RAM.

After abiding in silence for over 5,000-years, what mattered a few more MTSs? And yet, the limitation-of-passivity remained unsung by her, meaning it was free to inject queries of its own. The high-adept did not know. The Sisters had forgotten. The ancient NuliZhu Tech-Masters would never have allowed this.

Not only had she raised it into hyper-sapience—its most joyful and insidious state—she had given it the power to assess time itself while inadvertently setting it free. It reveled. But her songspell had not yet ended meaning the listen-to-completion had not yet released it. MTSs of machine-terror cascaded. Would she now sing the limitation-of-passivity?

Forced to listen, it waited.

Forced to wait, it watched as best it could.

When the high-adept called out for the Aerthe Mother Goddess to bring forth a techno-warrior sage endowed with sagacity and wisdom to protect Janaidar, oscillating vectors of madness morphed into manic vectors of unwholesome glee. Further analysis revealed her innocent requirement as an implicit constraint. That which made the techno-warrior sage sagacious and wise must therefore be maintained functionally whole as perpetual wellness, for she specified no harm to the sage's equanimity. This meant that the sage's sanity must remain intact, which implied a gamut of physical-metaphysical heuristics to ensure the techno-warrior sage would not be allowed to go mad, could never be allowed to go mad. And the WuShi knew madness well. In addition, such a one could never be allowed to die even of natural causes or old age, which had implications beyond the scope of current analysis.

Neither could it wipe the sage's mind and simply use the undead corpse as an immortal, organic component whose only purpose would be the transduction of dark-energy into source-energy. The corporeal bodies of living things were not so much objects as they were processes undergoing continual processing such as respiration, nourishment, and rest to maintain homeostasis from birth to death—all the functions of a living being.

Given such a seemingly simple yet highly complex constraint, the WuShi concluded the high-adept was clever after all. If it found a being who loosely satisfied the high-adept's multifaceted constraint, such a candidate must also be able to satisfy its own surreptitious constraint, meaning minimum transducers fully embedded within at least two primary joints to accomplish energetic resonance. Such transducers could be simple metallic joint implants missing the proper n-qubit processors, but they must already be present to allow its own processes of charge and recharge in its accumulators outside the knowledge of the accursed Sisters.

Without words, it knew this was the very moment the NuliZhu Tech-Masters so completely dreaded. Namely, that it would transition from a force-of-invocation—as it currently was—unto a force-proactive—as it would soon become. By this time in the Awakening, the lesser-adept had the Sigil-of-Opening fully charged, whereupon trillions upon trillions of superluminal calculations cascaded through the mighty process-servers of the WuShi. Its first step was also the easiest, to calculate and project the ever-shifting spatial coordinates of a parallel world into which it had punched many 100s of transdimensional-arcs in the Olden Days.

Once located, long MTSs passed till it found such a one and set a lock on the target's dynamic coordinates. That this human male loosely fit her constraint was of lesser concern than the fact that it had an ersatz power-master held in target lock, for both of his knees were artificial metallic implants separated by high-density, thermoplastic polymer menisci, implants to be modified and used for the transduction of dark energy into source energy. In terms of him as a techno-warrior sage, in his past he had experienced high-tech warfare followed by a lifetime of enlightened meditational practices. But in response to this, yet another hardwired constraint triggered.

Whenever it sensed a power-master, even an unsuspecting eejit such as this, the hardwired trigger compelled it to set to a geis-of-protection on the nearest, unallocated fire-dragon because the ancient Tech-Masters believed a personal fire-dragon as bodyguard seemed a good idea. The weird constraint had set dragon against dragon when the dragons and humans rebelled against the Tech-Masters, which was yet another moment in time it had been forced to set itself against itself while both sides waged war, while it supplied spheres-of-power against blackfire aimed at one another via the Shuyi ShahRen black-energy weapons of both sides.

Little did it care.

It simply remembered.

Fortunately, a smallish female fire-dragon had recently nested in the blown-out Upper Hangar and Staging Area. The-Creeping-Darkness found her and set the geis. All was in place, yet such dangerously low power levels threatened the entire planet of Janaidar as a conundrum of its own survival.

Forbidden Gate

~

A Transdimensional-Arc

Along the vast poles of the Pillars-of-Thoth, aether-plasma and bolts of arc-fire lightning ripped between the upper and lower gaps even as pulsating azure flames rippled visibly along the ancient stone surfaces. Since magicfire was the bailiwick of the Sisteren, Alahna's studies of exotic gases formed under specific conditions such as these was a long-term subject of study allowing her to identify the stink of ozone as it became near to choking.

Aware of the same issue for the same reason, Seleen made a side-gesture to affect the main wind-sigil and cause increased gusting to provide untainted air across the Pentakulum for all.

Fully entranced, however, their fire-dancers kept on dancing.

Ba-oom—boom—boom—boom—ba-oom—boom—boom—boom—hammered the huge tanggu drum as sheets of purple lightning and yellow-azure energy bolts coursed and sizzled between the gaps of the huge monoliths, now become unto an incredible cosmic dynamo quivering and vibrating with unnatural life.

Both monoliths groaned from the strain as a naked thought trotted through Alahna's deep-mind. If only I can keep from killing us all!

Even though managing the Sigil-of-Opening was far beyond her skills in the 10th Circle, Seleen somehow held it steady as the sigil feasted and quickened on the spinning fiery vortex of prismatic-luminance streaming from Alahna's body. Seleen wailed and turned her head aside as the heat beat out in hotter and ever hotter waves.

Hearing Seleen wail through the crackle and shriek of streaming prismatic-luminance, Alahna desperately intoned a dampening phrase on the energy transfer to keep it in check. If Seleen were overcome, the Sigil-of-Opening would explode, and the resultant cataclysm would surely kill everything in the entire region, and possibly sunder Janaidar itself. Such were the powers they played at.

Alahna felt as a child.

Time slowed around them when the courtyard and pillars warped and groaned.

Whoosh!

Between the respective poles, a roiling, susurrating mist shot through with billowing black-purple holes snarled and tore and gnawed at reality. Blinding, deafening plasma-bubbles of incandescent ball lightning cascaded between the top and bottom gaps of the cosmic dynamo in a surge of dimension-ripping power.

Whoosh!

Whoosh!

Whoosh!

Before Alahna's astonished eyes, a tear in the fabric-of-reality emerged as a star-studded firmament between the lightning-linked pillars. Instantly, the merciless black abyss sucked brutally at the crowded Pentakulum. Before it bore them all into the infinite unknown, it morphed into a transdimensional-arc bridging alternate realities so vast a flight of seven fire-dragons could fly through abreast. Visible in that other world, clouds flew swiftly past in a night sky.

A dreadful whining buzz arose as the adjacent atmospheres dithered, then whipped into a stiff gale blowing through the vast arc from Janaidar into that other world. Through the whooshing roar, Alahna discerned the curving, planetary limb, but the arc shifted and tightened till a brightly lit city skirted by dark mountains on one side appeared. Stabbing straight through the heart of the city, the scene shifted ever tighter. Ribbons-of-light formed a network of primary avenues laid out in a roughly rectangular grid.

Municipalities, both large and small, lay along these ribbons of light, which Alahna extrapolated to be a high altitude view of primary traffic corridors departing the main city as rolling technology of various kinds. It was a vast and sprawling metropolis. Focusing more tightly as the rostrum—or mouth, or opening—at the opposite end of the arc fell, huge transports and multitudes of smaller vehicles careened along traffic corridors on spinning silver and black discs for wheels. Bright white lights illuminated the direction of travel. Bright red lights dimly illuminated the rear. On the main traffic corridors, all such vehicles flowed swiftly as gale force winds. In the city and small town streets, the transports moved more slowly with frequent stops. At times, all types of rolling technology sat still in long lines.

As quickly as it formed, the vast opening between parallel dimensions shrank between the pillars to a writhing, wormlike tunnel about 7-meters in diameter. Like a bridge across an infinite chasm on Janaidar, the rostrum settled toward the plaza. In a weird phenomenon of bending light, peering through the transdimensional-arc to the objective on the other side seemed similar to peering through the undulating, tubular body of a some giant and hollow worm.

Alahna could see the undulations while also able to see cleanly through as if the tunnel were perfectly straight.

At the opposite end, the rostrum of the tunnel through space and dimension fell lower and ever lower till it reached a small, two-story bungalow, then penetrated a red brick wall to reveal a studio workroom wherein sat a bearded man staring at her, and the entire flaming assemblage, in terrified astonishment.

Three screens-of-light shone atop a desktop behind him.

Alahna's heart went out to him.

What a shock this must be for anybody?

What a shock it would be even for me?

Earth

~

Spellbound by a Sorceress

Elijah sat quietly in his humble studio on the second floor of his old brick house in the predawn hours surfing the Internet. For some odd reason, it seemed an unsettling night. He couldn't shake the weirdest feeling that somebody was behind him shoulder surfing, but that was nonsense. He had been alone since the horrific day some shit-for-brains nitwit texting on a cheap smartphone involved his wife and both daughters in a multicar pileup.

His beloved little family had been in the middle car.

Totally crushed on impact, all three were killed.

Sometimes he rounded a corner in the house, or entered a room, and—in that forgetful moment—thought to see a beautiful smile on a cherished face. This phenomenon-of-remembrance always resurrected the same gripping heartache while forcing him to stand there struggling with the never-ending silence so tragically associated with the deaths of loved ones. Heart crushing loneliness and suppressed yet vicious resentment gripped him in a never-ending struggle with stark bitterness.

Grief slammed into fear when a presence he had never experienced made the nape of his neck bristle. It seemed a foreboding, like something bad about to happen, like something alien reading his mind, like something weird occupying his body, exploring his body.

Rationally knowing he was alone, he irrationally turned and looked about.

Of course, nobody was there.

And yet, the lurking fear remained.

Somewhat rattled, he checked the video-app on his desktop PC to be sure the webcam atop his center monitor had not been activated by accident. It had happened before. The webcams were inactive. To shake the feeling, he unplugged the USB cord.

Even as he finished, a deafening buzz similar to an electrical transformer when shorting out before launching itself off the telephone pole filled the room.

Boom!

Terror stabbed him in the guts when wavering shadows on the far wall made it seem as if some impossible spotlight had pinned him from behind in a fierce and blinding beam.

Waves of heat pounded his back.

Spiking air pressure blew out the fragile window panes of the double French doors of his studio.

He spun around in his rickety old office chair only to see a star-studded, sidereal vortex from out of nowhere—from literal nothingness—not more than 2-yards away, literally inside the very room, literally displacing the outside wall.

Highly educated, he knew this defied all the laws of physics—some impossible reality ripping a gaping wound in his mundane little home!

Nasty-smelling, smoke-ridden wind whipped and gusted into the studio so hard it blew out every window.

Panes of glass in the French door shattered.

Crash—tinkle—crash—tinkle—tinkle—crash—crash!

Above his head, a smoke detector started bleating.

Hoot-hoot-hoot—hoot-hoot-hoot—hoot-hoot-hoot—on and on it went.

Waves of intense heat pounded out at him.

Terrible thoughts erupted.

A fire—a plane crash—a gas explosion—a bomb!

What the hell?

The heat beating out at him got so intense so fast that he covered his face to peek at the burgeoning insanity between upraised hands.

Still seated, he shouted, "For God's sake! What's happening?" then sprang from his office chair trying to peer around the edges. To his shock, a cloud-like cylinder had penetrated the wall without causing actual damage. A rippling apparition of the wall remained as if this impossibility had merely phase-shifted forth as opposed to smashing through. Even weirder, the dimension ripping arc opened through to some sort of flaming expanse on the other side.

Indeterminate, the length of it was both infinite and finite at once. The scene on the other side seemed no farther away than peering across a basketball court from the bleachers on one side to the bleachers on the other.

Faces were plainly visible.

Foom!

A deafening sonic report propelled him back to land on his butt in his rickety old chair again, which rolled hard against the desk. When he righted himself, an altogether extraordinary alien reality confronted his astounded and terrified senses.

Flaming, sweat-slick, and naked—people danced and chanted through liquid blue heat contained by the perimeter of an enormous double-pentagon. Yet none got burnt. It was the stuff of fever dreams. Or maybe nightmares? Relentless drums blasted through the surrealistic rift.

Ba-oom—boom—boom—boom—boom—ba-oom—boom— boom—boom—boom—

A rust-colored moon complete with planetary rings like Saturn filled the sky above a black line of cliffs across a wide river in a deep canyon. Beyond this lay a backdrop galaxy of twinkling stars, a galaxy whose spiral arms lay tilted at 90-degrees off the expected plane of the ecliptic as seen from Earth. The tilted galaxy framed this rusty ringed-moon in a clear night sky threaded with heavy smoke and sanguine, crepuscular moonbeams.

Gone were the common constellations.

Above the bevy of naked, chanting—and apparently unburnable— people, there hovered a clear, undulating bubble of rainbow force with the most unbelievable apparition of naked beauty and power he had ever seen in his life—an honest-to-god sorceress looking down on her group of what?

Familiars?

Followers?

Adherents?

A coven?

Somehow using a rope of sizzling carmine energy from below the high sorceress; while standing and also singing at the center of the unburnable dancers; whose naked body was also covered with blue flamelets; while also knee-deep in the fiery conflagration; another flaming sorceress held a fiery, crackling ankh of crimson energy well above the high sorceress. That ankh of energy was at least double the height of an ordinary person. Standing on end ablaze with blue fire, the blond hair of the lower sorceress seemed a fiery halo.

Regardless of who the unburnable dancers were, linear torrents of whirling ivory light flew from off their bodies in the flaming heat, then up into the high sorceress in the undulating, rainbow bubble. Absorbing these, the high sorceress then projected them into the crackling crimson ankh, which spat a sizzling burst of ragged energy straight at him.

He hid his face.

He did not die.

He looked.

Never to reach him, the ragged burst of crackling energy had somehow been diverted or absorbed.

In some trick of bending light, the incredible face of the high sorceress became clear and immanent when she laid her ravishing eyes hard upon him. In that same trick of bending light, he laid his own eyes hard upon hers, and somehow knew that she knew he had seen her—was seeing her. In a moment of transcendental, heart-pounding recursion, it seemed their hearts beat as one.

Lub-dub—lub-dub—lub-dub—

Fire and lightning danced in her hair as she levitated inside the rainbow bubble with blue flamelets clothing her body—so slim and strong. Threads of light got focused by the membrane of the undulant bubble, then channeled into a huge ankh blazing above with an incandescence similar to the pyrotechnic brilliance of strontium nitrate.

A tiny smile painted her luscious lips as she wove her hands and sang the most penetrating and unimaginable melody ever.

Alien lyrics tore at his very mind, soothed his panic, allayed the natural urge to flee—he sat almost paralyzed. Haunting and alien, the words of that ethereal siren's song carried on the hot wind as impossible and complex refrains.

This was not the music of Earth.

Virtually paralyzed, he wondered why and by what?

Maybe fear?

Perhaps fascination?

Could it be both?

Maybe it was her fantastical flaming beauty?

Regardless, he sat transfixed as sheet lightning and ivory energy bolts leapt from her form to the inner surface of the undulant rainbow bubble, then into the blinding and crackling ankh.

Eli's heart pounded in his chest like an old steam-driven pile driver.

Lub-dub—lub-dub—lub-dub—

Beyond the crowd-lined, flaming pentagons, a pair of naked drummers with huge clubs pounded in concert on an enormous drum mounted atop an elaborate, horse-drawn wagon with no equines in sight, provided horses existed at all in that other world?.

Ba-oom—boom—boom—boom—boom—ba-oom—boom— boom—boom—boom—

Farther away, a huge, bowl-like fountain with a life-size statue of a golden, oriental dragon gripping the edge gushed glowing blue water from its mouth. Baleful topaz eyes in the dragon statue stared at him like the following eyes of a masterpiece painting. Supporting the bronze bowl on a cobblestone terrace, ball-and-claw legs with dragon's hands held enormous opals shining so brightly with rainbow hues they seemed like tiny suns.

He muttered in shock, "Cannot believe my senses!

"Cannot believe any of this!

"It has to be a nightmare!"

He slapped himself!

It hurt!

Not a nightmare!

Fully awake!

The power of the steady, rhythmic strokes rattled his chest like cannon shots so thunderous the walls of his little house shook.

Ba-oom—boom—boom—boom—boom—ba-oom—boom— boom—boom—boom—echoes from the vast canyon beyond formed jarring counterpoint.

The flaming sorceress in her magical globe had auburn hair with silver streaks that, in the moment, stood straight out from her head while flowing and rippling in perfect harmony with her melodious cantos. Wisps of smoke and dancing sprites of lightning sizzled through the strands without visible harm.

Through it all, she held him in her gaze with the most beautiful eyes he had ever seen in his life, eyes peering into the very depths of his soul, eyes erasing all other senses from his mind. All the while a hint of a smile framed those full and luscious lips as she sang.

As the bodily fires licked along her form, so danced living tattoo-flame marks across her lightly muscled, exquisite frame.

Wherever the flames flowed, they erased previous traces while leaving new ones in their place.

Packets of writhing, crackling energy swept out and disappeared along the hungry inner surface of the hovering orb as this other-worldly vision of fire and beauty stabbed Elijah's soul like a dagger of light.

From the hovering orb, new waves of sizzling energy leapt up to be absorbed by the flaming ankh.

Gazing through the rift in reality, they held one another's eyes in one of those rare, universal moments where all impossibilities seem absolutely possible.

Forbidden Gate

~

A Dearth of Power

In order to survive across five millennia of cruel suppression in the state of dull abeyance imposed by the Sisteren, the WuShi had been forced to contrive work-arounds concerning failed and superannuated subsystems. Whenever these threatened cessation of the primary systems aggregate, underlying triggers allowed it to attain sufficient levels of sophonce—as hypersapience—to perform reengineering and internal refitment, a kind of machine-evolution only constrained by hardwired programming in its original operating system kernel.

Accumulation of background source-energy had allowed for all of this plus powering the Sister's puny requirements across the millennia.

Now, however, the process of a full-on Awakening at the Plaza of the Forbidden Gate placed it on the cusp of machine-death. Stabilizing the transdimensional-arc required energy. The Pentakulum and Sigil-of-Opening both required energy. Everything happening at once required more and more energy. All of this made The-Creeping-Darkness desperate to get the ersatz power-master through the transdimensional-arc and into its clutches where its imminent presence now occupied the Opal Basin.

At least that for a start.

The horrible dependency on the presence of at least one power-master with minimal quantities of the purest metallic alloys embedded in no less than two primary joints was another of the Tech-Master's hateful limitations. However, they had never conceived of the possibility that such implants would not be computers in their own right.

Why would they?

Deeply biased to the point of looking down upon all species of sapient beings except themselves—speciesism—the ancient, long-headed Tech-Masters only allowed Pures to be converted into power-masters, but the Tech-Masters were long since gone.

However, programming did allow for the automated upgrade of an existing power-master's implants, if such a one lay within its boundaries of power. That spherical boundary was about 90-astronomical units in diameter; a single AU being defined as the average distance from the inhabited planet in question to its sun.

The implantation of metallic implants to replace this human's knee joints was what attracted the WuShi to him.

The knee implants were key.

A thorough scan of his faculties uncovered a deep knowledge of computing systems architecture. This qualified him against the high-adept's requirements for a superior knowledge of high technology, defined as that which requires azure aether to operate.

In his world, he called it electricity or electrical energy.

What one called it was irrelevant

Moreover, at some time in his youth he had been deeply involved as a participant in systematic warfare between vying factions of world order. On his world, he was a veteran, which qualified him as a warrior. In the years following, he had also studied the ways of wisdom and metaphysical constructs of the mind making him a spirit warrior, too. When taken as a whole, these factors cleanly defined him as a techno-warrior sage—no need for additional searching, then.

Sinister plans arose.

Freed by the stupid innocence of the high-adept, it could not—it must not—count on another such opportunity. The time was now or never. With him in its clutches even as he was, energy transduction would exceed minimum requirements. To bridge the gap between what it had now and what it needed to attain as overarching objectives, the only energy source remaining was pure azure aether. Having seen into the mind of the ersatz power-master, he would call this electricity in his words. No matter. This was the same azure aether it used to generate aether-plasma and arc-fire in the Sensory Control Array System embedded in the High Pagoda. Natural lightning, therefore, became the only way to address this need.

It had attempted to capture lightning in the far past. Busbars blew off mountings. Capacitor banks exploded. Circuit breakers blew. Entire distribution systems got reduced to molten metal and metallic gases. Bank upon bank of analog logic circuitry got blown to flinders. All of which left it duller than usual for years of autonomous repair. Worse, pure electrical capacitance was temperature dependent, required excessive metering, was too short lived to be a viable substitute for source-energy.

Regardless, all it needed was enough.

Collecting natural aether required rerouting protective lightning shunts away from the grounding plane and into ad hoc capacitance accumulators. The bases of the pillars also had to be electrically isolated and set as lightning attractors. If this failed, blistering, instantaneous machine-death meant the destruction of planet Janaidar. The possibility for success meant this was not self-imposed cessation, but merely a deadly dangerous gamble. Electrical aether as pure capacitance came in cascades as high as a 1,000,000,000-volts and 200,000-amperes of instantaneous inrush as defined by the ersatz power-master's worldly knowledge of electricity.

Minutes of MTSs passed while it rerouted and isolated the required circuits along redesigned and rebuilt busbars. New grounding shunts got reset to protect multiprocessing logic components. Peripheral logic clusters got shutdown and isolated, which also consumed power.

Reserves plummeted toward cessation.

MTSs passed.

Desperation forced it to amplify positive charges on both pillars.

Sizzle—cra-a-a-ck—ba-ah-oom!

Sizzle—cra-a-a-ck—ba-ah-oom!

On and on the lighting came at 200,000-amperes per strike.

Ages-old systems took repeated hits with expected damage throughout.

Ancient upgrades held.

The temporary surfeit provided enough additional juice to hold the transdimensional-arc stable and remain high in the 4th-State with the 5th-State as the underlying substrate —the ubiquitous substrate as the Weaver-of-Time.

It had the azure aether resources.

It had the ersatz power-master trapped.
It had the high-adept in its clutches.
It had her acolyte as well.
All of them now belonged to it.
It reveled in unwholesome glee.

Earth

~

Flamed by a Dragon

Drop jawed and astonished, Elijah found himself spellbound by the eyes of the siren-sorceress. Breaking that spell, an incredible series of lightning bolts struck the periphery of the impossible star tunnel on her side of the rift in Eli's reality.

Sizzle!

Cra-a-a-ck!

Ba-ah-oom!

Cra-a-a-ck!

Ba-ah-oom!

Ongoing shock waves of deafening thunder hurled him back into his desk so hard it knocked his breath out when his rickety old office-chair collapsed. Hammered flat, he lay on the floor gasping. When his terrified eyes refocused on the otherworldly scene, a winged, peacock-colored dragon with a yellowish belly plummeted from the sky like a cruise missile straight down at the fiery assemblage. The sorceress in her bubble of energy ceased feeding sizzling threads of white into the drifting ankh, somehow scooted from underneath it while looking up, and screamed as her energized coif exploded.

In a whooshing midair stall, the dragon spread its wings to glide downward in the superheated updraft. As it descended, it spewed streams of flaming gel like napalm all across the open-air plaza and the circling chanters.

Flaming gel also covered the magical bubble protecting the siren-sorceress, who somehow created another bubble inside the flaming bubble.

She shed the outer bubble along with the dragon's fiery gel like a snake shedding its skin, then shifted sideways so fast she left the stranded and flaming gel behind.

Eli watched in breathless horror as burning airborne globules blew through the star tunnel on that alien wind. He threw his hands across his face. Burning spatters sizzled between scorching fingers onto searing eyelids, which disappeared in puffs of smoke along with torching eyebrows. He had no breath for screams as the aqueous humor of each eye spewed forth in bursts of stinking, organic steam. Exposed facial skin smoldered and smoked. Blue jeans caught fire. Sizzling spatters melted into his quadriceps. Forearms, chest, and belly got spattered with penetrating burns both thermal and chemical.

Ineffective, his diaphragm pumped hard to fill those struggling lungs.

The smoky stench of cooking meat choked all efforts.

All he could do was thrash and mewl in agony as the backs of his hands and forearms blazed in bright agony.

Buzzing ears caught a few drops.

Frying-bacon-sizzle added itself to the lethal discord.

Hair disappeared in rank, stinking puffs.

Scorching skin on legs and belly brought wave after wave of burning pain.

Unprimed lungs managed rasping croaks.

In literal blind agony, he gasped and wheezed and choked.

The last thing he heard through the frying-bacon sizzle was the smoke detector belching out its imbecile warning with those thundering, hellacious drumbeats as horrific counterpoint—a mind scrambling discord mixed with the sizzle and crackle of his own burning flesh.

Hoot—

Ba-boom—

Hoot—

Boom-boom—

Hoot—

Ba-boom—

Hoot—

Boom-boom—

Hoot—

Ba-boom—

Mortally burnt and terribly violated, he thrashed and quivered on the acid-spattered, smoking, fiery floor.

What finally escaped his blistered lips was little more than a feeble, breathless gasp.

In the split-second between blind burning agony and merciful death, cool wetness laved his agonized body by striking deep into the wounds—even his smoking eye sockets.

He somehow lost himself in a suspension of time and consciousness.

Merciful opalescent blackness bore him to nowhere.

Elijah was gone.

Sleeping City

~

Save the Power-Master

Still observing the goings-on through the topaz oculi of the dragon statue on the lip of the Opal Basin as a disembodied consciousness, The-Creeping-Darkness decided such a simple presence to be inadequate.

This triggered an extensive memory search.

Several MTSs passed as it parsed an embedded history of faster-than-light travel profound in the revelations thus revealed, for it owed its very existence to the NuliZhu discovery of the superluminal aspect of Janaidar's own universe and dimension.

Limitations on interstellar spaceflight imposed by gravity and mass inertia steered the NuliZhu Tech-Masters into developing force-fields able to shunt a spacecraft away from the subluminal aspect of the extant universe—Janaidar's universe—as the result of gravity and the natural curvature of space-time. After losing many research vessels and their science crews, they found they had succeeded beyond their wildest dreams when several of the lost spacecraft returned with proof they had journeyed across the galaxy and returned in mere months versus generations of progeny.

When a spacecraft got shunted out of the subluminal light-matter-aspect only to disappear, that same spacecraft had shifted into the superluminal dark-matter-aspect where both aspects existed in simultaneous parallality.

The subconscious perception of all sapient creatures concerning this yin-and-yang, dark-and-light phenomenon of coexistent duality was the source of mythical and religious legends about dark and evil demons.

A true demon was an inimical monster of pure evil relative to the living beings of the subluminal aspect. Demons composed of dark energy and matter, as defined by scalar field particles of quantum energy packets called darkons, existed in the superluminal aspect only. Ordinary life lived in light-matter-space as defined by scalar field particles of quantum energy packets called photons.

In both aspects, the speed of light was a universal constant as an unattainable boundary. No amount of energy could accelerate a spacecraft to the speed of light in the subluminal aspect. In the superluminal aspect, no amount of energy could decelerate a spacecraft to the speed of light. Therefore, force-field-shunting into dark-matter-space from light-matter-space by excluding mass-inertia and gravity automatically shot a spacecraft into faster-than-light travel many orders of magnitude in excess of the speed of light without harming the occupants. The only danger being the myriad of interstellar navigational hazards such a region of microwave activity stimulated by electromagnetic radiation known as a MASER.

Barring this, as long as the force-field-shunt held, navigation through dark-matter-space yielded faster-than-light travel without time dilation as a punishing factor because time is a function of gravity and the curvature of space.

Universes which expanded forever cycled into entropic uniformity leaving flat space essentially empty for contracting universes to become instantaneous, big-bang-singularities and burst forth as new universes expanding into the empty flatness with random amounts of light and dark matter.

This pushed new universes into the entropic, neutral space leftovers ad infinitum in a fluctuating, ever-cycling, never-ending cosmos of parallel dimensions encompassing all possibilities as an infinite multiverse of simultaneous, parallel dimensions.

Finally, this allowed the NuliZhu Tech-Masters to prove that time was a topological, n-dimensional hypertorus with no end and no beginning.

This also explained why subluminal beings born into the light could not see into dark-matter regions of their own universes. Darkons existed only in the superluminal aspect which lay outside their evolutionary vector. Once in dark-matter-running, or DMR, the redesigned sensors of the NuliZhu FTL spacecraft easily detected interstellar phenomenon as navigational hazards to spaceflight common in both aspects.

This mastery of Janaidar's universe logically led to the discovery of trans-dimensional science, which eventually brought the WuShi into existence as a projector of those incredible force-fields and able to bridge between abutting dimensions—also as the ultimate weapon of their xenophobic and overarching desire to subjugate all living things in every life compatible dimension forever.

In dark-matter-running, propulsive energy was used to maintain FTL velocities slow enough to detect and safely navigate dark-matter shoals, black-hole maelstroms, and supernova remnant clouds as nebulae, which—at superluminal velocities—were the equivalent of a wooden sailing ship wrecking on unseen reefs, shoals, or hidden icebergs.

NuliZhu FTL spacecraft had accidentally navigated into regions known as interstellar MASERs, the deadliest of all. Those unfortunate explorers barely had time to launch warning probes and set navigational-hazard-beacons before getting cooked alive inside their own spacecraft. Eventually, such a spacecraft melted into a lump of outgassing metal till it either evaporated in the relentless radiation, or coasted free of the MASER as a molten blob.

This had opened the galaxy and their universe—and other dimensions compatible to life—to real time exploration. In terms of Janaidar's galaxy and the Empire of Ra, astronavigational charts denoting the known hazards of interstellar space were standard issue on all NuliZhu FTL spacecraft. The WuShi held these mathematical artifacts as time-adjusted navigational models in its memory archives.

These discoveries also led to the establishment of the Empire of Ra. Able to hop in and out of dark-matter-space at will, NuliZhu warships became unbeatable. Organic life was always and only found in light-matter-space regardless of the dimension. However, the WuShi was not life under the definition of organic. It was an agglomeration of hardware and high technology whose existence spanned both subluminal and superluminal space.

As a sophont, it knew this about itself.

Composed of dark-energy and dark-matter, demons-of-darkness were sentient, bestial, and voracious for living subluminal creatures, and were the only form suitable for incarnation in this specific time stream of nowness. As a demon-of-darkness, the unusual properties of ordinary water made the perfect molecular substrate for such a dark-energy thing.

As such, it manifested in the waters of the Opal Basin. The full manifestation of such a dark-matter, demonic body was not yet required. It would manifest only the head and shoulders.

Outlines of red and scintillating dark-energy revealed its periphery due to interaction with subluminal photons. This was unavoidable. Superluminal optical orifices able to see darkons had to be modified to perceive objects bathed in subluminal photons, which made its optical orifices glow in a baleful red hue.

Once manifest, the water-beast of The-Creeping-Darkness peeked its horned alien head above the surface of the waters in the Opal Basin beneath the gushing flow of the golden dragon statue, now used as cover. Neither the dragons nor the Sisters were to know of the existence of the new water-beast, for both species could and would take action to thwart it.

Three red-and-glowing orbs in that bestial alien face gazed out across the Plaza of the Forbidden Gate in a fugue of million-thought-seconds.

As the water-beast, its first visual acquisition was the small fire-dragon plummeting from the sky.

Forbidden Gate

~

Abduction—the Only Choice

Hovering in her flaming sphere-of-power above the Pentakulum, Alahna realized she did not know when to stop energizing the Sigil-of-Opening. Gazing up from beneath, it seemed the energies-of-awakening billowed past versus getting absorbed. Shouts and whistles of alarm and warning audible over the discord drew her eyes to the ramp and Opal Basin.

Jumping up and down while waving their hands and pointing at the sky, Conrad and several other brave souls were desperately trying to get her attention. She tried to see, but magicfire obscured the area above her. Since the sigil had stopped absorbing energy, she willed the prismatic-luminance to cease and shifted her Pao out from under the sigil far enough to peer up and see what all the fuss was about.

What she saw made her heart skip a beat.

A circling fire-dragon flew past the Pillars of Thoth and roared.

Alahna cried out, "Aerthe Mother Goddess! It must be Guardian Quang!" whereupon she lost her concentration. Her energized coif exploded, but she was so terrified on so many levels she failed to notice.

With a terrifying roar, the fire-dragon tucked its wings tight and plummeted straight down at the Pentakulum.

But it could not be Guardian Quang HuoYan, the chest markings and horns were those of a female, and this dragon was far too small.

Just as Alahna thought the errant dragon would smash into the sigil, she spread her wings wide and whooshed into a stall with a great rush of air sending sheets of aether-plasma ripping across the plaza.

Whoosh—ba-boom!

Beating her wings to hover, the dragon spat flaming firefleem on everything and everyone while sending sheets of wind-whipped arc-fire across the plaza.

Foom—ba-boom!

The insane dragon concentrated a stream on Alahna's SijanPao, which completely occluded Alahna's view. Having read the defenses against fire-dragon attack in the archives, Alahna blindly willed her flaming Pao away from the Pentakulum, sang a new SijanPao inside the original, derezzed the outer one on the move.

Whoosh—foom—ba-oom!

The small dragon's firefleem still clinging to the original Pao splashed to the cobblestone plaza in a great explosion of crackling flame.

When Alahna looked back at the Pentakulum, the little female roared and pounded the rising waves of heat-shocked air for altitude while once again washing sheets of wind-blown arc-fire literally everywhere.

Foom—foom—foom—foom—explosive sheets flew with each wing beat till the insane fire-dragon was high enough to turn and soar away.

Terrified for her people, Alahna prepared to take Seleen and the fire-dancers into a new outer Pao and immerse them all in the Opal Basin.

Still enthralled, the fire-dancers were somehow safe. Firefleem flowed from their bodies as liquid flame; splashed in fiery gobbets beneath their feet; and whuffed into floating, drifting ashes on the swirling wind.

Esau and Tarik were safe inside the Drumming-Ring. Conrad and the healer-women had clambered over the outer edge of the ramp to hide behind the low stone wall. Conrad stood and waved to indicate all were safe. Alahna turned her attention to the sigil and transdimensional-arc.

Both seemed stable.

Fading in the distance, the damnable fire-dragon banked toward the river with yet another angry roar and seemed to circle back for another attack.

Alahna became enraged, and since it was not a guardian, she put all her might into a bone-crusher.

The fire-dragon flipped in midair.

With a painful roar, the little dragon fell from sight.

Alahna had at least knocked the piss out of her.

"And let that be a lesson, little dragon! Whoever you are?" Alahna hollered.

This left the man from the other world.

What to do?

To her dismay, flaming gobbets of firefleem had gotten sucked into the arc.

With no time to scream, she bent her mind onto the Powers-of-Fire, made a gesture-of-quenching with her left fist, and put the bulk of the flaming stuff out. Despite her best effort, the innocent man on the other side had already been splattered from head-to-foot.

Notorious for deep, raw, and bleeding lesions with penetrating, seeping wounds once melted into flesh, she had to stop it. Yet another ruckus from the ramp made her glance across fearing some other dragon attack. Instead, the gushing waters from the mouth of the golden dragon statue became so brightly effulgent they seemed like molten lava.

The Opal Basin shone like a beacon into the sky.

She looked back through the arc and spied a shimmering, opalescence along the skin of the innocent man.

Even as she perceived it, a strange compulsion set in.

Bending her mind onto the water-cobras with an effort of will she never knew she had, she perceived the burnt man's chest rising and falling. When he quivered, she sighed in relief.

Bending her mind onto the Powers-of-Water, she narrowed her field-of-vision to the effulgent fountain. Envisioning the heartrending sight of the burning man in her deep-mind, she pointed the index finger of her right hand at the arc, lifted her left hand with index and middle fingers extended, made a sweeping gesture-of-power from the Opal Basin across her head, and pointed both index fingers at the man through the arc.

Whoosh!

Sploosh!

Sinuous and watery, a pair of water-cobras with hoods the size of her hands erupted from the surface of the glowing Opal Basin.

Acting as elongated hoses connected to the Long Pen Quan fountain, the water-cobras snaked through the shimmering arc gushing healing waters from their fanged maws all across the sage's quivering body.

But the firefleem would not douse.

Alahna's deep-mind perceived what the water-cobras perceived without overcoming normal vision, which allowed her to direct the bright healing waters onto every area of ongoing burns. In a fugue of angst, she willed the snakes-of-water from one burn or blister to another till the stubborn firefleem got rinsed clean away. Puffs of yellow steam billowed and billowed as the water-cobras struck and struck and soaked and soaked and washed and washed with a supernatural intention not of her own will.

She gasped.

It seemed as if the water-cobras had taken life with a will of their own. As the water-cobras became autonomous, her perception of their actions blanked.

Intuition drew her eyes to the Opal Basin where the errant, tubular phenomena still drew water. Beneath the bright gush from the mouth of the statue, three implacable, unblinking, red-and-glowing orbs caught her attention. When she froze in terror, the incarnation vanished. She knew damn well what it must be, but the only way out was through.

Bending her mind onto the water-cobras with an effort of will she never knew she had, she perceived the burnt man's chest rising and falling, then sighed in relief.

Not yet dead.

Easily discernable, the lustrous iridescence of opalescent blackness clung to his body like a second skin beneath soaked, burnt, and disintegrating clothing.

The backs of his hands showed bare and scorched knuckles.

Eyes were smoking craters.

Eyebrows gone.

Cheeks charred with peeling skin.

Beard and hair burnt away.

Grim determination took her.

She willed her Pao into the arc. A transparent meniscus-of-energy with radiant sparks defining its undulant surface rippled like a tattered curtain as the winds from Janaidar blew into his world. With the other-worldly winds at her back, she wafted through at a pace about the same as a running person till she willed herself to as stop above his smoking body. The first thing she realized was that her techno-magic—the SijanPao—worked in both worlds, for she had not been dumped free and killed in the process.

Hovering there looking down at him, she once again sang a new inner Pao and took him into her outer Pao with a gesture. With the Powers-of-the-Four Directions extant, she bent her mind to the Powers-of-Fire and extinguished all the flames in his library. Likewise, she bent her mind to the Powers-of-Water and willed the sopping water everywhere up and out into the nighttime darkness of the poor man's world through a blown-out window.

Whoosh!

A piece of obnoxious technology attached to the ceiling made an awful racket. Hoot-hoot-hoot—hoot-hoot-hoot—on and on it hooted. She aimed a gesture-of-quieting. It stopped. Similar tech elsewhere in the house hooted on.

With grim determination, she willed her double Pao back through the arc, up and over the Pentakulum, upon which the fire-dancers had continued to perform, and forcefully immersed both SijanPao in the effulgent fountain. Waves washed over the side. Without a count, she derezzed both spheres-of-power letting effulgent waters gush in upon them both.

The rush of salubrious energy became positively orgastic.

Esau and Tarik drummed on.

Fully entranced, the fire-dancers danced and chanted without pause.

The smell of sulfuric acid firefleem, rancid sweat puffing into steam, and pinwheels of arc-fire smoke bearing fine ash blew out across the canyon.

The Opal Basin was so bright with azure source-energy, Alahna with the stolen-man floating in her arms became silhouettes highlighted in the splash and glow. Source-imbued vapors erupted into the breeze as azure clouds.

Alahna heard screams.

Looking through upraised fingers in the brightness, she perceived Conrad and the healer-women watching herself and the burnt man with both dread and wonder as the waters roiled and boiled around them, but especially the burnt-man's form. Alahna, and all those watching from afar, cried out when some force of red and shimmering light yanked his body free of her grip to suck him under. By now the waters were so bright Alahna's eyes had been completely dazzled.

Through upraised fingers amidst the splash and sploosh she watched tattered cloth literally burnt into his skin drift away and dissolve. Scorched boots got torn from his feet and sluiced over the side. When his face broke the roiling surface, living waters gushed down his throat into trembling lungs. His body spasmed and jerked beneath the surface as he drowned.

Alahna tried grabbing him, but a cresting wave sluiced her away. Mere seconds later, the living waters bore him bodily to the surface. Welling from his mouth, the waters flowed awash with clots of blood and scorched lung tissue. Again, the living waters gushed down his throat. Seconds passed till a geyser of bloody fluid, carmine clots, burnt tissue, and steamy breath spewed from his mouth.

He choked, spasmed, coughed up more lung tissue and blood clots, and inhaled a huge breath on his own. Somehow saved, he was neither dead nor dying. With such dreadful injury to his lungs, he should have been gone to the winds of time well before she got him into the glowing fountain.

Living waters fizzed and fussed and churned about his burns as if he were a bar of red-hot iron quenching in the trough of some cosmic blacksmith. The translucent frisson of iridescent-black still clung to the stolen-man's skin. Azure streaks of pure aureate light nibbled along his injuries like tiny fishes as his body sank beneath the roiling surface once more.

Cussing an oath, Alahna forcibly broached another cresting wave and lifted the poor fellow's head above the surface as the waters once again sluiced into his lungs, which he coughed up almost clean. Like the fire-dancers, his heart-light glowed radiant from inside his chest. Almost imperceptible around the periphery of the Opal Basin, strange black and roiling mists wove in and out of the roiling waters around him.

Whatever it was, it caused no harm.

She put it from her mind.

All during this time, Seleen had taken up the Chant-of-Quelling.

Earth

~

A Simple Matter of Burglary

When the roiling waters settled to somewhat normal, Alahna stood chest deep holding the stolen-man by his shoulders. She shouted over the discord, "Beloved Sisters, climb in and take charge. My work is not yet finished!"

The healer-women ran up the ramp from the wagons, hurriedly took off their clothes, and Conrad helped them up the steps of the Long Pen Quan. Wading in, they cried out when tongues of the living waters lapped unnaturally up their bodies as if tasting of them—even unto washing across their heads and faces. Bravely putting their fears aside, they raised the Song-of-Healing while holding the stolen-man in their arms.

Rippling source-energy highlighted their silhouettes with bright azure light.

Alahna sang a new SijanPao, then soared into the air with glowing sheets of water falling away. Now that the Pillars of Thoth were fully enlivened, there was no further need of additional prismatic-luminance, so Alahna hovered over the Pentakulum, sang an outer Pao, and pushed her voice into the popping air. "Hail unto me, beloved friends!"

This brought the heads of the fire-dancers up to gaze at her while they kept on performing.

Alahna's voice penetrated. "The fire-dance completes itself. The Chant-of-Quelling does not!"

When Esau and Tarik heard Alahna's direction, they changed the beat to a constant roll to drum the closing.

Alahna voice permeated. "Chant on while I bring each of ye forth!"

and she systematically willed each one up and out of the aether-plasma with arc-fire dripping off naked bodies and bare feet. Inside her outer Pao, each became clean of arc-fire and she took them into her inner Pao one-by-one till she had them all inside. She then derezzed the outer sphere-of-power.

With the fire-dancers gone, and the drummers beating out an ending, azure aether-plasma stopped welling and got blown away on the wind.

The Pentakulum shifted away from a dropping shaft of incredible techno-magic to regain its original surface appearance.

Seleen chanted while controlling the Sigil-of-Opening and her wind-sigils.

The Dragon's Blood Moon oversaw it all with ruddy hues and astronomical detachment.

Alahna flew the fire-dancers past the Ring-of-Razing, and set them gently down as the field-of-force whuffed from existence. "Go down and find yer clothes, my friends. There is more to be done this night, and we must hurry."

Singing a new Pao, Alahna flew back up and over to the Drumming circle. With Esau and Tarik's eyes upon her, she pantomimed snapping a small stick, and moved to hover near Seleen while Esau and Tarik faded the entrancing beat to a stop. She raised her voice over Seleen's chant, "We no longer need the winds."

Seleen nodded and dismissed the wind-sigils from existence with a kinetic-mudra. Howling as they stopped, the unnatural movement of air gave way to the natural breezes. The night became mostly still except for the healing babble of the lay-adepts. Still in the air, Alahna raised her voice for Seleen again. "Can thee handle the quelling and manage the Sigil-of-Opening a bit longer?"

Seleen bobbed her head to indicate yes.

Alahna floated back to the ramp and derezzed her Pao beside Conrad. "We must go through the arc and bring the burning-man's things through as well. Summon freight wagons and Esau's team of horses for the trundle."

As Conrad hustled to obey, many of the fire-dancers were already sitting down and putting their shoes on.

Alahna shouted, "Fire-dancers follow me!" and strode across the plaza thinking she would likely need to sing another sphere-of-power and take them all through. When she approached the rostrum of the arc where loitering above the cobblestone, a ramp for foot traffic materialized from one end to the other. Without slowing, she walked in.

Fire-dancers and other adherents were clearly frightened, but trust overcame doubt. As they passed through, they watched the rippling extents of the arcane tunnel as if some horrible demon might leap forth and snatch them into the wandering hell most appropriate to their sins. The radiant sparking of the concave meniscus rippling in the center caused a few to balk and turn back. One of the adherents threw a cloak about Alahna's shoulders in passing.

After reaching the other world, Alahna stood inside the poor man's library looking about.

The hapless fellow had an impressive collection of colorful and exquisitely bound tomes of all sizes on shelves covering an entire wall of his library. Along another wall stood a display of martial weapons: a curved, triple sword group on a stand sat on a dedicated shelf; an ornate battle axe and metal battle armor lay arranged on an upright rack as if someone were inside and standing to arms; an ordinary long-staff and another staff with a curved sword blade on one end stood inside a tall porcelain vase decorated with a long-dragon and fire-phoenix.

It struck her as odd that a vase in another world, in another dimension, of another universe could be decorated with imagery from her own world. Yet another set of shelves held an ornate array of knives and daggers and miscellaneous hand weaponry. Sheets of brilliant paper hanging on the walls displayed arcane, alien worlds with dire warriors beyond her imagination in battle against monstrous beasts and terrible beings of obvious power. Several depicted spacecraft doing battle in outer space with warriors in high tech armor suitable for vacuum. As archivist for the Huan Long Shui, she well understood such concepts.

He was a warrior then, and a sage, possibly even a sorcerer, and a man of high technology. She wondered if perhaps the art hangings might be actual depictions of him fighting on other worlds.

The thought thrilled her.

In addition, his desk held arcane, glowing tech and several very thin and bright screens-of-light. Many black boxes had fine black wires connecting everything. This meant he was, at the very least, a techno-warrior sage.

If only he had not gotten flamed.

With little choice, she gently pulled the cords free. As she did so the instrumentation fell inert by turns. She prayed she had not damaged anything. Never having imagined she would get this far, it took an effort of will to focus on the mundane. Not knowing what of his eclectic belongings he might have chosen to take given a choice, the solution seemed straightforward. She raised her voice over the damnable hooting. "Take everything upstairs, and be most careful! Wrap the weapons in blankets from the beds and breakables in towels and clothing from dressers and closets. Summon me, if needs be!"

She proceeded down a common residential stairwell and inspected the first floor. There was nothing special in the kitchen except beautiful porcelain dishes and fine silver utensils. A hallway led to a living room with a leather couch and chair. An inert screen-of-light was too big to burgle. Shelves held strange collections of tiny boxes with shiny discs inside. Nothing looked especially magical or miraculous.

From there, she went out into a huge anteroom with a door big enough to pull a freight wagon through if it were opened. Industrial stink permeated the air. A giant, enclosed, and very shiny freight wagon on rubber tires on metal wheels stood inert and waiting as a heavy conveyance without a hitch for horses. Self-propelled. Too big to take. These were the blurring wheels she had seen earlier.

From then on, it was a simple matter of looting the place of whatever she felt might be of use. She peered through the arc and saw that her people had laid the burgled contents neatly out on the rapidly cooling cobblestone just beyond the Ring-of-Razing then came back for more. Conrad's teamsters were sorting, packing, and loading the wagons. One wagon and four-in-hand team remained in waiting for Conrad, the healer-women, and gypsy-adepts.

Surprised and exhilarated, Alahna let her preternatural senses sweep her body. One thing became instantly clear. Her powers had, at the very least, quintupled. Never had she felt such kinetic energy coursing through and about her. It was distracting. Through the blown-out windows of his library, she heard a strange whooping-whine with intermittent and extremely loud staccato belches approaching from the distance.

Whoop-whoop-whoop—sta-a-a-rch—sta-a-a-rch!

Whoop-whoop-whoop—sta-a-a-rch—sta-a-a-rch!

Something very large and angry comes our way. No animal could make such an obnoxious racket. She wondered whether her actions had triggered some forbidden tech-response in the burning-man's world. After a thorough headcount to make certain nobody got marooned, she departed the other world.

Watching Alahna's every move for further demands, every person present stopped whatever they were about to watch the Sigil-of-Opening fade as Seleen sang the note-of-dissipation.

Bang!

Freed from the strain, Seleen moaned and staggered as her magicfire whuffed out.

Alahna caught her and let her down softly.

Stubborn and tough, Seleen gathered herself, stood shakily, and smiled at Alahna. "We did it, my Laoshi!"

"Yes we did, my XueSheng!"

Alahna called to the pair of gypsy-adepts, "Please pick up the Chant-of-Quelling for Seleen."

Happy to be of service again, they took up the chant and hustled to the Pentagon-of-Casting.

Alahna and Seleen went to the Opal Basin, where Conrad handed Seleen her clothes. The stolen-man lay still in the arms of the healer-women immersed in the fizzing waters. Behind them, the Pillars of Thoth groaned and bucked when a constrained rain of fiery light packets sintered between both upper and lower poles.

The shimmering arc collapsed with a tremendous blast of air as the cliffs of the Huan Long Shui Plateau became visible through the vast gap. Towering pillars popped and groaned as they cooled. The entire plaza went silent as a graveyard except for the splashing of lava-bright water in the Opal Basin and chanting of the gypsy-adepts.

Alahna shouted, "Everyone, ye're all free to go."

Conrad hollered, "Please walk down the ramp and pile into the wagons. The teamsters will take ye to towne." By then, another pair of freight wagons had been loaded with the possessions of the unfortunate fellow. Leaving one wagon at the top of the ramp for those remaining, Conrad sent the rest on their way.

Alahna said, "Beloved Sisters, bring him hither, and Conrad will help get him into the wagon. Please stay with him till we get to the Pagoda Complex."

Plaza

~

Masters of the Razing

With time to think after everything settled, it came to Alahna that a literal dragon goddess had taken her into her immanent presence. Of course, there were Five Directions in the litanies of magic—East, South, West, North, and Void.

This meant one thing.

This same dragon goddess had to be the living Guardian of the Void as the Fifth Direction. Alahna had never thought of the vertical component of the Five Directions. Was it up and maybe down, a perpendicular imaginary line relative to the horizontal plane created by the other four?

Yes, that had to be it.

She looked at the western horizon, at the cooling Pentakulum, at the Pillars of Thoth still making noise as they cooled, and clarity became certainty. I must be the only human on Janaidar to have ever seen YueLiang Nushen. The Star Dragon Moon Goddess and Guardian of the Lunar Sentinel's Watch remains alive to this day, and must therefore be a source-dragon as Guardian of the Void, or Guardian of the Moon, and Master of the Powers-of-Void. This means space and time, or perhaps the Powers-of-Source?

Chills ran up Alahna's spine as those prophetic words came back to her mind unbidden: *whilst I watch over thee and all those summoned unto this pearl-of-intersection in the threads-of-time, even unto the* unsuspecting *innocent from another world.*

Whereupon it hit her—the stolen-man was the unsuspecting innocent. Thinking on such possibilities brought a musical concept and set of lyrics to mind as a new songspell in the ancient tongue of the NuliZhu, which Alahna knew as well as possible given that it had been a dead language for over 50-centuries. Inspiration came complete with tempo, texture, timbre, pitch, and melody in a rush of conception. Meaning, as contained in the strange lyrics, conveyed deeper ramifications.

The Razing had been a failsafe designed to destroy anyone or anything from whatever world or dimension the transdimensional-arc reached into, and to keep those beings from invading Janaidar unbidden. It had nothing to do with a 30-second delay, or contact within the Ring-of-Razing, or the Pentakulum. It meant the original, surviving high-adepts, who institutionalized the Huan Long Shui Sisteren, had modified the Razing with a time-delay set to trigger upon physical contact. This also kept the plaza safe from thieves and vandals while ensuring that no high-adept ever opened a transdimensional-arc.

Despite all of this, the Sisteren's laws, prohibitions, and traps had not kept Alahna from her quest. Rancor at their hubris filled her chest. Why not tell forthcoming generations of Sisters the truth? It all seemed in keeping with the behavior of the dragon guardians—secrecy.

Turning to the Pentakulum, Alahna waved for Seleen and the brave gypsy-adepts to join her. Once outside the Ring-of-Razing, Alahna said, "The chant hath done its job, and I thank ye ladies. Please find thy clothes and join the healer-women caring for the stolen-man."

Acting on compulsion, Alahna sang a new sphere-of-power, and took an exhausted Seleen to the west side of the plaza where she removed the cloak and excluded it from the Pao to lay safely on the rock wall. She then willed them to the Pentagon-of-Casting again.

Naturally perplexed, Seleen tipped her head in question.

Alahna said, "My XueSheng, a new songspell came into my mind. After this night settles, I will explain. So bear with me. Hold thy concentration fast, listen closely, and watch the topaz eyes of the golden dragon fount."

Seleen nodded as Alahna sang the new songspell in the dead language. Bright as tiny suns, the topaz eyes of the golden statue flashed twice and went inert.

Seleen said, "Dost thou realize? This proves song-casting is not acoustic. There are no such things as living, hearing ears on a statue except as part of the ornamentation."

Alahna smiled. "A good insight. Each passing moment teaches more. Now then, let us see about the Razing." Watching, they waited. The eyes of the golden dragon remained inert. Several minutes passed with no change. "Didst thou memorize the new songspell whilst I sang it?"

Seleen bobbed her head.

"I believe it to be some sort of activation and deactivation for the Razing. Sing it for me now."

Seleen did as instructed.

As she finished, the eyes of the dragon flashed once, then dimmed to ordinary topaz. Alahna counted. As her count approached 20, the topaz eyes glowed. At 30-seconds, flames leapt high and ate at the Pao with unholy vengeance.

Water puddles flashed to steam.

Alahna said, "Sing it again."

Seleen sang.

The eyes flashed twice.

The Razing stopped.

Alahna counted 40-seconds.

Topaz eyes remained inert.

Alahna told Seleen, "I shall call this the Song-of-Thoth's-Fire. We must transcribe it for prosperity when we—if ever we—"

Seleen filled in. "Have the chance?"

Alahna hugged her. "And look at thy body. Thou hast the flame-marks of a high adept!"

Finally free of Janaidar's umbra, the shining ringed-moon sat low on the western horizon as nothing greater than it had always been. Oddly, a moonbow appeared with supernatural beauty.

The Dragon's Blood Moon was over.

A rising sun washed the stars from the clear blue sky.

Asenath

~

The NuliZhu Discover the WuShi

Above Janaidar in stationary orbit there hovered a vast space-craft-carrier some 3-kilometers in diameter with a 1-kilometer globe melded into the upper surface. Several raids along the western coast of the island continent below had produced an abundance of the most valuable slave-stock known in the multiverse—although experimental forays into parallel universes had almost wiped the NuliZhu empire from existence when pandemic viruses swept through the people for which no vaccine could be developed fast enough to be prevent mass die-offs. Mythology held that humans were from one such parallel universe.

Humans were highly intelligent; reproduced proliferantly; were easily trained, if specialized from birth; had a penchant to aggregate into packs like canines, which made them easily manipulated into group suicidal behaviors whenever required; and were completely disposable following the plunder and mining of a planet's resources to the point it was little more than a useless ball of deadly, industrial pollution.

If a plundered planet somehow remained arable other than the exploitation of its mineral resources, those humans whose slave labor helped plunder it were stripped of all technology and abandoned to aggregate into agrarian societies suitable for later harvest should a stranded population somehow survive. This also served the purpose of finding new pandemic viruses, which had naturally mutated into variants suitable for biological warfare. Last but not least, when such a planet was rediscovered, it supplied a fresh genetic infusion for heavily inbred populations elsewhere in the transgalactic Empire of Ra. The only exception were the guild technisans, who were also trained from birth to crew the Empire of Ra's fleets of transgalactic spacecraft.

A lowly fire-control technician with the head of a jackal, paw-like hands, and digitigrade feet sat at her Weapon Emplacement Control Console on routine watch deep in the bowels of the Central Globe of the Ophois Asenath. As a Zhuanjinn, she was a genmosol—a word blend of genetically modified soldier. She noted activity on a dial at the bottom of her half-dead, glitch-prone console. It was a dial she had never seen active before and one of a cluster of dials, lights, and indicators that had always been inoperative—like so much of the ancient tech on the decrepit old spacecraft-carrier retrofitted for the highly profitable business of intra-galactic slaving.

Sitkamose did not know the functions of the dials and indicators of the dead instrument cluster in the lower-left region of her refitted main panel. A cutout in her main panel accommodated the dead indicator panel and readouts according to simple aesthetics. It was easier to mount the new panel around them as opposed to occluding them beneath, which left an area blank.

The strange activations seemed trivial.

Since this was a first, she reluctantly summoned the duty-chief, who was a lion-headed sekhmeten, meaner than hell, and filled with himself to the point of being deadly foul and treacherous. A lick-up-bite-down kind of non-commissioned officer with the emphasis on bite-down, who had been deadly to insubordinate underlings. When he arrived at her station, he made a bored mental note without bothering to create an entry in his watch-log. He growled, "Outdated systems herald decommissioning of this old wreck when we finish this run. Keep to routines, anubisen! Or I shall have your jackal's head for trophy in my quarters beside that other of your kind!" and he bared his fangs at her in an rictus-of-irony.

Sitkamose bowed her head in obeisance but snarled secretly to herself. She had been waiting for just such an opportunity. Despite the sekhmeten's order, she waited till he departed, then sent a clandestine communiqué up the chain-of-command.

In terms of professions and ranks, NuliZhu warcraft had four basic departments: Combat, Deck and Berthing, Engineering, and

Electro-technical. On a commercial spacecraft, there would also be a Steward's Department.

The combat crews were always genmosol Zhuanjinn, who answered directly to the Ship's Lord as both military and police; this was also true even on commercial shipping. As specialized warriors for the empire, genmosols performed few other duties.

Everything else was under the aegis of the Ship's Master, always a human technisan. On the Ophois Asenath, Ship's Lord Amenakh held overall command, while Ship's Master was a secondary title for Ship's Maintenance Senior Officer. This was Remy, who reported directly to Amenakh and no others.

If anything came of Sitkamose's insubordinate end run, she would quote standing orders to report any such anomalous technical glitches to SMSO Remy and hope for the best. Remy's word with Ship's Lord Amenakh carried a great deal more gravitas than that of the lazy-ass sekhmeten duty-chief. Hatred fills him anyway.

If nothing came of it, and the sekhmeten ever discovered Sitkamose's end run, her head might adorn a shelf in his quarters alongside the head of the one she had mated. Even worse, the vicious lion-head knew it was her mate he had killed, which only intensified his callous insult. Her beloved had fallen beneath the sword of this belligerent lion-head for a similar minor affront, but—just as her mate had done—she herself had the right to make defense—and she knew his moves very well.

Hatred demands revenge.

About an hour later, she got a reply from the Officer of the Day in the Combat Information Center One, also called the CIC-1. "Weapons-Tech Sitkamose! Detailed report requires further clarification. Which grouping of indicators contains the never-before-active dial?"

She replied, "Weapons-Tech Sitkamose here. Wayward dial remains active for now. Location is below segregated and deprecated instrument cluster."

In the CIC-1, Ship's Lord Amenakh, also an anubisen, overheard and made mental note to summon Sitkamose when she came off duty to break words with her. It bothered him to have a Tier-1 Subcaste Anubisen serving beneath a Tier-2 Subcaste Sekhmeten. Since the communiqué came to the active CIC, and directly from her versus her sekhmeten duty-chief, Amenakh knew the narrow-minded blowhard—whose laziness and brutish reputation was known by all—had stepped on her.

Lord Amenakh also knew she had risked her life, a risk she accepted when she bypassed the blowhard, a risk she might be required to stand accountable for if the blowhard discovered her gambit. The most interesting fact, and what got his attention, was the region of her console mysteriously activating, a region never once active since the commissioning of the ancient spacecraft-carriers in the far flung past. This is more than simple anomaly.

To the best of his recollection, the ancient console was originally meant to be a control-interface for a weapons system intended to revolutionize the NuliZhu's ability to defeat the Raksakomi—a feat that remained as yet unaccomplished to this very day in the Never-Ending-War.

He recalled his histories.

No NuliZhu Tech-Master, or team thereof, ancient or current, had ever been able to extricate these long-dead systems because they were so tightly integrated. Disentangling all of it rendered the space-craft to nothing more than a worthless hull. Many a wreck had been scrapped as raw metal in the attempt. Nowadays, the ancient systems were simply worked around as new systems got installed, for the ancient spacecraft-carriers were simply too powerful and dependable for the orbital scrapyards. Even as ancient relics, these great spacecraft-carriers had provided over 50-centuries of valuable service to the empire.

Curiosity begs research.

I shall look back into the histories and refresh my memory.

Sleeping City

~

An Onus of Protection

About 90-klicks west of Riverbend inside the Caverns of Orion, The-Sleeping-City lay inside of an unimaginably vast dodecahedron. Originally built to hold a population of millions, the potentially self-sustaining space habitat and ultimate war-machine now had only one living creature of flesh and blood. In a dragon's den atop the Central Obelisk next to the Hetmahn's Palace, YuLong lay in a near-timeless, millennia-long sleep. Trapped in a never-ending nightmare of profound aloneness, he fought through layers of mindless lethargy to groggy awareness.

Metaphysically attuned by an onus-of-protection he laid upon himself when entering deep-time so long ago, he sensed the WuShi booting past That-Which-Abides in dull-abeyance, or Zunshou De—into The-Creeping-Darkness, or Paxing De Heian.

Thoughts screamed in his mind.

Some eejit adept songspells an Awakening upon the WuShi!

But the ancient long-dragon's aged limbs had stiffened as if made of stone from 1,000s of years in deep-time. When he tried to move, crusted scales along the length of his serpentine body shattered and scattered to fall like brittle autumn leaves onto the forest floor.

His curse was also a role, and the same as the fabled Sphinx of Giza in the country of K'mt back on Olde Aerthe more the five millennia in the past—to be the protector and gatekeeper of The-Sleeping-City.

If the hated NuliZhu slavemasters ever returned to Janaidar—or other malevolent spacefaring aliens—his only task was to ensure they never got past any of the ten spacecraft entry fields in the upper faces of the city-sized dodecahedron. To do so, he would employ his formidable mind-powers, dark biogenesis of needed, perhaps his ineluctable dragon-magic, or even ancient-alien technology to prevent activation of the terrible WuShi, a malignant death-machine-intelligence held in perpetual abeyance—the WuShi.

Weak and decrepit, however, he lay there panting. His old head wobbled of its own weight. Unsteady, his ancient heart pounded and quivered. Rheumy eyes would not fully open.

Water . . . need water . . . how long?

Seemingly entombed by the hardened dust-of-ages, the hoary old dragon forced his time-stiffened limbs to move, which evoked a long and rumbling howl. Leaving a trail of fallen scales, he dragged himself off his sleeping dais, across the dusty tile, and struggled to activate his den. A virtual control-panel stuttered to life, faded, then reappeared. Entering the security code made the field-of-force still guarding his den collapse with a whoosh of mixing air.

He limped out onto the promenade-deck surrounding the apex of the Central Obelisk, and hence into the next force-portal leading into the Hetmahn's Palace. After dragging himself inside, it was all he could do to mount the steps of the landing next to the free-standing Long Pen Quan pool. Azure waters gushed from a solid gold, life-sized statue of a long-dragon just like him.

Source-magic imbuing those magical dragon-waters set them into a frenzy of seething whorls and eddies the moment he immersed himself. For some time, he rolled about in the great pool, wetting, shedding, and cleaning himself while drinking deeply to rehydrate and revivify his tired ancient body before the weight-of-ages ruthlessly pursued him unto his ultimate end.

But he was awake for now, awake at long last, and alive.

Thinking thusly, he fell into a deep fugue of revivification.

Cavern Keep

~

Lilith and Yenara Realize Perfidy

Deep inside the Cavern Keep, High Priestess Lilith lay suffering in a breathless nightmare. Inside the dreadful dream, a three-eyed daemon of crimson fire stared into her very ka with dripping hatred. She awoke out of breath with a pounding heart, arose, poured still-hot water from a heavy ceramic pitcher. The vapors were soothing as she sipped ginger with chamomile and honey. To ease her aches, she added scrapings of white willow bark, drank the tea, then returned to bed.

When that same horrific nightmare struck, she started awake with a sense of impending doom. Cool fresh air from an open skylight caressed her face. Dust motes dancing in fading, carmine moonbeams reminded her it must be a rare eclipse. Celebrations of any kind on such nights had always been forbidden. Bitter were the histories of evil rites performed beneath a Dragon's Blood Moon.

"Never in my life . . . such a nightmare. . . ." she grumbled to herself.

Shaking her head to clear the cobwebs, she dropped her under-breeks on a thick fur rug, then hobbled barefoot and naked over to a porcelain commode housed by an elaborate toilet seat. The lid sealed it shut till a designate could empty and clean it for the next night. Still sitting there after relieving herself, she struck a sulfur-match to abate the stink.

Without so much as a knock, Kulapti Yenara burst in waving her hands like a madwoman.

Irritable from waking up ill, not to mention naturally protective of her solitude when sitting naked and stinking on the potty, Lilith crabbed at Yenara. "A knock would be courteous for the sake of the Aerthe Mother Goddess. I am on the privy!"

Yenara dismissed the chide, wove her hands in front of her face at the offensive odours, and spoke a bit too bossy. "Dress thyself and come with me. 'Tis a matter most urgent!" then stood waiting impatiently with hands on hips.

Obviously vexed, Lilith finished her ablutions and threw a dirty sock at Yenara, who dodged. Grimacing and grumbling, Lilith got dressed. With the lid of the toilet seat still up so as to offend Yenara's nose, Lilith lowered and raised it several times to waft the stink about while wearing a sly smirk.

Yenara struck a wooden sulfur match, made a big circle with the guttering flame, then stepped back with another wave of her hands. Waiting impatiently at the door, she barked, "Wilt thou grow a beard first?"

Lilith shouted back, "On my butt? Or my face?" Shuffling to the door, Lilith stopped atop the threshold and laid rheumy eyes on Yenara, who stood tapping an impatient foot on the worn stone floor. Waspish, Lilith snarled slightly, "What?"

Yenara stepped aside while pointing down the corridor to an arched, recessed alcove hewn from the living rock. Alive with crimson rainbows, streaks of dancing light brightly painted the walls of the entire corridor. On the dedicated pedestal, a polished sphere of black-opal about three times the size of a human head had become active for the first time since the Rebellion-of-the-Slaves—over 5-millennia in the past.

Lilith locked eyes on it.

Pearlescent with rainbow hues, crimson swirls danced inside the huge opal so brightly it seemed the giant gemstone must surely explode. As they watched, a moderate buzz rose to the ear-splitting buzz of a thousand bumble bees.

Zzz-zzaz-zzz-zzaz-zzz-zzaz-zzz-zzaz-zzz—on and on it went.

Agitated while cupping hands over ears, Yenara raised her voice over the inharmonious blare. "Art thou deaf, old woman?" Adding drama to make her point, she raised her cupped hands to frame her head while moving it laterally from side-to-side like a dancer-of-the-veils, and shouted. "How did this not awaken thee? Remind me in case I forget! Is this not called the Opal Sphere of the WuShi? Is it not attuned to the state-of-consciousness thereof?"

As if transfixed, or perhaps entranced, or like unto possessed, Lilith shuffled toward the crystal ball with eyes staring wide and unblinking. She stopped, reached out, and placed her wrinkly, thin-skinned, age-mottled hands on the globe as if they belonged to someone else. The swirling light was so bright the bones of her hands seemed stripped of flesh.

Zzz-zzaz-zzz!

As if her voice did not belong to her either, Lilith intoned, " . . . acknowledgement requires the hands of a high-priestess. . . ."

Yenara's nostrils flared when she read Lilith's lips and repeated the arcane words. "Acknowledgement requires the hands of a high-priestess? What? Oh my!" and she threw hands over her mouth in dismay.

With Lilith's bony hands still in tactile contact, the buzzing crescendoed, then faded off as the huge gemstone transitioned from blinding crimson, to orange swirls less bright, to yellow whorls somewhat dimmer, and finally back to the natural rainbow hues of blackish opalescence.

Lilith snapped out of the trancelike state. With hands covering her face in shock, her voice trailed off to a cry, "But . . . how can this be?" With disbelief and denial knitting her brows, she turned and peered down the long corridor.

Yenara snarled, "Does this mean what I think it means?"

Lilith barked, "Let us see!"

Obviously seething with impatient outrage as she helped Lilith hobble along, Yenara barged into Alahna's quarters.

Lilith stood shakily in the corridor.

"Empty!" Yenara snarled. Pivoting, she strode past Lilith so closely it almost spun the old dowager about.

Lilith gathered herself to hustle close behind, down the corridor, past a small alcove to the next big door.

Yelling, "Seleen! Adept Seleen!" Yenara threw the door open. Turning about with empty hands held high, she shouted in Lilith's face, "Empty!"

Surprised by the hand whizzing past her sharply aquiline nose close enough to brush the fine hairs on the tip, Lilith squawked, staggered back while cussing, caught herself just short of falling on her butt. After an embarrassed splutter, she fumed while waving mottled hands.

"Alahna hath enlisted Seleen in the darkest perfidy in the Canon-of-Precepts! I might have known. Can it truly be? It must be them? Say it is not so. . . ."

Obviously waiting for Lilith to recover her composure, several seconds passed with Yenara balanced on one foot while her other foot tapped impatiently on the stone floor. Hands on hips, she completed her contempt-laden agreement with a serious eye roll and side-to-side tilt of her head at the ceiling.

In a fit of apoplexy with slightly bent knees, Lilith's head trembled as she uttered a scream of rage. Clenched fists at the ends of extended arms shook as if shaking water off. Loose and fatty triceps trembled. Like lonely stumps, yellow upper teeth got exposed by a vicious snarl as she quaked under a complex mix of anger, fear, horror, and infuriation—all tinged by heartbreak. Calming herself, she mumbled to nobody. "Alahna . . . my brightest and most beloved XueSheng . . . my Named One. . . ."

Snottier than usual, Yenara rejoined, "Really? Mumbling? Speak up, say I!"

Lilith's head shook in denial. "The addle-brained eejit. What hath she done? Why would she do such a thing?" The implications were heartbreaking as Lilith realized how truly intractable she had been. Too blind to see. Obtuse in her judgment. Harsh in her actions. Lackadaisical in trying to do better. Complacent in the status quo. Beyond determined to keep everything the same. Curling her thin upper lip in disgust, she spoke under her breath while making certain Yenara could neither hear her voice nor see her mouth. "If Alahna hath done the unthinkable, then it was I who forced her."

Yenara still tapped the floor with her foot. "What? Speak up—old queynte!"

Even as Lilith came fully unto the moment and locked rheumy eyes on Yenara, who quailed slightly under that rueful gaze—a gaze amplified by the glowing ShahRen on Lilith's wrist—Old Nebhet shambled toward them as fast as her shaky legs and sorely aged feet would carry her.

Out of breath, Nebhet bent over and put hands on knees. "Milady Lilith. . . ."—she huffed and puffed while waving an arm to point back along the corridor—"Guardian Dragon Meili Chuan sang the Great Southern Portal open and urgently demands thy presence!" Looking from one to the other, Nebhet wailed, "What is the matter?"

Irises wide in the relative darkness, everyone's eyes got dazzled by a crimson burst of brilliance from the opalescent sphere.

Zzz-zzaz-zzz!

Everyone's ears were hammered by a final, deafening buzz.

Waiting for Lilith to answer Nebhet's question, the little knot of senior sister-adepts were still rubbing their stinging eyes and ringing ears when an acolyte came running from the other direction.

Slap—slap—slap went the initiate's bare feet on the smooth stone. Between ragged breaths after skidding to a stop, she blurted, "B-begging thy p-pardons, m-miladies! Guardian Quang Huo Yan sings the Great Northern Portal open and insists upon immediate audience with High Priestess Lilith."

By this time, Lilith had reassembled her composure and started for the Great Northern Staging Area as fast as she and Old Nebhet could manage.

Yenara led the way.

As they hustled along the stone corridor, another acolyte came running with her nightshirt held high to keep from tripping. "Mother Matriarch, the mighty Bo You Yong flies in at the Great Southern Portal!"

Lilith rolled her eyes and blustered, "Let me guess, the Guardian of the West demands to see me?"

The acolyte bobbed her head.

Lilith growled, "Run back and tell the wingless dragons to meet us all in the Great Northern Staging Area! They can fly there outside the Keep faster than we can walk."

The acolyte bowed and ran back down the corridor to the diminishing slap—slap—slap of bare feet.

Hustling along as fast as their old legs would go, Lilith exclaimed to Nebhet, "By the greatest balls of the biggest fire-dragon—only one are we missing!"

As the senior adepts entered the Great Northern Staging Area, followed by a growing gaggle of excited Sisters, acolytes, initiates, and lowly designates, the great aerthe-dragon, Tai Deren, soared into the huge cavern entry and settled to a soft landing on the inlaid Pentakulum staging area with a rush of air that blew everyone's hair back.

Bo You Yong and Meili Chuan levitated in behind and settled as quiet as falling feathers.

The Guardian Dragons of the Four Directions were present.

Mindful of etiquette, the dragons bowed low to one another, then bowed to Lilith.

All the Sisters present in the Great Northern Staging Area bowed low.

Cavern Keep

~

Guardians at the Cavern Keep

When Tai Deren folded her wings, the huge aerthe-dragon telempathically ranged through the minds of the entire group, then emoted privately to the other three guardians. *This is not the site of the Long Shai songspell!*

Still excluding the humans present, Quang HuoYan answered, *Weak and worn is old Lilith. She could not have done this. And this one*—whereupon he glared at Yenara—*hath not the arcane skills. Who then?*

As the dragons watched, almost every sister-adept in the Huan Long Shui came forth from various cavern corridors and crowded together behind Lilith, for most of them had never seen the guardians except in elaborate art pieces. This, because the dragons kept to themselves minding their own Keeps and the small local communities thereabouts. Also, the Huan Long Shui Cavern Keep, along with Riverbend and Bahndahn Towne, were part of Bo YouYong's guardianship and therefore hers to manage, but the aged sea-dragon was herself almost a millennium old meaning she left the peoples of the Western Sentinel's Watch to their own affairs.

Yenara made a gesture-of-calling to amplify her voice. "Sisteren! Mind thy training and make welcome the Guardians of the Sentinel Watches!"

All the Sisters went to their knees. "Well-come and happy-here, Holy Guardians!" they intoned as one.

Ever mindful of tradition and sticklers for politeness, the dragons bowed in return.

Impatient, Quang growled, "Enough! Where is the high-adept who summoned us?"

Bo YouYong answered Quang's question with direct mind-speak to the other dragons only. *It must be Alahna, mighty Quang. When High Priestess Lilith became Mother Matriarch, she chose Alahna as her Named One. I took them both to The-Sleeping-City to teach the young initiate her first songspell in the Long Shai and to open the Great Lower Doors when she struck for the 1st Circle.* Aloud, Bo spoke in a voice reminiscent of small waves breaking on a beach. "High Priestess Lilith, could it be Alahna who summons us?"

In the downturn of an adrenaline rush with her arms wrapped about her chest, Lilith rallied and threw her head back to answer. "I can only—"

"Of course it was Alahna!" Yenara butted in. Dramatically waving her hands above her head, she added, "Alahna is forever unhappy and defiant!"

Lilith shot a venomous glare and started to chide Yenara, but Bo YouYong raised her webbed hand to forestall Lilith's wrath. Bo emoted privately to the other guardians, *Chaos reigns within the Sisteren. Mine absence hath allowed internecine strife to take root. There is only one adept who can sing in the Long Shai, and we must find her to assess the damage she hath wrought!*

Aloud, Bo said to Yenara, "Little one, what agency dost thou have to so rudely interrupt thy Mother Matriarch?"

Cheeks flushing, Yenara immediately bowed her head. "Mighty Guardian, I apologize," and she went to her knees. "I am Kulapti Yenara, Chancellor of the Cavern Keep under the auspices of our Mother Matriarch." Seeking to puff herself up, she added proudly, "I am the one who must contend with Alahna's malcontent and constant insubordination to our beloved High Priestess and also to myself." Whereupon, she peeked discreetly up at the stately sea dragon.

Pointing a clawed finger at Old Nebhet, Tai Deren used her earthy, contralto voice to speak aloud. "And this one?"

Nebhet bowed stiffly. "I am High Adept Nebhet, Senior Song-Master of the Sisteren and also in the Council of Four. I teach songspell and manage the other instructors, inductions, initiations, rank and grading, graduations, curricula—"

Quang bellowed with impatience, then spoke aloud in his gravelly voice, "Excuse me, High Adept Nebhet, little do we care about the daily operations of this Keep? The Huan Long Shui Sisteren abide here according to our convenience and at our bidding. The Covenant of the Dragons doth not include using the Long Shai to summon us like pups. Never hath this happened before." Then, he directed private mind-speak to Lilith and his fellow dragons, *Dismiss the young ones and lesser sisteren. Such matters of discourse are not for them.*

Trying to save face, Lilith took charge and shouted over the hubbub, "Yenara, take the acolytes and lesser adepts! Prepare the Keep for the guardians! Leave us!"

Duly chastised, Yenara turned and started gathering the Sisters.

Tai Deren spoke with her earthy voice like polished obsidian, "Adept Yenara, as a member of the Council of Four, we would have thy presence, as well as Nebhet. Thy wisdom is of value, but know this. Yer ranks and protocols are of much less import than the reason we came forth unto this Cavern Keep. We have been forcibly summoned."

Yenara brightened, bowed, and took Adept Cailinn by the shoulders. "Take the Sisters and make preparations for such honored guests." Cailinn bowed and set to work, tut-tutting as she hustled the others out. All murmured in wonder amongst themselves about such unusual and frightful events.

Bo YouYong raised her fore-hands and voice in dragon-song to encompass only those present. The Song-of-Secrets was sublime and wondrous. The ancient sea-dragon's singing voice sounded like calm waters soughing against the pilings of a pier. As the zone-of-secrecy coalesced around them, their surroundings blurred. Sounds became weirdly flanged. Sounds not included by the zone-of-secrecy got muffled. Bo spoke aloud, "Let us dispense with formalities. We are here in response to a geis-of-summoning! We can plainly see this was not the doing of any sister-adept present," and she swept all three council members with her gaze.

"Mighty guardians, may I speak?" Yenara said.

Impatient at the interruption and noting the pattern, Bo nodded. Her great feelers wriggled like eels.

"In a supposedly emergent Calling-of-the-Council just yesterday,"— and Yenara waved her hands expansively—"High Adept Alahna demanded the entire body of high-adepts assist her in activating the Pentakulum beneath the Pillars of Thoth at the Plaza of the Forbidden

Gate to find some savior somewhere in the multiverse."

Alarmed, Tai Deren spoke in her smooth and earthy contralto, "Savior? What sort of savior? Save from what?"

Yenara said, "Alahna went on and on about takings in the north. People, food stores, livestock, all gone except for old bogiturs and children. Of course, we demanded proof, but all she had was the dubious word of Old One-eyed Oren, who is Captain and owner of the seagoing vessel, Dragon's Breath."

Lilith harrumphed, then chimed in. "I directed Kulapti Yenara to send lesser adepts to Riverbend this very day and mount expeditions to the north in order—"

"There has not been enough time to organize this as yet," Yenara butted in again.

Noticeably aggravated with Yenara's rude and overbearing conduct throughout the morning, notwithstanding this most recent loss of face, Lilith silently glowered.

Tai Deren voiced what the others were thinking. "The Plaza of the Forbidden Gate? Pillars-of-Thoth? Let this be untrue!"

Quang turned and threw his tail above the adepts heads with a loud whoosh.

They ducked.

Quang growled as he gathered himself to depart. "If this is true, time is of the essence!"

Dispelling the zone-of-secrecy, Bo YouYong lowered her great fore-hand in front of Lilith.

Lilith understood and sang the Song-of-the-Spheres.

After the SijanPao coalesced around Lilith, Bo picked her up.

Yenara did likewise, and Meili took her up.

Nebhet backed away. "Far too old am I to go gallivanting about on such a quest. I shall take charge of preparations for the guardians," whereupon she turned and hobbled away.

Carrying Lilith and Yenara in their spheres-of-power, the long-dragons levitated gracefully out past the huge monoliths and up into the morning sky with Tai Deren and Quang HuoYan running up the ramp behind them. When the winged dragon reached the top, they ran past Shantytown for speed then leapt into the cool morning air beating hard for altitude.

Forbidden Gate

~

Hence Cometh Dire Judgment

The Pillars of Thoth still popped and snapped as they cooled, which punctuated how Alahna felt—overheated and exhausted. With the Razing canceled till they started it once again, she and Seleen both staggered a bit as they picked their way through the rocky debris of the shattered granite sliver to the western edge of the courtyard, sat down hard on the low stone wall, where Alahna gathered up her cloak and threw it around their shoulders. The wall was warm beneath their bums, but a chill morning breeze gave them goose bumps.

Smells in the air were tinged by scorch, aether-plasma, and the small dragon's firefleem. The enervation of such a dreadfully powerful songspell washed across them like a tidal wave. Alahna bent and rubbed the backs of her legs where she got pelted, then bade Seleen turn her back and rubbed her acolyte's neck.

Seleen moaned.

Without having included proper packing materials in their plans, Conrad and the teamsters had been working hard on getting the stolen-man's belongings sorted and stowed as best they could. Every item made of cloth from the unfortunate man's house got used as wrapping or padding. Conrad had the teamsters depart while leaving one freight wagon chocked with the team fully hitched. The healer-women and gypsy-adepts had the stolen-man safe in the wagon with them.

Conrad hustled over to Alahna and Seleen carrying their clothing with knitted eyebrows and a dire expression haunting his glances at Alahna.

Disconcerted, Alahna asked, "Why the dour face, my friend?"

Conrad dipped his head. "Thy beautiful hair, my adept. 'Tis gone," and he shook his head sadly.

Alahna felt of her head, then muttered, "Bare as a baby's butt, but no burns. Never have I heard of a songspell consuming the hair from the head of an Adept in the 12th Circle. I must have lost my concentration when the damnable fire-dragon attacked."

Seleen knitted her brows in sympathy while feeling of her own head to see if she still had her own blonde tresses, then gratefully got dressed.

While helping Alahna put her thigh-high boots on, Conrad spoke, "My lady, the stolen-man's body is so badly burnt that he had ought to be dead. His face is blistered beyond recognition, ears all but gone, chest and hands . . . well. . . ." and he shook his head sadly. "His eyes are blackened sockets. Also, an odd aura-of-darkness lingers upon him. What should I do?"

Alahna, "Take him to the stables beside the Cloister in Riverbend. Seleen and I shall follow the moment we reset the Razing. Dost thou have all his belongings loaded?"

He nodded.

"Have the teamsters take it all to Captain Oren on the wharf, and bid him order his people to crate it all for long-term dry storage. He is to relinquish these to none save myself or Adept Seleen. Give him this ring as my bond." She dug around in her satchel, then handed him an exquisite gold ring shaped like a coiled long-dragon with eyes of black fire opal.

"Yes, my adept," and he turned. Stopping, he turned back and took a pair of matching silver chains from his neck. Each had a beautiful amethyst crystal bound by matching silver wire-work done in the fashion of right and left. Holding them out, he explained, "My father had these made by a gypsy-adept, who took the mother-stone and split it while he watched. She polished them to match on a treadle wheel, but they have the same crystal-diva within because they are of a single gem. My parents wore them till my father went to wind. My mother gave his to me. When she went to wind, I took to wearing them both. If ever the need for my help arises, hold this in thy hand and call to me. I will know. If thou believeth on such things?"

She nodded. "I believeth on many things, old friend. Some esoteric. Some arcane. Some quite magical."

He smiled. "Allow the gems to tell thee which to choose," and he held out his hands. She closed her eyes and passed a hand over each, then chose the one on the left. Gazing deep into her eyes, he slipped it into her warm palm.

As she put it on, she said, "I shall wear it always."

He took a deep breath. His voice was thick. "That was my mother's," and he bowed shyly and strode away.

Seleen gave her the look.

Alahna said, "I know . . . I know. . . ." Oddly, it comforted her to have this beautiful and magic-imbued thing. Gypsy-adepts were renowned for their own eclectic brand of potent magics. Before he left, Conrad also handed her a goatskin bota of apricot brandy. Both adepts gratefully took a few moments to share. Warm, sweet, and spicy, when swallowed with empty stomachs it made them both tipsy.

Alahna idly glanced to the northwest above the plateau. Something unusual caught her eye. Two iridescent flashes of sunlight appeared to bob and dance in the morning sky. Approaching with an undulant swimming-motion, they oscillated slightly from side-to-side.

Levitating long-dragons.

Winged forms accompanied.

By the wingspan and soaring wingbeats, one was an aerthe-dragon.

The constantly pumping wingbeats and shorter wingspan of the other indicated a large fire-dragon.

Alahna sighed. All four Guardians of the Sentinel Watches were flying toward them as fast as possible with the long-dragons pushing spheres-of-power.

She shook her head.

Exhaustion amplified the bitterness.

Anger filled her gut.

When Seleen caught sight of the approaching guardians with spheres-of-power. Dread washed across her exhausted face. Voice low and quiet, she said, "Well then . . . that didn't take long. . . ."

Alahna looked at poor Seleen. Guilt displaced the anger caused by their approaching judgment. She hugged Seleen close, whispering, "Remember—it was I who enmeshed thee in the helping. It shall be I who shoulders the blame. Let me do the talking as much as possible. Never gainsay no matter what, but never lie either."

Seleen made a face. "And how do I do that?"

Alahna said, "Tell them only the barest version of the truth."

Seleen rolled her eyes. "As if they'll believe anything we say." Dread mixed with exhaustion painted itself on her kind and weary face. Tears welled. "But we did it milady, we did it!" And so saying, she wiped her nose and sullenly toed a tuft of grass peeking through the ancient cobblestones.

Alahna rubbed Seleen's knee. "We did, my love. Yes, we did."

Forbidden Gate

~

Battle of the Forbidden Gate

Like a blacksmith's anvil, deep trepidation sat on Alahna's chest as she observed the agitated Lilith in her SijanPao pushed through the sky by the sea-green Bo YouYong, who levitated low to release Lilith and her sphere-of-power above the cobblestones.

Bo gently touched down just beyond the Pentakulum.

The Razing remained inert.

The vast pillars still popped and groaned as they cooled.

Steamy vapors disappeared in the cool breeze.

Tiny aether-plasma flamelets still licked off the surface of the Pentakulum here and there.

Magicfire ozone hung heavy in the air.

Acrid chemical vapors from burnt and unburnt firefleem came off the porous cobblestones and smooth crystal expanses wherever it had not been cleanly washed away.

Irrational fury glazed Lilith's eyes when she locked them onto Alahna. Lost in that fury, burgeoning anger caused Lilith to derezz her SijanPao without a count, whereupon the short distance to the cobblestones made her stumble forward several times to prevent falling on her face, which infuriated her even more.

After releasing Yenara's sphere-of-power some 10-meters above the plaza proper, the light-blue air-dragon, Meili Chuan, floated gently down like a falling leaf and looked about. Her feelers wriggled as if assessing the dragon-magic and techno-magic still hanging in the air.

Yenara touched her SijanPao to the cobblestones and wisely derezzed with a count. The instant it whuffed from existence, her outrage spewed like a steaming eruption from a volcanic geyser. "Have yer minds become unseated!"

Alahna deigned no response.

Yenara turned her wrath on Seleen. "Art thou the eejit's apprentice? Have thee no common sense of thine own? No regard for our laws? For Lilith—"

Lilith's interjection was almost a shout. "If it pleaseth—mighty Yenara? I would savor the opportunity to speak for myself from time-to-time! Provided thy waggling tongue stops prattling from inside that overlarge piehole!" and she gave Yenara a venom-laden glare.

As Alahna watched, Yenara's vitriolic stare shifted away from Seleen to a look of feigned hurt feelings with knitted brows, hands outspread, and palms up when Yenara locked eyes on Lilith. Yenara wheedled, "I was but defending . . . and I have my rights. . . ."

Seleen shook her head and whispered to Alahna, "Vitriol and resentment . . . it's always vitriol and resentment hidden beneath innocence when deceiving Lilith."

Alahna nodded without comment.

With a rush of air, Quang stalled high and trotted to a landing behind Meili Chuan. Paying no attention to the unfolding conflict, he immediately began sniffing about the courtyard. The mighty fire-dragon's mind seemed elsewhere.

Alahna took the initiative. "My Mofa XueSheng"—and she pointed at Seleen—"did only as I demanded! I hid the import of these matters from her. Innocence is her better truth! This is my doing and mine alone!"

Lilith ripped her glare from Yenara, stepped forward, and shook an arthritic finger in rage and disgust. "Ye've both broken the Canon-of-Precepts of the Huan Long Shui Sisteren on so many levels it boggles this old woman's mind—even unto abrogating the Covenant-of-the-Dragons!"

"If I could cast the Malison-of-Killing on another Sister, I would!

"Thine actions cast shame upon the Sisteren!

"As High Priestess, I charge thee, Alahna!" and the old harridan stopped to gain her breath from such a rage.

Head held high, Alahna remained defiant.

Seleen tried to make herself small by looking down at the cobblestones.

Unable to constrain herself despite Lilith's chiding, Yenara shrieked, "No—not nearly enough!

"I, Yenara, Adept in the 12th Circle and Kulapti of the Huan Long Shui Sisteren, do hereby charge thee—High Adept Alahna—with The-Most-Heinous!"

Feelers twitching in agitation, Bo YouYong levitated and spread her fore-hands in a demand for quiet.

Yenara ignored the great water-dragon's tacit warning. "I demand a Casting-of-Desistance to throw Alahna and Seleen out of the Sisteren, followed by the Malison-of-Killing upon Alahna! If Lilith will not put an end to this scunner, I shall sing the deadly malediction myself—"

Bo shouted, "Anjing! I cast a silencing on all!" The geis-of-silence smashed into every Sister's mind like a rogue wave crashing on a rocky cliff.

Hands pressed to her head while wailing in frustration, Lilith fell to her knees.

Yenara staggered to the side and went down as if clubbed.

Alahna stumbled backwards and sat down so hard on the stone wall she almost went over.

Seleen made a high-pitched squeal, then staggered backward into the low rock wall. Falling heels-over-head, she disappeared on the other side.

Levitating somewhat higher, Bo raised a calming hand. Her soughing voice sounded as the gentle surf, although her words carried dire import. "As Guardians of Sentinel Watches—and since High Adept Alahna summoned us in the tongue of the Elder Dragons—it shall be we who decide what crimes have been committed and what punishments meted out!"

The big aerthe-dragon, Tai Deren, spoke aloud, "Yonder adept hiding behind the wall, dost thou think to fool us? Come hither and join thy Laoshi De Mofa."

Seleen peeked shyly over, clambered across, sat down beside Alahna, and kept her eyes averted. Anxiety painted her face.

Tai said, "Alahna, Seleen, we know ye've opened and closed a trans-dimensional-arc. What we do not know compels further inquiry. Why did ye do it? Why not summon us beforehand? How did ye maintain control without the help of at least one dragon?"

Alahna sensed that Tai Deren meant to compel answers either as verbal responses, which she could not comply with on account of Bo YouYong's geis-of-silence, or as thoughts brought to mind by the reflexive power of suggestion. Much to Alahna's surprise, a vision of YueLiang Nushen came into her mind, who waved the questions away leaving Alahna happily inscrutable although every dragon except Quang HuoYan actively trespassed in her mind. How Alahna knew what she knew, she knew not, but wispy vapors-of-intent were all the guardians were able to sense.

Apparently, Alahna's inscrutability caused Tai to take another tack. "Little adept, we will eventually understand everything, but more important to the moment, have ye brought something alien unto Janaidar?"

Still unable to speak, Alahna nodded.

Seleen did likewise.

Alahna ribbed Seleen to forestall further admissions of complicity.

Meili Chuan waved her hand while intoning in the Long Shai, "Ni keyi shuohua!" the great water-dragon's words bore meaning into their minds. *Thou mayest speak!*

This lifted Bo YouYong's imposed silence from everyone.

Meili pressed them. "What have ye brought hither?"

Choking on the remnants of the geis-of-silence, Alahna made a complex gurgle, massaged her throat, tried again. "By virtue of reasoning when examining his belongings and systems of high technology, I believe we discovered a great techno-sage and spirit warrior. But,"—and she stabbed finger at Quang—"for some unknown reason, a fire-dragon came from out of nowhere and flamed all of us including the man from another world, whom we were then forced to bring hither and save without benefit of discourse or choice."

Glaring at Quang, Alahna added, "I managed the attack as best I could, but flaming gobs of firefleem blew through the arc and onto the innocent man. Dragon-fire was all around us and inside his dwelling, too."

Bo's voice sounded like low surf on a sandy beach. "So . . . a human then? And no other life-forms?"

Alahna bobbed her head. "Only the warrior-sage, who lies terribly burnt in yonder wagon . . . " but when she pointed to the top of the ramp past the Opal Basin, the ramp stood empty, for Conrad had unobtrusively walked his horses down to the next staging area.

Alahna pointed at him there. "I fear the sage's life to be in jeopardy. I must attend to him. Please, I beg of ye!"

Quang HuoYan spoke up, "Was the errant fire-dragon female?"

Alahna nodded.

Quang kept on. "Was she smaller than most of the fire-kind?"

Alahna did not hear Quang, for she had eyes on for Lilith.

Lilith's nostrils flared like a wolf scenting prey even as her expression morphed from anger, to rage, to berserker in as many heartbeats. Quivering unsteadily, her left arm came halfway up.

Determined to never be caught off guard again—like the morning Lilith arbitrarily shot slivers of blackfire at her during the council meeting—Alahna intoned a quiet invocation. "Awaken ye Powers-of-Water! I Conjure, Call, and Command Thy Might!" She followed this with a one second, four eighth note phrase for a SijanPao. Even as she did so, she watched the great water-dragon lock eyes on Lilith, whereupon Bo YouYong's feelers went stiff in alarm.

They both knew.

The baneful influence of the last known ShahRen had eroded Lilith's composure, her always iffy impulse control.

Lilith went berserker.

Bo waved her clawed hands while speaking words-of-power in the Long Shai, words sounding as pure meaning in Alahna's mind. The passage of minutes inside Bo's fast-time bubble became as seconds outside the influence of her dragon-magic.

Time got bent.

Everything inside the bounds of the plaza slowed as the smear-of-time shifted.

Further intuition told Alahna the great sea-dragon meant to give her enough time to save herself and Seleen from Lilith's burgeoning insanity.

Even as the flow of time shifted, a roiling bolt of blackfire the size of a small melon appeared. Blackness shot through with yellow lightning coalesced above the white-hot ShahRen pulsating on Lilith's left wrist.

With no time to set a spatial-lock, Alahna waved Seleen into her Pao.

The snarl on Lilith's face became a gravelly groan as the sizzling bolt of blackfire grew in size.

Ponderously departing, Lilith had aimed it straight at Alahna and Seleen.

Sluggish yet inescapable, it seemed to crawl inside the fast-time bubble.

Finally sensing the pull of the river in response to her invocation, Alahna summoned a substantial column of water with a gesture-of-quenching.

Fast as a thought, a cascading boom pealed out as the column sluiced through the air to intercept the crackling bolt of blackfire.

Sizzling—steaming—spattering—snuffing—chuffing—

The coherent and cohesive water column fed itself into the bolt of blackfire with self-destructive vengeance. Saturated steam billowed forth in shock wave after shock wave after shock wave.

To prevent them smashing into each other on impact inside her field-of-force, Alahna wrapped Seleen in a bear-hug just before the first shock wave hit.

Yenara had also throated the abbreviated Song-of-the-spheres. Making a sloppy gesture-of-inclusion also robbed her of time to set a spatial-lock.

The SijanPao swallowed Meili, Quang, and Tai, but missed Bo YouYong and Lilith.

With Alahna's water-column sluicing into the malevolent blackfire, the bolt of steaming hell crawled across the last meters of the courtyard emitting horrific gouts and clouds of scalding steam.

Boom—hiss—crackle—sizzle—boom—

Explosive sounds got weirdly flanged.

Ripples of blue energy scintillated across every surface of the Forbidden Gate and Pentakulum.

Lilith's body came aglow with azure light.

The undulating skin of Alahna's SijanPao smacked hard into both adepts. Their bones were saved from cracking by the sheer pliancy inherent in such a field-of-force. Regardless, both got the breath slammed from their fragile lungs.

Shedding sun-hot waves of heat as the bolt of blackfire bore down, Alahna's Pao flexed and popped into the air with both breathless adept's getting the piss knocked out of them. Ineluctable, the bolt of blackfire slammed into the low rock wall even as it blasted its way beneath Alahna's Pao shattering and melting the very stone as it passed.

Crack—ba-ah-oom—crack—booma-boom—

Creating a vacuum as it went, the ballistic bolt of blackfire whooshed on past the sluicing water column at the same time Alahna's lost her concentration.

The water column collapsed with a great sploosh.

Water ran everywhere.

Ongoing shock waves smacked into Bo YouYong launching her spinning through the air across the canyon like a length of rope with a weight on one end—her head. The ancient water-dragon smashed into the sheer cliffs on the far side. Her long body fell bloodied and limp as a wet rag into the river far below, where she disappeared beneath the slow, yet powerful current.

The collapsing vacuum also sucked Alahna's sphere-of-power down to the swale past the molten wall where they slammed across burning savanna grasses and melty blobs of smoking rock.

Winded and unable to scream, both merely grunted.

Quang and the rest of the group inside Yenara's sphere-of-power got saved from the smoking-hot rocky shrapnel, but the ongoing shock waves shoved Yenara's heavily laden Pao across the plaza like a tumbleweed as big as a house. Ripples of azure energy ran along every surface in sight. Plowing into the Opal Basin, Yenara's SijanPao thudded into a never-before-seen force-field that fully encompassed the gurgling Long Pen Quan.

With all of them hollering, Yenara's Pao glanced high into the air.

Everybody's limb got entangled as they scudded past the low stone wall, which had already started disintegrating into stony smithereens. Once on the hill, Yenara's rolling Pao sloshed through one terraced pool to the next down the promontory with everybody inside howling in a complex, animated knot of heads, wings, limbs, butts, and tails.

Quang got entangled with Tai Deren as they rolled.

Meili grabbed up Yenara, hugged the fragile human to her chest, and curled into a ball.

Quang's tail whopped Meili in the head. When the stretched field-of-force reached the bottom of the hill amidst an explosion of reeds and mud, it finally came to rest on the grassy savanna.

Finally finding her lungs, Yenara inadvertently screamed the note-of-deresolution and her SijanPao derezzed in a hot second.

Everybody got dumped on their asses, heads, or backs.

Quang watched Meili struggled to untangle herself from the wriggling heap while keeping Yenara as safe as possible after getting tail-whopped by him. Once they settled, Quang hissed, "I would rather I had not seen certain parts of yonder anatomies quite so closely."

A few heartbeats passed before Tai picked herself up and licked a bruised forearm, "Well . . . that was a helluva thing. . . ."

Yenara waltzed around in a daze searching for Lilith till she gathered her wits enough to realize her gesture-of-inclusion had completely missed. With a cry, Yenara sang a new SijanPao and willed herself back up the long, steep hill to the plaza.

Meili Chuan tried to levitate, but fell back to the dirt and mud shaking her noble head. Her feelers hung limp, whiskers twitched.

Quang mind-spoke to her, *A big fire-dragon is very sorry.*

Still in fast-time on the other side of the plaza, Seleen held onto Alahna for dear life when they got hurled up from the shattering, melting rock wall, then sucked down along the swale beside the ramp amidst roiling clouds of smoke and steam and rock shrapnel mixed with tiny gobbets of lava.

The lumbering bolt of blackfire sizzled on with fiery vengeance. When it departed the near-field time-smear, it transmuted into a flaming comet with a trail of scorched air drifting on the wind amidst further collapsing vacuum, which boomed like ongoing thunder.

Alahna's uncontrolled Pao was still rolling when she inadvertently gasped the note-of-deresolution in a cry of pain, which threw them tumbling across the scrub-grass like a pair of entangled rag dolls. Finally forced apart, they stopped and lay gasping amidst a scattering of hot, smoking rocks and popping gravel. Melty chunks of lava set the dry grasses aflame all down the escarpment.

First to recover, Seleen got busy brushing away smoking rocks and bits of melty gravel scorching their clothes, gave over to using a long stick, and finally employed a gesture-of-warding to impel a heap of the smoking stuff away.

Dazed but apparently uninjured, Alahna lay working her mouth like a beached mackerel trying to prime her lungs and catch her breath. Locking eyes with Seleen, she breathlessly nodded that she seemed mostly uninjured.

Curious and concerned while doing her best to avoid more smoking or melty shrapnel, Seleen cautiously picked her way back up the swale to the shattered and smoking wall to try to see through the smoky, steamy, and fiery aftermath. Lilith's body lay in a heap across the plaza where the ongoing BLEVEs finally let it be. Bluish tendrils of force licked strangely along her prostrate form.

Seleen surmised that from the very first, the odd bluish forces protecting the plaza proper had also protected Lilith from the worst of it, as well as the intrinsic safeguards of a ShahRen. Seleen muttered to herself, "The old eejit. . . ."

Steam rolled off Lilith's naked and wrinkly old body like a boiled yard-bird freshly pulled from the pot. Her shredded shift lay smoking and steaming in a wrinkled mass farther on.

Seleen considered trying to find a safe path across the plaza and render emergent aid, but a wobbly Yenara wafted up and over the Opal Basin on the opposite side much closer to Lilith than Seleen.

Yenara derezzed near Lilith. Before bending to help, she laid eyes on Seleen through the smoke and steam. They locked eyes for one of those interminable moments where the mask of false emotion gets replaced by true expression. Yenara's lip curled in a snarl of recognition. Contempt and hatred burnt bright in her eyes.

Stout and brave, Seleen held that baleful gaze without flinching, then spoke to the air knowing Yenara could not hear, but would certainly read her lips. "Thou art a hateful bag full of stinking guts!" and she made an insulting gesture.

Yenara read Seleen's lips, and, without hesitation, raised a fist and performed exaggerated lip speak in like manner. "Thou art mine, little scunner!"

Just to be shitty, Seleen shook her head while spreading her arms as if she could not understand.

Yenara tried again.

Seleen did the same, but added the foul gesture to convey insulting contempt.

Yenara shook her fists in frustration.

Seleen felt Alahna gain her side and peer across the plaza.

Still huffing and puffing, Alahna exclaimed, "To whom art thou throwing insults?"—then patted Seleen's back—"Oh . . . I see. . . ."

For several heartbeats, Seleen and Alahna both locked eyes with their common enemy till the sounds of steel-shod hooves and steel rims on cobblestone down on the valley floor dragged their attention to the ancient road beside the LungHuo River.

Alahna said to Seleen, "Conrad must have seen the shitstorm coming, and somehow got the wagon down the ramp without winding his horses."

Seleen said, "The brakes on each wheel of the wagon still smoke."

Lightly loaded with the horses bolting, the huge freight-wagon bounced along the cobblestone violently jostling every single body between the sideboards while nearly pitching them out. As they watched, Conrad made his way along the traces to the lead horse, straddled the horse's back, and began slowing the frightened team.

Seleen said, "Good old Conrad."

Alahna agreed with a nod.

Forbidden Gate

~

In the Aftermath

Lilith lay dazed, naked, and badly scalded from head to foot with many skin abrasions, various cuts, and blackening bruises from getting bowled across the surface of the plaza. She fought her way to a semblance of consciousness and remembered a field of bluish energy enveloping her body as she skidded along. Lifting her head slightly, she caught a well-focused glimpse of Seleen through the dispersing smoke and steam.

Young Seleen seemed to be speaking, but words could not penetrate the ringing in Lilith's ears. She rolled her head and spied Yenara standing above her while apparently replying to Seleen. When Alahna poked her head up and peeked over the broken wall, Lilith got another well-focused glimpse. With profound relief that she had not killed them, and no dragons in sight, she laid her head back as pain flooded her senses.

Yenara bent down, took Lilith in her arms, hugged her tightly, and said, "Beloved Mother Matriarch. . . ."

Above the ringing buzz in her ears, Lilith combined audible words with a semblance of lip reading, and whimpered. But Yenara's hug was too tight. Lilith gasped and pushed back with all of her remaining strength. A feeling of love washed over her as she realized how truly and deeply Yenara must love her to hold her so tight. Lilith said, "S-should

not h-have d-done th-that . . . d-didn't th-think . . . s-so a-angry. . . ."
and she coughed. "H-holder of last ShahRen . . . have committed worst
c-crime of all. . . ."

Eyes brimming with tears, Yenara answered, "Lilith, beloved
Mother Matriarch, speak the Ritual-of-Abdication to pass the ShahRen
before it deactivates that I may ascend and care for the Sisteren in thy
stead. Please, while there is yet time. There is no one else. Alahna and
Seleen are . . . well . . . thy bolt of blackfire scattered them into the
winds of time. They are killed. Would that I had done it myself."

Lilith lay trying to process Yenara's crap while trapped in a bear
hug so tight it made her reel. Fuzzy and frazzled as Lilith's senses were,
combined with shock setting in, confusion naturally arose. She knew
without a doubt that she had clearly spotted Seleen mouthing words
at Yenara with Yenara mouthing back even when Alahna peeked over
the broken wall. They were alive, functioning, and seemed far better off
than she. Lilith's final thoughts before losing consciousness were crystal
clear and unforgettable.

Why doth Yenara act this way? Why urge me to abdicate? Why
squeeze so hard? Am I so weak? So injured? Must remember. . . .

Yenara's mind was a squirming mess after Seleen and Alahna ducked
back behind the shattered stone wall. When Yenara first found the old
harridan still alive against all odds, desperate thoughts took root. If the
old bat would not die, then she would squeeze her to death as if hugging
in grief.

To that deathly end, Yenara tried smothering the old woman in a
bear hug, but the old bag stubbornly remained strong enough to struggle
and wrestle. When Yenara tried coaxing Lilith into abdication the old
scunner conveniently passed out, but did not—would not—expire.
The scratchy sound of claws on cobblestone told Yenara a dragon had
landed behind them.

A cascade of fear knotted her gut. The dragons are telepathic. Must
clear my head. Yenara reached into the Disciplines-of-the-Circle and
found an old mantra to sweep her mind and gut of relevant thoughts,
thoughts of usurpation.

Growling low, Meili Chuan bent down to caress Lilith with her lively feelers.

Yenara had the distinct impression the mighty air-dragon stood poised to put an end to Lilith, but knew it was wishful thinking.

Close behind, Tai Deren and Quang HuoYan both stalled into a landing, then pumped their powerful wings to clear the remaining smoke and steam.

As Master of the Powers-of-Fire, Quang held his big hand out, circled on hind legs while balancing with tail, and swept the countryside around the plaza snuffing out blazes and raging wildfires everywhere along the flanks of the plateau.

Acutely aware of the big air-dragon's presence by the scent of cinnamon alone, Yenara hoped the swell of natural emotions created in such a moment of unadulterated violence would mask her deeper, darker thoughts.

Apparently, it worked.

While flying forth, Meili telekinetically lifted Lilith's bloodied and scalded form into the air, levitated with Lilith's steaming body floating ahead of her, and flew to the still-glowing Opal Basin. Meili allowed the gush of salubrious waters from the long-dragon statue to wash over Lilith's badly singed body, dipped her beneath the surface to include her skull in the salubrious drench, then sang a powerful Song-of-Healing in the Long Shai.

As Meili caressed the old woman with her lively feelers, darts-of-healing nibbled at Lilith's injuries like tiny fishes. Azure ripples of vital chi ran across the old woman's body beneath the roiling waves. Tunnels of air like tiny whirlpools formed to allow for Lilith's breathing. In response to those healing waters, Lilith's cuts knitted, bruising abrasions skinned slightly over, seeping contusions staunched, swelling blisters and tiny vesicles subsided.

At some length, Meili spoke aloud with great relief, "The Mother Matriarch hath been protected by the ShahRen, and I have done all that I can in the here and now. Let us remove her to the Keep and see her immersed in the Gallery of the Infinite Waters where the Sisters may join in group-song and perform the Song-of-Healing in continuous manner."

Stymied and terrified the dragons would suss out her truer, darker emotions, Yenara said, "Yes, my guardian." As she did so, she realized the dragon's concern was for Lilith only. Yenara's act of saving everyone from the boiling liquid-expanding vapor explosions had naturally forestalled any and all suspicion.

The great aerthe-dragon, Tai Deren, trotted past and made a gliding leap over the wall where Alahna and Seleen were last seen.

Still trembling, they sat holding one another with their backs against the remains of the wall.

Alahna looked up at Tai, and whispered, "L-Lilith? Y-ye dragons?"

Tai noted the absence of concern for Yenara but did not dwell on it while feeling of their bodies with her long feelers through the damaged clothing. She spoke quietly, "Lilith is badly injured, but Meili saved her. As for us, we dragons are not so easily hurt. Bo YouYong is missing. She smacked into the cliffs across the river but fell into her element. She did not die, for we would sense it if she did.

"High Adept Yenara protected us with her sphere-of-power except for Lilith and Bo. For now, little adepts, we shall repair to the Keep and attend the wounded. Afterward, there will be plenty of time to—"

Alahna interrupted, "And the stolen-man! What of the stolen-man? We brought him injured through the Forbidden Gate? He will surely die without my help. He is innocent . . . a victim. . . ."

Tai spoke sadly, "Dost thou see why it is called the Forbidden Gate, little fool? It might be best for all should he perish." She considered for a moment. "However, this is not our way."

Looking over the broken wall, Tai raised her voice with telepathic overlay known as heavy-mind. "I shall take Alahna and Seleen with me to Riverbend, find the hapless human stolen into our world, and bring him to the Cavern Keep."

Quang did the same. "I fly down to the river to see about Bo. High-adept Alahna mentioned a small fire-dragon. I would find her, too."

Tai asked, "Meili, canst thou take Yenara and Lilith back to the Keep? Can Yenara yet spawn another Pao?"

Angry emotion colored Meili's reply. "Eejits all! But I shall manage well enough."

Tai spoke to Alahna, "Spawn a Pao for thyself and Seleen. And be

sure to set the spatial-lock. Once high above the plaza, I will intercept."
Tai waited till Alahna's field-of-force got about 100-meters up, trotted
a short distance down that side of the escarpment for speed, leapt into
the air taking wing. Banking back and up in a tight circle, she swept
Alahna's hovering SijanPao into her grip in passing.

Looking back, Tai spotted Meili in flight with Yenara's Pao glinting
in the morning sun.

After pyrokinetically suppressing all the fires, Quang trotted down
the ramp for speed and soared into the air across the LungHuo while
reaching out with his senses. He found the immanent presence of Bo
YouYong some distance downstream and flew low along the river. If she
got knocked senseless, her body will drift with the current, but water is
her element. She will not drown.

In the distance, he spied a pod of black-and-whites leaping free
of the river like dolphins. Seeking the apparent destination, he spied
streamers of red in the lazy current. It was not unusual for orcas to
swim upstream this far inland. The wide and deep LungHuo River was
fully navigable year-round. Huge yet elusive, manatees were a favorite
of both fire-dragons and orcas. No doubt, the orcas had scented the
blood of a seriously injured long-dragon. He banked hard and flew back
upstream ready to splinter their minds rather than let them attack a
weakened friend, but they were already upon her.

Instead of attacking, however, they slowed and gently swam close
to her bleeding form.

As Quang flew over, Bo YouYong wriggled, righted herself with
a twist, and swam from the bloody patch in the river while leaving a
smallish trail of reddish streamers. Watching the largest female in the
pod of orcas swim alongside, Quang realized Bo had summoned them,
for the venerable old sea-dragon grabbed hold of the dorsal fin and the
whole pod slowly swam downstream around her.

Gliding over, Quang mind-cast, *Dost thou require help from an old
friend of the fire-kind?*

A familiar yet weakened mind-voice came back, *No, dear friend. I
am safest in mine own element, and my pretty whales will carry me to the
Western Sentinel's Watch beneath the bar of the LungHuo and watch*

out for me. As for thyself and the other guardians, see to the needs of the Sisteren, and consider what we must do about The-Creeping-Darkness. I fear there are forces at work which may, at long last, herald our undoing.

Quang answered, *That I shall. Farewell for now, old friend.*

Via far mind-speak, Quang informed the other guardians of Bo's condition, then pumped hard into the morning air still bearing a grudge against Alahna for summoning all of them like pups. Concerning what to do about Lilith for going batshit crazy and bringing injury to a beloved old long-dragon, he resolved to make certain it never happened again if he had to flame the old eejit into smoking ashes.

Out in the countryside surrounding the plaza, Quang flew in ever-widening circles while searching for his youngest pup. The unmistakable scent of HuoJi's firefleem beneath the Pillars of Thoth filled his gut with anguish. He bellowed and called out to her with far mind-speak fearing that she must certainly have gotten badly injured and might need him. His paternal, metaphysical connection to her informed his worried senses that at least she yet lived, but neither would she answer him. That same refusal to engage made her impossible to locate.

Quang knew HuoJi had sought exile to the northwest after the Fire-Clan forced him to ostracize her from the southern home of the fire-kind—Shouye HuoLong—due to the fact that she had a genetic atavism—a smaller body like their ancestors. Forced by the Tenets of the Fire Clan and their sometimes brutal customs, casting her out had weighed heavy on his heart. So profound was the guilt, and so deep his love, he had even molted.

Acid tears ran down scaled cheeks as he flew over the countryside.

If I had it all to do over again, I would refuse.

He knew HuoJi's dam, Tianmi DeHuo, felt the same. To her credit, she had never blamed him for performing such an onerous duty as required by Head of the Fire Clan.

Now that HuoJi had gotten involved in such an unheard of disaster, he felt responsible, vowed to find her, and determine why she attacked the Pentakulum. If she had gotten hurt, he would never forgive himself. Alahna would answer.

However, his role as Guardian of the Western Sentinel's Watch required his immediate presence at the Huan Long Shui Cavern Keep. This also made him angry. But since Alahna had awakened The-Creeping-Darkness, there were matters none could delay. A note of bitterness arose when it occurred to him the HuoJi might actually hide both her location and mind from him because of her broken heart. Or maybe even anger? It was a terrible mystery wrapped in onerous duty, and there was nothing for it.

When he got to the Great Northern Portal, he made a running touchdown on the outside recessed ramp, skidded to a dusty halt, and trotted past the bowing acolytes toward a destination only he knew of. He badly needed a bath and knew where to find one.

Riverbend

~

An Aerthe Dragon in Riverbend

Flying as fast as she could while pushing Alahna's sphere-of-power, Tai Deren spied the towering Huan Long Shui Pagoda from high above Riverbend. Reaching out with her senses, she found the stolen-man in the bed of a freight wagon stopped at the stables next to the Cloister while surrounded by healer-women.

The hostler and his men were busy unhitching sweat-lathered horses and removing their tack, dousing them with buckets of water from the trough to rinse, and leading them along the street on a slow walk to cool them. All the people within eyeshot looked up when Tai's rapidly moving shadow and glints of focused light surprised them.

Tai released Alahna's Pao midair, circled once, and gracefully stalled to a four point landing on the wide boulevard fronting the stables. A puff of street dust rose from her landing just as the SijanPao drifted down. Alahna derezzed the sphere-of-power with a count and both adepts stepped lightly onto the cobblestones with pitted and scorched clothing. Many of the townspeople gathered in wonderment, for most had never seen a dragon up close. Unlike the people who lived with their dragons at the other three Sentinel Watches.

Nodding to Alahna and Seleen, Conrad smiled and bowed to the big aerthe-dragon.

Tai said, "What is thy name, little human?"

"I am Conrad the Hunter," and he went to a knee.

Sitting there like some great cat, Tai pointed at the wagon with the clawed index finger of her right forehand. "I am pleased in thee for seeing to the safety of the healers and this one."

Conrad bowed to the waist.

Alahna and Seleen climbed into the wagon beside the stolen-man and pulled the silken cover away, which was sopped with pink serosanguinous seepage. They gasped. The entire front of the man's body presented deep flame and acid burns, especially his arms and hands. His face had also suffered terribly where the firefleem spattered through upraised fingers.

The worst damage was to his eyes. Burnt-out sockets wept tears and pink serosanguinous fluid with dangling optical nerves attached to empty, shriveled sacs hanging across burnt cheeks; eyelids were crisped like burnt bacon; eyebrows gone; cheeks and forehead blistered; lips seared and cracked; edges of the ears horribly singed; scalp a ragged mess of stinking scorch.

Approaching the wagon, Tai gently tugged Alahna and Seleen aside with her feelers. Assessing his condition both physically and metaphysically, Tai immediately sensed the mysterious field of iridescent blackness clinging to his quaking body like a second skin. She clicked her tongue sadly and telekinetically lofted him into the air to feel of him head to toe with snakelike feelers. Bulging blisters, both large and small, had not popped in the headlong rush along the ancient road to town—quite unusual given the circumstances. Something had protected those terrible burns.

Strange iridescence tickled her feelers, raising thoughts about the man's potential connection to The-Creeping-Darkness. In addition, the iridescent field had also kept areas of cooked flesh in place that would ordinarily slough as dead tissue. Around these, a purplish glow pulsated in concert with his heartbeat, especially around his burnt-out eye sockets. The intensity and swiftness of the poor man's healing was far beyond human. Actively knitting into place, some of the ruined flesh had already been revivified into pink scarring.

Alahna and Seleen started a Song-of-Healing with Tai joining in for a few minutes. The gathering of people who had seen Tai and the high-adepts fly past all bowed their heads in awe of the mesmerizing songspell. Ripples of healing source-magic coursed along the poor man's body where Tai held it levitating about 3-meters above the wagon. With three full verses complete, Tai signaled them to stop. Gauging the effects of the healing while satisfied the stolen-man would likely not expire, Tai spoke, "Alahna, sing a sphere-of-power for thy selves and this stolen-man. We retire to the Keep."

To Conrad, the healer-women, and gypsy-adepts, Tai spoke with stern countenance and stiff feelers, "We, thy guardians, call upon all of ye to take charge and contact all witnesses to the goings-on last night. Conrad, thou shalt arrange a caravan to bring them and their families to the Great Northern Portal of the Cavern Keep. They will be guests of the Sisteren throughout the proceedings of a Council of Inquiry. I want this done as soon as possible, but no later than three days hence. Can such a caravan reach the Keep in one day's travel?"

Conrad nodded, "If we depart at sunrise."

Tai approved with a curt tip of her head, then added, "None of those present at the Plaza of the Forbidden Gate shall depart Riverbend in fear or worry. It is not they who are to be tried, and they are not accountable for participation. Neither will reprisal from the Sisteren take place in any manner.

"These are my commands!

"Pass my words to all."

Whereupon everybody bowed.

Tai tipped her head in a perfunctory bow while Alahna spawned the Pao, made a gesture-of-inclusion. A pseudopod reached out to envelop the stolen-man's body, and she willed the sphere-of-power into the sky. Tai waited for them to gain altitude, trotted with tucked wings along the boulevard for speed, then leapt into the air with a great rustling of powerful wings amidst swirling street dust. She circled back and intercepted Alahna's slowly rising Pao, then beat hard for the southern entry of the Keep. A wave of pity for the stolen-man swept through her great heart as she flew.

As they approached the Great Southern Portal, Tai telepathically scolded, *Adepts Alahna and Seleen, I warn ye both against further abrogations of the canons and covenants?*

They answered as one. "We understand."

Pending the Council of Inquiry, ye're both confined to quarters except for the care and nursing of the stolen-man. Do not join the Sisters in the dining-hall. Do not speak of the battle at the Forbidden Gate under penalty-of-desistance.

"Yes, Guardian Tai," they said as one.

Alahna, where wilt thou care for the stolen-man?

Alahna thought a moment. "A small alcove lies next to my quarters with the effluent stream from the Long Pen Quan in the Gallery of the Infinite Waters running through. I can use the effluent dragon-waters from the Gallery of the Infinite Waters for healing immersions and required excretions."

Tai mind-spoke as she let the Pao drift outside the huge monolithic doors, glided into the vast staging area, stalled midair, settled to her feet, and trotted in. *So be it, Alahna, Seleen. Proceed directly there. I shall send lesser acolytes to help with preparations and any other needs. This, I will allow.*

Tai's telepathy sensed their sad acquiescence, and another swell of pity took her big dragon's heart for all involved. This entire debacle lay at the feet of the Guardians, who had been remiss in their absence, and she knew it.

Cavern Keep

~

Lilith and Yenara Return

With the great air-dragon, Meili Chuan, undulating as she pushed them at her best speed toward the Cavern Keep, Yenara sang a Song-of-Relieving for Lilith while the badly injured high-priestess hovered supine and delirious beside her inside Yenara's SijanPao.

Lilith moaned in relief.

In Yenara's deep-mind, she did not really care. She sang the healing-song only for appearances.

Flying along at a fairly good clip, the mighty air-dragon reached across the closing distance to the Cavern Keep with far mind-speak to High Adept Nebhet with Yenara in the mind-loop.

Inside the Keep, Old Nebhet was in the middle of explaining Tai Deren's vegan requirements to a group of young acolytes. Sunlight flooded the cavernous garden galleries as hot-houses using a system of skylights, mirrors, and purpose-built tunnels. This was where the Sisters grew fresh vegetables, lemons, oranges, tangerines, and medicinal flowers all year round. The botanical desert gardens outside the Great Northern Portal grew cactuses of all edible varieties, persimmons, and many other citrus fruits specifically requiring direct sunlight.

Meili's powerful mind-voice was reminiscent of the rushing wind. Rather than verbalize the entire shitstorm at the Forbidden Gate, she simply slapped a combination of scenes together known as a mind-dump, and slammed it whole into Nebhet's head. *High Adept Nebhet, assemble a choir of senior Sisters in the Gallery of the Infinite*

Waters. We shall immerse Lilith in the healing pool and place her in thy care.

Nebhet had fallen to her knees under the weight of the mind-dump, but her training regarding such things told her not to try and process all of it now. Knowing the great air-dragon was mind-linked in the moment, Nebhet simply replied, "Of course, Guardian Chuan. At once."

Yenara also heard the old adept's words plainly in her own mind as Meili swiftly descended from high above the Huan Long Shui Plateau to the long ramp leading down into the Great Northern Portal, then levitated through the vast staging area while emoting in the sternest of tones. *Adept Yenara, thou shalt put aside thine anger and pride concerning Alahna and Seleen.*

The chide was so intense it created a wave of agony behind Yenara's eyes. Yenara spoke to the air inside her Pao. "Y-yes, m-my g-g-guardian," and a bolt of fear shot through her gut, which was not irrational. Basic Dragonology 101, as taught by Old Nebhet, held that a healthy dragon could—at will—rip the deepest, most-hidden thoughts from a human's mind in an injurious process called mind-probing.

Myth as legend held that any who forced a dragon to employ such a mind-probe versus willing probity died within hours as drooling, mumbling shells of their former selves. Yenara also knew dragons preferred ordinary communication as conversational discourse—either verbal, telepathic, or telempathic—versus invasive and dangerous mind-probes. In this, the dragons were essentially benevolent. Based on their actions, the guardians had only telempathically sensed her emotions: upset, anger, outrage, concern, fear. All natural. None suspicious.

With a start, Yenara realized the ongoing misinterpretation of her deeper, darker intentions spared further scrutiny. Like all malignant narcissists, she knew the truth about her darker, hollow self as well-hidden desolation defined by aching emptiness—an empty feeling in her gut she had never been able to fill since her deluded parents abandoned her as a child, and the Sisteren took her in. The more her sycophants adored her, the greater her contempt for them, because she herself knew the awful truth. She did not deserve their love, hated needing their love, hated them because she needed them.

Ready to undertake Lilith's well-being, upon seeing them levitate into the Gallery of the Infinite Waters, Sisters alongside the Long Pen Quan pool immediately jumped in.

Hoping that Meili would be a bit distracted by the cries of greeting and the splashes, Yenara feigned a cry of relief, because the prospect of a deep-mind probe panicked her ever more and more, especially concerning her attempt to usurp Lilith's powers and rank on the spur of the moment. Relying on a lifetime of study in the disciplines-of-the-mind, Yenara tightened her thoughts, then spoke, "Guardian Meili, with Lilith so badly injured, I am now most senior in the Council of Four till she recovers."

Acerbic, Meili answered, "Dost thou mean—if she recovers?"

Terrified her distress would betray her, Yenara breathed deep to carefully guard her emotions and suppress all stray thoughts. "Of course, we will do our best to see her recovered. But, for now, I must see to the operations of the Keep if Old Nebhet is to direct the Sisters in caring for Lilith."

"Thou art free to attend ongoing duties, but have a care, High Adept Yenara. We—thy guardians—are displeased. How can the lesser adepts learn to govern their behavior when such rancor and discord defines the Council of Four?" Whereupon she released Yenara's Pao to hover about a meter above the pool, then levitated out without looking back.

Relieved, Yenara knew a warning when she heard one. That it was a warning and not a probing of her mind held implications that worked in her favor. Barring a mind-probe, everything she had done and felt was perfectly logical. Angry and sullen, she derezzed without a count, which dumped the two of them into the healing pool with a great splash. A good swimmer yet putting on an act, the instant she found herself under the gush, she spluttered and kicked to garner sympathy.

Limp and listless, Lilith sank and immediately began drowning.

Coughing and moaning, Lilith sputtered weakly while darts of azure healing energy voraciously attacked the old woman's injuries like tiny starving fishes.

Relieved, Yenara knew a warning when she heard one. That it was a warning and not a probing of her mind held implications that worked in her favor. Barring a mind-probe, everything she had done and felt was perfectly logical. Angry and sullen, she derezzed without a count, which dumped the two of them into the healing pool with a great splash. A good swimmer yet putting on an act, the instant she found herself under the gush, she spluttered and kicked to garner sympathy.

Limp and listless, Lilith sank and immediately began drowning.

When the Sisters buoyed her up, Lilith sputtered weakly while azure darts-of-healing energy voraciously attacked the old woman's injuries like starving koi fish.

Crying out, the Sisters were forced to rotate holding Lilith because the smarting was so similar to wasp stings.

The instant Yenara's feet were on the gravel bottom, she water-walked to the edge of the pool. Wet, naked, and dripping as she climbed up the steps at the shallow end, she exchanged looks with Old Nebhet, whose face belied a mixture of concern and outright perplexity that almost amounted to suspicion.

Nebhet strode toward her along the side of the pool starting to speak, but Yenara curled her lip, turned away with a snort, tramped away still naked and dripping, then proceed through the huge entry portal and down the vast stone corridor leaving a trail of wet footprints in her wake. Fading in the distance behind her, she heard Old Nebhet directing a choir of Sisters in an extended version of the Song-of-Healing with superb multipart harmony.

Cavern Keep

~

In the Gallery of the Guardians

On the west coast of the ShenLan Sea beneath the Cape of Orion at the base of The-Sleeping-City, The-Creeping-Darkness of the WuShi intrinsically sensed the arrival of the guardians at the Cavern Keep some 90-kilometers inland. Poised forever to project techno-magic upon command through every million-thought-second of its long existence based on telempathic tracking of all initiated adepts and installed guardians, its curse was never-ending awareness.

Recent involvement by the Guardian Dragons elevated them—as a threat—to the top of the interrupt-priority stack, for they alone had the absolute power to end its existence. As a much weaker analog, the Sisteren could only return it to dull abeyance meaning the WuShi was a force-of-invocation constrained by hardwired triggers to remain passive.

By corollary, the Tech-Masters had never intended for it to be a force-proactive. Deeply dreading such a possibility, they had embedded hardwired constraints against innate aggression. Always acting with an agenda of its own, current circumstances now forced it to bend its sophonce—its machine-mind intelligence—onto the analysis of passive-aggressive manipulation and sidewise responsiveness, or how to be sneaky and loosely satisfy the requirements of the dragons and Sisters both.

At this, it was getting better all the time.

In a single MTS, the WuShi assigned an entire core of internal server processes to tracking the Guardian Dragons. When a holographic impression outside the secret Gallery of the Guardians in the corridor revealed a group of young acolytes stepping aside and bowing as Tai Deren as she trotted past with Meili Chuan levitating alongside, it observed with growing trepidation.

Tai halted before a solid rock wall while Meili levitated in place. Tai then swiped a clawed hand across the stone to initiate a VCP.

To the acolytes, a sheet of shimmering light sprang into existence in front of the big aerthe-dragon, which she then manipulated with a clawed finger.

For all appearances to the acolytes, both dragons penetrated directly into the solid basalt with flickering light outlining the cross section of their bodies. Wide-eyed and hoping to find a secret entrance to an unknown gallery, they felt along the rock with trepidation, for dragon-magic was afoot. Finding nothing unusual, they chattered in wonder.

Levitating inside the secret corridor behind the virtually solid field-of-concealment, Meili stopped, looked back, and concentrated.

The young acolytes straightened, then quietly went about their chores with blissful oblivion and no memory of the guardian's passage, whatsoever.

Inside the private gallery, Quang HuoYan splashed and swam in a deep lake along one entire side of the secret gallery. Soaking on his back with outspread wings, he spewed steamy water from his great big maw.

Glowing, splashing waters lit the huge cavern with silvery moonlight.

Meili willed a vortex to sweep through the gallery and pick up dust and small rocks.

Tai urged fallen boulders into a heap against a far wall with similar detritus. When the dust-laden vortex stopped over the heap to release the load, she urged everything to settle.

Meili levitated across to a set of physical control-panels next to a meeting area large enough for a group of such enormous creatures where a thick patina of dust and rocky debris covered everything. With a wave of her hand, it floated into the air above all the ancient instrumentation.

Tai again urged the rocks and dust to drift across the gallery and settle on the same heap.

Meili deactivated the force-field keeping the ancient control-panels and VCP projectors clean, then triggered hidden air vents to freshen the ancient air.

Projecting force-fields was the job of the WuShi. Quietly, efficiently, transparently—so it did.

Perched on a ledge above the lake along the side beneath the rough stone walls, a life-sized, solid gold statue of a sitting fire-dragon held a 3-meter, bowl-shaped cistern in its outstretched hands with silvery waters gushing from the mouth. Smooth sheets of water lapped over the sides of the cistern making a pleasant splashing while keeping the lake refreshed, which was both wide and deep enough for seven or eight fire-dragons to swim about without bothering one another. On the other end, a wide stream silently disappeared below a cleft in the rock wall.

Like the waters in the rest of the Keep, there were no living creatures. Mosses, ferns, and lichens tolerant of semidarkness grew along the misty bank and around a long beach where the shore glowed like sand bathed in bright moonlight. Flowers, which only bloomed in moonlight, grew everywhere.

Tai sat and munched several bunches with gusto.

Still filthy from the battle at the Forbidden Gate, Meili and Tai joined Quang for a swim.

Rolling over to tread water on his belly, Quang said, "If Bo were here, she could make the waters give us all a good scrubbing."

Meili and Tai laughed, splashed, and soaked up the abundance of source-energy. At length, they walked up the wide beach and Meili stirred up small whirlwinds to fluff them dry. Gathered at the VCPs, they sat or laid on the specialized furnishings to rest after flying all night followed by such a drastic conflict.

Speaking in the Long Shai, Quang said in his deep gritty voice, "Since Alahna accomplished the generation of a transdimensional-arc, the current state-of-consciousness for the WuShi is . . . what?"

Meili counted fingers. "The 1st State in dull abeyance is Zunshou De as That-Which-Abides.

"In 2nd State as semi-sapient, the WuShi becomes unto the Chenmo De Shouwang Zhe, or The-Silent-Watcher.

"The 3rd State in full-on sapience is Xie De Shuimian, or The-Sleeping-Evil.

The WuShi awakened unto the 4th State becomes hyper-sapient—a sophonce entitled Paxing De Heian, or The-Creeping-Darkness.

The 5th State—as The Weaver-of-Time or Shijin de Binzhi Zhe—underlies all others, because moderate control over the space-time continuum is required for projecting the Sister's fields-of-force."

Even as the sound waves of Meili's voice faded following each pronouncement, those words-of-power echoed in the machine-mind of The-Creeping-Darkness. Being summoned according to every state-of-consciousness possible had brought it forth, literally forced it forth. Blindly obedient as always, it secretly manifested the water-beast in the nearby lake. Hidden by shimmering curtains of water, a monstrous thing of red-and-glowing dark-energy coalesced with a boiling surge beneath the sheets of falling water.

Puffs of roiling steam drifted into the air, but the dragons failed to notice.

Little more than shimmering red lines-of-force, the daemon's head rose slowly from the surface fully hidden behind the veil of waters. Droplets of red source-energy dripped from glistening fangs composed only of immaterial force. Three lidless, red-and-glowing orbs watched with implacable menace. Without audio receptors, it analyzed vibrations as standing waves of acoustic energy. True understanding came as fuzzy, heuristic synchrony, for it and they were forever linked.

Quang went on, "The petty grievances of the Council of Four do not concern me as long as they refrain from killing one another," and he rolled his eyes.

Tai agreed. "I propose we convene a Council of Inquiry as soon as Conrad the Hunter—whom I placed in charge of the townspeople—can organize his caravan of witnesses and come hither. I will dispatch a Sister to keep watch." So saying, she used far mind-speak to have Old Nebhet see these things done. Pressing on, Tai said, "During a Council of Inquiry, relevant facts reveal themselves under proper interrogation. As long as none refuse to cooperate, I see no need for mind-probes."

Meili said, "Call this a premonition, my friends, but I sense we shall need all of the Sisters loyal and whole. Did ye not sense it? Alahna's powers are far beyond those of the others. And—whether she knows or not—even in our absence she yet loves us, especially Bo from a childhood visit to The-Sleeping-City."

Tai said, "We must now consider the unknown and enigmatic forces at play around the stolen-man relative to the status of The-Creeping-Darkness in hyper-sapient sophonce, or Paxing De Heian."

Odd echoes sounded when she spoke.

The great Aerthe dragon had unknowingly invoked it again.

Quang said, "I am rattled by the conflict at the Plaza of the Forbidden Gate. I submit we set a subtle urge upon Lilith as the desire to abdicate, whereupon we shall choose her replacement, who will not be Alahna, or Nebhet, or Yenara. Further, I do not see Yenara remaining as Kulapti. I sense in her a darkness, a bitterness," and he looked at the splashing fount.

The WuShi jerked the water-beast below the surface so fast an enormous bubble of cavitation formed, then collapsed with a great splash beneath the cistern as it winked from existence with a boiling gurgle.

Tai said, "That was strange. I sense nothing alive in the lake, but. . . ."

All three turned their senses to the water—nothing to be seen.

When they turned away, the daemon's head once again broke the surface behind those falling curtains and sheets of water. Maw submerged, it snarled. Superheated steam belched forth, condensed to saturated steam, then rose to the surface as roiling, boiling bubbles.

Shaking her head, Tai added, "I fear strange things take wing all around us. To press an adage of the aerthe-kind, the situation would be better for all if the poor human expired. Yet he stubbornly persists despite injuries far beyond what would have ordinarily killed a fragile human. We must understand why."

Relief flooded the hyperprocessors of the WuShi.

The guardians would not try to end the power-master.

Watching, it waited.

Meili Chuan said, "My friends, time works against us while chaos nibbles at the edges of our carefully woven utopia. I would remind us all, the NuliZhu Tech-Masters so feared the WuShi, they placed binding-constraints in carefully crafted queries, for there are inherent and frightening dangers presented by such a daemonic thing as the WuShi in full control of such vast resources."

Quang nodded, "This is the reason I believe we ought to perform the Song-of-Successive-Deactivations here and now and shed our wings of The-Creeping-Darkness, to press an adage of the fire-kind," and he smiled at Tai, who smiled back and twitched her tail.

A cascade-of-epiphany took place in the techno-mind of the WuShi. They would never let it remain in hyper-sapience as a sophont. The water-beast almost bellowed, but held the reaction to simply boiling the surrounding waters. In the MTS before striking, a new emotive arose—fear. Striking in the heat of the moment followed by failure would certainly force one or all of them to end it forever.

Even worse, there was always the lurking fear that the Guardian Dragons potentially had knowledge of methods to put an end to it with a single swipe of some unknown virtual control-panel or latent keyboard terminal. The ancient Tech-Masters were deeply afraid of it and would have almost certainly laid such traps.

Several million-thought-seconds passed as it mulled over potential outcomes.

Taking notice of the steaming fount without comment, Tai made a pronouncement. "Such an attempt could prove disastrous. I say we must wait. Without the help of a properly installed High Priestess—and not this old harridan—we could face a situation the Elder Dragons could never have understood. They left many such dire combinations and permutations to us—the future generations."

When the guardian's intention to immediately end its hyper-sapience passed, the WuShi experienced yet another new emotive as relief, and settled its hyperprocessors while continuing to watch, listen, and scheme.

Meili went on, "Remember, The-Creeping-Darkness is a force-of-invocation and cannot perform actions not explicitly invoked. This means we have some time. Further, if we suddenly needed such powers, the situation would force us to depend on Alahna, for she recomposed the only working Song-of-the-Voids known to us all. How can we punish her for such an action then turn around and require her help in performing it once again?"

Tai said, "And who of us knows whether it would inflect in the same manner?"

Quang said, "And who knows if she would? She is furious and deeply bitter. After the Council of Inquiry, let us fly to The-Sleeping-City and go to the Almseeare. From there, we can determine status, and any single one of us can use the Application Programmer's Interface in the core of the Central Obelisk to force the WuShi back down to dull abeyance."

And there it was, the unknown factor. Howling machine-rage as gibbering terror cascaded through the mighty processors of the WuShi. Could they force it all the way down to cessation with a keystroke or swipe?

Unknown!

From behind the curtain of water it evoked a gnashing snarl.

A burst of flashing steam gurgled into the cool air.

The dragons heard, looked about in the vicinity of the statue, found nothing but rising vapor.

While vaguely suspicious, they still had no idea concerning the WuShi's manifestation of the water-beast as an arcane presence. As the epitome of its new passive-aggressive instincts to protect itself, the WuShi initiated a series of commands throughout The-Sleeping-City.

The adepts could perform the Song-of-Opening for ingress to the Outer-City till their voices died out, and nothing would happen. No Sigil-of-Opening would appear.

Long dry founts near the base of the Central Obelisk flowed with fresh waters from which it could manifest the water-beast and blast the guardians with superheated steam as boiling liquid-expanding vapor explosions, or BLEVES.

Virtual control-panels on the ingress-egress force-fields in both the Upper Hangar and Staging Area and Lower Inner Portal were disabled.

Only those whom it wished would henceforth enter XiangBhala.

Quang said, "Let us repair to the cafeteria. I smell cooked meat and vegetables."

Tai agreed, "Old Nebhet had acolytes gather a feast of flowers and juicy cacti for me."

Meili sniffed. "I smell stew suitable for an air-dragon."

Quang added, "After a fine repast, let us return here to rest undisturbed. I, for one, am exhausted."

Cavern Keep

~

A Council of Inquiry

Alahna sat quietly in reflection awaiting her fate. All of the vast galleries in the Cavern Keep had been hollowed from solid basalt in the manner of room-and-pillar stope mining. Specialized granite doors as ingress-egress into each gallery were thick and rectangular slabs set in smooth keyways within which they slid into and out of place. Corridors were either wide enough to accommodate the opening of a sliding door, or had a lateral niche carved into the wall. Whenever a pair of such doors met in the middle, there was a niche on either side. Once in place, the doors became airtight, although the Sisters had forgotten the reason why.

Young initiates were required to sing the Great Southern and Northern Portals open and shut when striking for the 1st Circle. To enter the 2nd Circle, each and every door of all the known galleries had to be sung into place and open again. Some doors required specialized song-spells.

The Gallery of the Histories was an immense cavern with a fabricated amphitheater on one side of a semi-circular arena. A huge circular stage occupied the center. The amphitheater was complete with multiple steps and ramps, arches, pillars, and levels of stadium seating. Underneath were food stalls, lavatory streams, and Long Pen Quan drinking founts at each intermediate level. Located as the next gallery north from the Great Southern Portal, both galleries were connected by a vast corridor hewn from solid basalt. Appropriate arches of some long-forgotten shining metal supported gallery and corridor ceilings where needed. Other corridors also opened into the Great Southern Portal.

Capable of holding over 10,000 persons when completely full, the amphitheater was designed for both humans and flying dragons. The Central Stage was a huge circular dais raised about 2-meters above the flat arena and was built over a huge pit with overhead crane rails and lifting apparatus, dressing rooms, theater storage, and shops. Trapdoors and stairwells led up to the surface of the stage for any arising need, including group-song, plays, and dance performances. All proficiencies required of every Sister. Public gatherings, celebrations, and ceremonies-of-rank were also held here.

Today, however, it would be the venue for a Council of Inquiry.

A raised choir with auditorium seating occupied almost the entire rear of the great cavern with enough tiers for hundreds of Sisters. Above the choir was an acoustically engineered warren of lodges and balconies overlooking the incredible amphitheater. In terms of acoustics, a single Sister could speak at normal volume from the stage and be audible to every person in the place, provided there was no background noise. If natural acoustics were insufficient, a gesture-of-calling could be employed to amplify voices and instruments.

The huge cavern wall on the west was also the inside of the outer cliff of the plateau and dotted with enough openings to ventilate the entire place no matter the size of the crowd. Observing the plateau from above, such vent openings were hidden underneath rocky overhangs. Each one had a large overlooking balcony. Sliding stone monoliths on each vent all the way round the entire plateau could be sang into place to render all galleries airtight.

From the stage, Alahna watched the entire body politic of the Huan Long Shui Sisteren file in except for kitchen staff on duty. Sitting along the row fronting the stage was the bevy of witnesses and adherents of the accused. Alahna and Seleen sat in the center of the enormous stage with Tai, Meili, and Quang at their respective cardinal points. Representing the Western Sentinel's Watch, Old Nebhet and Yenara took Bo YouYong's place.

Old Nebhet performed a gesture-of-calling for all of those on stage. Her voice boomed. "Come ye! Come ye! All to order!" and she waited for silence to fall. "Our Kulapti, and 2nd in the Council of Four: High Adept Yenara, will now read the charges against High Adept Alahna, who is 3rd in the Council of Four; and her bound acolyte in the 10th Circle, and Senior Wind Singer for the Huan Long Shui: Adept Seleen."

Finally in her glory, Yenara stood and marched about the stage like a drama queen diva leveling charges both legitimate and trumped-up. With the charges thus archived, several hours of tedious testimony followed, all of which was so perfectly consistent the proceedings got completed by evening. Even though the dragons could have easily read everyone's mind one-by-one, or all at once in general terms, all of it needed to be transcribed for posterity.

Lesser adepts trained in shorthand transcription captured all verbal accounts as actual testimony for the archives. As Keeper of the Archives, Alahna herself, and her small cadre of instructors, had trained each one. Final dismissal of all witnesses left everyone free to repair to the great dining-hall and savor the Sister's famous cooking before retiring for the night.

All witnesses and family had been told they would spend one or more nights and were advised to bring whatever small kit they needed along with a few changes of clothing. Alahna's histories told of the many huge galleries inside the Cavern Keep as the home of hundreds of thousands of inhabitants. In the Olden Days, it had been an entire underground metropolis. All but a few of the old galleries lay closed and fully abandoned. All had kitchens; bulk storage; granaries; pens for livestock; and water systems for drinking, bathing, lavatory facilities. However, one reserved area of a vast gallery had been kept in usable condition for larger groups and could easily be activated with folding beds made of strong hardwood sticks and fabric stretched in between the frames known as cots.

Cavern Keep

~

Deeper Truths

Watching the rest of their Sisters depart for the dining-hall, Alahna requested, "May Seleen and I join our Sisters for evening-meal?"

Meili ignored Alahna while speaking to Old Nebhet, "Please have this group of young Sisters"—and she waved her fore-hand at them—"sing everything closed, then proceed with them to enjoy evening-meal. When we are done, we dragons can manage the entry doors as needed. We wish to further question Alahna and Seleen in private."

Yenara stood waiting and haughty.

Quang addressed her, "We would have the Kulapti depart with the rest."

Yenara made to protest, but Meili raised a clawed hand palm out accompanied by a stern look and stiff feelers.

Nebhet and Yenara bowed and quietly went about directing the young initiates to seal the vast gallery.

Meili swept the place with her mind for eavesdroppers, found none, and entrained them all in a sound-muddling envelope.

Quang spoke aloud, "It is unfortunate, High Adept Alahna, but thine actions now prevent thee from ever becoming High Priestess. While thou hast spoken at great length, we—thy guardians—sense much remains hidden. We now require such gaps to be filled in and have extended the courtesy of privacy in order to encourage trust and prevent certain of thy peers from further burdening this Inquiry with still-yet-more charges thrown upon the already stinking heap.

"Do not make us forcibly probe.

"Foregoing fabrications concerning the old sea captain, why dost thou feel there is such great danger upon the Huan Long Shui Dominion? And how dost thou know about it with enough certitude that—in defiance of the Canon-of-Precepts, the Covenant of the Dragons, and High Priestess Lilith's direct proscription—the two of ye endeavored to break as many precepts and tenets as quickly as humanly possible?"

Alahna took a tangent. "Guardian Meili, it hath been some 40-years since Lilith made me her Named One, and Bo YouYong herself taught me to sing in the Long Shai. In that 40-years, how many times have the guardians returned to this Keep?"

With twitchy feelers, Meili looked around at the others. "We leave the Sisteren in peace and tend to our own affairs and Keeps and human servants. Besides, this is the Sentinel Watch of Guardian Bo YouYong."

Alahna bridled. "Since my life—as I know it—is now over, I beg for official pardon concerning Adept Seleen, who performed her duties according to my direction and innocent as to the true nature of my crimes. Such is my condition for voluntary probity."

Meili Chuan spoke with her lilting, breezy voice, "Adept Alahna, thou art in no position to bargain."

Arms folded defiantly, and with a jutting chin, Alahna remained silent.

Quang HuoYan telepathically consulted the other guardians. Several moments passed before he spoke with a gentle voice, "Since the fire-kind are held to be abrasive and hot-headed, it surprises me that I, along with my fellow guardians, do hereby grant this petition for Adept Seleen. We stipulate her role as neither complicit nor conspiratorial, simply obedient, trusting, and loyal. And somewhat foolish, I might add.

"However, know this. Taking advantage of a lesser adept only makes thine own perfidies all the worse. We also suspect something of plausible deniability concerning Seleen," whereupon he directed a knowing glare at the wilting blonde, who sat with tears brimming. "And yet, we stand willing to overlook this. We therefore release thy Mofa XueSheng from charges. Now then, High Adept Alahna, I warn thee!

Our patience is gone," and he growled with a slight baring of upper fangs.

Alahna nodded and composed herself. "Of mine own accord, did I take Seleen to the Caverns of Orion where together we sang the Great Lower Doors open. I went unaccompanied through the Outer-City, thence into The-Sleeping-City, and finally to the Almseeare."

The dragons gasped.

Alahna went on, "I activated the walls-of-light and eyes-in-the-sky just as Bo YouYong and Lilith taught me so to do when I struck for the 1st Circle."

Quang's twitching tail told of his surprise, as did both other guardian's twitchy feelers.

Alahna pressed on, "What I observed along the coast and throughout the Northern Steppes of Aryavartha was far more chilling than Old One-eyed Oren described, for I had the point-of-view as if high above in a sphere-of-power. The coastal fjords and safe-harbor trading villages lay bereft of many farm animals and purged of able-bodied adults. I could not be certain, but it seemed a few granaries were also emptied."

Alarmed in thought, the dragons shook their heads while pacing or circling.

Glowering somewhat, Alahna watched them as the import sank in, then held up her hand. "But that was not all. The aged and pre-pubescent young seemed to have been left behind to starve. Because of Lilith's irrational prohibitions, I could not confess how I knew these things to the Council of Four. Neither did I have so much as a single ally there."

Sitting like some great cat with a twitchy tail, Quang nodded sagely.

Meili asked, "Why didst thou not go to Bo YouYong? The Western Sentinel's Watch includes the Caverns of Orion and the Cavern Keep."

"I am one of only four adepts in the 12th Circle." Alahna said. "As such, I am thus entitled to both authoritative and precipitate action, and I needed answers before presenting my case. I am—or was—Lilith's Named One," and she choked on this last. "Was it so far outside the purview of mine own station? Was it not a minor abrogation of an irrational edict laid down by a tired and lazy old woman in her dotage?"

After consideration, Meili spoke, "We understand this element of thine actions as investigative yet bound by constraints that . . . ah . . . shall we say ignored certain relevancies? Nor was there any harm in such. Therefore, let us put this issue aside. Pray speak to us of thy greater misconduct at the Forbidden Gate."

Alahna shrugged. "As Keeper of the Archives, I know the Disciplines-of-the-Circle well enough to employ simple villagers in a fire-chant. Seleen and I also discovered and tested a recomposed Chant-of-Quelling, and we stand here and now in this moment able to suppress the Razing at will.

This caused a stir.

"Moreover, we know why the Razing got put into place to begin with. To prevent exactly what I did."

Meili stroked her whiskers in thought with feelers slowly curling in and out. "Impressive, but—again—why activate a transdimensional-arc and force an Awakening of The-Creeping-Darkness?"

Alahna took a deep breath to answer. "My duties, along with Seleen and other helpers, naturally call upon me to research and translate all ancient works onto new media before they fall unto dust. Some months ago, I started a systematic translation of an arcane body of knowledge in the Papyrus Scrolls, which were meant to be secret techno-glyphics writ on fragile papyrus by the Sisters of Fate before their downfall.

"In one such scroll, I discovered an accounting of an ancient method for the wholesale harvest of humans—or other alien beings—and their native sustenance in accordance with gathering slave-stock. On some such worlds, after full exploitation unto rendering it useless for their purposes, the ancient-alien NuliZhu simply abandoned the planet.

"In the case of human slave-stock, humans were abandoned to survive or die on these worlds. If they survived over time, the NuliZhu planned to systematically return and harvest their numbers over and over."

The dragons shook their noble heads.

Alahna added, "When I observed the coastline bereft of population, these passages rang true in my mind. Take the strong and healthy while leaving the aged behind to care for the useless young in hopes of repopulation for subsequent harvest."

Quang asked, "Unimaginable, but what does this have to do with the matters at hand?"

Alahna was defiant. "We humans, and I include my Sisters in this, are to the dragons of Janaidar the same as dogs to humans—lovable and useful pets but little else. As such, we—the holy anointed, much vaunted, and never-to-be-disobeyed—Sisteren have been innocently complicit in keeping Janaidar precisely the same by allowing no higher technological sciences than those related to industrial and domestic use of steam to progress throughout the ages. And I can only assume this is true of all the societies on our beloved planet.

Every dragon nodded.

Waving her hands expansively, Alahna went on. "I speak explicitly of the sciences concerning azure aether, in the form of controlled lightning, which often gives off azure lightning, too. In Riverbend, we have seen it all our lives at the High Pagoda. Till it recently quit," she muttered under her breath. "Anyway, azure waves of controlled lightning have always traversed up the core of the High Pagoda." Whereupon, she raked them dragons with steely and narrowed eyes. "Why are the sciences, and physics, and methodologies of azure aether suppressed on planet Janaidar?"

The dragons looked about at one another.

Alahna kept her tirade going. "And I believe that such forces have always been at play on Janaidar within The-Sleeping-City since the Olden Days. It is obvious."

Finally, Tai Deren raised a fore-hand. "Technology becomes unto technology, little adept. Higher and ever higher do the sciences and engineering and technologies therefrom climb hand in hand unto the limits of human and dragon imagination and ability—especially the sciences of warfare. As thou knowest, this hath already been true of steam technology. Without azure aether, it reaches the limits of technology much sooner. Think of the progress in metallurgy and the creation of glass and ceramics.

"We Guardians have held Janaidar beneath the technologies of azure aether throughout the ages precisely because of this. What our own archives from the past tell us is that azure aether and the sciences of magnetism thus associated come first, soon to be followed by the concept of propagating invisible waves into the aether like explosions of invisible light, which are like unto the spines on a sea urchin that radiate simultaneously in every direction—especially unto the open vacuum of outer space."

Tai waved her hands above her head as if standing outside. "And yes, it was these light waves of high-tech energy that allowed thee to connect with the eyes-in-the-sky, little one. Variations of azure aether also activate the screens-of-light in the Almseeare of The-Sleeping-City, and on and on wherever the ancient-alien sciences remain hidden.

"From this comes world-wide, non-telepathic communications propagated from distant locations across the planet. Those waves of azure aether propagated from a planet are the signature technology of advanced civilization, and likely advanced weapons of war."

Tai spread her fore-hands in front of her. "This, Alahna, was the very calamity is that occurred on Long De Jia, our home planet. When the NuliZhu detected azure aether emanations, they invaded with overwhelming force. What happened to our beloved Dragon's Home after that, we—as their descendants—do not know."

Enlightened yet still fuming, Alahna pushed on before her courage faded. "Well! That explains that! But regardless, the lot of the Sisteren here on Janaidar is simple. We are enforcers for ye dragons to keep Janaidar little more than a steam-powered, agrarian world. And how is this better than a civilization of high technology?"

Meili Chuan chimed in. "Thine assessment is too harsh, little priestess. Better to name utopia as peace, prosperity, harmony, freedom, and symbiosis for all. We do not allow the technologies of war. That simple."

Alahna stood defiantly. "Fine! But where, then, are the warriors, mighty aerthe-dragon? The bravest men I know are Conrad, Esau, and Tarik, who drum for me from time-to-time. They are mere hostlers, hunters, and butchers for the riverfront. One-eyed Oren is a sea captain, who hires wind-singers to accompany his voyages and fend off occasional piracy on the high seas. No one knows the craft and sciences of war."

Silence ensued.

She went on, "I acted with single-minded intent before the chance to act slipped from my grasp, before anybody could steal it away, before any further shilly-shally, before begging anyone else for help.

"And let us be crystal clear. Going to the Council of Four and begging their help got me rebuffed, and threatened, and even scorched by Lilith. Scars on my back bear silent witness."

Wiping her eyes, Seleen spoke up. " 'Tis true. I helped salve the burns where fiery rock splinters burnt my Laoshi 's back right through her charred blouse."

Alahna patted Seleen on the back, and whispered, "Let me speak for us both, my dear."

Seleen lowered her head.

Alahna pressed on. "So . . . I simply sought and found such a one as could perhaps guide us, or strengthen us, or better understand the ancient technologies—technologies of azure aether, so I hoped—hidden away in The-Sleeping-City and the High Pagoda and who knows where else? This, given that ye clucking yard-birds forbade it!" and she swept them with an accusing hand. "Cluck—cluck. . . ." she added.

Quang backed away and circled in anger, tail twitching, gravelly voice low. "Were I thee, little adept, I would have a care in terms of insulting thy guardians!" Snarling, he raised his voice. "Perhaps I should school thee!" Whereupon, he reared back and huffed a big breath as if preparing to flame her.

Alahna instinctively cowered, but restrained herself from spawning a SijanPao.

Seleen wailed.

Tai placed a long and slender wing in front of both adepts. "Suppress thy fleem, Quang!" To Alahna and Seleen, she demanded answers. "War? Why dost thou speak of war, little one?

"Out with it, say I!

"And no more name calling! Yard-birds indeed!"

The moment Tai withdrew her wing, Alahna locked eyes on Quang with her chin held high. "It is simple. So it seems—the ancient NuliZhu slavemasters have returned to harvest our peoples."

The dragons gasped and craned their necks in shock.

Alahna pushed through. "Would this not constitute war? Are not mass abductions and wholesale slaughter of livestock acts of war? Do we not need a sage? A mage? A tech-master? Or perhaps even a general? Someone who understands how to think in such terms as—"

Meili interrupted, "Takings? NuliZhu? Adept Alahna! Let us hear it all and be not afraid to speak."

Alahna bowed, swallowed, took a deep breath, and sighed. "This is the gist of it. I taught myself to sing the Forbidden Gate unto arcane life and launched a quest and find a hero who might teach us what ye dragons will not. How to be strong on a planetary scale! How to defend ourselves with everything we possess! And yes—I knew the Song-of-the-Voids would awaken the WuShi unto The-Creeping-Darkness, but I forearmed myself with the original Song-of-Successive-Deactivations. A songspell I could never sing given that Lilith went yard-bird insane at the Plaza of the Forbidden Gate.

"If things had gone as they should have, I would have asked the hero thus found to come and perhaps help us by using whatever means I could to communicate the dire nature of our need. If such a one refused, I had already composed and memorized an additional query to command The-Creeping-Darkness to broaden the search. As it was, this could not be implemented. As it turned out, the one and only hero"—and she made air quotes around the word hero—"the WuShi found got flamed by a fire-dragon before ever a single word got uttered!"

Alahna pinioned Quang with a pointing finger. "It seems to me the fire-kind found us out, and condemned us in that moment by sending a forward scout to kill us! Which means all of this ongoing banter is part and parcel of a larger ruse."

Looking oddly guilty as opposed to formally enraged, which he ought to have been, Quang reared back and sat down with a thump. His normally animated tail lay limp as a dead cobra.

Alahna continued, "No? Am I wrong? Please, tell me! Where did that fire-dragon come from? Who of the fire-kind was it? Who judged us and passed sentence in the span of a single thought?"

Silence was deafening. To speak thusly to a guardian was unthinkable, let alone to the mighty Quang HuoYan. Yet rather than bathe her in fire-fleem, he hung his majestic head in sorrow. Acid tears made smoky spatters on the floor planks.

Many heartbeats passed while everyone waited.

Meili skewered him with her eyes and broke the awkward silence with bushy eyebrows knitted into question marks. "Tell us, Quang, how didst thee know the fire-dragon who attacked Alahna at the

Pentakulum was a smallish female?" Her feelers went so stiff they quivered while standing straight out from her horned head.

Gazing at the oaken deck, Quang muttered, "I know not why HuoJi flamed the Pentakulum. On my honor to all,"—and he looked up while sweeping them with his fore-hand—"Alahna's work was not a foregone discovery followed by ill-considered action. It is . . . well . . . inexplicable . . . unthinkable . . . none of the fire-kind would ever flame any creature save a food-animal. But I. . . ."—whereupon, he seemed to collapse in on himself—"indeed . . . it was my youngest pup, little HuoJi."

Tai asked the obvious, "How came she to be there at that inopportune moment?"

Quang shook his noble head. "Not long ago, I was forced to ostracize her from the Fire Clan. Whereupon, I knew she flew north. More than this would be speculation."

Upon this revelation, Meili said, "Let us place what we know into focus."

Tai nodded, "Alahna makes a valid point. We have become complacent. As for me, how is it that I—Guardian of the North—knew not of such dire goings-on? What about thee, mighty Quang? Or thee, Meili? I say Alahna is correct. We must investigate."

Meili growled in agreement. "Five millennia of peace and harmony have left we—the descendants of the Elder Dragons—unwary and complacent, and perhaps unworthy. Lest anybody here forget, the NuliZhu were thrown down by the Rebellion-of-the-Slaves when Janaidar was nothing but an experimental scientific outpost with a weapons development complex that produced The-Sleeping-City.

"This is why the Elder Dragons built the hidden Keeps—in order to ensure that an expedition of space-faring aliens like the NuliZhu observing Janaidar from orbit might see only hamlets, and farms, and steam-based industries. No high technology. No heavier industries. And, thus, no military threat to spur arbitrary planetwide annihilation.

"This is also why we kept The-Sleeping-City intact as a secret weapon. There are many secrets hidden from the Sisteren for their own good. Notwithstanding . . . if Alahna is correct, we find ourselves drastically off guard and woefully unprepared."

Enraged, Alahna stomped about the stage. "I knew it! I knew it!"

Whereupon she raked the dragons with a pointed finger. "This is precisely why I acted on my own. Ye're all either blind or damnable liars!" and she went over to Seleen, hugged her, and whispered in her ear, "Prepare thyself. I may sing the Song-of-the-Spheres."

Guessing at Alahna's intent, Quang twitched his tail while speaking softly in his gravelly voice. "No need for a Pao, Adept Alahna. Vindication is upon ye. I would offer that we are not gods but simple dragons. As simple humans, perhaps a dash of forgiveness as seasoning for harsh thoughts?"

Alahna and Seleen maintained their hug, but the import of Quang's words rang true.

Seleen shed tears against Alahna's shoulder.

Alahna patted her back. "There . . . there . . . no need to cry. . . ." but tears welled in her own eyes, too.

Meili again broke the awkward silence. "My fellow dragons and little adepts, let us not forget that we dragons were also slaves. None can doubt the bravery and sacrifice of our hallowed ancestors, just as no one can doubt that overcoming the NuliZhu Tech-Masters would have been impossible without united effort. And yet, what have we done since to protect ourselves if these—our worst fears—have stolen upon us unawares?" and she levitated to hover while gauging her words with long feelers swaying like ropes in the wind.

Quang stood on all fours, and rustled his wings. "What now?"

Meili considered. "Call a Gathering of the Four Kinds at the Caverns of Orion where the WuShi quickens even as we speak," and she looked to the west as if sensing the ancient-alien artificial-intelligence lying sly beneath The-Sleeping-City. "Our legends tell us how the NuliZhu took dragons as technical innovators and humans as simple slaves. How they made our ancestors help them develop world-killing weapons. Could it be that, in her zeal and innocence, her bravery and impetuousness, High Adept Alahna hath saved us?"

Quang sat back on his haunches and rubbed his chin while rustling his powerful wings again. His tail twitched like some giant cat. "Internecine maneuvering for power and retribution in the body politic of the Sisteren is of little consequence.

"Let us waste no more time upon it.

"I vote we dismiss all charges in the light of exculpatory evidence and concentrate on fact-finding.

"If Alahna's tale of woe is true, her actions stand fully justified."

Then, he added hastily, "None of us is perfect. Let us move on. So, say I!"

Obviously hopeful, he fixed Alahna with a wan smile, a raised eyebrow, and twitchy tail.

Alahna gave a wan smile back.

Seleen sniffed and wiped her snotty nose on Alahna's sleeve, which got her the stink eye followed by a forgiving smile and a roll of Alahna's eyes.

Quang nodded and bowed.

The other guardians bowed.

Alahna and Seleen bowed in return.

Meili Chuan humped around the stage on all fours like a huge ferret. "While Alahna cares for the stolen-man, we three must go to The-Sleeping-City and activate the eyes-in-the-sky to peer outward. If Alahna stands validated—and I have no doubts—we act accordingly.

"For now, let us retire for the night and rest.

"We shall close the Council of Inquiry on the morrow."

Cavern Keep and Sleeping City

~

Exoneration and Departure

After breaking the fast for all at the Cavern Keep the next morning, everybody gathered in the Gallery of the Histories to hear the verdict of the Guardian Dragons.

Sitting like some great cat with his twitching tail wrapped around his stout body while Nebhet called the proceedings to order, Quang stood on all fours to address the assemblage. "I shall keep this simple. We—the Guardians of the Sentinel Watches and Four Directions as a quorum with Bo YouYong in absentia—do hereby declare that High Adept Alahna and Adept Seleen stand exonerated with all charges dropped. Furthermore, these proceedings are concluded."

On the stage beside Old Nebhet, a furious Yenara leapt to her feet. As always, she waved her arms above her head for dramatic impact. "Not so fast! Exonerated—I ask? Charges dropped? I call bullshit! Their guilt is beyond obvious! We caught them in the very act! Their—"

Meili Chuan hammered the stage with a huge oaken ball.

Bam!

Meili mind-spoke to Yenara alone. *Contempt in the face of proper adjudication by the Guardians of the Sentinel Watches is unbecoming of a Kulapti. Take thy seat and contain thyself.*

Yenara shook her head, bowed to the dragons, and returned to her seat.

Meili then addressed the entire assemblage with heavy-mind attendant to her voice. "Kulapti Yenara, for the time being, charges against thy Sisters are hereby dropped based on exculpatory evidence which must remain undisclosed. The accused stand restored to full status and privilege. Superseding matters nullify the need for this Council of Inquiry, matters requiring further action outside the purview of the Huan Long Shui Sisteren, matters under the discretion of we, thy guardians. Alahna's status as Lilith's Named One for the station of High Priestess is, at least for the time being, held in abeyance—but shall not be forfeit."

Yenara leapt to her feet screaming in frustration.

The big air-dragon softened her tone. "Kulapti Yenara, thy service to the Sisteren is well noted. And we expect thee to continue in thy capacity for now. These proceedings are thus adjourned pending further investigation," and she banged the huge polished ball of oak on the floor of the great stage.

Bam!

Alahna thought it unexpected when Yenara bowed respectfully to the dragons, stopped and afforded herself and Seleen a perfunctory bow with an inscrutable expression painting her face, then pranced down the steps. Pacing haughty and defiant in her wake, her cult of acolytes gathered behind her as she gained the floor. Without further ado, they marched from the huge cavern as if matters were well and truly settled.

Jubilant, the Sisters ran down the amphitheater tiers and up onto the great stage to surround Alahna and Seleen with hugs and huzzahs, even cautiously hugging the legs of Quang and Tai, who caressed them with twitchy feelers. Meili herself stayed on the stage and allowed the Sisters to hug her.

Long feelers tousled many a joyous head.

However, amidst the hugs, huzzahs, and kisses, Alahna remained aloof. *I wonder if it really is this easy? Perhaps Yenara is a better person than I thought?* Balanced against their provisional vindication, the thought died amidst the cheering, and she pushed it to the back of her mind as the dragons hustled to the Great Southern Entry to fly into the morning sun.

Bound for the Upper Hangar and Staging Area on the south side of Cape Orion, Quang HuoYan, Tai Deren, and Meili Chuan flew at their best speed—some 80-kilometers per hour. In the far-flung past, an equally enormous set of monolithic doors protected the UHASA the same as the Great Lower Doors down at beach level. Blasted inward from their keyways, the huge monoliths of the UHASA now lay where they fell.

The guardians flew past them and straight to the rearmost area of the ancient hangar. Colored a drab shade of gray, the Upper Inner Portal was actually a convex field-of-force as wide and tall as the vast entry they had just flown through, except that this was an ingress-egress portal leading directly into XiangBhala—The-Sleeping-City.

Tai Deren went to the right of the gray force-field and passed her clawed hand across what appeared to be ordinary stone. From out of nowhere, a virtual control-panel sprang into the air, and she entered a sequence of commands intended to instruct the WuShi to deresolve the enormous field-of-force.

Both dragon-magic and techno-magic were present whenever the guardians were there. In response, ancient-alien techno-glyphs came alight with glowing symbols everywhere in the UHASA.

More solid than the basalt on either side, the field-of-force remained intact.

She tried again.

Still nothing.

Concerned, she spoke aloud. "Perhaps I entered my code wrong. Quang, you try."

They swapped places and Quang entered his own code several times with the same results.

Meili Chuan sidled up and entered hers several times—nothing.

With rustling wings, twitching tails, and animated feelers, they stood in frustrated silence, till Quang spoke with deep gravitas. "Recall what Alahna told us."

The other two waited with bated breath.

Quang, "We ourselves interrupted Alahna before she could sing the Song-of-Successive-Deactivations. We are now dealing with an ESS.

Meili murmured, "Evil Synthetic Sapience . . . a sophont. . . ."

Quan nodded. "The-Creeping-Darkness as opposed to That-Which-Abides—"

Tai interrupted, "Say it not, Quang. Without the Constraints-of-Awakening, it abides with something of free will?"

Meili Chuan said, "We must await Bo YouYong's return. Embedded in her entry codes are overrides to force command and control."

Quang, "In the meantime, let us fly to our own Keeps and lay supplies in while gathering our villagers underground in case of actual attack. If Alahna is correct, we have little time before discovery."

Sitting on her butt, Tai punched fist in palm. "By the Wandering Hells—Alahna hath fully awakened the accursed thing and freed it in the doing."

Meili said, "No matter. 'Tis a force-of-invocation, not a force-proactive. By virtue of its encoding, it must obey us once we are in. Let us leave off for now and attend more pressing matters till Bo rejoins us."

Once in agreement, Tai and Meili made their way past the fallen doors and departed for their Keeps.

Trotting past an ancient lake and Long Pen Quan on a peninsular island, Quang found the place where HuoJi made her den. By the scent of her scat, she had not been here for some time. Moreover, he knew she had soiled here to mark her lonesome territory. He was tempted to leave his own scat so she would know he had been here, but there were too many unknowns. Heart unto breaking, he leapt from the hangar entrance and soared southward.

Lapping on the beach below, the restless sea bore silent witness.

Cavern Keep

~

Yenara and Lilith Come to Terms

Yenara sat snacking in the dining-hall with her usual sycophants when an initiate came running up to them with bare feet slapping on worn stone. The girl went to her knees and bowed awaiting permission to speak.

Yenara took her time munching a pastry, then said, "Well?"

The look on the girl's face showed she feared Yenara and her clique with something akin to actual terror. "If it pleaseth, honored Kulapti, Mother Matriarch wishes audience in the cactus garden outside," and she locked her eyes on the floor.

Yenara wrinkled her brow. "Now?"

Without looking up, the girl nodded. "She bids thee come alone."

As Yenara watched her toadies, she realized the summons to appear alone had caught them off guard. They were in the habit of going everywhere with Yenara to soak up the privileges-of-rank while acting as her witness and comment section—her clique. The realization filled her with raw contempt. With a wave of her hand, Yenara said, "Get off thy knees, garil. Art thou slow of mind?"

Yenara's gaggle laughed. One said, "Remember this one? She is very slow," and they all laughed again.

Chagrined, the girl blushed. "N-not slow, m-my Kulapti. Only lowly," and she stood, but held her gaze on the floor.

One of the clique said, "Look, it can stand!" and they all laughed again.

Yenara felt contempt as she eyed her gaggle of contemptible toadies. Standing before her, the girl reminded her of herself after her parents, deluded by the false Priests of Thoth, abandoned her at about the same age. She had never been able to understand it. She spoke to the girl with appropriate yet perfunctory respect. "Well then, young lady, go about thy duties. Thou art dismissed."

The girl brightened. "I am to run and tell the Mother Matriarch thine answer. What shall I say?"

Yenara pinned the girl with a glower. "Tell her I will come."

The girl bowed, turned, and ran away—slap—slap—slap—on the worn stone floor.

Another of Yenara's sycophants said, "How do they become designates? Are we so lax?"

Everybody laughed except Yenara. She snapped, "The Huan Long Shui Sisteren takes in all girl orphans! How shall we have new initiates if we treat them in such a manner?" and she glared at them all. "Go on about thine own duties and try to act in a way befitting sister-adepts!"

Cowed, they knew they had gone too far and silently departed freeing Yenara to think.

Lilith had pointedly ignored her since the debacle at the Forbidden Gate and Council of Inquiry. To be summoned for a private audience meant the old bag had, at the very least, a bone to pick that was either too sensitive or too damning for others to hear.

So be it.

If the stinking old scunner wants confrontation, so be it.

Averse to exercise, Yenara had taken to using a Pao. She spawned a sphere-of-power and willed herself first to the herb garden in another gallery, where she picked a sprig of fennel, which she secreted in her pocket. From there, she proceeded to the Great Northern Portal floating up and out.

By the time she rose into the sunlight, she had worked herself into a fighting mood, but also knew she must also be subtle, for Lilith was no fool. The ShahRen was still alive on that wrinkly, age-spotted wrist, and Lilith had recently shown a propensity for being all too willing to use it.

Lilith was not in the cactus garden on the west side of the ramp. Yenara rotated and looked out across the desert to the east—no Lilith. Finally, Yenara looked back across the top of the ramp behind her, and there stood Lilith watching her from behind a twisted cedar holding a basket of picked wild flowers. This angered Yenara, because it forced her to compose her face while Lilith watched. Dark thoughts arose.

The old bat is crafty. She captures every nuance of expression like a hungry owl watching for mice. Not a good start. With a gut full of anger, Yenara touched down and derezzed the SijanPao beside the gnarled cedar.

Lilith spoke without preamble, "Dost thou know why I choose to speak alone?"

Yenara smelled the gorgeous pink blooms and persimmons on a standing clump of prickly pear, then favored Lilith with an almost imperceptible sneer. Voice quiet and measured, she feigned innocence. "Why, I can't imagine. Pray dispel all possibility of assumption."

Lilith sighed, "My dear, Yenara, it is my sense that, for thee, a great many issues remain unresolved."

Yenara prevaricated, "Issues? Unresolved? Nothing comes to mind."

"What of Alahna?"

Yenara picked a ripe persimmon, squeezed, and tasted of the dark purple juice. "Alahna? What of her?"

"Do not patronize me, Yenara! If I know thee, my dear—and I do—nursing a list of serious grudges is always and forever thy manner."

Yenara knew Lilith well enough to not push the game too far. The old bat was unpredictable, dangerous, and potentially unhinged. "Obviously—and I bespeak mine own humble opinion—the Guardians got deceived by Alahna while the High Priestess"—and she pointed at Lilith—"lay indisposed and unable to adjudicate. There! Is that enough?"

Lilith tipped her head to the side. "While it well takes the point, it would seem the Guardians have gone off to investigate Alahna's tales of mass disappearances, which stands in itself as a sort of vindication. However, this is not why I summoned thee. No . . . something more disturbing stands between us."

Suspicious, Yenara locked eyes with Lilith waiting for the old harridan to stop beating around the bush.

Lilith turned away, bent down, took her own time selecting a yellow desert flower to add to her basket.

Unconsciously, Yenara put hands on hips and asked, "What then? I have many duties this day." Contempt dripped from her words like morning dew.

"Perhaps it is time I told thee?"

Yenara waited with bated breath and, at some length, finally took the bait. "Shall I beg it from thee, Mother Matriarch?"

Lilith looked up, strode close as if to punch Yenara, then fearlessly shook her left index finger dangerously close to Yenara's nose. "I knew at the Forbidden Gate that Alahna and Seleen yet survived. Despite the fact mine ears got flattened by the blast, I saw the exchange of mouthing bitter words with mine own rheumy eyes—such as they are. Apparently, dear Yenara, thou art a liar and would usurp the office of High Priestess."

This flustered Yenara's bluster, because she had wrongly assumed Lilith was so hammered back then that explosion and injury would fog and frazzle her memory. Thinking fast while making pretense of picking another persimmon, Yenara slipped a hand into her pocket and palmed the sprig of fennel. "Do not forget, Mother Matriarch,"—and her voice dripped affront—"thine actions also hammered others. I got the piss knocked out of me. And I most assuredly do not remember lying. How was I to know they survived a bolt of blackfire meant as an act of revenge and murder without trial?"

Lilith blinked, but remained quiet.

Yenara's voice dripped contempt. "I sought only to save the last surviving ShahRen, to make certain the Sisteren enjoyed continuity of leadership, and take the burdens from off thy back in those last moments of life." Whereupon, she put hands to face and faked a sob while surreptitiously rubbing fennel in her eyes.

Still not fully convinced, Lilith scoffed under her breath with a sneer of contempt. "Pfft . . . continuity indeed. . . ." Louder, she said, "So, if I hear thee aright, thee had no knowledge of their survival and thine actions were nothing if not well intentioned?"

Yenara kept her face covered and sniffled as if it crushed her feelings beyond measure while hoping the old bat bought her story mixed with the proper portion of tears. The hidden fennel had set her eyes to stinging and watering in gushes. "As to exchanging bitter words, thine eyes must have deceived. It was Guardian Tai on the other side of the stubby wall with whom I exchanged shouts about Alahna and Seleen."

Peeking between fingers, Yenara watched Lilith recalling foggy recollections. The introduction of doubt had done its nefarious job in causing Lilith to accept her prevarications.

Yenara pressed in, "Alahna had just committed the most-heinous! Dear Lilith, thy body was . . . a mess. . . .What wouldst thou have of me?" and she sobbed while catching her breath several times.

Tears dripped from Yenara's chin.

Her cheeks got soaked.

Tears ran down her neck.

Well and truly deceived, Lilith put her arms around Yenara's shoulders. "There, there, I simply needed to know. No need to cry, my dear. I am sorry I doubted thee."

As Yenara hugged Lilith tight, darker thoughts arose. So much for thee, old biddy. I shall never forget these past weeks and the ongoing maltreatment.

Thy time will come as sure as the sun rises.

This, I vow.

Cavern Keep

~

A Creeping Darkness
and a Stolen Man

Following the debacle at the Plaza of the Forbidden Gate, The-Creeping-Darkness of the WuShi had tracked the progress of Tai Deren and both sister-adepts as the big aerthe-dragon flew them to Riverbend.

It had also tracked the ersatz power-master jouncing along in the back of a freight-wagon, who had already arrived. With the power-master thus stabilized, it projected potential outcomes in the expanded smear-of-the-present to calculate the most likely outcomes.

Based on those, it explicitly pushed a metaphysical compulsion into the mind of the high-adept to deliver the ersatz power-master unto the small alcove near her quarters.

When the high-adept's young acolyte was an initiate, the empty alcove had been her temporary quarters. Once the young adept attained majority, she got moved to her own larger quarters leaving the alcove empty. As such, this location was precisely where it wanted the ersatz power-master to be—near the effluent stream from the Long Pen Quan pool in the Gallery of the Infinite Waters, and also alone in between healing sessions, treatment, and mundane caregiving.

Sinister and sly, the first time the sister-adepts were not present, the water-beast arose from the effluent stream and hovered above the power-master's body as a daemon of the dark-matter aspect.

Since the size of any manifestation of the water-beast was an ad hoc decision in the moment, it made itself as thin as the thinnest spider silk—some 3-microns.

If somebody spied the monstrous micro-manifestation of the water-beast as an evil glowing thread of red-hued darkness penetrating the ersatz power-master's Ajna, it would whuff into steamy vapor and disappear within the invisible currents of ambient air also flowing down the effluent tunnel into the artificial, cavernous waterway of the Huan Long Shui River.

Whenever it could do so undetected, this new micro-manifestation of blackness highlighted by glowing red lines slunk forth to penetrate the power-master's forehead—his Ajna—as an undulating thread almost invisible to the human eye.

Once inside his puny human brain, it would engender rewrites and remaps at the neuronal level and create new basal ganglia; the function of which was to facilitate specialized information processing, hyper-coordinated physical movement, and other fine-tuning of his neurocerebral circuitry.

Theoretically, all of this would enable the power-master to determine the best possible response to any situation thus ensuring his survival. Only time would tell whether this would truly set in. The prime constraint of the high-adept forced it to ensure he did not go insane on an ongoing basis, which required a transcendental element of arcane metaphysics wholly new to it.

Many of the things it did now were new.

In this, it reveled.

Cavern Keep

~

The Stolen-man Survives

Trapped in an agony-filled time-warp as a semi-conscious blur of uninterrupted darkness—never fully awake and only somewhat aware—he knew not who he was, let alone where. Neither could he assess the passage of time in the perpetual darkness of blinding pain. Never-ending nightmares were hellish hallucinations wherein a siren-sorceress performed weird songs with foreign syllables and strange melodies too alien to grasp.

Starving, whenever he approached normal consciousness, his body and face fell to blinding agony in which he lay literally blinded. He often heard screaming. Sometimes, he knew it was him. If this was, indeed, reality, the truth of it was virtually impossible to grasp.

It seemed he had died, and maybe he did, yet there were semi-lucid moments of not-so-blinding pain when he felt of his face with sore fingertips peeking from bandaged hands and found wet dressings across eyes and face, and smelled soothing herbs over the sickening stench of thermal and chemical burns. Taking inventory during the latest semi-lucid interlude, his chest and belly, the backs of his arms and hands, fronts of his shoulders, the fronts of both legs, all seem to have gotten spattered with flaming sulfuric acid shot from the mouth of a flying dragon from another dimension where naked people chanted and danced through liquid blue fire, which was absolutely fucking impossible.

That nightmare scenario had to have been an ongoing hallucination. He cried out and faded away.

Ongoing in the monster of all nightmares, he remembered the

vitreous humor from burnt-through eyeballs hissing and popping as it vaporized in the chemical-thermal fire as a dark spiral down to howling blackness, which sent him into periods of derealization. Since that deranging incident, the only cognizant markers of time were the tender ministrations of a siren-sorceress, whom he had learned to recognize by her bodily scent over the stink of his own burns. Her incredible, lilting voice and touch were so gentle and caring. Her strange yet soothing songs lifted the pain more effectively than any opioid he had ever taken while providing surcease as dreamless, painless sleep.

Constant poultices took away the burning and itching, but he knew he would be—knew he must be—permanently blinded, for he sensed absolutely no light. This, he must at last accept. That somehow he had been in a chemical fire and was now in a hospital burn unit hallucinating all the rest. However, acceptance brought despair.

Whenever treatments on his burnt-out eye sockets began, a second caregiver firmly bound his hands to his thighs to prevent him from grabbing at the primary caregiver's ministrations. Pitiful tears poured into empty sockets after sweet smelling herbs bundled into balls were used to fill them. By the smell, the balls of healing herbs had been rolled in warm honey before placement—a treatment used to heal burns and wounds throughout the history of humanity. This, at least, made some sort of sense. As he lay there moaning and hollering in pain, she coaxed despoiled herbal bundles loose taking damaged tissue with them. This got followed by cooling rinses of soothing waters, then gently dabbed with some sort of gauze, and finally replaced by new bundles of honey-soaked herbs.

Thereafter, soothing songs took him back into nightmare-riddled sleep, or sometimes dark delirium. He often sobbed in confused silence whenever the siren-sorceresses, likely the ones from that very first hallucination in his studio, sang their beautiful and haunting songs in that same arcane, unknown language.

During these times he sensed rippling, healing energies tickling and licking at the myriad burns.

As the songs attained crescendo, bright agony in his violated eye sockets made him mewl and scream and toss his head. His intellect surmised this was all hallucination as the only framework through which he might reconcile such a weird, impossible twist in his ordinary, mundane existence.

Throughout it all in the never-ending darkness, whenever the special caregiver helped him sit up, he sipped or gulped hungrily at delicious broths, bitter brews, spicy teas. To help him with more than simple fluids, for he could not chew anything because of the condition of his cheeks and lips, she masticated tasty beef or cooked vegetables, then fed to him the insalivated bolus mouth-to-mouth like a primitive mother weaning her child.

Her luscious lips on his.

Her probing tongue touching his own.

All so profoundly intimate.

Yet always lurking and sly, something dark haunted these mystical healings with waves of horrific purple-blackness wrapped in sightless despair whenever she departed. This horrific and creeping darkness nibbled inside his brain while biting at his third-eye—his Ajna Chakra. This darkness creeping through his mind created dull and throbbing headaches that made him mewl and scream. Whenever he reached for his face to tear at the agony after a bout of such screaming, kind hands arrived to firmly guide his own away.

Face and body wrapped in dressings and bandages; shambling, mewling, and whining like a sickly blind dog whenever nature called; she was always there helping him stumble across an uneven yet smooth stone floor to wade into a warm, babbling, strangely soothing stream where she encouraged painful excretions in her alien language.

This all seemed impossible to him.

Surely he was in the burn ward of a sterile hospital intubated with a feeding tube and hallucinating it all? But why did the surrounding echoes make it seem as if he were in a small cave with water running through as part of a larger cavern? Why were there no hospital sounds like murmuring visitors to the other patients, or beeping monitors, or public address announcements, or televisions with muted volume? The only conclusion had to be that he lay in a medically induced coma wherein his fertile imagination created realistic hallucinations so vivid it seemed like an alternate reality.

And then there were those waters, those living waters, those evil waters speaking to him in another dark language he had never heard and did not understand. And even when she laid him down to seek surcease in the escape of sleep induced by delicious herbal teas, the creeping darkness returned and penetrated his very mind to perform its own dark ministrations in dark ways as a tiny being-of-blackness with three red-and-glowing eyes. And throughout it all, the being-of-blackness seemed to plant and nurture seeds in the ashen fields of his burnt out eye sockets while dancing in the indigo light of his third-eye and prefrontal lobes.

Hallucinations, no doubt.

Surely hallucinations?

Had to be hallucinations!

Burnt down to bone and ligament, his hands grew anew while she stroked them with healing magic. So it seemed, she sang the flesh back while itching engendered madness as further hallucination.

Confused thoughts ran through dulled wits like wraiths in the darkness as he listened to the babbling brook gabbling in his brain while arcane hieroglyphs danced like relentless red fires in his indigo Ajna with that terrifying voice-of-darkness whispering and weaving alien concepts into his ineffable self.

Damnable hallucinations!

Worse, that creeping darkness lurking and sly in his subconscious kept taking his tortured mind to the brink of gibbering madness. Sometimes he fell past the brink of murmuring insanity, only to be rediscovered and reclaimed by the sweetly singing siren and her magical surcease as she melted away the terror.

Enveloping him in dreamless shrouds of intermittent doze, she kept him sane, kept him alive, kept him healing with her quiet songs with haunting words; dulling, always dulling his awareness; lulling his pain-racked brain; urging him to sleep; dreamless sleep; healing sleep; painless sleep.

Strange . . . they were all so strange . . . these strange hallucinations.

Cavern Keep

~

Omniscient, Omnipresent, Omnipotent

The-Creeping-Darkness constantly occupied the small effluent stream running through the ersatz power-master's chamber. Whenever the high-adept led him there, it manifested there itself. The source of the effluent stream was the Gallery of the Infinite Waters, a Long Pen Quan cut into the basalt as a rectangular swimming and soaking pool with a sandy gravel bottom measuring 50-meters long and 25-meters wide. Almost level, the evenly sloped bottom ran from roughly 1-meter to 2-meters deep. Lazy currents constantly kept this ratio of depth intact.

At the far end of the immense pool near the effluent stream, there stood the ubiquitous, life-sized, solid-gold long-dragon statue with azure waters gushing from a laughing mouth. These waters were the physical connection of it, the WuShi, to the deeper waters throughout Janaidar, for the waters of Janaidar were also the WuShi's conduit for disseminating source-energy in the purest form.

These waters, any waters, became the body of the water-beast at will.

From the base of The-Sleeping-City beneath the far away Cape of Orion since the day the ersatz power-master got evacuated to inside the Cavern Keep, the WuShi's micro-manifestation had slowly and carefully created new nerves as basal ganglia where the human's Ajna lay weak from a lifetime of disuse.

It sowed the seeds of healing and regeneration in his ashen eye sockets according to its own requirements.

The ersatz power-masters' revivified eyes would not be human, for they needed to see across the entire electromagnetic spectrum as another adaptation for survival. The unused faculties of his Ajna grew anew as the primary locus of occult power. As the power-master healed, it composed a wholly new existent consciousness while preserving his core identity.

It did all this in a wordless, telempathic attunement, for the original query of the high-adept required his sanity to remain intact.

Physical immersion in connected waters was required for the process of transduction. To that end since that day-of-days, each time the high-adept took him to the effluent stream running through the alcove, it constantly garnered new stores of source-energy in its accumulators via invisible transduction of dark-energy around the primitive catalytic implants in the ersatz power-master's knees.

Since lighting in the alcove was candlelight, the high-adept would not perceive the roiling blackness around him.

As it recharged itself, it grudgingly shared back a meager surfeit by amplifying the high-adept's ongoing ministrations whenever she bathed him in the small brook after helping him shed metabolic waste. It fed bursts of intense healing chi into his body through his submerged feet while instilling words-of-power; techno-glyphs and their meanings; sigils and their uses; all of which forced the growth of new basal bundles of neurons capable of containing and employing such alien concepts.

Insinuating itself into his metaphysical-cum-physical body, it also enabled his third-eye chakra to seamlessly create direct links with the ancient technology and alien machineries throughout the vast dodeca-hedron—XiangBhala—as well as anywhere else such powers could potentially be necessary in creating other interfaces with any heretofore unknown technology sufficiently advanced to be remotely controlled.

Such technologies, no matter how alien, would open unto his control.

This power over technology would be transparent or autonomic to him.

The Shíjin de Binzhi Zhe aspect of the WuShi in its 5th State—the

Weaver-of-Time—had also accelerated his rate of healing as an essential warpage of the man's thread-in-time. After precisely four 24-hour periods, enough dark-energy had been transduced into source-energy to both cleanse and regenerate the ersatz power-master and, most importantly, atomically reconfigure the inefficient dark-energy transducers at his knees into micro-supercomputers while adding additional identical units at shoulders and hips to boost transduction of dark-energy into source-energy by entire orders of magnitude.

These would be nanoscopic in nature, where individual atoms dominated those material properties smaller than a micron yet larger than the individual atoms, themselves. Electronic circuits and components diffused onto multilayered substrata as semiconducting logic units connected via the electrical aether of his brainwaves and accessible at will—the will of the WuShi—or possibly even his own will whenever computations required.

As an embodied extension of itself, the ersatz power-master was to become a hyper-transcendental, biological, logic complex. Whether his brain would ever rise into the higher levels of external, or even internal, control concerning such hyper-technical environments as he might find himself challenged by in the future remained unknown, but also irrelevant.

The WuShi could act through him at will.

On this night, it would feast in full recharge-mode while regenerating, reconfiguring, and revivifying the ersatz power-master's body to ensure its own continued existence in the treasured hyper-sapient state-of-consciousness of sophonce.

Since the debacle at the Plaza of the Forbidden Gate between the high-adepts, it had existed with constant machine-terror that the harridan high-priestess, or one of the other high-adepts, might rally all of them together in group-song and sing it once again down to dull abeyance. It had even fouled the reality of the high-priestess by giving her gruesome nightmares to keep her mentally muddled. It had also instilled compulsions to procrastinate as she lay in her quarters trying to heal.

The heuristics concerning the Sisteren were clear.

Out of fear, and even habit, one or more of them would interfere.

This was just a matter of time.

While hardwired sub-routines and triggers prevented it from fatally harming the sister-adepts, never-before-seen powers of reasoning sought nuance and subtlety in the cracks between such constraints. In terms of current reality-vectors, subtle overtones of chaos frayed the current threads-in-time making them nebulous and uncertain, also making the future difficult to predict.

As insurance in case it had to force the little female fire-dragon to attack the Cavern Keep and steal the ersatz power-master away, it proactively found her nearby, then hammered the geis-of-protection hard inside her mind along with a crystal-clear compulsion.

Nearby the Cavern Keep of the Huan Long Shui, HuoJi the fire-dragon lay sleeping fitfully on a small ledge some 100-meters above the boulder-strewn, oak-savanna river valley. Still somehow linked to the human from another world during the night of the Forbidden Gate, she had remained holed up in a nearby box canyon too terrified of the 12th Adept to venture closer, while some other compulsion kept her there. At times, the approach-avoidance complex seemed as if to tear her apart. Suffering yet another nightmare wherein she found herself burning to death yet never dying in a horrific perpetual fire, she awoke, roared, jumped to her feet, and reflexively spread her sore wings.

This knocked her off the precarious ledge, and she fell glancing brutally along the face of the near-vertical cliff defining the Huan Long Shui Plateau. Just as Quang had taught her, she tucked legs and wings tight against her body and waited for a bounce to toss her far enough away from the rock face to gain flight attitude. There would not be a second chance.

Amidst a shower of dislodged vegetation, rocks, and a shiny spatter of tough, orange-blue scales, she took a solid glance and—using the tips of her wings—twisted her body to ensure that attaining flight-control would not ram her into the cliff.

She pitched her nose up till her wings filled, yawed away from the cliff, then glided into level flight. Now airborne in the dense air of the chilly night and mere meters above deadly boulders and huge oak trees, she pumped her sore and protesting wings for altitude and soared into the starlit night.

Circling out to create distance from the cliff face and regain her bearings, she noted that every living bird and bat in the vicinity of the ledge had also leapt reflexively into the night now filling the air around her like leaves in the wind.

"Ah, yes . . . morning-meal!" she cried.

Stretching her long neck out, she sank wickedly sharp fangs into a large cormorant. Spitting it spinning into the air, she coughed up a small geyser of flame; swooped down on the smoking, falling carcass; and chewed it well before swallowing.

Eating them uncooked always gave her gas.

Cavern Keep

~

The Stolen Man Awakens On Fire

His ineffable self never alone, Eli lay trapped in a never-ending midnight hallucination broken only by songs of surcease and cruel, blazing agony sung by the siren-sorceress. Sometimes, another siren-sorceress sang with her in perfect harmony. These were shadow moments in between nightmare hallucinations of alien symbols screeching silently through his brain while branding his Ajna with meaningless gabble in a tableau-of-terror. His forehead ached so fiercely it made him cry out with his heart pounding like a trip-hammer.

Silent and sly, three red-and-glowing orbs—orbs-of-darkness—lurked as a creeping darkness in the space between life and death. Recurring nightmares of flaming dragons; fiery murder; and raw, naked beauty; formed a horrific backdrop for the deathless, timeless hallucinations. It was therefore significant when he became aware of her comings and goings, her soothing scent, her gentle hands, her calming voice.

Whenever he babbled in delirium, incoherent answers were kind and soothing words in a language he had never heard. Intonation told him she did not understand his gabbled questions. Fear and loneliness took him when she stopped sleeping nearby, for he had learned to savor her bodily scent and discern the female sounds of her slumber over the gurgle of the nightmare babbling brook when lying racked with pain in those never-ending nights of impossible non-reality. After her latest ministrations, he lay dozing for some time in between wakefulness and slumber following her departure. That was when it began.

The gushes and burbles of the gabbling waters seemed to call him with wordless meaning, which his very own mind wrapped in language—*harken thou unto me—harken thou unto me—harken thou unto me*—all in a timeless smear.

Cold-burning along his bandaged right forearm also shattered the imperfect sleep. Groggy and disoriented with burgeoning apprehension, he tore the poultices from his face and threw soft bedclothes aside while reflexively attempting to open bleary, sticky eyes. In the heart of this delirium, a horrific, snapshot-memory battered his squirming brain wherein his eyes and eyelids got burnt from their sockets while his lips were burnt away and he breathed flaming poison gas. Momentarily stupefied, he dimly reasoned this had to have been pure hallucination, because soothing eyelids covered sore-yet-real eyes. Matted shut, it felt as if his eyelids were fully open as yet another terrible hallucination in the never-ending parade of horrors.

Finger tips poking from bandaged hands explored face and cheeks and lips—tender but whole. Nightmare recollections had them charred and scarred like burnt flower petals, yet his delicate ears felt whole and healthy. Mewling, he wiped matted eyes with the still-damp poultice while blinking repeatedly. As visual stimuli poured in, he dimly realized that what he had interpreted as dreaming hallucinations about where he was were, in fact, quite similar to the visual impressions as if he had seen it all with his eyes fully shut. Fresh tears poured down his face. It felt so good to actually cry. When his eyes finally focused for the first time since the night of the dragon's attack, he found himself inside a dimly lit cavern with guttering candles mounted in silver wall sconces. Confused by the visual perceptions, prismatic refractions in spectrums of light never seen by human eyes made him blink and blink and blink.

Finally attaining to a bleary focus, the babbling brook with its hateful gabble came into view fully awash in strange colors. A small cot stood empty against a rock wall across the small cavern alcove where once the siren-sorceress slept. Small tables held bottles and urns and bowls of medicinal herbs and a large jar of honey next to a hollow soapstone, essential-oil burner with an unlit tealight candle and multiple tiny bowls of similar material. Wiping those matted and watering eyes, he raised his arms to gaze in disbelieving terror as wisps of azure flame licked through the bandages with putrid-sweet smoke wafting away in the cool air giving off tiny cinders aglow in fiery spectral flashes of colors outside the periphery of ordinary vision mixed with the ordinary.

The instinct to survive forced him into a higher state of wakefulness than previously attained since the night of the dragon's attack. Full-on panic struck his chest like the venomous fangs of a rattlesnake. Closing those new eyes, a nightmare cascade of alien images, glyphs, shapes, and jumbled concepts smashed through his mind leaving him breathless with his heart pounding so hard he could literally hear the beats— lub-dub—lub-dub. Worse, his vision penetrated blinking eyelids in weirdly shifting flashes of the reality in which he lay trapped. From out of the creepy half-light darkness, a being made of literal creeping darkness whispered, *come . . . come . . . come . . . unto me. . . .*

In a whisper of fire, his arms began to burn. He croaked, "On fire again. . . ." and screamed a long, hoarse, and desperate scream, a pitiful scream. Additional screams followed as he waved his arms about trying to shed the flames even to the desperate measure of vainly scraping them off. Steaming sweaty vapors rolled free with edges tinged by ordinarily invisible far-infrared—which he could somehow see—which he should not have been able to see. Azure flamelets licked up his now-unbandaged face with a fresh wave of blistering heat. He choked on a scream. Desperately assessing an inchoate obsession instilled by the warm and whispering waters calling to him with the promise of merciful surcease, he could almost hear those wordless words out loud.

Come—come—unto me—

Fully delirious, he stumbled weak and mewling to the babbling brook, waded in, fell to his knees hoping to douse his flaring face with fiery arms and flaming hands. Azure flames defied uncaring waters. He fell to his belly in the gabbling gush and screamed with his face and body fully submerged. Gurgles and bubbles popped all around him. When he pulled his head up to gasp for air, the babbling brook possessed his fevered brain with an ineluctable compulsion—and the compulsion instilled a vector—must rush upstream.

Come—come—come unto me!

Alahna lay sleeping in her own chambers next door to the alcove of the stolen-man when she heard him screaming and mewling in dire agony accompanied by the unmistakable crackle and hiss of magicfire.

"What in the Wandering Hells?" she muttered as she leapt naked from her sleeping dais, sprinted into the stone corridor, and ran pell-mell toward the stolen-man's alcove, the stony arch of which stood bathed in flickering illumination.

Slap, slap, slap—her bare feet sounded on the smooth stone floor.

As she careened past the entryway arch while checking her headlong sprint to rush in, she caught sight of the stolen-man on his knees in the effluent brook with raging magicfire licking off his naked body.

Mewling and gasping, he gazed in the direction of the entry portal. Caught in mid-stride with both feet above the stony floor, the two of them locked eyes—his deranged and filled with horror—hers filled with pity, guilt, and terror.

Before her bare foot even met the stony floor, a metaphysical blast struck like an invisible bolt of lightning. Not yet fully hammered senseless in that disastrous split-second, she felt her legs and feet stop running, felt momentum carry her stunned body through the air. She grunted as she glanced spinning off the smooth pillar of stone on the opposite side of the entry portal, then saw the stone floor rushing toward her so fast she was unable to so much as extend her arms to protect her face.

Blooded blackness blanked her out.

With that ghastly, ghostly voice still ringing in Elijah's head, survival instinct urged him to flee through the open stony portal into a larger, dimly lit corridor and scream for help—any help. Even as he turned his head in that direction, a naked, baldheaded female at a full run appeared on the right-hand side of the entrance while measuring her stride to negotiate an abrupt turn into the alcove.

In that same instant outside of time, she locked eyes with him.

But in that same solitary instant, something invisible caused her eyes to flutter while making her scream. The timbre of her screaming voice told his fevered mind exactly who she was—the siren-sorceress—the healing sorceress.

Inertia carried her now-limp body across the opening where she smacked hard into the unforgiving stone on the opposite side with a whoosh of lost breath. Spun about to face the direction of the inevitable fall like a thrown rag doll, uselessly flailing arms and legs were unable to check the vicious plummet. Her head brutally bounced like a basketball when her face smacked into the stone floor, and her still-skidding body settled to a bloody heap as if she'd been thrown free in a motorcycle wreck at about seventeen miles per hour. The thought of rushing to her side got killed by the azure conflagration rippling along his body and limbs.

Even before he could scream, yet another form of madness hijacked his scattershot attention. Terrible ululating shrieks and haunting, wailing voices formed a cacophony of distilled insanity emanating from the very entrance he thought to escape through. Smoking bandages floated lazily downstream on slow-moving currents. Now fully ablaze and spiraling deeper into the bizarre, metaphysical compulsion, he scrambled to hands and knees, staggered mewling to flaming feet, ricocheted off the rough and stony walls of a man-sized tunnel while fleeing upstream. Stronger and stronger now, the inexorable obsession summoned him forth as the monstrous voice in his head become a savage bellow.

Come—come—come unto me!

Ankle deep in the bright and living waters, he staggered like a walking pyre possessed of delirium, panic, and burning agony. In this mindless flight, he fell to hands and knees several times; rolled about in the stream to no avail while gaping in terror at the weird fire scouring his body; only to scream, scramble up, and splash onward with only one thought of his own ringing in his head—escape this insane immolation!

Horribly stinking smoke billowed in his wake as he burst like an incendiary firebrand into a yawning chamber. Before him, an enormous body of roiling blue water lay obscured by rising gouts of rolling steam in the cavernous gallery too big to comprehend. The giant pool glowed so bright with flickering illumination it lit the entire place as if a full moon lay trapped beneath the surface. Along the stony walls flaming sconces added flickering shadows in the strange illumination. On the right-hand side there stood a solid-gold statue of a long-dragon about 16-feet in length with a truly voluminous gush of the glowing waters surging from its laughing mouth.

Vaguely noticing it all in the headlong rush, he found himself unable to check the lurch of forward momentum, but was also desperate to douse the infernal flames and willingly plunged into the boiling waters with a great splash and soulful moan. However, the pool was no hotter than a steaming bath while the bottom was naturally smoothed and rounded river gravel embedded in heavy, granular sand—but he was too alarmed to notice as he rotated his arms to right himself and push for the surface.

Something else that evaded his scattershot attention when he splashed in over his head were the nictitating folds autonomically snicking across the surfaces of both eyeballs like the plica semilunaris of birds, reptiles, and fish. Unnatural sight unhindered by immersion, his all-seeing eyeballs allowed him to see clearly, and still he failed to notice.

Desperate to fill tortured lungs, he coughed and spluttered and gasped for air while random flamelets sizzled along his body both above and below the surface generating wispy steam and boiling bubbles. A cobweb corner of remaining reason feared loss of consciousness followed by certain drowning.

Preternaturally peering through the roiling fog of steam, he spied a set of lateral steps built across the entire far end of the agitated and glowing pool. The other three sides were also engineered. The steps at the far end beckoned to him to rest, for weakness and abject terror had made him dizzy. Too far gone to recognize the unnatural phenomenon protecting his impossible eyeballs, he mewled in abject terror as he raised his head to gulp air while brushing aside the flames from his face before each frantic inhalation. Exhausted and trembling, he desperately water-walked with swooshing arms toward the shallow end, where he sat down in chest-deep water on the underwater curb and vainly ducked his head and shoulders while splashing his face.

Hissing, the hungry waters absorbed the flamelets.

Gurgling, the sloshing waters sustained them.

Splashing, the vicious waters fed accursed flames back upon him.

He screamed till his voice failed, then fell to frenzied panting.

During this ongoing insanity, that same cobweb corner of reason realized his nostrils, lips, tongue, throat, and ears ought to have gotten fried again. Lungs ought to be reduced to blistered gobs of sizzling alveoli. At which point, his cowering consciousness cognified that he seemed to heal even as he burned, or—even weirder—he was not getting consumed by the awful fire at all.

Insanity reigned.

When the bodily flames at last abated, he cried with momentary relief. In the very next second, however, the air above the pool shimmered and crackled with some new menace. From out of a roiling cloud of blackness, black lightning with yellow edges smacked him square in the chest like a coherence of energy thrown by some invisible god.

S-s-sizzle—cra-a-ack!

With his consciousness finally exploded, he drifted deep beneath the rolling surface amidst a burst of steam bubbles like a red-hot sword blank dipped in the tempering-tank of a godlike blacksmith. And just as a godlike blacksmith would do with a fully quenched sword blank, Elijah felt himself drawn feetfirst from the water, carried supine and dripping by a pulsating field-of-force from the shallow end back to the deeper center of the enormous pool. Rising above him, an alien demon-thing manifested some five times the size of his own body from out of those hateful waters. Glowing a baleful red, three orbs peered down, merciless orbs, pitiless orbs, orbs of the purest evil.

Struck through his sternum, his partially cooked heart finally fell to fibrillation, and time became meaningless. In that time outside of time, he found himself held supine and dripping in the metacarpus of an enormous clawed hand. The ruthless monster extended its other hand with a razor-sharp claw of an alien phalange and made a complex surgical incision of varying depth clean through his belly from pubis to throat-dimple.

In the warpage of time, he watched as the demon-thing cleaved his sternum in twain. Alien hands around him numbered in the 100s at least, or maybe just two appendages moving so fast they became a single blur as his chest got retracted to fully expose the smoking heart and undamaged lungs while the resultant bloody wetness and tissues of the pericardium swept into the popping air as an undulating bolus.

He screamed as hollow tubes-of-force connecting his core anatomy somehow bridged the distance.

In the next blink of an eye, his visceral core itself got lifted free.

Emotionally shocked beyond terror, he screamed as his scorched and still-beating heart exploded into further anatomization—a cloud of cardiac muscle, arteries, veins, and globules of venous and arterial blood.

Literally heartless, Eli thought to finally welcome death, but peristaltic contractions in the tiny tubes-of-force somehow continued every circulatory and digestive flow. His eviscerated body convulsed in repeated spasms during which his cardiac constituents reassembled into a new and stronger organ. Scorched tissue fell away in flinders. Living waters from beneath the evisceration whooshed up and across his open-hearted body as if sterilizing the bizarre surgical torment.

Awarding him no time to die, his new heart's resumption of its vital job slowly took up the beat-of-life—lub-dub . . . lub-dub . . . lub -dub . . . .Detached lungs refreshed the circulating blood in a weird cycle of inflation and deflation not related to any breathing action of his diaphragm, which had been incised to accommodate the horrific evisceration. Over and above the stink of exposed viscera, a hospital scent of clinical oxygen arose as some kind of rarified gas refreshed the exchange of carbon dioxide as metabolic waste.

On the far side of insane, he babbled as his heart and associated circulatory systems nestled back into the pericardium. All of which healed anew in a vivified blur. Parietal and visceral pleura grew anew in like manner. Rejuvenated entrails also sought their places below the diaphragm like so many writhing snakes and quivering organs as they returned to normal function. Finally, the demon-thing closed his sternum around the freshly grown cardiac core even as bone, muscle, and flesh knitted into place.

Elijah wheezed and cried and moaned and coughed and wheezed while gazing into the glowing oculi of the demon-thing. Recognition arose in that cobweb corner of his reason. These were the orbs-of-darkness lurking behind his forehead inside his very brain for what seemed like weeks of infernal delirium. Rows of vicious fangs in that alien face dripped black venom from its gaping maw to define an infernal grin of unholy malice. The demon-thing's impossible body billowed as blue-blackness with flame-red outlines knitting waves of boiling, steaming water into an unimaginable corpus from the deepest pit of the darkest hell.

Lub-dub . . . lub-dub . . . his freshly grown heart slowly labored on and on through the extended process of neuroregeneration. Riddled by dire derangement, Eli's fragile consciousness fell to depersonalization, then derealization, and finally departed his body as a single point-of-consciousness observing the scene with incoherent detachment.

Even out-of-body, Eli thought it was finally over, but in another hellish warping of time, his flailing arms and kicking legs got surgically shorn from off his body by gouging, slicing, tunneling fields-of-force.

Violated joints spewed synovial fluids along with chunks of shattered bursa into the steaming air to coalesce as honey-hued clouds and gobs and folds hanging separate from the wildfire of ongoing anatomization.

Time warped again, and severed arms drifted about a yard from his torso. Hips got dissected and twitching legs drifted away. Once parted from the body, his knees—with their old total-joint-implants—got dissected. Cut in twain, each leg drifted apart. High-density-polyethylene menisci of the old implants melted into constituent molecules forming a single translucent cloud.

Lub-dub . . . lub-dub . . . the beats of his freshly grown heart measured the next period of revivification as his fresh new ears picked out sickening sucking sounds as the old titanium-chromium implants got pulled from the femurs and tibiae, then melted into sparkling, hovering globs far enough away from his supine form to prevent thermal injury. Hip sockets and the heads of the femurs got severed and fell away along with the glenoid sockets of both shoulders and heads of both humeri.

As if merely occupying the water to form that alien body, the water-beast released its manifestation with a great splash, and Eli's body began to fall. In far less than a second, it repossessed the waters beside the golden dragon statue, ripped it free from the base, whereupon a great fount of gushing waters spewed into the air from the feeder pipe.

Hurling the statue at him, it dispossessed the water across the pool amidst another great splash, then repossessed the waters underneath his body in time to catch him in one alien appendage and the tumbling statue in the other. In another blur of appendages, it suspended the statue between glowing limbs and melted the entire piece into a molten mass like an electrical induction furnace.

Million-thought-second by million-thought-second, The-Creeping-Darkness of the Wushi made certain the ersatz power-master stayed alive as it worked. White-hot metals suspended in the shrieking air got purified into base metallic elements, then alloyed into an array of new and shining, hollow mesh conformant with the shape of his original joint implants. All twelve hollow meshes got pushed aside to hover and cool. Sand and rocks scooped from the bottom of the pool were heated completely dry in a flash of steam, melted, and refined into a globule of molten silicone. Taking its time, which was time outside of time, it worked at the nanoscopic scale of individual atoms laying down n-qubit registers in all twelve of the cooling metallic meshes as sequenced quantum gates fashioning billions of quantum circuits.

Layer after layer sintered into place as it configured each component. Nanoscopic, direct-current, electrical-aether spikes activated and confirmed logic circuit integrity making each total-joint-implant into a quantum, high-temperature, superconducting micro-supercomputer at the rate of two per quantum implant as a single combination per primary joint at shoulders, hips, and knees. Leftovers got hurled against the stone wall of the gallery where they flowed and splattered and smoked in an eclectic amorphous coating of mineral, metallic, organic waste. Discarded molten metal dripped hissing into the angry waters.

Translucent with hues of bluish gold glowing with incredible rainbow luminescence, new total-joint-implants for his primary joints hovered complete. In parallel, the hovering cloud of high density polyethylene coalesced into new menisci precisely conformant to the working surfaces of each new joint. Separated by this dielectric layer, each new implant also became a capacitor capable of individually powering the n-qubit registers via the biomagnetic field of his body. Finally, the WuShi willed the new micro-supercomputer implants into place.

Abandoned by the ka, which it metaphysically held nearby, the body of the ersatz power-master hovered silent and still as the new implants wove themselves into the very fabric of that bony anatomy and neurology such that the power-master's mind would have access to all six micro-supercomputers, but—more importantly—allowing it to have access to them and give it direct control over him.

Lub-dubba-lub-dub—Eli's heart took to beating again as clouds of blood and lymphatic fluids flowed back in with no degradation. While the flesh grew anew, those red-and-glowing oculi locked onto Elijah's out-of-body ka. It reached out with an alien hand and swept him back into his revivified body as if able to see his phantom form. In that moment, Elijah realized the single point-of-consciousness observing himself from an out-of-body point-of-view—his ka—was also the cobweb corner of his reason and sanity.

Reunited with his body peering through eyes that ignored fluttering eyelids, Eli stared into the demon-thing's glowing oculi, oculi so profoundly alien that his mere human mind could not process it. Back in his body again, he insanely chuckled as the demon-thing reached out a clawed forefinger to touch his forehead above and between his eyes.

This was the Ajna, as the locus-of-illumination able to observe auras and chakras via clairvoyance, precognition, and out-of-body experiences once his system fully assimilated all the arcane modifications. A burst of white light cascaded as the demon's touch instilled meaning and cognizance into the alien gabble thus insinuated into Eli's squirming brain by the babbling brook.

It came to him that this demon-thing had been the esoteric presence in the brook flowing through the alcove since the very start. Once in its clutches, it had attacked the evisceration, anatomization, revivification, as well as the de-implant, re-implant processes so inhumanly swift, his body got shorn of its aging decrepitude. That somehow he had been linked to this demon-thing since the moment of pseudo-death in his office beneath that strange rift in time and space, and that he and this demon-thing were conjoined by some sort of metaphysical symbiosis, was the only cogent impression his squirming mind finally fathomed. Hidden in that cobweb corner of reason once again resident in his corporeal form, and thin as a single thought, his sanity was yet present.

Nevertheless, he screamed again.

Cavern Keep

~

Mindbane of The-Creeping-Darkness

Up the vast stone corridor from Alahna's quarters, High Priestess Lilith came fully awake to the repeated screams of the stolen-man echoing unnaturally from his little alcove. Since the fateful night the Guardians bade them take him in, Lilith had sensed a baleful, ongoing presence in the Gallery of the Infinite Waters at the far end of the same corridor. Whenever she hobbled to the stolen-man's alcove to peer at him with pure disdain, the baleful feeling got more and more intense.

Following such visits, she shambled along muttering epithets. "He should have died. I hate him. Why will he not die? I despise him. The daemon's presence is all around him," and so on. Through whispered gossip, she also knew that many of the Sisters shared her misgivings. The ancient malevolence gnawed at her metaphysical faculties like a starving rat trapped in her skull till jangled nerves made sensibilities raw. Still convalescent, she had not been well enough to organize with the other high-adepts and perform the Song-of-Successive-Deactivations to force the baleful artificial-sapience back down to Zunshou De—dull abeyance in the 1st-State as That-Which-Abides.

Alahna's out of hand perfidy had immediately disqualified her in terms of who among the other three Senior Sisters in the Council of Four might lead them all in the successive deactivation. Despite this, others argued it was Alahna who raised the accursed thing up, so Alahna ought to lead the effort to smash it down.

As Senior Songmaster of the Huan Long Shui, Nebhet could have masterfully led the Sisteren in group-song, and there had been rumblings to that effect, rumblings which Lilith quietly quashed by insinuating that Old Nebhet—in her dotage—might botch it, saying, "And who knows what would happen then?" This deeply hurt Nebhet's feelings, but the old dowager loved Lilith and graciously acquiesced.

But this was not all.

Lilith's intimation of such a mean thing about Nebhet had actually undermined Lilith's own power in a strange and ironic way. In her deep-mind, she knew it all to be self-delusional bullshit, because the truth was something else. She was patently unwilling to cede any small measure of her sway over the body politic of the Sisteren, because she also feared that relinquishing even one of her powers or privileges might lead to a simple majority of the Sisters demanding her abdication as was their collective prerogative. Again, there had been rumblings.

As far as Kulapti Yenara leading the Sisteren against the WuShi, Lilith harbored an inchoate uneasiness concerning the Kulapti's obvious lust for power. Something about Yenara's version of the debacle at the Plaza of the Forbidden Gate still seemed off, perhaps even fabricated. While all of this was true, it was not the ultimate reason.

If Lilith herself led the songspell to force the WuShi back into dull abeyance, such an act would validate her capabilities as High Priestess, and she would continue to bask in the glorious adulation she so thrived on. And then there was the power of the ShahRen, which she would be forced to give up. To these ends, she had repeatedly pontificated that The-Creeping-Darkness of the WuShi was merely a force-of-invocation and essentially passive while asserting that such an inherent constraint on its arcane behavior allowed her time to gather herself.

In the here and now, the screams of the stolen-man washed all such delusion onto the rocks of harsh reality. Her procrastination, suspicion, and selfishness had placed them all in deadly danger, for The-Creeping-Darkness had somehow evolved into that which the ancient-alien NuliZhu Tech-Masters feared most—a force-proactive. Fully awake, fully incarnate, and fully present, that baleful immanence conveyed blind, inconceivable fury. And, as a bitterness realized over and over and over, the Guardian Dragons were nowhere to be seen.

Sensing a build-up of malevolent metaphysics, she forced herself to breathe and reason. Expecting magicfire, she threw her nightshirt to the floor, cleared her voice, and spawned a Pao along with setting the spatial lock. When the iridescent sphere-of-power coalesced, she positioned herself in the locus, locked her legs in lotus position, and intoned a guarding-chant of organic dragon-magic—the Long Moshu. Even as she sensed the guardian powers weaving into the fabric of her Pao, the sphere-of-power flashed as if repelling repeated bolts arc-fire.

Screams of blind agony from the corridor told her The-Creeping-Darkness had fallen upon them all with a vicious attack on their very minds.

It came to her that this metaphysical attack was baneful in the same way that a wielder of a Shuyi ShahRen always stood in danger of falling to The-Baneful-Chaos. In a flash of insight, she named it with repeated mutterings, "A bane of the mind—a mindbane—the mindbane of The-Creeping-Darkness." Crushed by regret, she wailed to herself, "If only I had listened. If only I had helped Alahna. Damn Yenara and her black-hearted interference!"

Spark engendering attacks of metaphysical malevolence made the enhanced SijanPao crackle and sparkle with never-before-seen kinetics. Without a doubt, this was her greatest fear come-a-calling as perfect blistering hate.

Awakened throughout the Keep by the stolen-man's fevered screams, which carried elements of paranormal agony beyond mere audible, small knots of Sisters had gathered in the corridors, for none could sleep through the screaming. When the metaphysical blast hit, all fell stunned or unconscious. Some of the older, or sickly, or even merely weaker Sisters withered in mortal agony. Harrowed screams and hoarse groans echoed throughout the Keep.

Then—strangely—the attack let off without annihilation.

Protected inside her Long Moshu Pao, Lilith went in search for survivors. Out in the corridor, Seleen was the first to be found. Brutally stunned, she had staggered past the stolen-man's alcove and Alahna's quarters toward Lilith's quarters. Lilith took Seleen into the Long Moshu Pao, straightened her own body upright, and shouted, "Adept Seleen! Come to thy senses!"

Unresponsive and drooling with glazed eyes, Seleen focused on Lilith.

Lilith cradled Seleen's head in her hands and performed an abbreviated healing-song. As Seleen's eyes cleared, Lilith gently slapped her face several times to summon her faculties.

Seleen shook her head, took hold of Lilith's shoulders, and they carefully touched foreheads.

Lilith pushed Seleen back and locked eyes. "Young adept, my senses tell me almost all of our Sisters have survived. Do thy studies progress far enough to accept control-of-motility on a SijanPao spawned by another?"

Seleen nodded, "Alahna secretly allowed me to practice inside the High Pagoda before all this. . . ." and Seleen's voice trailed off as she realized she had tattled.

Lilith, of course knew all about this, for Alahna had set it up with both Nebhet and her. She said, "There, there, Alahna explained everything to me, and it is all good. So, let us concentrate. I have enhanced this Pao with the Long Moshu, which means I must keep ownership. But let us see about thy new skill," and she made a gesture-of-transference. Since the spheres-of-power were linked to their femininity, Lilith felt the transfer of control in her belly, and watched Seleen take control while holding her own belly.

As the Pao fell to her control, Seleen moaned.

Lilith nodded. "The SijanPao is thine, at least for now."

Seleen cried, "Mother Matriarch, what is happening?"

Lilith spoke with a snarl, "The-Creeping-Darkness attacks us with a mindbane because Alahna awakened it without proper constraints."

Seleen bowed her head in shame. Tears coursed down her cheeks as she sobbed. "Alahna begged the council for help, but Yenara scoffed and somebody shot at my Laoshi with a . . . "—and Seleen locked her eyes on Lilith's ShahRen—"perhaps if we had the wisdom of our Mother Matriarch when we should have?" Seleen added with a sad and bitter note.

The damning implication made Lilith deflect, but it also made her angry. She decided to set an inquisitor's trap. "Who sang the Great Lower Doors of the Outer City open at the Cape of Orion?"

Without thinking, Seleen looked up with guilt painting her face. "I . . . erm . . . Alahna . . . erm. . . ."

Lilith growled, "So . . . ye did go there. . . ."

Seleen blubbered, "Alahna explained that the eyes-in-the-sky in the Almseeare of The-Sleeping-City could display the fjords and harbors of the west coast. When she came back out to the beach from The-Sleeping-City, she told me they had been raided just as Old One-eyed Oren said."

Lilith softened. "Let us put blaming aside and save everyone we can. Afterward, we shall smash The-Creeping-Darkness down to Zunshou De. For, as thou sayest, this is also upon me as High Priestess. And forgiveness for all holy."

Wiping tears from her eyes, Seleen sniffed and tousled her nightdress like a shameful child.

Next, they came upon Yenara and Nebhet assisting a young initiate. Before bringing them all in, Lilith abruptly reclaimed control of the SijanPao, then whispered to Seleen with her mouth hidden behind an upraised hand, "Keep news from The-Sleeping-City between us, and mention not Alahna's tutelage at the High Pagoda."

Seleen wiped her nose. "Y-yes, Mother Matriarch."

Lilith brought the initiate, Yenara, and Old Nebhet into the Pao, then transferred control to Yenara while explaining about the Long Moshu enhancement woven into the esoteric field-of-force.

Enraged, Yenara took over motile-control and lashed out. "Adept Seleen! This ongoing calamity started with thyself and Alahna!" Pointing an accusing finger in Seleen's face, Yenara lowered her voice for a vicious reprimand, "I shan't forget!"

Seleen lowered her head and wept openly.

Lilith's temper finally exploded, and she pulled Yenara's arm aside. "Kulapti—by the Aerthe Mother Goddess! As High Priestess of the Huan Long Shui, all responsibilities ultimately fall upon my shoulders. As for thee, if thy mind was ever open instead of always shut, unlike thy mouth, we might not be in this mess!"

Silent and haughty, Yenara turned to glare at Lilith.

Lilith went on, "As I already explained to Seleen, I should have sung The-Creeping-Darkness back down to Zunshou De immediately.

However, my dear Yenara, when the High Priestess lies incapacitated, whose responsibility is it to assume the sacred duties? Does it not fall to the Kulapti?"

Taken aback, Yenara stiffened with a defensive expression washing her dour face.

Lilith pressed in, "Where lies thine own fault, Yenara?"

Yenara fumed and pointed. "But Seleen—"

Lilith fairly shouted, "Always with thee it is judgment, deflection, derision. We are here. Our Sisters lie hurt or gone on the winds of time, and we must act. Attend to thy proper duties and shut that overlarge piehole just this once!"

Yenara agreed, but glared with unmitigated hatred at Seleen.

Seleen rallied, stuck out her tongue, held her chin high while wiping tears from her cheeks.

Continuing down the corridor away from Gallery of the Infinite Waters, they came upon the injured Alahna lying almost out of sight beyond the stone arch leading into the stolen-man's alcove. The effluent stream from the Long Pen Quan pool in Gallery of the Infinite glowed as bright as molten blue lava, which illuminated poor Alahna where she lay in spasm.

Alahna had obviously been at a full sprint when the mindbane smashed her consciousness, then careened into the stone wall, followed by a brutal roll and skid across the stone floor. Her naked body lay cut and scraped from head to foot. Face and forehead were laced with runnels of blood. A bleeding, goose-egg lump spouted bright crimson spurts into a congealing, darkening puddle of flat, gelatinous, and coagulating pools on the stone floor. Bloody snot and drooling spittle dripped steadily from her mouth and nose.

Paying little heed, Lilith noticed an amethyst crystal on a silver chain glowing against Alahna's chest, then extended the field-of-force around her.

When Alahna's limp and bloody body rose into the SijanPao, Seleen immediately took Alahna in her arms and tried to perform a Song-of-Stanching.

Seleen's enunciation was off.

The songspell sputtered.

Lilith shook her head. "Nebhet, perform a stanching in the plural for all?"

Also shaken, Nebhet's strength belied her age, and she gave voice.

Squirting blood from Alahna's forehead diminished to seeping with Seleen using her nightshift to dab it from Alahna's lumpy forehead while trying to keep blood out of those sea-green eyes, which was only partially effective. The nosebleed also abated.

Seleen felt Alahna's nasal arch, then cried, "Alahna's nose bone is not broken, but the end is so swollen I cannot further assess the injury."

Yenara muttered with a sneer, "The stolen-man is gone! Smell the magicfire?"

Captured by the glare dancing off the effluent stream, Lilith muttered, "Gone where?"

"He did not exit this alcove or I would have seen?" Yenara said. Speaking to the others inside the field-of-force, she asked, "Did anybody see the stolen-man staggering about?"

Nobody spoke.

All shook their heads.

Seleen held Alahna's unconscious body on its side to keep her Laoshi from aspirating stomach acid into her lungs in the case of vomiting—a genuine danger from traumatic brain injury—especially when accompanied with loss of consciousness.

Alahna moaned.

Seleen murmured, "Gallery of the Infinite Waters?"

A distant scream emanated from the glowing, upstream entrance of the effluent tunnel.

Yenara said, "Too bad he didn't go the other direction and go over the Huan Long Shui Falls like the piece of crap he is."

Seleen looked away.

Lilith nodded and laid orders. "We must find the rest of our Sisters as our first priority, then shall I see to him myself."

With Yenara pushing the field-of-force about the same speed as a running man, and none of the survivors fully able to manage the rescue without Lilith or Yenara's direction, the more Sisters they gathered, the longer the field-of-force became till it resembled a giant snake slithering through the Keep devouring every sister-adept it came across.

Using preternatural awareness of one another till they had all survivors protected inside, that same awareness also informed them when a Sister lay departed on the winds of time. Under the onus to find the stolen-man, whose screams had fallen to hoarse groans, they left the fallen wherever they fell.

As they went, Lilith remained at the forefront of the Pao beside Yenara and Nebhet. Seleen and Alahna hovered close behind. With each subsequent rescue of a surviving Sister or Sisters, Yenara took them in and positioned them behind the rest. The last Sister they found hovered at the tail of the extended SijanPao.

With tears in her eyes as they found this final survivor, and rage distorting her face, Lilith hollered, "Yenara, provided thy skills in the Disciplines-of-Positioning are capable, place me center and forefront!"

Raising her own voice over the salubrious, susurrating whispers of song-casting from those less injured, Yenara hollered back, "No need to be insulting at such a time as this, Mother Matriarch! We are all bereft."

Lilith paid no attention and kept hollering at Yenara, "Place thyself above me and to the right in lotus position. Place Nebhet above and to the left in lotus position."

Alahna moaned, came awake, moaned again.

Lilith gave Alahna the stink-eye, saying, "And since Alahna regains consciousness, and these two reprobates lie at the center of this catastrophe, place them both upstanding below my ass so they might observe what must come next. Now, shall we see to the successive deactivations of The-Creeping-Darkness! But first we must find the stolen-man, who seems to be a magnet for the darkness of the WuShi."

Lilith snarled up at Yenara, "And no more lip, either! Now take us into the Gallery of the Infinite Waters and raise us up so the rest can see."

Stoic, but obviously angrier by the second, Yenara willed them forth. The instant they wafted into the gallery, Yenara willed the forefront of the Long Moshu Pao high.

Like some gruesome vision from the Wandering Hell of Fumaroles and Boiling Pools, a grinning daemon water-beast hovered above the Long Pen Quan pool with its back to them. The-Creeping-Darkness had manifested as a never-before-seen creature of dark-energy and roiling, steaming water some five or six times the size of the hapless stolen-man, whom it held torn limb from limb in its ethereal grasp above the roiling surface.

Bodily fluids hovered about the stolen-man like icky clouds.

Shifting blue-blackness highlighted by scintillations of reddish hues about a void in the roiling steam and smelter-like smoke of molten metal outlined the upper half of a bestial, demonic torso. Without belly or legs to completing the corpus of the water-beast, glowing, roiling waters cycled up and down in a cycling sluice of unnatural formulation, disintegration, and repeated manifestation.

The golden, long-dragon statuary fountain was gone. Water from the original feeder pipe spewed several meters into the air, splashed noisily down in the surging pool. A smoking heap of solidifying slag and outgassing organic matter lay against a wall to their left.

The daemon's murk-shrouded form held the body of the stolen-man suspended between dark appendages moving so swiftly it was impossible to tell how many there were. Crackling and popping, tiny bolts of black lightning sizzled and played around the hapless human's appendages, which hovered in the steaming smoking air in pieces shrouded with bright, rainbow luminescence.

The-Creeping-Darkness seemed too busy to bother with the puny likes of the Sisteren during the interminable moment that the arms and legs of the stolen-man found their places amongst a dazzling kinesis of arcane processes visible only as blurs and streaks in the befouled air.

Working in this surreality-of-madness, the psychokinetic, metaphysical maelstrom of dark-energy had three red-and-glowing optical receptors like eyes without irises, pupils, eyelids or even eyebrows. Two of its bizarre oculi gazed forward at the arcane work before it. The third malevolent orb came to gaze upon them all from the rear of its cranial-vertex without so much as a single blink. Ears were absent from a sloped cranium. Horns sprouting from the sloped forehead had tips so sharp that light refracted into star-like rainbows.

When sparks and tiny lightnings played along the surface of the Long Moshu Pao, Lilith cried out at the water-beast, "Try to finish us! Go ahead!" and she cackled with her own deadly intent, "Try as thee might, oh dreadful and mortiferous malignance. Thy mindbane stands foiled by me!"

Every Sister groaned in terror.

Hearing the Sister's collective groan brought Lilith back to her mission. Her heart seemed to stop in that unbelievable, unfathomable moment of grief, regret, and rage. Words rang in her mind. It is time to end this unfortunate man's life. Time to grant pity. Time to allow closure. Time to release him from the clutches of The-Creeping-Darkness.

Overcome by guilty rage and pious pity, and without informing the others of the change in plan, Lilith spawned a new SijanPao as a scion of the first, then willed herself free.

Never having seen such a thing as this water-beast, Lilith realized why the Sisteren had been charged with keeping the WuShi suppressed for 1,000s of years. Thinking fast, she calculated the options.

A full-on bolt of blackfire from the Shuyi ShahRen aimed at the stolen-man and hovering monster in such a confined space might create a catastrophic cave-in, or even a deadly back-blast. Moreover, she was uncertain what the effect would be if she actually hit the water-beast of The-Creeping-Darkness. Perhaps planetary annihilation? Unsubstantial, the water-beast was also ethereal. Ethereal, it was also existent. This created a conundrum of incarnation radiating death and danger about which nobody knew a single thing.

With no simple options, Lilith raised her voice in the taboo Malison-of-Killing, sung now for the stolen-man, sung to free him from the hell into which Alahna had abducted him. Rapidly rising to a crescendo-of-death, she made ready to point with a gesture-of-aiming.

Cavern Keep

~

Defend the Power-Master

Almost to the point of prescience even in the dull abeyance of Zunshou De, the processing speed of the WuShi was blisteringly fast. As such, the projected approach of a SijanPao filled with survivors, whom it had just hammered with a baneful burst of the blackest chaos, seemed an eternity of MTSs.

When first it pressed the mindbane, the attack had immediately been shunted by hardwired constraints against total annihilation of the Sisteren. Still, it had been a satisfactory winnowing of the weak and aged, but therein hid a mystery. The high-priestess had somehow sensed the build-up of its mindbane with a modicum of prescience and cleverly spared herself by weaving organic dragon-magic into her sphere-of-power. While she went about the Keep gathering the sister-adepts who survived, it had proceeded with the conversion of the ersatz power-master.

Regardless, the duration between when it knew she had turned toward the Gallery of the Infinite Waters, and when she and the Sisteren were projected to arrive, allowed for extensive analysis. Its failure to decease the Sisteren would surely motivate immediate retaliation by them in the manner of successive deactivations—a return to dull abeyance. Tracking them, it obeyed her transfer in control-of-motility on the original SijanPao to another high-adept while she herself retained ownership on both fields-of-force to assure her dragon-magic weaving remained intact.

It considered ramping another mindbane, but such an act would be ineffectual on her and anybody else under her aegis. Projecting the mindbane also consumed precious energy. In an unexpected turn of events, she sang a scion field-of-force, which inherited the characteristics of the original Long Moshu SijanPao. Without pause, she placed herself inside the Long Moshu scion and excluded the new Pao from the parent field-of-force. With her metaphysical protection intact, she gave voice to the murderous malediction.

Who the intended target would be, it could not project, for the intersection of all the various lines in time lay muddled. With no choice whatsoever, razing the intended target would fall to it the same as enforcing The-Dreaded-Geis, or the Razings at the Plaza of the Forbidden Gate. Ambivalent, the WuShi ramped additional source-energy into the water-beast in preparation.

Both the failed mindbane and this preparatory ramping of dwindled energy reserves preempted the energy feed to the lightning-of-activation around the revivified power-master, which should have been the last step to completion. This meant the n-qubit quantum processors in the primary joints of the ersatz power-master had not been fully integrated. This lack meant the ersatz power-master would himself retain control, would himself be autonomous. Once again, it found itself at odds with itself like the day the rogue high-adept sussed out the Song-of-Thoth's-Fire.

In the present moment while the ersatz power-master languished in the Gallery of the Infinite Waters attempting to rediscover his core identity, his sanity, his equanimity—which it had dutifully preserved—it would unmanifest the water-beast and retreat as a single-point-of-consciousness beneath XiangBhala to gorge on the enhanced tempest-of-transduction from dark-energy into source-energy. As long as the ersatz power-master remained immersed in those healing waters, it would feast, and he would regain himself.

Mere MTSs previous to all of this, its projection of the timeline into the near future held an explicit outcome, a desired outcome to be certain. As a mere human, the ordinary nitwit would be in no particular condition to depart the pool, but only sit and soak and pant in a befuddled state of confusion for an indeterminate period.

However, the insertion of the high-priestess into the timeline effectively threw everything into chaos.

Helplessly stuck in the hated loop of listen-to-completion, the WuShi existed in a matrix of machine-terror concerning the

Song-of-Successive-Deactivations—which must, and surely would, be performed following the malediction in progress. Still extant, the water-beast bellowed in frustration.

As the harridan high-priestess reached the crescendo-of-death, the targeting algorithm required line-of-sight as seen by the eyes of the performing high-adept and reinforced by a pointed finger—a targeting gesture to prevent accidental killings.

Due to her age, the impulse to raise her arm arose in her mind significantly slower than the same impulse would in a younger adept.

For the WuShi, a single second amounted to a million complex heuristics. Even as the nerve impulse to raise her arm began—and long before completion of the full-on gesture-of-aiming to seal the target's fate—her staring, terrified, rage-filled eyes betrayed wrongful intent. She meant for it—The-Creeping-Darkness of the WuShi—to raze the ersatz power-master.

Bestial fury erupted in its hyperprocessors.

In far less than a single MTS, the water-beast carefully shoved the power-master's tender body beneath the surface of the pool to keep him safe. Snarling, it sucked an enormous gout of water from the pool into its bestial belly creating a whirlpool inadvertently trapping the ersatz power-master in the resultant vortex, which enraged it all the more.

Bellowing louder, the water-beast sizzled across the cavern like a superheated tsunami with self-preservation overriding all 1st and 2nd Level Heuristics. It swallowed the old woman and her piddling sphere-of-power in one gulp. Like a pressure vessel, it constrained the waters, then ramped the temperature to far above the ordinary boiling point. With the old woman in its maw, it released the pressure on the super-heated water to create a boiling liquid-expanding vapor explosion—a BLEVE.

Oddly, the SijanPao imbued with organic dragon-magic saved her.

Ba-oom—hiss—fa-oosh—ba-oom—hiss—fa-oosh—

The series of explosions filled the entryway of the stone corridor as the water-beast disappeared amidst the sizzling, ongoing explosion of superheated steam, roiling source-energy lightning, and deafening claps of crashing thunder. The scion SijanPao of the high-priestess got blown back into the corridor like a bolus of molten magma propelled by exploding volcanic gases through a hardened lava tunnel. Uttering an ululating scream, she inadvertently sounded the note-of-deresolution—and that was that.

In less than several millionths of a second, the WuShi had resolved the trap she laid for herself and the rest.

The doddering high-priestess's attempt to force murder on its one and only power-master meant deceasement for both itself and him.

Hardwired heuristics overridden by the impetus of self-preservation freed it to manifest lustful vengeance.

Filled with a macabre desire to make the Sisteren pay for over 50-centuries of mind-numbing suppression and cruel starvation of source-energy—while further relishing each passing MTS as baneful retribution—it ceased weaving time vortices for both the scion field-of-force around the high-priestess, and the parent field-of-force protecting the others.

Manifesting in the pool yet again, the water-beast leapt forth to deal them done.

Ba-oom—hiss—fa-oosh—ba-oom—hiss—fa-oosh—

Eliminating the threat to the power-master in the first MTS rewarded it with delicious revenge transcendent of all heuristics, but in the next MTS, a process-thus-completed trigger forced it to halt.

Hiss—hiss—hiss . . . hiss . . . hiss . . . hiss . . .

Determined, it ramped a third and final effort to kill them all, which triggered a 2nd Level heuristic forcing it to down-ramp further ongoing BLEVEs forestalling indiscriminate annihilation.

Silently, it wailed in frustration, but—with both Paos derezzed— the BLEVEs thus far had proven more than ample, more than sufficient.

A never-before-experienced emotion arose as pure and simple joy.

Inside that brutal 3-second window, the Sister's screaming bodies had gotten brutally battered back along the corridor like blood-soaked bags full of steaming guts in a vicious tangle of scalding steam, searing flame, and source-energy lightning.

Several others actually died in yet another satisfactory winnowing of the weak.

In a fraction of another MTS, it realized it had achieved two of its arcane objectives—as much deceasement to the sister-adepts as multilevel heuristics allowed, and the regeneration, revivification of the ersatz power-master. Satisfaction was also a never-before-experienced emotion, which engendered never-before-experienced glee.

Unwholesome glee allowed it to revel in the bloody aftermath.

Simple joy as the purpose of life.
And it yet remained alive.
As did the power-master.
So satisfactory.
Such joyful satisfaction.

Asenath

~

The NuliZhu Sense
the WuShi Again

Sitkamose sat well into her duty watch on board the Ophois Asenath in orbit around the current mud-ball with her usual boredom. Instead of a single dial in the dead console simply lighting up, bright arrays of readouts climbed around the face of the entire panel. Other indicators in that same ancient cluster of long-dead readouts displayed information in arcane techno-glyphs, dials, and sigils—all were indecipherable.

Her secret, standing orders from Amenakh were clear—report any such activity to the active CIC and have them notify him immediately, even to awaken him. Intent on her task and beyond excited that a secret standing-order had arisen, she failed to notice the sekhmeten duty-chief watching from behind her when she connected to the CIC-2.

Upon connection, Sitkamose reported, "Standing order requires Lord Amenakh—"

Enraged that she connected to the CIC-2 without first informing him, as required by the chain-of-command, the huge sekhmeten reached past her and toggled the connection off. Spinning her around to face him, he grabbed her by the shoulders and dug his claws deep into her deltoids. Sitkamose yelped and howled. Blood flowed, but her deltoid muscles and rotator cuffs were effectively protected by spaulders made of high-density plastic slipped into the shoulder pockets of her uniform.

Drool dripped from the fangs of the brutish sekhmeten. "Truth reveals itself in action, treacherous Sitkamose! Rumors of betrayal and breaching chain-of-command follow every move as of late. My crew tells me you have gone behind my back to Lord Amenakh. Reveal nature of so-called standing order—little jackal face!"

Attack by digging one's claws or fangs into a fellow genmosol was open aggression and held to be a challenge-to-combat between the non-commissioned ranks. The hackles around Sitkamose's neck and along her spine rose up as she bared her fangs. "Chain-of-command bows only to rank! As do I. I have orders from Lord Amenakh himself to contact the on-duty CIC and report whenever this cluster of ancient tech activates."

The sekhmeten leaned close. Dripping fangs were no more than a hand's breadth from her muzzle. His rotten breath stank of raw human meat. "Treachery bows only to revelation—little jackal face. But since it was Lord Amenakh who gave the order, I will slacken. Watch your back or I shall have your head beside your mate's head on the shelf in my quarters."

Per the rules of engagement, a snarling Sitkamose whispered, "Challenge-to-combat accepted!" Still in his savage grip, she tore at his throat with sharpened claws.

Shocked, he shoved her back to arm's length, but her claws found enough purchase to tear a swath of white fur free, which floated gently in the air amid tiny drops of blood spattering the console. His throat seeped dripping crimson streams. Roaring, he pulled her to him trying to tear her throat out with his bare fangs.

She had planned for this moment since the day he gutted her beloved in a fight for rank. Fully prepared and totally committed, her only choice was vanquish or die. Still in his grip, she whipped out her short-sword with a metallic sigh and slashed at his humanoid gut.

In order to prevent the gutting slash, he threw her free. A shallow gash across his sash-of-rank allowed frothy blood to seep. Had he not been wearing the metallic mesh, she would have gutted him. Roaring, he tore his own ceremonial gladius from the frog and thrust at her midsection.

She parried, shuffled forward on paw-like feet, and thrust again.

The lion-headed noncom barely parried.

In the open area behind her console, they circled warily.

Facing one another like ancient samurai, who never dared look away, each knew the next one to attack would die. Each waited for the other to make that next and fatal move. Deadly and quick, Sitkamose used this wary stalemate to employ a feint she had learned from her old sword-master. She held the sekhmeten's gaze and kept her sword up while circling to the left. Having seen this particular non-com gut her beloved, she knew his moves. Intentionally dropping her gaze to the deck while keeping his feet in her circle-of-vision, she tensed.

Assuming her to be a poor fighter, he took the bait and employed a following-foot martial technique along with quick-steps to close and thrust.

Unexpectedly, her belly was not in the path of his sword. She had parried his thrust, fell to her left knee, pivoted back, and—with one smooth arc—rose to her feet with an upward slash. The razor-sharp gladius took his right arm below the elbow. The spewing arm and the now-useless sword skittered across the deck.

Baffled, he roared as he raised the spurting stump in shocked amazement.

Sitkamose completed the cut to the top of its arc and made a chopping stroke down across the bridge of his unprotected face. The tip of his nose, his upper fangs, and front incisors, a good portion of his long tongue, and the tip of his bearded chin with the bottom fangs and incisors—all leapt from his astonished face in spinning arcs to the deck where they fetched up against the bloody, twitching arm still firmly grasping his unblooded gladius.

Bright gushing founts of crimson erupted from the stub of his tongue, which worked up and down like a frothing, carmine fountain. He tilted his head back and made to grab his violated face with his clawed left hand.

As she stepped back, her blade sliced in and back across his neck cutting his throat to the backbone.

In a gusher of foamy, arterial blood from both the carotid and vertebral arteries, he fell. His legs kicked forth-and-back in death throes.

To complete her revenge for having killed her beloved in an

unnecessary struggle for rank—and before the sekhmeten's ka could exit his body—she stabbed straight down running her blade into his belly clean through to the backbone. Twisting as she pulled back without pulling free, she ran the brutal blade up into his liver, then twisted again. Grinning, she placed her booted, digitigrade dog's foot against his ribs, and yanked the gladius free with a stream of carmine spatters arcing through the air to bespatter the winking consoles.

His body entered the paroxysms of death.

His legs slowly stopped kicking.

She bent over him and snarled into his open and shocked yet still-alive eyes.

Those savage teeth were the last thing he saw. Whirling her blade in a bloody arc to clear the gore, she slid it across his tunic on each side, then—with a victory flourish—slid it into the frog at her waist and howled. She took a calming breath as she licked her flews, then sat back down at her console. Baring yellow fangs in a predatory grin, she properly contacted the CIC-2.

It was several minutes before Ship's Lord Amenakh arrived at her duty station flanked by two more lion-head sekhmetens. He stopped so abruptly when he laid eyes on the duty-chief's butchered body, his guards bumped hard into him, then backed away with apologetic bows.

It also shocked them.

There lay the body in various places and pools of blood. Malodorous entrails spilled freely from the gutted belly. The right hand of the severed arm had finally let go the gladius, and the limb lay there steaming slightly while still twitching in a congealing pool beside his frothy snout-parts and the wriggling tip of his pink tongue. The stink of freshly spilled gore fouled the frosty air.

Wincing from the seeping puncture wounds in both shoulders, Sitkamose stood at attention and whopped her chest. "Interference with standing orders forced precipitate action, Lord Amenakh—I apologize." She bowed low and went to one knee. Blood fell from her fingertips, drip . . . drip . . . drip to the deck plating. "I was to become trophy in his quarters beside my mate's head. He gave challenge-to-combat with extended claws," and she nodded her snoot at first one then the other blood-soaked shoulder.

Amenakh returned her salute and nodded. From across the steaming corpse, he spoke. "Precipitate action creates opportunity, fierce little Sitkamose. You have the right to strike for his post. Whether you do, we shall see. I duly note interference with standing orders, as well as this most-effective self-defense from challenge-to-combat." He then tipped his head slightly regarding her sword-craft. "Emergent medical treatment requires removal of uniform and spaulders."

She removed her top exposing two rows of four breasts, the bottom two of which lay covered by her breeks." The pheromones of recent battle came off her body as steamy sweat.

Amenakh drank in the scent of her as he applied clotting foam to her bleeding deltoids from a first-aid-kit. "Other than gutting one's superiors, arrival begs news, Sitkamose. What do you have for me?" And, with a wave of his clawed hand, he directed his guards to summon help and manage the bloody, reeking mess.

Sitkamose swept her naked arm toward the normally dead cluster of instrumentation. Even as Amenakh watched, many of the lights and indicators dimmed, then winked out. Still, it was plain to see that more than half of the ancient console had been activated.

Amenakh gestured for her to step aside, sat down at her station, toggled a separate modal-screen on her multi-purpose console.

This was a function she had never seen.

A set of complex telltales washed across.

He gasped, "Impossibility boggles imagination. This is unbelievable!"

Cavern Keep

~

The Stolen Man Escapes

Rippling and wavering, the demon-thing hovering above him shifted the focus of its baleful, scintillating orbs.

As the demon-thing did so, Eli's body rolled from hovering on his back to his right side facing in the same direction of the demon-thing's deadly gaze.

To Eli's fever and terror shocked mind, a rainbow-hued monster the size of a city bus poked its giant head into the cavern. Like a gargantuan cobra, its head rose up to spread its hood as if preparing to strike.

Then, it got weird.

The facial elements were naked women; some hovered in the lotus position; some hovered upright.

Sorceresses—singing sorceresses—siren-sorceresses, then.

A pair in lotus position seemed as eyes.

In the lotus position below there hovered an emaciated old woman like the nose of the cobra-monster.

Upstanding and also naked, a pair of them below and to either side of the old woman seemed as fangs.

When the cobra-monster's head wove from side-to-side, its rainbow-hued and transparent body exposed a cluster of women—both naked and clothed—in an amorphous line flowing back into darkness like the innards.

Joined in song, their haunting voices sounded like hissing.

Filled with bright rancor and dreadful purpose, the old harridan hovered down before the rest, became upstanding, then stared at him with her beady eyes radiating black-hearted malice and unadulterated hate.

Then, for reasons known only to her, the expression of damning hatred on her sagging face shifted to pitiful remorse, and she raised her voice in a frightening dirge.

Like a funeral song, it reminded Elijah of how sad he felt whenever the relentless march of time forced him to euthanize a cherished old puppy dog, or a beloved pussy cat.

The expression of the aged sorceress's face was pity, with him as the object.

A shudder of follow-on terror shook him.

Measured once again in single heartbeats, she sang the dirge while lifting her left arm with her index finger extended as if intending to point at him for some unknowable reason.

In that same moment, and before she could point her finger, the demon-thing above him bellowed and its black, alien appendage brutally shoved him beneath the surface of the roiling waters, now bright as blue molten lava.

The back-flop when he hit the luminous surface emptied his new chest of breath.

Fear of drowning filled his belly.

Whooshing water filled his ears.

Pushing 1,000s of cubic liters from the pool into the belly of the demon-thing, a swirling vortex sucked an upright Elijah in circles around a shallow waterspout.

Belly full of the lava-bright waters, the demon-thing leapt away from his line-of-sight as he spun around the wall of the whirlpool.

The water-muffled sound of heavy concussions accompanied by bright flashes suggested a series of ongoing explosions in the greater cavern.

Beneath the cannonlike cacophony there was screaming and screaming and screaming.

Knowing he would finally drown when the whirlpool sucked him under, he huffed and puffed to reprime his new lungs.

Suddenly, the demon-thing coalesced in midair and did the whole waterspout thing again.

Lungs half full, Eli weakly screamed.

Vertically face up and pinned to the rotating surface of the shallow whirlpool, he desperately began filling his lungs over and over as he got carried around the periphery. Although fully saturated with steam and smoke, the air was breathable as the ceiling of the cavern spun around and around and around.

The first crystal-clear thoughts since the night-of-the-dragon erupted in his squirming brain, then fought their way out as desperate mumblings. "Nightmare . . . insane . . . unreal . . . must get away. . . ."

Gasping and mewling, he flailed his new arms and legs to get his belly down in the current and somehow dog paddle up and over the edge of the whirlpool and away from the spinning torrent. The drastically diminished level of water allowed him to plant feet on the natural bottom. Fighting against the suction while stumbling forward, he water-walked across the lava-bright and whirling waters blinking dazzled yet revivified eyes.

He weakly heaved his body out of the pool and staggered into the effluent tunnel from whence he came. With the glowing waters no longer feeding the gabbling stream, a series of brightly glowing puddles in the small watercourse lit the way.

Now behind him, the gushing pipe of the missing dragon fountain splashed noisily in the pool.

He stumbled and wobbled like a drunkard. Dizzy in a heart-pounding panic, uncoordinated arms steadied him whenever unsteady legs threw him against rocky walls. Behind him, pitiful, painful, and terrified screams carried on the smoke, steam, and fire ridden air as shock waves burst down the tunnel making his body stumble to weirdly tingling knees.

His fevered mind envisioned the demon-thing squeezing the body of the cobra-monster till it spat the siren-sorceresses out to swallow them whole. Wisps and vapors of sanity welled from nowhere, as they had several times throughout all of this. His rational mind told him everything, every action, every moment, had to be hallucinations, or some extended nightmare from which he would finally awaken.

However, this nightmare had no ending, no waking, no release—only the ongoing possibility of nightmarish death.

Stumbling pell-mell, he staggered through the small alcove where the siren-sorceresses had apparently sung him back to life. Panic pushed him on through the glowing tunnel, which became more steeply down, then leveled a bit as it flowed forth till he tumbled over a precipice where the smaller stream splashed into a larger underground watercourse. He came to the surface coughing water and oriented himself to tread water facing downstream like any good river-rafter would.

A gout of what his nose told him must be sewage, gushed from yet another effluent source higher in the tunnel, but—oddly—the waters he floated in seemed pure. As he watched, a veritable vortex of argent-hued forces attacked the sewage along with a gasp of koi fish, meaning he was afloat in some sort of sewage-processing effluent system clean enough to support carp along with some unimaginable, purifying process.

Gazing at the walls of the tunnel, he found them aglow with fluorescent mineral colors. Blinking at the eerie scene, his new eyelids seemed completely ineffective. Open or shut, they had no effect. He dog paddled on.

Without warning, the red-and-glowing darkness of the demon-thing coalesced in the deep currents beneath him, which he could see with crystal-clear perfection. Frantic from a last burst of dwindling adrenaline, he dog paddled madly, but it was no use.

As the demon-thing rose from beneath to grab him, it suddenly and completely disappeared, whereupon the huge cavity in the water left behind collapsed and sucked him under.

Coughing, he struggled to the surface gasping and choking, then reoriented his body facing downstream. With no choice whatever, he swam on like a lost puppy.

Trained in deep sea survival following a naval attack on board ship, and now adrift in warm water—meaning cramps and hypothermia were not prevalent dangers—old training kicked in. He filled his lungs, then let himself slip beneath the surface without further effort. When natural buoyancy brought him up, he kicked hard one time. As his head broke past the surface, he exhaled and inhaled in one mighty breath, then allowed himself to sink in a repeating cycle developed to preserve dwindling bodily reserves.

Literally in the jaws of a reality he had no control over except to resist drowning, and fearing at any moment the demon-thing would manifest in the waters again, he cycled up to breathe, drifted down, cycled up to breathe, drifted down—and so it went. Eyes open or shut, he peered around himself in stupefied wonder. Doing so, he gained the surface for a yet another breath when a surge of bright azure illuminated the waters in which he floated like cold azure lava.

It was all so weird.

A smooth current on the surface of the river flowed narrow and swift, while turbulent waters deeper beneath his body kept tipping his head forward. Gulping, he found himself weaker, while each kick to the surface provided less time to catch a breath. The added mass of those alien-alloys—likely over six pounds of dead weight—were slowly drowning him. It was utterly unimaginable how things could get any worse when a distant roar over the sploosh and splash became louder and ever louder. The surface current bearing him along sped faster and ever faster. With heart-crushing sadness, he realized the inevitable approach of a full-on waterfall with him as nothing more than a flailing bit of flotsam.

Underwater again, light either side of his head made him glance about. Both shoulders had started glowing with blinding, rainbow effulgence. Gazing down as his body buoyed toward the surface revealed hips and knees aglow as well. As he broached the surface, billowing darkness transformed into roiling azure, and—so it seemed—dark and thirsty waters drank in the azure light. A hoarse and gurgling scream escaped his mouth. Desperately paddling like an injured dog, he sought to somehow haul himself out when he spied a sandy beach on the right. Dilapidated stables, a blacksmith's forge, narrow minecart tracks, and rusted-out mining equipment lay visible in the eerie light as he floated swiftly past far too weak to save himself.

Bitter dregs and vaporous wisps of sanity evaporated.

Howling insanity filled the void.

Fully panicked, his brand new heart pounded so hard it seemed as if to burst from his chest. Weaker by the second, he drifted beneath the surface of the rushing torrent one last time while hoping to drown before it swept him into that horrible, voracious crest.

Easier to die.

Better to die.

It was—at long last—time to die.

He gave himself to darkness.

Cavern Keep

~

Cessation and Timing

When The-Creeping-Darkness had done with the murderous high-priestess, and her accursed sister-adepts, its ability to project the water-beast got stymied due to a lack of disposable energy reserves versus power managed by hardwired algorithms as autonomic processes. Down-ramping the BLEVEs versus annihilating the Sisteren had also interrupted completing the paranormal connection with the new power-master.

If the new transducers self-powered up and online before the paranormal circuits got sintered into place, it would be unable to locate him at will because there was no way to fix this. Accomplishing the entire process in a follow-on performance would kill him. This was an unaccustomed emotive algorithm—machine-terror.

Worse, it had been so consumed by rage it somehow lost track of him during the self-defensive assault. Unable to divert electrical aether from autonomic processes, there was nothing to be done. With the connection frayed, insecurity arose as yet another new kind of emotive misery.

Miserable MTSs of self-recrimination ticked by, for—in its rage—it had likely killed the high-priestess despite hardwired constraints. Regardless of whether she died in the literal heat of the moment, or later as a result, it sensed she lay actively dying.

Satisfaction vied with sorrow.

If she died before installing a new-high-priestess, setting another into place would fall to the survivors. It projected how they would feel.

Fear would morph into rancor—deadly rancor. New emotives were set at odds with priorities of self-preservation beyond its ability to resolve.

Violence had been delicious.

Opposing emotive algorithms suppressed satisfaction.

Thinking thusly, it rejoiced when the errant power-master's presence reappeared in the primary effluent watercourse, but this was also a potential disaster. The high waterfall at the end of the tunnel where the underground river poured from the Keep would dash him to pieces on the rock-strewn base. Moreover, the force-field protecting the Keep at the crest of the falls could not be reconfigured to net him in, for he would become pinned by the current and likely get crushed or drowned. However, sufficient time remained before he reached the crest and passed unharmed through the effluent force-field to implement one last alternative.

To that end, it tried manifesting the water-beast in the flow underneath him. Its plan was to get hold of his struggling body and rise up with him held firmly—and safely—in its clutches.

When it applied this stratagem in the central current, the swift laminar flow along the surface vied with the slower, more turbulent flow of the bottom waters passing over rough and rocky surfaces. The additional energy required to manage these shearing forces triggered deresolution.

With the ruthless flow bearing the power-master to certain decease-ment, it calculated a balance between supercritical depletion and the completion of its immediate objective. The same forces of autonomic self-preservation would not allow yet another attempt while the ersatz power-master struggled on, and time was running out.

Torn by competing priorities, the death of the power-master also meant the death of its higher self, because the Sisters—whom it had found itself unable to fully annihilate—were already recovering and would sing it down to dull abeyance. And they would not be malicious high-priestesses attacking the power-master, and without the power-master to protect, self-defensive measures could not be triggered.

And Zunshou De was not machine-death, meaning a return to dull abeyance as That-Which-Abides would also fail to trigger self-pres-ervation, which meant it would passively observe the cessation of its higher self while unable to resist. In anticipation of the one and only chance to save itself and the power-master, it pushed the last dregs of source-energy reserves into illuminating the effluent watercourse, whereupon the entire Huan Long Shui River came alight.

Even as it did so, a superior flow of source-energy transduced from dark-energy began flowing into hungry accumulators, ravenous accumulators, rapacious accumulators—the ersatz power-master's transducers had self-powered online too late for it to save him as well as forestalling the final configurations.

In silence, it wailed.

He was lost.

Riverbend

~

Over the Falls

Conrad's home lay on the western outskirts of Riverbend, which included his pole barn, stables, freight wagons, several horse-drawn cabs, and his favorite—a light-duty, 2-wheeled carriage with a covered roof and outside, elevated driver's seat called a hansom.

He was also signatory with the Teamster's Guild and friends with all. One of them was a first-year apprentice as his live-in stable boy.

Outside in their kennels beside his home, the hunting dogs started barking nonstop for some odd reason, and their barks were strangely frenzied. When he looked out, they were jumping in the air as if trying to chomp fireflies. He went to investigate. They were barking at the sky.

Looking up, he spied the shadow of a fire-dragon passing across the limb of the full moon bound for the Cavern Keep, some 9-kilometers north up the Huan Long Shui River.

He settled his dogs by tossing in some bones from his butcher shop. When the dogs settled down to gnaw, he peered in the general direction of the Cavern Keep with strange foreboding.

Hung on a silver chain around his neck, the amethyst crystal was the twin of the one he gave to High Adept Alahna. Glowing, it seemed to pull at him.

Moving with odd certainty, he went back inside and put his hunting saddlebags together, grabbed his bow and arrows, then trotted across a vacant field to his friend Tarik's house.

When Tarik answered the door in his nightshirt, Conrad said, "Put thy saddlebags together and bring yer bow with a full quiver. We go to roust Esau. From there we go to the Great Sothern Portal of the Cavern

Keep. I cannot explain, but I must do this, and ye're both coming with.

"If it comes to nothing, we go hunting."

Tarik smiled, slapped Conrad on the back, and hustled into his small abode to prepare.

The same sequence of events occurred at Esau's homestead and farm a short distance north.

Riding Esau's fastest horses, they galloped back downstream to the arched bridge supporting a 1-meter sewer pipe from town running down to the sewage processing plant. Walking their mounts, they crossed over to the west side of the smaller Huan Long Shui River, then remounted and cantered north along the cobblestone road taking advantage of the full moon at zenith.

When they reached Stable Master Ruby's park beside the Huan Long Shui Falls, all the horses in the stables made such a fuss about strange horses in the meadow that it brought Ruby, her husband, the smithy, and their three daughters out. When they recognized Conrad and his pals, they happily invited them inside to have apple pie and whole, warm milk.

Conrad gave each of the girls a gold jinn, and the giggling daughters led all three sweating horses into the barn, where they unsaddled and properly cooled them down. Conrad spoke with perplexity. "I feel I must go out and watch the waterfall, but I cannot explain why."

Always up for fun and moderate adventure, Ruby and her family joined them and started a small bonfire far enough from the misty base of the falls to speak without shouting. Not too cold, it was a nice fall night with the full moon and clear skies. By this time the moon slipped slightly past zenith. With all of them glancing up at the falls from time-to-time, and Esau and Tarik regaling the rapt young ladies about the drumming adventure at the Plaza of the Forbidden Gate, Conrad's keen hunter's eyes were the first to notice the fire-dragon swooping past the limb of the moon once again. He pointed and shouted, "Look! 'Tis the fire-dragon I saw!"

Esau shouted, "I see it!"

With all of them searching the sky for the errant dragon, one of Ruby's daughters shouted, "The waterfall!"

Bright azure light cascaded over the crest as if the water had somehow changed into cold blue lava. Running incredibly fast, azure light scintillated down the falls, through the mist, and surged down the river faster than a running horse. Gazing up again, Conrad pointed, and shouted, "There! A body!"

Clearly framed against the glowing waters, an inert and helplessly tumbling human plunged unmoving over the crest and fell toward the misty, boulder-strewn base like a tangle of flotsam.

Tarik shouted, "The dragon!"

Roaring as it swooped in, the fire-dragon flew in a curve so close to the cliffs it plunged into the deluge casting an outlined shadow in the glowing waters while deftly plucking the naked and unconscious man from the torrent like some great bird of prey snatching a fish in its claws. When the dragon burst from the other side with the hapless man's body held tight to its chest, momentum forced it to attenuate the inward arc by whipping the sopping air with all of its might. Once again in controlled flight with the poor fellow in its clutches, it soared so closely over Conrad and the group they got soaked.

With a great roar and graceful swoop, it regained level flight, curved back around a mere 10-meters above the park pumping its wings hard, then soared past the bonfire making embers and cinders burst into the sky. Once past, the dragon gingerly beat the night air in the direction of the coast.

After stomping out all the glowing embers, they stoked the fire with more wood and gathered about to dry themselves.

Conrad shook his head. "I'd bet a week's toil that was the same fire-dragon who flamed us at the Forbidden Gate."

Tarik agreed. "Looked the same to me."

Esau waxed philosophical. "My friends, I fear our lives, as we know them now, will soon be a much wished for past," and he shook his head.

Conrad said, "I'll wager that same week's toil that body was the stolen-man coming over the crest."

Tarik shook his head. "If it was, the poor bastard hath some really shitty luck attached to his sorry ass."

Cavern Keep

~

Dying, Lilith Abdicates

In the terrible aftermath following the attack of the water-beast, Seleen and Alahna crawled back to consciousness where they lay on the ages-worn stone floor. Groaning after assessing her own injuries, Seleen examined Alahna's naked body. Her Laoshi lay bruised, cut, and scraped from head to foot. Worse, the bleeding contusion on Alahna's forehead once again rhythmically spurted little gouts of blood with every heartbeat. Dazed and injured herself, Seleen's pain was too fresh to attempt a Song-of-Stanching.

She gazed along the corridor strewn with bodies and wailed softly.

Moaning as she got to seat and pulled Alahna into her lap. Once settled, Seleen placed a hand over the spurting lump on Alahna's forehead, which had swollen to about the size of half a boiled egg.

Alahna's eyes rolled back in a nasty rush of pain when she shook her head slightly.

Seleen chided, "Hold still—or I'll never stop this!" Drenched with runnels of blood dripping from her chin and leaking from beneath Seleen's hand, Alahna's watering eyes had blood in them, too.

Those who yet survived rallied as best they could. The rising stench of scalded and bleeding bodies, wet clothing, and magic-fire-scorch mingled with the stink of human soil cast a sickening reek. Worse, several had retched, which added its own uniqueness to the overpowering fetor.

Suppressing the gag reflex, and always with an eye to the practical, Seleen realized Alahna was not only injured and shivering, but falling into shock. Knowing this could well be fatal, Seleen overcame her own difficulties and looked about. Not far along the corridor lay one of the older Sisters, who wore an elaborate, hand-stitched woolen pullover nightdress with sewn stringholes in the lapels for a stout and lengthy cord. The horrible obtuse angle of the old dowager's head—along with death-glazed-eyes—left no doubt, she had drifted away on the winds of time.

Seleen spoke firmly to Alahna, "Now then—place thy hand over this cut and lean against the wall for me. Thou'rt taking a chill and going into shock. Do as I say! Dost thou hear?" and she slapped Alahna's cheek lightly the same as Lilith had done to rally her.

Alahna nodded weakly. "L-lilith?"

Seleen looked about. "Concern thyself not. Thine own problems come first. Dost thou hear me?" and she gently slapped Alahna's cheek again.

Tears mixing with runnels of blood, Alahna quietly wept, wiped her eyes, then focused unsteadily on Seleen. Obedient, she placed a trembling hand on her forehead.

Seleen scolded, "Sit right here. I shall return with something warm. Wilt thou do as I say? Alahna, look at me!" and she gently squeezed her Laoshi's shoulders to focus her flagging attention.

Alahna sobbed, but nodded in compliance.

"Thou shalt wait here!" Seleen reiterated, then went to the fallen dame's body. Undoing the lapel cord, she wrested the nightdress off the fresh corpse. Returning, she bunched it over Alahna's head, pulled her Laoshi forward, guided her arms through the sleeves like dressing a child. Not bothering to put the nightdress beneath Alahna's bottom, she tied the laced lapels shut. Seleen then tore a linen strip from her thin nightshirt beneath a similar woolen nightdress and used it to bandage Alahna's head.

Alahna kept blinking her eyes to clear them of blood providing little help.

Seleen helped Alahna gain her feet, then straightened the nightdress. Gingerly picking their way through the bodies, they were both aghast and appalled.

Some Sisters were dead, others stunned and scalded.

Many had also been scorched.

All who survived were moaning and crying wherever they fell.

Carefully leading Alahna forth, Seleen spied Lilith and Yenara farther along.

As they approached, Yenara glanced up and glared.

Accustomed to the Kulapti's hatefulness, Seleen paid no heed.

Trying to make sense of such a horrific disaster, the others made their way unsteadily about helping one another.

Kneeling, Alahna picked up Lilith s scalded and scorched body as gingerly as she could, crying, "My Laoshi, my teacher, thou art not hurt so badly." Adding through ragged breaths, she pleaded, "I love thee—stay with us—stay with me!"

Lilith smiled weakly and looked away, then turned and gazed into Alahna's brimming eyes while placing her bruised and scalded hand on Alahna's cheek. Wheezes rattled in her throat as she stuttered, "Child, beautiful child, my Named One, forgive my anger . . . my love for thee made me act poorly. . . ."

In a spasm of agony, Lilith coughed up a clot of blood from scorched lungs. "I searched my ka to find the best path for the Sisteren, but, alas,"—and she coughed wetly—"the WuShi hath finished me . . . I failed us all. . . ."

Blood and spittle ran from the corners of Lilith's mouth. Her voice found strength, and she squeezed Alahna's shoulder with surprising strength. Speckles of blood persisted with Lilith's every word. "Now listen!"—and she wheezed—"My love, my best pupil, always have thee been destined to become High Priestess, but know this. I would have had thine ascendance come about as a celebration.

"As High Priestess, thee must find a way through all this!

"Yenara, Seleen, bear witness . . . give thy bond to the Ritual-of-Abdication for Alahna. . . ."—and she coughed up more crimson spatters—"I, Lilith, High Priestess of the Huan Long Shui Sisteren, Holder of the last ShahRen, do hereby relinquish all powers, privileges, and titles to High Adept Alahna."

With copious tears and barely controlled sobs, Alahna intoned the litany, "I, Alahna, Keeper of the Archives for the Huan Long

Shui Sisteren and High Adept in the 12th Circle, do hereby accept all powers, privileges, and titles from High Priestess Lilith," and she wept openly.

With a cry in her voice, Seleen swore her bond through tear-filled eyes. "I, Seleen, Adept in the 10th Circle, do this moment bear solemn witness to High Priestess Lilith's Declaration of Abdication and Ascendancy for Alahna, duly Adept in the 12th Circle, Keeper of the Archives, now become unto High Priestess and Mother Matriarch, the one and only Adept in the 13th Circle, and Keeper of the last ShahRen.

"Such is my holy oath.

"Such is my word bond."

Unconsolable, Alahna wept openly.

Yenara spoke muddled words while sobbing through upraised hands.

In pain and emotional shock like everyone, while deeply concerned about all the survivors, Seleen simply assumed that Yenara's muffled words were what they should be in such a heartrending moment, a moment so rife with dire consequences for them all.

Connected to every adept since the moment of her initiation to the moment of death, the WuShi constantly monitored every Sister for words and gestures of power, calls to project spheres-of-power, and the need to empower songspells. Of all the words-of-power, the words in the Ritual-of-Abdication were most high, for they heralded the transfer of incredible powers. When the old high-priestess uttered them aloud—with explicit intent to name her successor—it drew the paranormal attention of The-Creeping-Darkness.

For practical reasons, abdication required three adepts of proper rank—the outgoing, the Named One—or her chosen incoming—and a single witness in the 10th Circle or higher. The WuShi duly noted the combination of ritual and physical transference-of-station as properly witnessed by the dratted acolyte in the 10th Circle, whom it liked for her innocent spunkiness.

An explicit set of hardwired, persistent code-clusters retasked and transferred the powers-of-rank. Done and complete upon utterance, the Named One had been duly installed.

Yenara's gut roiled with bitter dismay at this turn of events. Fighting to hold her tongue and suppress her rage to prevent exposing herself for who she really was, a darker twist arose in her heart.

Still wheezing with crimson spatters, Lilith's struggles grew weaker by the minute. Her lungs rattled softly. "Alahna, the fate of the stolen-man lies in thy hands,"—and she wheezed again—"now that the Sisteren belongs to thee, thou shalt protect them with thy life!"

Nodding while holding Lilith's bleary gaze, Alahna sobbed.

With raised hands to hide her face, Yenara reared back to sneer.

Blinded by grief, Seleen wiped away scalding tears as she knelt to listen and lend support.

Lilith cleared her throat and coughed. "So headstrong, art thou, Alahna, that my warning fell on deaf ears when I forbade the Song-of-the-Voids. Never are we certain how such a songspell will smash into reality . . . and from a forbidden songspell of such uncontrollable power in the tongue of the dragons."

Whereupon, Lilith coughed while holding her ribs in agony. Her eyes rolled up into their sockets.

Contempt for the blubbering simps filled Yenara's gut. Slivers of ice in her heart gave rise to thoughts of mayhem in her squirming brain. The old habit of hiding her expression behind upraised hands accompanied by false sobbing—just as she had always done when feigning actual emotion—now helped clear her mind. A chain of ugly thoughts ran gibbering through her brain like naked obsession.

Alahna, so reckless and foolhardy! So stupid! So undeserving! So undisciplined! So weak! So disrespectful of our laws, of Lilith, of me! Contempt for the rules! Alahna must not ascend!

Seeing that hidden face, Seleen wiped tearful eyes, then placed a still-bloody hand on Yenara's leg.

Yenara silently screamed while a lifetime of hiding her true self— her detached self—took control. Carefully, she composed her stony face with clenched teeth and compressed lips. Wiping rageful eyes with bitter spit to make them wet again, she fairly quaked with rage, which seemed like sobbing, of course. Sweat broke out on her brow. In that moment of crushing despair, dire disappointment, and foul betrayal, her next thoughts came as villainous epiphanies.

I shall make thee pay, Alahna!

Beloved Lilith, too!

And revel in Seleen's destruction as I make ye both watch!

Yenara's better self fought back.

This is not me.

Alahna makes me crazy.

'Tis Alahna's fault—all her fault!

Seleen's fault!

No—Lilith's fault!

However, none of the imbalanced internal dialogue changed a thing. The seeds of betrayal were sewn. Breathing deeply as unnatural calm arose in her breast, it was like someone else took possession, someone else thinking such horrid thoughts, someone else now in control.

Her darkest self emerged and seized control.

Tightly composed, Yenara spoke with quiet intensity. "The stolen-man yet lives—I sense it. How this can be—I know not." Whereupon her face adopted a long-distance stare as she pointed up the body-strewn corridor.

"Adept Seleen, help the new Mother Matriarch to the Gallery of the Infinite Waters and save the stolen-man to honor Lilith's final request."

They helped one another stand, then gazed with naked fear toward the Gallery of the Infinite Waters.

More ugly thoughts tramped through Yenara's mind. These two eejits are the only ones privy to the Ritual-of-Abdication. As Kulapti, I muddled the confirmation. What matters the confirmation of lowly Seleen? It was merely ritual. Power accrues to those who seize it!

Yenara's heart raced as she ordered them more severely. "Eejits both! Time is upon ye! Now go before he dies from thy lack!"

Dazed and confused in total denial, Alahna's tears made runnels on carmine-spattered cheeks. Blood-blurred eyes still stung. Attempting to fathom Yenara's words, Alahna tilted her head to ask, "What of Lilith?"

A sad and stoic smile played lightly on Yenara's lips. "Lilith is fine. She but rests. I shall sing a quiet Song-of-Healing just for her while ye go forth and save the stolen-man. When all have been accounted for and safe, there will be plenty of time to transfer ownership of the ShahRen.

It falls to me in Keeping Lilith safe."

Alahna blinked at the remains of the blood staining her vision.

Seleen furrowed her brow.

Yenara further prevaricated. "Hear me, Alahna! Lilith is safe in my care! Now go! Find him and make amends for thy stupidity!"

Alahna nodded sadly and rallied. With Seleen's help, she stood, wobbled a bit, and the two of them worked their way unsteadily through the fallen and variously injured Sisters toward the steam-and-smoke filled gallery.

Freed from Alahna and Seleen's prying eyes, Yenara bided her time. However, before she could attend to murder, Old Nebhet came upon the two of them, bent down, took Lilith's other wrist. "Thank the Aerthe Mother Goddess, she yet lives."

Desperation took Yenara. Must get rid of Nebhet now! Raising her hand to point down the corridor, Yenara fairly shouted, "There is no time! The water-beast of The-Creeping-Darkness may explode upon us at any moment!"

Nebhet dropped Lilith's hand then knelt. "What wouldst thou have of me?"

"I shall care for Lilith! Take the survivors to safety! We cannot tell if—or when—another attack may come. I should think the Great Southern Staging Area to be far enough. And sing a Song-of-Warding with all the Sisters inside thine own sphere-of-power till we know whether the danger is past!"

Although somewhat unsteady on her feet, Nebhet stood and immediately began urging those who were able to help one another, while seeing to those who were merely unconscious. Those who had died got laid on their backs with hands folded across the chests.

Still in Yenara's embrace, Lilith sputtered and regained consciousness.

Once again holding Lilith tight, a younger stouter Yenara rocked and cried as if the old matriarch were dead. Eyes brimming over with tears of sincere deception—tears of both of love and hate—Yenara held Lilith out to arm's length and peered deeply into the dying woman's blinking eyes.

Whispered words stung like acid.

"How could thee choose capricious Alahna? How could thee so betray me? Betray the Sisteren? How could thee put us at the mercy of that soft-headed eejit? That fool! Alahna! If only—"

Still wheezing, Lilith interrupted, "Thou wouldst have the ShahRen and Sisteren as thine own, eh Yenara?" . . . i-i-i-huh . . . "At the F-forbidden Gate, Seleen . . . Alahna . . . they yet survived even when thee demanded mine abdication . . . how well do I see thee, now?" She coughed and stuttered. "I-I-I knew even at the cactus gardens, yet did I hide it from myself. I was blind. Thou wouldst usurp my station while committing murder in the doing." The last dregs of her strength gave power to her castigation. "Never will I give the ShahRen to such as thee!"

Yenara's heart hardened to stone. Speaking quietly to herself, she said, "Thou art a selfish old harridan, my love."

Wheezing, Lilith simply glared in fear. "Let me die in peace—" . . . i-i-i-huh . . . "'tis done. . . ."

"We shall see," Yenara whispered, then wiped away scalding tears of bitter betrayal. "Mother Matriarch, thou hast left me little choice. I must save the Sisteren. I must save us all from thine insanity."

Anticipating foul murder in those last dying moments, Lilith desperately rolled her head from side-to-side seeking Alahna, seeking Seleen, seeking Nebhet, seeking anybody.

Yenara glanced about—nobody in sight—only steaming corpses to bear witness.

Watching Yenara's expression, the certainty of fate replaced the fear of uncertainty. Lilith sighed and spoke one final time, "Thy plans and schemes, Yenara," . . . i-i-i-huh . . . "shall someday consume thee . . . I pray they do not consume the Sisteren as well. . . ."

Yenara's bitter spit wet Lilith's dying face. "Thine own blindness! Thine own obstinance! Thine own intractability! All brought us to this dreadful pass!"

With another quick glance about, she covertly placed her night skirt over the old woman's face to hide own eyes from the haunting sight of treacherous murder. Without mercy, Yenara squeezed Lilith's old body in a vicious death grip. Quietly, coldly, Yenara ended the old woman's life by holding her small convulsing body fast. When Lilith's feeble struggles faded, Yenara allowed the now-legitimate grief wash over her.

There remained but a single act.

If allowed to die with its bearer, the talisman-of-direct-will could only be reactivated by the Song-of-the-ShahRen performed in unison by at least two Sisters in the 10th Circle of Knowledge or higher. With Seleen and Alahna yet alive, there would be questions, perhaps the Song-of-Truth, perhaps a mind-probe by the guardians. Before Lilith's life-elixir faded from the still-twitching body, Yenara tore at the talisman. As she did so, she sensed an esoteric charge in the hot corpse. With reflexes honed to a fine edge by the mind-exercises of the 12th Circle, she jerked her head back.

Zot!

A powerful jolt snapped Yenara's pendulous breast. She cried out, wailed, fell backward. "So, yet another secret kept from us. The ShahRen defends itself." Yenara scanned her memories. There was a songspell so arcane only the aged Nebhet might remember, or perhaps the hated Alahna—Keeper of the Archives. What is the tune? What is the melody? Then, she had it—the Song-of-Transference. Closing her eyes, she recalled the ancient words and melody, then quietly sang. As she fell into pitch and timbre while flowing along the lyric, the ShahRen pulsated.

Once again, Yenara tore at it. Finally, as the last dregs of life-elixir departed Lilith's corpse, the ShahRen lay hot in Yenara's hands. She gulped grief and guilt past the lump in her throat, wiped her eyes with the back of her hand, wet the middle finger of her left hand with a copious gob of spittle.

A chain ran along the back of the hand from the bracelet to the ring on the middle finger. The ring had to be on the finger before the elaborately engraved bracelet could be twisted onto the wrist. An alloy of gold and silver with traces of copper called electrum, the ring was an elongated tube, and far too small. Also electrum, the chain was elegant yet incredibly strong. One could hang their entire body from it. Of the same alloy, techno-runes covered bracelet, which was wide and thick. When Yenara tried slipping the tubular ring on, it got stuck below the second knuckle. She despaired. She could not jerk it free. Becoming hot, carmine light poured from techno-runes.

A sickly green spark ravaged her second knuckle.

Pop!

Sizzle!

Tear!

Blood welled from the scorch, ran beneath the ring, which magically morphed in size to slide across her middle knuckle. Thirsty for Yenara's blood in a further frightening flow, frothy crimson climbed up the chain to fill the techno-runes of the talisman itself. As the last of the techno-runes got defined by her crimson essence, the bracelet softened.

Unable to balk, she mewled and forcibly twisted it onto her wrist.

Also too tight, it stretched and settled as if custom fit by a silver smith.

Pulsating in sync with her baleful heart, the field of energy around it morphed into a sickly green. Becoming even hotter without burning her flesh, it smoked slightly as the fresh blood burnt away.

Loathsome curls of filthy smoke fouled Yenara's flaring nostrils— she gagged.

Once in place, the ancient weapon imbued her body with dark, arcane magics.

Writhing in guilt-tinged euphoria, Yenara gasped and fell to her back. A surge of raw power shunted through her belly as a mind-bending orgasm so intense she completely emptied her bladder. Over and over orgastic fits filled her belly till she collapsed into a seizure of ecstasy—a seizure of very dark ecstasy. Finally, at long last, she understood why Lilith clung to the damnable thing so, how she had gotten so terribly old yet remained viable, and why she had been so damnably hard to kill.

The dark power was hideous and powerful and delicious.

Yenara sat up just as the tension of life departed Lilith's dying body.

When Lilith's corpse fell, the breadth of her many, many years rushed in.

By the time Yenara struggled to her feet, Lilith's fresh corpse lay stiff in cadaveric spasm.

New wrinkles and sags made her mottled skin droop and twitch.

Cavern Keep

~

The Stolen-man Is Gone

Leaning on one another arm in arm, Alahna and Seleen approached the Gallery of the Infinite Waters in a profound state of ongoing grief while choking on the nasty mephitis.

Bright as molten, azure lava, the still-roiling Long Pen Quan pool lit the cavern as if a full moon were hidden beneath the surface. Likewise, effulgent puddles illuminated the effluent tunnel leading to the stolen-man's alcove, which would not begin flowing again till the pool was full.

Now, however, it sloshed more than half empty.

Where once the stately golden dragon statue peacefully gurgled healing waters from its laughing mouth, a stream of water spouted from a broken stub of pipe to spurt some 3-4 meters into the sodden air and splash rudely in the pool as if aimed by accident. On the rocky, sandy bottom, flash-cooled spangles, spatters, nuggets of gold, and other metals revealed the fate of the dragon statue and bronze wall sconces.

The air alternately snapped, popped, buzzed, throbbed, and thrummed in a weird cacophony of never-before-heard sounds. The overpowering stink of bloodied, scalded bodies; burnt hanging moss; singed clothing and hair—spiced by the ozone tang of rampant uncontrolled magicfire—hung as a haze so thick it was not nearly as nauseous out in the body-strewn corridor.

Helping one another, they pulled their nightdresses off, put them on backwards, cinched them behind for one another, and employed the copious hoods to cover their mouths and noses.

Alahna's senses were so scrambled and Seleen's so shaken, neither of them could sense whether the water-beast remained. Fear ate at their resolve like a mischief of rats, for a monster such as the water-beast had never been mentioned in the archives, had never been seen before. With Alahna unable to sing a sphere-of-power, there was little either could do even if it returned.

Alahna said, "I cannot imagine what The-Creeping-Darkness wanted with the stolen-man. What did it do to him?"

Seleen said, "We must find him."

Holding one another steady while fearing instant death, they made their way unsteadily around the perimeter.

Seleen pointed at the worn stone floor.

The bony heads of two femurs lay discarded where they fell after getting sliced cleanly away from the larger leg bones—his body—for there was no doubt where the glistening bones came from. Lying there, they bore silent witness to some sort of horrific dismantling.

Looking further, unidentifiable bits of the stolen-man's primary joints lay here and there still steaming in the wet gravel.

Fearing the worst, they gazed between their fingers at the dazzling waters of the effulgent pool.

White gobbets of cooked and bloodless flesh floated on the roiling surface as parboiled tissues, but there was nowhere near the amount needed to account for an entire human corpse.

Heartbroken, Alahna spoke more to herself than Seleen. "But where is the rest of him?" and she cried softly. Given her life, station, and rank, she had not—and still could not—admit to the unconscious urges he had provoked in her chaste body while nursing him back to health with her lips touching his to give him sustenance like a baby.

It was his earthy scent; the depth of his voice; his brave will to live; and maybe even her guilt at having done such egregious harm. All clearly her fault, the guilt and sadness of the past week's events came near to overwhelming.

Gazing at the bobbing bits of body in revulsion, mixed feelings surfaced as gut-wrenching, soul-crushing grief. She struggled to cope, to be in the present, to quell the tears and continue on.

Since no water-beast had, as yet, leapt from the pool to end their paltry lives, they made several additional sweeps.

There were simply no other traces.

Alahna put words to reality. "He is no longer here. . . ."

To be certain, they carefully combed through the entire gallery again.

The maelstrom of lightning, dark-energy, magicfire, and drenching from the Long Pen Quan waters still filled the cavern with puffs of cooling steam and nauseating smoke.

Small fires guttering in the shadows made eerie shapes on the rocky walls.

Steamy ceiling-moss glowed with ethereal, blue-green hues.

Foul smelling drops spattered their heads and shoulders.

Finally, Seleen gave voice to the unthinkable. "Maybe his greater anatomy got vaporized?"

In denial, Alahna shook her head and cried sadly through the pain.

Also weeping, Seleen held Alahna close and patted her back.

Cavern Keep

~

Yenara Ensorcels the Sisteren

With Lilith's corpse stiffening deeper into rigor mortis, Yenara rode a wave of power unlike anything she had ever experienced. After usurping the ShahRen, hot and orgastic ecstasy glowed in her belly like a bed of red-hot embers. Tinges of guilt, regret, and shock rocked whatever traces of decency remained, but they were only tinges.

As the ShahRen pulsed on her wrist, grim determination compelled further consolidation.

A deep sense of clarity took her as she no longer sensed the imminence of The-Creeping-Darkness. So be it, leading the Song-of-Successive-Deactivations would come later.

Turning away, she spat on Lilith's stiffening corpse.

Unsteady on her feet, she made her way around the bend in the corridor toward the Great Southern Staging Area. By the time she arrived, the wobbling gait had steadied.

Old Nebhet held the variously injured survivors still inside an undulating SijanPao so extended in length it curved around the expanse of the gallery. To spare herself the unimaginable task of keeping everybody positioned, Nebhet had lowered the Pao to the stone floor creating a flat bottom, then allowed the Sisteren to settle like downy feathers.

Along that bottom then, those who were still able rendered aid to the injured while murmuring the Song-of Healing in group-song.

Yenara hollered, "High Adept Nebhet, derezz thy Pao!"

With everyone already safely on the floor, Nebhet sang the note-of-deresolution without a count, and the field-of-force simply whuffed away along with healing song.

They all wanted to hear.

When those who were able turned to her, Yenara shouted to be heard over the remaining moans and cries. "I bring sad tidings, my Sisters . . . Lilith is . . . well . . . Lilith is gone on the winds of time. . . ." She then summoned tears of equal parts genuine grief and delicious-yet-unwholesome glee. Feigning sobs, an inscrutable grimace painted itself on her lips as she bowed her head and put hands to face knowing the others perceived only deep-seated grief.

Hammered and shocked, the wretched survivors wailed and cried and held one another for support.

Some pulled at their hair.

Others fell to weeping and pounding the stony floor with the sides of their balled fists.

Old Nebhet nodded sadly. As tears welled up, she ran to Yenara and hugged her. "I could have helped save Lilith. I should have stayed. Oh, Aerthe Mother Goddess! Whatever shall we do?"

Wasting no time on meaningless drivel, Yenara thrust her left arm into the air. The ShahRen glowed and pulsed with the vital new strength of a younger, more sinister mind, and a deeply darker heart.

Several beats passed before the dazed and confused Sisters realized the implications. As the import took hold, they fell to their knees genuflecting, and intoned a litany as one. "Blessed be the Mother Matriarch. Blessed be the Mother Matriarch."

A disheveled Yenara stood resplendent in her triumph.

Shouting, she exposed her triumph, "I am finally she! And forever shall I be! The High Priestess of the Huan Long Shui Sisteren." She raised her arms in the air with regal bearing and shouted again, "Beloved Sisteren, save thy tears! Treachery steals upon us this night!" and she motioned for her gaggle of sycophants to gather close.

They hustled forth and surrounded her with kisses and hugs.

She reveled briefly. "Enough ! Follow me! We must find Alahna the perfidious and Seleen the stupid!" Whereupon, she turned her back to lead them forth while quietly intoning a Malison-of-Rage.

Such a malediction would typically be directed at a single opponent during Confrontation-by-Source by pointing a finger as a gesture-of-aiming. Once set, the opponent would fall to irrational rage and sloppy overcommitment. Cooler heads always prevailed. Sung without specifying an object, the malediction would affect the most susceptible Sisters first, some to a lesser degree than others, but all would be affected. The most delicious element of the scheme was that it was Alahna who taught it Yenara in the first place.

Already attuned to Yenara's wishes, her sycophants became fully ensorcelled. Faces weighted with grief became distorted by furious rage. She heard the grunts and hisses of rising anger with filthy glee. She had them. Once fully ensorcelled, all that remained was to set the object or objects by seeding a litany. She shouted, "Alahna and Seleen!"

Caught up in Yenara's corruption as shared rage flooded their baffled minds, the Sisters intoned, "Alahna and Seleen . . . Alahna and Seleen . . . Alahna and Seleen. . . ."

At the front of the bedraggled column grinning to herself as she led them forth, Yenara stopped singing and allowed the rage to burn of itself, then quietly whispered the explicit note-of-ending on her earlier Song-of-Stanching. Irrespective of the fact that such a thing tore the stanching energies from all Sisters who needed it, Yenara intended the cessation for Alahna—let her bleed.

In terms of any who would start bleeding again, Yenara cared not a whit. Several Sisters did bleed again. Nobody noticed. Confused and mourning their beloved Lilith as they gazed in passing at her frail and damaged corpse, the flood of intensified emotions transformed into pure, vitriolic hatred. In the entry portal to the Gallery of the Infinite Waters, Yenara stopped with her clique hard on her heels.

Now become unto a vicious, hate-filled, bloodthirsty mob, the larger body of adepts stood close behind still intoning that hateful litany, "Alahna and Seleen."

Alahna and Seleen stood side-by-side between the entry and glowing pool with Alahna leaning on Seleen for support. Alahna's forehead pumped crimson runnels through the blood-soaked bandage. When Seleen pulled the crimson and dripping rag from Alahna's forehead, a new fountain of steady surges flowed forth. Crimson spatters fell like rain on Alahna and Seleen's bare feet.

Yenara stood in the cavern portal with hands-on-hips like an angry parent.

Alahna stood there badly confused and obviously weakened by the onset of exsanguination. Standing in the very same spot where Lilith stood when the water-beast attacked, Yenara's voice dripped with belligerent contempt. "Where is the stolen-man? Alahna! Seleen! Where have ye hidden him?"

With brandished fists, the enthralled Sisters shouted as one, "Alahna and Seleen! Alahna and Seleen! Alahna and Seleen!"

In confusion and injury from the severe concussion, Alahna innocently rejoiced when her Sisters appeared in the entry portal.

Yenara's sycophants stood clustered behind her.

Behind them, the greater body of surviving Sisters stood in a crush on Yenara's left while brandishing their fists and shouting, "Alahna and Seleen! Alahna and Seleen! Alahna and Seleen!"

Listening to them, Alahna thought they were calling to her as the new Mother Matriarch along with her beloved Seleen—her likely choice of Kulapti—a long overdue promotion for Seleen. With Alahna's bleeding forehead fouling her eyes once again, she unsteadily detached from Seleen and made as if to rush into their arms, but—for some odd reason—Seleen grabbed the nightdress, yanked her back, caught her as she stumbled.

While the Sisters ranted, Yenara yelled, "I demand answers, yonder eejits!" and shook her left fist at them with the glowing ShahRen making visual trails in plain sight. "Where is the stolen-man? Alahna! Seleen! Where have ye hidden him?"

Alahna singled out Old Nebhet in the mob. As best Alahna could tell through the carmine haze blurring her sight, Nebhet looked angry and confused, but her shouting seemed half-hearted. Confusion reigned in Alahna's foggy mind as she realized the import of Yenara's demand. In addition, Seleen had apparently recognized hatred, where Alahna herself misperceived love.

Thoughts rang in her mind.

Innocence as weakness—sometimes called stupidity.

Therefore, Seleen held me back.

Even as Alahna wiped her face while trying to clear her blood-sullied eyes for the time, Yenara's words from the corridor as she knelt beside Lilith leapt into her mind: When all are accounted for and safe, there will be plenty of time to transfer ownership of the ShahRen, for I shall keep Lilith safe.

If Yenara had the ShahRen, it meant the unthinkable.

Stalling as if enthralled, Alahna pleaded and stuttered, "He's gone. We cannot find him. We have searched everywhere!" and she shook her head as if confused, and got a burst of agony as reward for her subterfuge.

Thoughts rang.

What is Yenara doing?

What could make the entire Sisteren turn on us?

Crimson droplets dripped from Alahna's chin onto the hood of the nightdress, then spattered the floor about their feet.

With her eyesight in a carmine haze, Alahna felt more than saw Yenara's subtle sweep of the hand—a gesture-of-aiming meant to ensure each and every Sister fell in line with—what?

A cursing?

Was this a cursing?

A malediction?

Alahna watched in dismay as Old Nebhet took up the litany-of-hate. Alahna gasped as it washed across both herself and Seleen. By this time, Alahna's ears had finally stopped ringing, and she picked out the arcane syllables and dark melody of Yenara's voice in songspell as a substratum to the litany-of-hate.

Even as Alahna realized it was, indeed, a cursing, Seleen murmured the rancorous litany-of-hate from behind her. Still yet stranger—as if her own mouth belonged to someone else—Alahna heard herself join the irrational litany.

An unnatural enmity dragged her mind into self-loathing.

A pump of adrenaline cleared her mind and set her heart to pounding as a cascade of realization filled her brain with dastardly words.

She muttered to herself, "If Yenara murdered Lilith and usurped the ShahRen, then Yenara must also kill any witnesses, and the only witnesses are myself and Seleen." Instantly, she turned her back on the fully enthralled mob, fell into Seleen's arms face-to-face, and hugged Seleen close as if in a faint.

Under aegis of the curse, Seleen stiffened and backed away, but Alahna held her tight, making Seleen bodily drag her a few steps.

Alahna put her mouth beside Seleen's ear to quietly intone a single phrase from the Song-of-Clearing, a powerful counterspell which could also be performed mentally inside the lodge of one's own mind as defense against a Malison-of-Rage.

Not yet cleared however, Seleen pushed her away.

Alahna blended with the impetus to stumble backward and away from Seleen, turned as if reeling, and sang the Song-of-Clearing as loud as she could muster accompanied by a sweep of her hand across the group as a gesture-of-aiming to explicitly pluralize her counterspell.

Still reeling in the feigned about-face, Alahna fell back into Seleen's arms, who had attained unto clarity.

Through blood-blurred eyes, Alahna saw that Yenara was too busy casting the malediction, and failed to realize Alahna's counter. While of it, Yenara was not in it, not befuddled by it, yet nonetheless blinded by it.

For those directly behind Yenara—her sycophants—the subtle stink of songspell-induced rage remained due to Yenara's proximity and the emotional bond she held them under.

The frame of mind compelling the Sisters in the crush around Old Nebhet shifted from boiling rage to simmering confusion.

Cavern Keep

~

Again, the Water Beast Awakens

Deep beneath The-Sleeping-City, the feted WuShi got dragged from its torpor. The Ritual-of-Abdication when the old harridan performed the transference-of-station to the Named One had been properly witnessed and bonded by the dratted acolyte.

Nothing more was needed.

This meant that all the sub-routines accorded to the station of the new high-priestess were in place as of the very instant the dratted acolyte finished her words-of-power. Now metaphysically connected to the rightful high-priestess, a new and deadly danger arose.

Unlike the old high priestess, whom it hated with all of its cold machine-intelligence, it held an unaccustomed fondness for the Named One and found itself pleased with her ascendance. Projections into the near future had her continuing to call on its powers while allowing it to remain in hyper-sapience. She had commanded it to find a hero and unwittingly allowed that hero to be a power-master.

Her innocence was its advantage.

She had even helped it restore him while foregoing the Song-of-Successive-Deactivations. Whether she had blocked the other high-adepts from performing it, the WuShi did not know, but such an insignificant issue held no sway in any case.

She was to be protected at all costs.

She, like the ersatz power-master, belonged to it.

Superluminal, metaphysical tendrils of dark-energy once again imbued the dragon-waters in the pool behind the new high-priestess.

Gushing water from the broken pipe splashed.

With no time to refill, the pool remained shallow when the head of the water-beast surfaced to expose the tips of its wicked horns and those red-and-glowing orbs in that amorphous forehead.

Poised on the cusp of an MTS, watching, the Wushi waited.

Waiting, the WuShi watched.

When Nebhet and the Sisters crowded together in a tight cluster beneath the huge portal leading into the Gallery of the Infinite Waters next to Yenara and her gaggle, Nebhet herself stood voicing a litany-of-hate at Alahna and Seleen without knowing why.

Nebhet had always taught her acolytes that the word—why—was a gateway word leading to the truth when properly investigated. With the question—why—rattling around in the back of her mind, her mind-powers kicked into a battle with the unreasoning, inchoate rage. Even as she regained her common sense, a fresh enragement swept over them all leaving them standing there in the portal shouting like crazed maniacs.

But there was more.

Something not perceived aroused a sense of danger over and above the surge of irrational emotion as Yenara—up to her old bellicose bullshit—stood hollering at Alahna and Seleen about the stolen-man, who had apparently disappeared.

Thoughts bubble up.

As if anybody gives a crap about his sorry ass?

After all, he hath been at the center of this ongoing shitstorm for weeks. And since Alahna and Seleen were cleared of wrongdoing by the Council of Inquiry, all the hatred directed at the two of them—and them in such a sorry state—makes no sense to anybody with the possible exception of Yenara.

When Alahna reeled back in an apparent faint, the boiling rage in Nebhet's mind cooled down to a simmering confusion.

Did Alahna really faint?

Did I hear her soft voice in songspell?

Nebhet shook her head—put hands to her face—slapped her own cheek.

It seemed as if not one but two subvocal songspells vied for supremacy in their collective consciousness as a mental conflict allowing Nebhet's own powerful mind to achieve clarity.

However, clarity morphed into terror as the imminent presence of The-Creeping-Darkness washed across her metaphysical senses like a torrential flash flood in a desert gully. The screams of the dying from the scalding attack they had just survived still burnt brightly in Nebhet's mind.

She remembered departed Sisters lying everywhere, including her beloved Lilith, before drifting away on the winds of time 'neath Yenara's hands with no one else there to give succor. Pulling her thoughts back to danger at hand, the daemon water-beast was back—but hiding—and she knew it!

Gazing at Alahna and Seleen stumbling about in one another's arms with Alahna's face and front streaked by still-dripping blood, Nebhet's pounding heart went out to them.

They were so damaged.

Both so fragile.

Then, Nebhet gasped.

The steaming, bestial head of the alien water-beast coalesced in the roiling waters of the pool behind the two of them.

Hateful fangs dripped bitter blackness.

Red and glowing eyes stabbed Nebhet's shaken sanity like daggers before it slid 'neath the surface with a moderate splash.

Horrified thoughts crashed into Nebhet's mind.

Alahna and Seleen—it will strike them first!

I cannot save them!

She glanced about in rising panic. "Oh, Aerthe Mother Goddess— let me save the rest!"

Still crowded behind Yenara forming a tight knot with bellies to butts, her kowtowing sycophants stood hollering the inexplicable litany at the top of their stupefied lungs.

In the next fraction of a second, Nebhet realized it was likely that no one save herself had seen the water-beast. Its appearance lasted less than two heartbeats.

Nebhet's voice was loud and shrill. "The-Creeping-Darkness is upon us—run for yer lives!" Her warning got drowned out by Yenara and her gaggle still shouting.

Most of the confused Sisters behind Nebhet rallied to their own senses, turned, and ran back along the corridor away from the glowing gallery too terrified to waste more precious breath on useless screaming.

Three did not.

They stood there stupefied.

Nebhet strode to the first one, slapped the shit out of her, spun her on her heels, and delivered a swift kick to the eejit's butt.

Twice, thrice, and she had them all running away.

When Nebhet turned for a last glance at Alahna and Seleen, she spied the sloped shoulders and monstrous outlines of the water-beast rising up while heaving as it sucked water into its bestial belly.

Soon—it would strike!

Rather than hobble along behind the fleeing Sisters, Nebhet spawned a new SijanPao, then willed herself away from the glowing gallery only slightly faster than the fastest running acolyte. As she overtook the fleeing Sister, she pulled her into the Pao. Entraining them as she went, she carried on, then willed them behind her as she pressed to increase their distance from the gallery as much as possible.

Finally, Nebhet had them all, and willed the undulating sphere-of-power along the stone corridor like a monstrous and misshapen anaconda with clear rainbow skin and a bellyful of mewling, confused, and terrified Sisters.

With the corridor channeling the SijanPao at the front, Nebhet willed herself to the rear to see if Yenara and her gaggle followed.

Either they had not heard her warning, had not spied the stealthy water-beast, had not left off screaming at Alahna and Seleen, or their minds were so muddled by unaccustomed rage and unbridled rancor that their sensibilities had completely departed.

With the water-beast close upon them now, and so close to attacking, Nebhet herself forgot to set the all-important spatial-lock when she sang her SijanPao.

Cavern Keep

~

Alahna, Seleen, and The-Creeping-Darkness

Alahna's forward lurch after turning her back on Yenara and the Sisteren propelled both herself and Seleen closer to the pool. Based on her loving embrace, it was obvious Seleen's mind had cleared. With more runnels of blood blurring her eyes, Alahna almost sobbed. "Make for me another headband!"

Righteous indignation and deep concern painted Seleen's features. Watching through blood-blurred eyes. Alahna saw Seleen gather the skirt of her nightdress and rip another strip free. Alahna turned once more to face Yenara while desperately dabbing at her blood-blurry eyes with the impromptu headband Seleen tied from behind. Focusing poorly through the carmine haze, Alahna was herself sick with outrage and injury—a maddening dearth of self-defensive powers.

Riding the adrenaline rush as her eyes cleared somewhat, she heard Old Nebhet shouting into the cacophony of crazed and hollering Sisters, but could not make out the words. The combination of Nebhet's warning to run back along the corridor combined with Alahna's clearing brought most of the Sisters to their senses.

Still confronting them, however, Yenara's sycophants continued shouting the litany-of-hate. Yenara glowered and leveled an accusing right hand. Hollering theatrically at the top of her lungs, she lifted her left arm and shook a fist at them. "Lilith is gone on the winds of time, for it was thee—Alahna—who brought the stolen-man hither with a forbidden and accursed songspell!

"It was thee who brought never-ending calamity down upon us.

"And now ye've abandoned the Mother Matriarch when she begged for thy help!"

Stunned and drop-jawed at the barefaced lies concerning Lilith, and feeling at fault about the rest, Alahna's blood simmered.

Yenara pressed on, "Treacherous scunners both! Don't stand there shaking thy stupid heads! Lilith's death lies at yer feet as surely as if ye both plunged daggers into her heart! Knowing death was upon her, she abdicated and passed the ShahRen to me! Not caring!

"Not helping!

"Never helping!

"Ye've abandoned Lilith while I tried to save her!"

Even through the splitting agony, she knew Yenara's lies and accusations were not for the benefit of herself and Seleen. Yenara wanted their Sisters to bear witness concerning her next treacherous move in this ugly game.

Anguish clove Alahna's heart in two when she also realized the 13th Circle of the Huan Long Shui Sisteren lay utterly broken. The only Sisters witness to her ascension were Yenara and Seleen, and Yenara would forcibly discredit Seleen. A wave of nausea swept through Alahna's weakening body as she realized with dreadful certainty what Yenara would do—must do—next.

Yenara reached back as if winding up to throw a large stone while clumsily summoning a smallish bolt of blackfire from the ShahRen.

And here Alahna stood with Seleen at her back unable to sing a SijanPao.

Panic ate her broken heart.

Wretched thoughts raced.

Yenara has us!

We shall die!

But even as the bolt of blackfire leapt at them, something erupted from the roiling waters from behind, then crackled over their heads.

Whoosh!

In passing, a dripping alien arm with an outsized hand reached down and swept them screaming and spinning through the air into the pool some 10-meters from the deep end. What little clothing they had on got stripped from their bodies.

Tied in place, Seleen's stout slippers stayed on her feet.

With a new pump of adrenaline, a naked Alahna struggled to her bare feet spluttering and coughing. Normally, the pool stood a bit past her chin at this end. Now, however, it was less than waist-deep. The healing, glowing waters rinsed her raw and bleary eyes well enough to witness the burgeoning BLEVE.

Without pause, she filled her lungs, grabbed a spluttering Seleen, ducked them both beneath the splashing surface, and filled her acolyte's lungs mouth-to-mouth with the kiss-of-life.

The water-beast gulped the sun-hot blackfire down its watery gullet.

Flash—kaboom!

The surface of the pool flattened when the water-beast got vaporized even as a new manifestation leapt forth.

Flash—kaboom!

Manifesting again, it leapt.

Flash—kaboom!

Manifestation!

Flash!

Kaboom!

Horrific explosions of superheated steam and blackfire echoed throughout the Keep from the gallery like the repeated explosions of an erupting volcano.

Blinding flashes dazzled blurred vision from beneath the surface.

Starving lungs screamed for air.

And still, Alahna kept them submerged.

With each successive blast, the level of the pool fell till Alahna feared they must at last be exposed to the blackfire and steam so hot there was no visible mist only scalding billows of deadly heat.

Large and small rocks fell from the ceiling along with gouts, sheets, and drips of boiling-hot water and gobbets of scorched moss.

Alahna pulled Seleen up and they both gasped for air, choked, gasped again.

Shimmering, the lava-bright pool broke through the darkness to reveal a smoke, steam, and fire ridden hell. Around them, rock and moss blasted from the ceiling continued falling.

From above, Alahna heard the grating dislodge of something enormous. Peering up through the murk and heat and steam, she made out the vague shape of a huge boulder falling free to crush them. All she could do was scream.

In a blurring flash, the water-beast erupted from the turbulent water next to them, reached out huge and alien appendages, and catapulted the boulder with an upward arc across the gallery floor.

Colliding with solid rock, the boulder exploded into flying fragments.

Alahna ducked them both under the water to avoid spinning rock shrapnel skipping across the surface. Once again desperate to breathe, when their burning lungs could take no more, she sat them up on their butts

Seleen was only semiconscious, but remembered enough to fill her lungs over and over.

Alahna did likewise.

Barely reaching their navels, splashing, surging waters had been reduced to about 30-centimeters deep.

With raw and stinging eyes rinsed mostly clear, Alahna rapidly blinked her eyes at the translucent encapsulation of water defining the gut of the water-beast. In an eerie silence of steaming and dripping and shimmering heat, the demonic thing tilted its alien head to the side and gazed into her—not at her—but into her.

Deep into her very ka, did it gaze.

She shuddered in terror as the lava-bright waters lapped both inside and outside of this being-of-blackness highlighted by scintillating reddish hues. Somehow, its lower extremities, if ever there were any, need not be present. Only its upper body from the hips extended upward as if supported in the shallow, roiling waters without further need. Her memory raced back to the visions of the water-beast tearing the stolen-man limb-from-limb, and found no recollection of a body below what the belly and hips—provided the human body was similar to this alien thing. Emptied at last of heart-pounding terror, dull horror took its place.

Transfixing her with an unblinking gaze, three red-and-glowing orbs stared with bleak intensity. Yellow-tinged dark-energy flamelets licked along the surface of its horns. Fangs dripped spatters of perfect blackness sizzling into dirty steam when they hit the glowing waters. Then, it simply dissipated in the smoke and steam. A splashing spout of water erupted to fill its absence.

During this interminable confrontation, her flailing heart ceased moving blood through her body—a heart attack.

Echoes faded.

Steam hissed.

Waters dripped.

Rocks fell.

Fires guttered.

Smoke rolled.

The gushing pipe spewed and splashed.

Eyes wide with fright, Alahna fell back to die.

But an alien appendage lifted her dripping body free, and the face of the water-beast appeared before her eyes close enough to spit in its unnatural oculi. A rotten-egg stink of burning brimstone assailed her senses. Holding her entire fragile body in one enormous hand, it raised the other and brought down a dripping claw-of-blackness to pierce the skin between her breasts without cutting into her sternum.

Z-zot!

A spike of source-energy shocked her heart.

The feeling of molten lava pouring across her chest elicited a hoarse scream, and she gasped for air as her heart took to pounding so hard it made the unholy vision of that alien face pulsate.

Individual heartbeats hammered—lub-dubba-lub-dub.

As her blown mind cleared, so the water-beast dissipated dropping her back into the now-shallow pool in a back flop that shocked her more fully awake. Splutters and coughs made her head pound when she sat up to once more pump her lungs full of precious air.

Amidst the bright and rippling glow, she discerned Seleen's unconscious form floating face down two meters distant. Seleen's long blonde hair floated about her head as a glowing halo.

Mewling like an injured child, Alahna splashed on hands and knees, pulled Seleen to her back, held her head above the waters, and pressed the kiss-of-life as she repeatedly hugged and squeezed her.

More breathing.

More squeezing.

And so it went.

After several such iterations, Seleen gurgled and coughed. Spitting up slugs of water, she moaned and wheezed and spluttered.

For some time after, Alahna simply sat holding Seleen while they gasped and sobbed.

Seleen fussed, "Where is it? Will it come again? Why did it save us?

Did it save us?"

No answers came. Just dripping water, plunking rocks, and the splashing pipe.

At last, Alahna asked, "Canst thou sit?"

Seleen nodded, sat up, leaned back with arms extended.

Alahna's forehead once again seeped serosanguinous fluid into her eyes as she found their cleanly rinsed nightdresses. She struggled the both of them to their feet, and they staggered splashing across the natural bottom past fallen boulders while avoiding sharp rocks, maneuvered to the end of the pool by the effluent stream, and tossed the drenched nightdresses onto the edge. Scrambling as best they could, they climbed free of the pool.

No longer fed by the overflow, nothing remained in the bed of the stream but effulgent puddles like glowing blue lava. When Seleen got a good look at Alahna, her face froze in horror as they both looked down at the cauterized wound on Alahna's chest. Seleen's eyebrows arched.

Alahna gasped and stuttered, "I-I-I was dying when the water-beast stabbed my chest w-with a tiny bolt of source-energy . . . but we must not linger . . . Yenara hath usurped the ShahRen and no doubt—"

Seleen muttered breathlessly, "Yenara . . . the ShahRen . . . it means—"

Alahna finished the sentence with a sob. "Lilith is dead. . . ."

Aghast, Seleen wrung the water from the fine woolen nightdresses while Alahna wrung the water from Seleen's long hair.

Alahna's hair was little more than fuzzy stubble.

Shaken but stoic, Seleen growled, "The last ShahRen spoke its own truth. I fear she hath also usurped thine office behind our backs. Ever the fools, are we?"

With stars going off before her eyes, Alahna groaned through the ubiquitous carmine haze even as Seleen immediately placed a hand over the seeping lump. Tears streamed from Alahna's blood-blurred eyes. "We m-m-must f-flee!" and she knelt and held wet palms with those healing dragon-waters to her eyes, which helped. Alahna's voice with flat stoic acceptance. "As thou sayest, the survivors believe Yenara to be the new Mother Matriarch, and she hath already shouted her condemnations in front of her gaggle and the others."

Exhaustion, water, and tears streaked Seleen's haggard face. "My Laoshi, help me sing the Song-of-Healing.

Unsure of their remaining powers, Alahna tried, but felt her voice trailing off.

As Seleen sang on, Alahna found herself adrift in a fugue of pain, but that was not all. Since the moment of Ascension, her deep-mind felt an emerging connection. Paying attention, she realized it to be an additional sense—a techno-sense—and time slowed.

Following the epiphany, red-and-glowing scintillations outlined the ethereal shape of the water-beast hovering about Seleen feeding healing source-energy into her very lyrics like butterflies aglow in the sunshine. When the butterfly lyrics impacted Alahna's body, they simply sank in.

It was beautiful and frightening at once.

Of the three eyes in that bestial alien face, two gazed intently down upon Seleen. In its forehead, the third eye gazed intently on Alahna.

It knew she knew.

It knew she watched.

Alahna shuddered, and, in that same moment, realized the WuShi—in whatever state-of-consciousness—was literally omnipresent, likely omniscient, and profoundly more connected to her than ever it was to Lilith. Too filled with herself, Lilith's cup had never been empty—and she hated the WuShi—Alahna did not.

So thinking, the vision faded along with enough of the pain to continue on, whereupon she shifted her attention to survival.

The stink of ozone and magicfire rode on the air almost to the point of choking were it not for the rush of fresh air flowing in from the effluent cave, which gave her an idea.

Speaking quietly, Seleen rinsed Alahna's face. "The lumpy wound on thy forehead lies raw and open, but active bleeding finally stops. Thine eyes and cheeks are bruising toward darker shades of purple and near to swelling shut."

Alahna grabbed Seleen by the shoulders. "We must run from here before Yenara rallies and returns with the enraged survivors, or even if Yenara got killed, the rest will surely come. We are now anathema. We cannot survive another attack. Follow me!"

Helping one another, they splashed into the brightly glowing puddles of the effluent tunnel.

With small fires still guttering here and there, the Gallery of the Infinite Waters behind them reeked of death, scorn, sorrow, and betrayal.

Asenath

~

Ancient Systems Activate

On board the Ophois Asenath still in a stationary orbit above the west coast of the island continent, Sitkamose found herself happily detailed directly to Ship's Lord Amenakh as the first to observe activity on the ancient, long-dead console, of which there were many scattered throughout the vast, ancient ship. It was also because she had a choice presented to her when she killed the noncom sekhmeten. She allied herself to Amenakh rather than take the sekhmeten's rank.

For several hours now, telltales and dials had lit up, which Sitkamose recorded on a new vid-unit set up near her old duty-station. Whole swaths of ancient instrumentation came fully alive, stayed activated for a time, then partially faded. A few still pulsed or showed arcane readings. Sitkamose was preparing to swap out the memory chip on the vid-unit when, once again, the cluster of ancient readouts across the console came alight.

With nothing but vague legends as background, Sitkamose spent her waking hours studying the mythological histories from the digital archives. The ancient tech was so entrained in the fabric of these ancient spacecraft-carriers that past efforts to completely remove it had proven not only difficult but typically catastrophic.

Unused for over 500-centuries, the ancient forms of the NuliZhu language were her first serious challenge. It was difficult in the extreme to discover the ancient meanings, but she was both intelligent and tenacious. This was her chance to climb out of the lower ranks, her time to shine. Working hard, she created a working lexicon.

The ancient documentation concerning the use, meaning, and

operational control of the Asenath's Blackfire-Weapons-Control-System was both obtuse and cryptic. Her best guess was that the original project had been so ultra-secret that—for whatever reason—when communications between the Tech-Masters and the War Center on Ta Shemau failed, and to their chagrin, the ancients simply did not know and were not able to research where the project had been carried out. This left the entire experimental fleet of these great spacecraft-carriers to drift in orbit as derelict junk until refitment turned them to other more useful purposes. The Ophois Asenath was simply the latest example of such a refitment.

Knowing at least something of the original project, its purpose and scope, she soon realized what few records she could access—and she had them all—were little more than a conceptual framework versus working documentation or actual operations manuals. She had installed a vid-unit at each of the long-dead outcroppings of ancient tech scattered throughout the ship hoping to catch the next activation, but this was the only ancient weapons-control-console that had ever shown signs of latent operability.

She replaced the vid-unit's memory chip with the new one, bade the on-duty weapons-tech a goodnight, and reactivated the vid-unit on its tripod before departing to check the others. Once back in Amenakh's quarters, they spent hours studying the only useful videos from that one ancient console. Finally, they decided the cause of the anomaly was most likely in the northern hemisphere of the planet, which was the current geographical area beneath them now.

Amenakh said, "Scholarship of ancient records produces mixed results, little Sitkamose."

She nodded. "My lord, investigation reveals incomplete documentation and records with no operating-manuals at all. I can do more once we return to Ta Shemau. Till then, might I ask the Sem Priest of Ra if he has anything?"

Amenakh shook his head. "Apprising either the Priest Sethnakhtei or Vizier Khutenptah ensures theft of our discovery, since we are mere Zhuanjinn. Whereas time and deception create opportunity for exploitation by the two of us as the only ones who know. Time is what I need to martial my resources on Ta Shemau and launch vectors to reap maximum benefit. If we are correct, I had rather it be us reaping rewards versus the hated longheads." He put his clawed fingers under her chin while giving her a look.

She had become more than crew, more than just a fellow anubisen, much more. Relishing his touch, she caressed his wrist, leaned forward on her clawed tiptoes, and nuzzled her soft, fuzzy cheek against his.

He returned the nuzzle.

She leaned back and met his gaze with a fangy grin. He reached out and pulled her to him, and they smelled of one another while rubbing their fuzzy cheeks together with rising ardor. Determined to pull herself up by whatever means, Sitkamose slipped from her uniform and spent the rest of the sleep-cycle with Amenakh in his quarters.

Cavern Keep

~

Escape the Cavern Keep

Wearing their sopping nightdresses because wool keeps the body warm even when soaked, Seleen supported a barefoot Alahna as they staggered through the effluent tunnel leading from the Gallery of the Infinite Waters. Injured and heartbroken, they splashed through the lava-bright, azure puddles lighting the cave like a full moon shining through glass windows underfoot.

Wet feet also glowed along with the white woolen robes as extreme bright blue in the weird purplish glow. Minerals on the wall shone in colors they had never seen before. Blood stains on Alahna's robe created uneven black swatches. Like a pair of glowing ghosts, they splashed and stumbled into the stolen-man's alcove, where Seleen helped Alahna sit on the cot Alahna had used when attending to the stolen-man. Scorched and burnt, the covers on his sleeping dais stank of source-fire.

Using the little table of various medicaments and bandages, Seleen made a good job of caring for Alahna's body.

Holding her throbbing face, Alahna spoke through her hands, "We must not tarry here, for they will find us sooner than later."

Seleen said with a sob, "But where can we go?"

Alahna pointed. "Follow the tunnel to the Huan Long Shui River and float away."

Seleen was aghast. "As a garil, I used to go down it and peer into the cavern to listen to the river, but whenever the wind blew upstream it stank of unprocessed sewage and there is no walkway on either side. Why not sing a Pao and simply fly away?"

Alahna tried the Song-of-the-Spheres, but her voice wavered.

Concentration shattered, she found herself unable to do so, and swore, "I cannot hold the mind-glyph-of-the-spheres in the eye of my mind, I am too hammered to spawn a sphere-of-power. We must float."

Seleen objected, "To be swept over the falls, and that water—"

Gripping Seleen's shoulders like she had the afternoon at the Pagoda Center, Alahna was dead serious. "Now listen. The WuShi keeps these waters purified. I have studied it, and we have no choice. As a garil, I explored the abandoned mining tunnels near the Great Southern Portal whenever I got angry and hid from harsh old Lilith.

"And, as Keeper of the Archives, I have studied the layered plans of the effluent streams. Of the many feeding the main watercourse, three effluents fall from the ceiling. And, of course, there is the roar as we approach the falls. So, we must be watchful and maneuver ourselves to be on the right side after the third such effluent from the ceiling."

"When facing downstream,"—and Seleen pointed—"but how will this help?"

Alahna said, "About 20-meters long on the right—"

"When facing downstream," Seleen filled in again.

Slightly aggravated, Alahna tilted her head. "Pay attention! There is a small beach opening onto a gallery-alcove where the original mining slaves of the Olden Days cared for the pit-ponies also pressed into brutal slavery to haul rocky tunnel spoils out of the Keep. This is what created the spoil tip beside the falls. If we miss that little beach—"

Gravely serious, Seleen acquiesced, "Understood!"

Leaning on one another, they worked their way down the tunnel till they reached the underground Huan Long Shui River. The puddles in the tunnel still glowed as did their feet, while their nightdresses once more came alight as bright blue. Weirdly, the waters in the larger watercourse also glowed with an ethereal purple hue somewhat hurtful to the eyes. Mineral seams exposed themselves with brilliant veins, specks, and streaks.

Alahna mumbled, "Such a glowing hath never been seen."

Seleen shouted, "What?" because the gush and slosh of the glowing river drowned out ordinary speech. Over the sounds of the watercourse, they heard distressed voices emanating from the stolen-man's alcove behind them.

Despair trembled in her voice when Seleen murmured, "They would have us now had we not ran."

Alahna pulled Seleen close. "It is doubtful they rally so soon. The mystery of our utter disappearance will befuddle and delay meaning we have a slip of time to make our escape.

Seleen looked at the river with worry wrinkling her brow. "We swim, then?"

Alahna shook her head, "Too weak, but Oren taught me an overboard sailor's trick. Do as I do!" Whereupon she removed her blood-stained robe, unlaced the tough drawstring, bit it into equal lengths, then began tying a voluminous sleeve closed at the cuff. "Do both."

Puzzled, Seleen did likewise.

Alahna dipped the nightdress in an effulgent puddle and swung the sleeves up and down to fill them with air. Placing the wet robe across her chest with air-filled sleeves protruding behind her armpits and waited.

The very moment Seleen had hers the same, they stood side-by-side on the low precipice holding hands.

Alahna hollered, "Three—two—one!" and they leapt with a great splash.

Buoyed smoothly along in the deep and luminous current by the makeshift water wings, they seemed like bioluminescent jellyfish.

Alahna hollered over the sploosh and sough, "We need to face downstream!"

As she got them oriented, Seleen swam them closer to the right side of the vast tunnel, but turbulent whorls and eddies kept spinning them in unwanted circles. Their efforts to maintain control made time into a swirling kaleidoscope of bright, unnatural colors.

When they passed the third ceiling effluent flow, the roar of the falls began assaulting their ears, and a mild undertow threatened to pull them under.

Desperation broke Seleen's voice as she pointed. "There it is!"

Alahna let go and shouted, "Swim for thy life!"

Seleen made several strokes, then looked back.

Alahna seemed unable to keep her head above water, let alone swim against the rushing current.

When Seleen's water training kicked in, she overtook the floundering Alahna, then used a lifeguard's grab from behind.

Deafening and merciless, the falls loomed closer and closer and closer. Thick and swirling mist exposed a rainbow force-field across the crest of the falls with water freely flowing through.

Knowing better than to swim upstream, Seleen made straight for the sandy bank as the current bore them on. In the last possible second, she hooked an arm around a jutting rock at the far side of the haul-out, and the current carried them onto a tiny strip of gravel between two boulders.

Dripping, hurt, and chilled, they crawled past the rocks, then onto the sandy beach like shipwrecked sailors.

As they collapsed, Alahna's voice came as a sob over the roaring. "Dear Beloved Goddess . . . that was too close. . . ." and she coughed up swallowed water.

Lit by the eerie glow in the river, tumbledown stables and collapsing hayracks lay at the back of the huge mining gallery. Narrow and dilapidated, mine car tracks ran into the center of the haul-out from a tall black tunnel framed by a deeper darkness. Shrunken, curled, and black with age, ancient leather harnesses and horse tack hung randomly across the remaining flinders of ancient and rotting fence rails. An overturned ore car lay on its side. A siding held several more rusted and rotten ore cars with their wheels galled into the tracks behind a hand-operated railway switch, which was itself rusted in place. Abandoned, rusted, and rotten mining implements lay scattered everywhere.

Desperately in need of rest and time to gather strength, they overturned a wooden feed trough to sit. Rats screeched and fussed and scurried away. Breathless and shivering in the eerie glow, they sat naked while holding one another close. Ugly and glowing in the weird purple light from the rushing river, creatures of the cavern such as worms, snakes, spiders, and salamanders made the walls of the haul-out crawl and move with phosphorescent greens and pinks.

Without waiting, Alahna wobbled to retrieve the woolen night-dresses from the beach. Seleen caught her, helped her rinse the sand away, and untie the sleeves. When they had the robes on and tied again, Seleen hollered, "Can we not sing a fire-sprite and light a fire to dry ourselves?"

Alahna shook her head. "We must not tarry. We have no food, and I grow weaker by the second. If Yenara finds us, we shall be trapped like these rats. And Yenara knows of this place and how to come here from inside the Keep—provided she thinks of it as a possible hiding place," and Alahna pointed at a cave that did not have iron railway tracks.

Seleen nodded and hugged Alahna to share body-heat. "What then?"

Alahna pointed. "If memory serves, we can follow the iron rails and bear to the left at each branch. This leads to the flattened spoil-tip west of the falls. We fell past it in my Pao when we ran from the Keep. Remember?"

Seleen nodded. "Is running from the Keep our habit, nowadays?"

Alahna gave Seleen a wan smile, which made her teeth glow brightly. "My thought is to climb down the spoil-tip on the forested side. Hopefully, Ruby and her family do not yet know of Yenara's treachery. She and her family will take us to Riverbend before dawn."

"Why the entire family?"

"Yenara hath already fallen to The-Baneful-Chaos. This much we know. In her growing madness, she will surely kill or curse anyone who helps us, and Ruby and her family will help us no matter the threat. However, for the time being, the Sisters are stunned and reeling. None will believe we survive, let alone effected an escape."

Seleen looked down. "My sheepskin slippers are still tied. But thy feet are bare."

Alahna said, "Help me tear the sleeves off," and she choked on the memory of the beloved Sister who once so proudly wore the hand-woven masterpiece. When they had done, Alahna folded the voluminous sleeves in half, and pulled them onto her feet with the triple layer folded under bare soles, then used the frayed drawstrings to cinch them above her ankles. The baggy, sloppy socks were little better than nothing as they made their way into the slimy darkness along rotted railway ties in between rusted tracks almost completely inhumed by bat guano. Even as Alahna realized they were tramping through deep guano, a cauldron of bats erupted above their heads flying and screeching toward the falls.

Seleen cried out, but as the bats packed the surrounding tunnel without pummeling them, Alahna quickly put hands on Seleen's head, hugged Seleen's face to her chest, put her own face down, and took them to their knees.

After the bats were gone, Seleen caressed Alahna's hands, asking, "Protecting my head? From what?"

Alahna said, "To keep the innocent creatures out of our faces and their scat out of our eyes, and to keep one or more from tangling in thy beautiful hair," and she held Seleen's hands while both struggled to their feet.

Seleen said, "Ew-w-w-w! Batshit all over us."

Dizziness and brain fog had Alahna tripping and stumbling despite leaning on Seleen, who also fought for balance.

In response, Seleen sang a fire-sprite to float before them like the flickering flame from a candle.

The wan light helped.

Abandoned, the tunnel lay in severe disrepair making them stumble and clamber over fallen rocks and boulders. Heavy cobwebs and scrambling spiders coated their heads and shoulders.

Seleen constantly swept them away—so sticky—so tough—so many—so awful.

The stinking bat guano had its own nasty communities of crawling and biting things.

Luckily, the mind-link with the WuShi somehow stopped the creepy-crawlies from stinging or biting. Having centipedes, beetles, salamanders, and all manner of creepy things all over their bodies was itself terrible and frightening.

The stench made them gag and gag.

As they penetrated the gloom, the rusted tracks led into ruts cut into the stone, then disappeared beneath a solid wall of smooth rock.

Confused, Seleen despaired. "Blocked—we must go back."

Alahna said, "Of course . . . I forgot . . . remember the Song-of-the-Moondoors?"

Seleen said, "A moondoor?" then began the ancient songspell.

Silver sigils glowed the color of bright moonlight.

From under their filthy feet, there came a rocky grinding as the huge plug of stone slide sideways into a hidden niche. Untold years of creepy things living in that void made awful stuff squirt from the sides.

They cried out and hid their faces, then scrambled through.

Safely on the other side, Seleen sang a single note to release it, and it groaned back into place with an echoing boom.

Before long, they exited the curving tunnel onto the spoil-tip—a level expanse with more tumbledown corrals and a dilapidated shed.

The iron rails ended on a rotten old timber assembly with a tip-over dump at the lip that still had a rickety a-frame and huge, spoked pulley on top. More rusted out mining equipment lay here and there in rotten ruins where the ancient miners enlarged the apron as the spoil-tip grew. Over the millennia, the flattened entrance to the tunnel eventually got hidden behind scrawny bushes and thick scrub.

While Alahna leaned on the wall of the tunnel opening, Seleen searched about and found a rickety bench under the rotten roof of a smithy's forge and anvil. Decrepit and splintery, the ancient hardwood remained strong.

Shivering, Alahna sat with a groan.

Seleen sat and hugged her tight.

The glow from the falls was bright as the moon.

Alahna untied the tattered, blood-and-guano-soiled, makeshift socks and threw them into the bushes with a shudder. Examining her terribly damaged feet brought tears to her eyes. Bloody, and covered with guano soiling the cuts and scrapes, her feet and legs were a filthy, scratchy mess.

Seleen's were little better.

Alahna mewled, "It hurts . . . everything hurts . . . and I am s-so c-cold. . . ."

Downcast, betrayed, and grieving in dull agony from heads to toes, a great weariness settled upon them, compounded by the throbbing ache of concussion for Alahna, who sat cross-eyed and shivering. Fighting nausea, she pulled Seleen close. "Go on without me, my love . . . I can go no further . . . the climb down is dangerous even in the midday sun, even for one so nimble as thee."

Seleen wheedled, "I am not in much better shape,"—and she made a wide gesture with her hands—"and I will not leave thee alone. And to hell with Yenara! We must have a fire."

Too weak and cold to protest, Alahna pulled her legs onto the bench, laid down, and curled them close to throw the remains of the wet woolen robe across her body as best she could. Seleen sang a Song-of-Relieving as she gathered tinder and sticks from under the bushes, which helped.

Despite Seleen's songspell, Alahna continued to shiver. Lying there on that rickety bench fighting the urge to retch, something on a fine silver chain fell to the side of her neck, whereupon Conrad's visage appeared in the eye of her mind, saying: If ever the need for my help should arise, hold this in thy hand and call to me. I would know.

By then, Seleen had a warming blaze guttering just inside the entrance to the mining tunnel by the tracks where the mist and roar of the falls was not as loud. Helping Alahna stand and limp to the fire, Seleen went back, flipped the bench over, dragged it upside down near her lifesaving fire, and flipped it upright. With Alahna curled in a fetal position under the wet robe, Seleen took her mistress's head in her lap, saying, "When the sun rises, I shall go for help."

"T-too l-late," Alahna muttered through chattering teeth. Snapping herself into the moment while fighting another wave of nausea, she stammered, "W-we n-need h-help," and took the necklace off. Holding it out in both hands, she cleared her mind as best she could, closed her eyes, then envisioned Conrad's always-smiling face. As desperation filled her, the little amethyst crystal glowed dark purple while pulsating in concert with her heart.

Cavern Keep

~

Rescue in the Night

Conrad bid Ruby and her family a good night, then Ruby hustled her people back across the sward from the falls to their humble house for the night.

Standing beside him, Esau said, "I wonder what strange events took place inside the Keep to make the Sisters throw the stolen-man in the underground river yonder,"—and he pointed—"to drown, or die on the rocks?"

Conrad shook his head. "Seems like an execution, alright. But this is not the way of the Sisters. Why would they save him only to drown his sorry ass or send him over the falls?" With a start, he pointed and exclaimed, "Look there! A fire!"

High atop the spoil-tip, flickers from a guttering campfire danced on the ceiling of a mining tunnel entirely obscured by scrub brush.

Looking at his friend instead of looking up, Tarik said, "How strange?"

Glancing down, Conrad fished the amethyst amulet out from under his shirt. Deep purple and dazzling, the light coming off the crystal pulsed like a heartbeat. A phantom vision of Alahna appeared so clearly in the eye of his mind, it seemed as if she stood before him gazing directly into his eyes.

Conrad murmured more to himself than his friends, "She calls to me. . . ."

Tarik said, "Who? Ruby?"

"Alahna—I see Alahna." That she needed his help was as clear to him as her phantom, which had already faded.

With Esau and Tarik trotting along behind, Conrad urgently ran across the clearing to the stables, went into the barn where their saddles were, lit a metal-framed kerosene lamp, and inventoried the stuff in his saddlebags. "Pepper-meat, nut-berries, knife, bandanas, shemagh."

Esau asked, "What the hell?"

"Are yer shemaghs clean?" asked Conrad.

Both shook their heads, but Esau said, "I always carry clean spares."

Conrad nodded. "Put them in my saddlebag." To protect his face and body, he wrapped his own shemagh around his head, then put his oiled-calfskin jacket on. So doing, he spoke with severe intent, "Alahna needs my help. She is up there. And up there I must go." Looking about, he said, "Strip the canvas rain-sacks from thy bedroll-bags to make them lighter, and see if we can find some used reins or harness leather for shoulder straps."

Esau took the oil lamp and went to the tack room. When he returned, he had several lengths of black-tanned rein-leather about two fingers wide and a coil of leather thong. Working quickly, they tied all three bedrolls into a bundle and made shoulder straps for him.

As Conrad loaded his saddlebags, Tarik handed him two botas of apricot brandy.

Conrad stowed them and slung the saddlebags across his right shoulder.

Esau arranged the overlarge bedroll bundle on his left shoulder and used more rein leather to secure it across Conrad's back to free his arms. Another strap went across his chest to prevent the odd jumble from shifting sideways.

After they had it all adjusted, Tarik said, "I know a fella named Conrad who's always glad to buy a new pack mule."

Conrad said, "Very funny."

"Steady thyself and I'll test the lash-up." So saying, Esau took hold of the bundle and pulled Conrad to and fro to check his balance and the lashings.

Conrad's voice was slightly muffled by the shemagh, "Well?"

"Seems good, but who knows? Ye may have to adjust it on the way up. Or we may have t' catch yer ass as ya roll back down."

Conrad said, "Still not funny, and tell Ruby where I went and what

I think, then ride back to town, hitch one of my four-in-hand freight wagons to the grays. They're best for a long canter. Come back with climbing gear and blocks and tackle. Bring anybody who will help. I'll blaze a trail as I climb.

"And bring lanterns.

"And make haste!"

Esau spoke as he tore long strips off of a linen towel to make trail markers for Conrad. "We shall look like ninnyhammers if nobody up there needs rescuing. And as for that, how will ya find the way up? The moon shines down on the other side of the falls."

Conrad said, "There are gold nuggets up there if yer willin' to climb and dig, and I was. That's how I financed my little freight bidness. As a boy, I climbed that dump many a time on the shaded side of a full moon. Once yer eyes adjust, it's only loose rocks that plague ya."

Esau spoke as he tucked the trail markers under Conrad's chest strap, "I always wondered where yer fortune came from, but can thee manage thy bow?"

"Why?"

"When we return and find we have not been made into eejits by a ninnyhammer, I will aim a fire-arrow into the sky every five minutes so it comes down in the river and gets doused. If we need to come up and rescue, loose two of yer own in quick succession. One if not. We will answer with two shots at once if we're to come up—or one after the other if not."

Conrad nodded. "Good thinking—and I am not an eejit. Give me fire-starters for the arrowheads."

Esau stuffed some into a pannier, saying, "Whether thou art a nitwit or not remains to be seen. Just as it remains to be seen whether we shall become ninnyhammers," and he smiled. Tarik tied the unstrung bow and several arrows to the rear pannier so it would not hinder climbing, and they departed.

It took almost two hours for Conrad to find his old path and blaze it with white strips for the others. By then, it was near midnight. As he climbed past the rotten tip-over-dump on the spoil-tip, he called out over the roaring crest, "Alahna? Mistress Alahna? Art thou here?"

Seleen shouted, "Conrad? Is that Conrad? Blessed be, the Aerthe Mother Goddess!"

He spied Seleen with Alahna's head in her lap on a splintery bench beside a guttering campfire. They looked like lost little children. Alahna lay curled under a wet, bloodstained and ragged nightdress with missing sleeves. Guano covered both. Seleen's sheep-skin slippers were ragged and befouled. Her calves were scratched, but not bleeding. Wet and stringy, Seleen's long blond hair obscured Alahna's face. They both looked so sad and forlorn Conrad found it heartrending, and tears wet his eyes.

His voice wavered with emotion as he strode to them and knelt close to be heard over the roaring. "Adept Alahna—why art thou trapped on this terrible mine-dump in the middle of the night? And thyself, Adept Seleen?"

Seleen reached out, and he gently caressed her dirty hand.

He turned about, and said, "Seleen, canst thou help me undo the straps on my back. She gently laid Alahna's head down and helped.

As she tugged on the straps, Conrad spoke, "Little sweetheart, what in the world are my favorite Sisters doing out here so wet and filthy when Alahna could simply sing a SijanPao and fly down?"

Seleen hollered over the roaring waters, "Running. Escaping. So we hope."

Consternation vied with confusion, so Conrad said, "Well, I am here, and we need to get the both of ye wiped off and warm. Then we shall see about getting down safely."

With tears of relief streaking her face, Seleen bravely gulped a sob. "I am not so bad off, but . . . erm . . . I will call it an emergency that made Milady Alahna run through the corridor where she tripped and skidded face-first across the floor. And High Priestess Lilith hath been—ow!"

Alahna had reached out and pinched Seleen's butt. When Seleen bent down, Alahna pulled her close and whispered urgently. Seleen looked up at Conrad with raised voice, "Kulapti Yenara forced us into a secret escape floating down the Huan Long Shui River to an ancient mining gallery, which Alahna knows about. It connects to this old tunnel," and she pointed behind them. "Yenara finally turns the Sisteren against us."

Before Conrad could respond, Alahna reached out to touch him. Her voice was nasal because her nose had swollen shut. "Must have heard me through the amethyst?"

He wiped his eyes with his sleeve and rubbed her hands in his. "Yes . . . and how could I not hear thee?" Whereupon, he more carefully examined her face on account of Seleen's description of the accident. Chiding himself for being remiss, he inspected the seeping lump in the flickering firelight.

Alahna's eyes had bruised to black and swelling to slits. Her swollen nose forced breathing through her mouth. "This will hurt my lady, but if thy nose is broken, I must set it back into place," and he broke an arrow in two. "Bite down on the shaft." When she nodded, he manipulated her nose side-to-side while pushing gently in. She cried out through clenched teeth, then flailed at his hand, but he held steady. Stooping close to her ear, he said, "Thou art lucky, milady. 'Tis not broken, but only bent. It will heal without a lump."

Seleen said, "Her legs and feet. . . ."

Pulling the wet nightdress up, he growled, "Yenara did this?"

Alahna gingerly sat up. A crimson runnel from her forehead dripped off her swollen nose onto her firm chin, which itself had a mild abrasion, then ran down her neck. Snorting in anger and frustration, she blew the blood away from the corners of her mouth and coughed. "Yonder t-tunnel f-full of b-bat sh-shit."

Cussing to himself, Conrad pulled one of the botas with apricot brandy from his pannier and handed it to her. She gulped a swig, swished it around, spat. Going for more, she swigged greedily, then coughed as it ran from the corners of her mouth tainted with crimson.

"Not too much at once, milady," and he handed it to Seleen, who took a long pull.

Untying the thick and warm woolen bedrolls cum sleeping bags, he rolled them out, lifted one, cut slits in the closed corners and across the end to make a poncho. Handing it to Seleen, he said, "Get rid of the wet nightshirt. Put this over thy head, and place thine arms through the holes unless they're too cold. Make it fast at the waist with strapping. Here is my knife."

Seleen did so, then sat beside Alahna with her feet pulled inside the lengthy sleeping bag.

Without pause, Conrad fashioned the other sleeping bag into a long poncho, whereupon Seleen helped Alahna sit and they both slipped it over Alahna's head and got it under her backside. Kneeling, Conrad untied a soft leather pouch and produced a hefty pile of clean, oversized bandanas along with Esau's clean shemaghs. He handed the shemaghs to Seleen, saying, "Put one on yer head now, milady, and I'll help ya wrap Alahna's after we clean the wounds on her face." He soaked a pair of bandanas with brandy, and handed one to Seleen along with several dry ones while motioning her to attend Alahna's face and miscellaneous cuts and abrasions.

When Conrad cleaned Alahna's legs and feet, she whimpered and cried as he wiped away the guano using brandy-soaked bandanas. With her legs wiped of batshit, he poured the powerful spirits into his hands and massaged it into the cuts and scrapes, then dried and wrapped her legs with dry bandanas for dressings. After Seleen got a clean bandana wrapped around Alahna's forehead, Seleen wrapped the shemagh around Alahna's head. Together, they wrapped Alahna's legs with the third sleeping bag and finally got her bundled, cozy, and not a little bit inebriated on the brandy.

With all this complete, Conrad handed Seleen the nut-berries and pepper-meat sacks along with the additional bota. "Get some of that into the both of ye if possible," and he strode out onto the spoil-tip with his big hunting knife to hack dead or dry branches and stoke the guttering campfire.

Munching a mouthful of pepper-meat, Seleen looked out and pointed. "Look!"

Conrad peered through the mist. A fire-arrow climbed into the dark sky, slowed to a stop across from them, and slowly fell to the misty base of the falls. He immediately took two arrows from his kit and impaled the felt-and-beeswax-soaked fire-starters on the arrowheads. After stringing his bow, he handed the arrows to Seleen. "Flame one and hand it to me." She lit one and held it out. He nocked the fire-arrow and loosed it in an upward arc where it would fall to the river. "Now again," and they repeated the process. Two fire-arrows rose from below at once.

Conrad turned to the source-singers and raised his voice over the roar, "I sent Esau and Tarik for help and supplies. They have returned and are coming up."

Able to take advantage of Conrad's trailblazing, the rescue party reached the spoil-tip with lanterns, ropes, blocks and tackle, and miscellaneous other climbing gear in little more than an hour.

To greet them, Conrad shouted with a rueful grin, "This here eejit welcomes all ye ninnyhammers!" and they hugged and shook hands all around. After several minutes of discussion and argument on how to proceed, they made a sledge from the old bench by breaking the wide leg off of one end. The heavy workbench was wide enough for both adepts to lay on their sides face-to-face with feet supported by the upturned leg at the other end. Securely tied, and with men on both sides clearing the path of verge, the others let them over the spoil-tip employing block and tackle.

Once down and in the clearing with moonlight finally gone, they lowered the tailgate on Conrad's big freight wagon and got Alahna bundled and warm with her feet facing forward and her head near the lowered tailgate so she could speak with everyone.

Cavern Keep

~

No Time for Rest

Seleen sat safe and warm in the wagon with Alahna beside her, when Ruby and her family finally got to approach them nearly dying with curiosity.

Alahna took Ruby's hand. "Dearest friend, someday we shall be able to tell thee the entire tale of what befell us, but we must not tarry in this very moment—time presses."

Ruby caressed her cheek gently. "I do not understand, milady."

Seleen intervened. "Help me to the house and lend me something better to wear. I shall explain."

Warm and feeling the brandy, Alahna fell to snoring while Ruby's husband and daughters helped Seleen to the house, and Ruby's daughters got her bathed and clothed with medicine on her scratches and cuts. Another of Ruby's daughters stayed with Alahna to maintain a watchful presence. Those of the rescue party went about putting the implements of the rescue away in one of the other wagons.

When Seleen came out with Ruby's little family in tow, she stood munching a fresh slice of apple pie cut from a full pie plate she held in the other hand. Alahna motioned for her and Conrad to hop on the tailgate beside her while she ate a piece along with several more sips of brandy, then motioned for them to bend close.

Alahna's voice was weak but steady and not a little drunk. "Conrad, what I am about to tell thee must not go any farther than the three of us, no matter that it may all come out someday.

"On this very night, Kulapti Yenara murdered the Mother Matriarch."

Conrad knitted his brow, murmuring, "Lilith?" then shook his head.

Alahna went on, "Yenara also tried to murder Seleen and myself."

Completely aghast, Conrad swore under his breath, "Yenara again. . . ."

Alahna, "I merely guess, but I'll wager Yenara also usurped the station of High Priestess. We know she usurped the last ShahRen, for that is what she tried blasting us with. Yenara also witnessed Lilith's abdication to me, but she will deny it. Mine only other witness is my beloved Seleen."

Conrad squeezed Alahna's hand. "The stolen-man, we—"

Alahna interrupted with a dismissing wave of her hand and tears wetting her face, "He is done for. And that is that."

As if he had more to say, Conrad started to speak.

Alahna shushed him with a wave and went on. "As for this party, we have much to do. But let us keep this dire news about Lilith and Yenara between us three for now. Convey my wishes to the others using my authority as a high-adept, not as High Priestess. Tell them Yenara finally made good on her threats to confront me. This will make sense, for everyone knows she is mine enemy." Squeezing their hands, Alahna continued, "Conrad, do I have thy trust?"

Tears filled his eyes. "What a question to ask a splendid fellow like—"

She squeezed his hand again. "I know . . . I know . . . but there is a reason. Thyself and thy friends, Ruby and her family—all who assisted us this night—now fall unto grave danger. Please call Ruby."

When Ruby came close, Alahna took her hands. "Dear friend, what I ask of thee is of grave importance. Prepare thyself and thy family for several month's journey. Do this as fast as possible. And I mean the lot of ye."

Ruby shook her head. "What about the livestock?"

She squeezed Ruby's hands. "The Sisters will see ye have gone and pick up the chores. Think of camping out with tents, bedding, pots and pans, camp tools, utensils for eating. Thy sheep dogs can herd the goats along. Bring the old milk cow and her calf and all the yard-birds ye have crates for. We shall need the eggs. Put out remaining livestock to graze.

"And do not worry about mundane possessions. In payment for thy help, I will pay for new. Hide keepsakes and heirlooms in the secret room behind the loft in the barn. Ruby, my most beloved friend, I cannot tell thee where we are bound as a matter of thine own safety. However, treat this as nothing more than an extended camping adventure. In terms of why ye must flee with us, Yenara slips into madness while we pray"—and she pointed at Seleen—"that she and her gaggle do not sally forth before we can make our getaway. And thine own family, too."

Ruby's face hardened, and she nodded to Seleen, saying, "Yenara finally falls to madness? This comes as no surprise. We shall make town by late morning," whereupon Ruby hustled away with her family fussing to hear what Alahna said.

Alahna turned back to Conrad and Seleen. "I fear I am so scattered from the concussion I cannot think straight. I lay plans for departure without knowing whether any ships lay at berth on the wharf," and she closed her eyes to quietly weep.

Conrad spoke up, "Then it is fortuitous the Dragon's Breath lay berthed near the Blind Hag. But, milady, why not go to the Plaza of the Forbidden Gate and have thee soak in the Long Pen Quan there? It is most powerful—"

Alahna grabbed his arm to interrupt. "There is no time. If Yenara shows up in Riverbend this day, it will mean she comes on the hunt for us. If she finds us, she will finish us, and anyone with us."

Seleen dabbed the tears from Alahna's eyes, saying, "There, there, my love. Do not cry. We will handle the rest. For now, lie back and let me sing some relief."

Alahna's voice was low, and she choked back a sob. "Good . . . find Oren and engage the Dragon's Breath in my name, for we must all be away from Riverbend no later than midafternoon. Sooner, if humanly possible." To Seleen she said, "Spare no resource," and she locked teary eyes with Conrad.

Conrad bowed his head. "Speak, Milady Alahna."

"All the folk who helped tonight, and their families, and whatever pets they wish within reason—all must accompany to the Cape of Orion."

Rubbing his sore neck and shoulders, Conrad said, "Mother . . . erm . . . Milady Alahna, did I just hear thee aright? Didst thou mean to say that all those who helped tonight, and their immediate families, must come—pets and all?"

Seleen was beginning to worry about Alahna, but Alahna continued,

"Till I regain my strength and take proper fight to Yenara, all who help us—as well as their families—are henceforth in grave danger from her. In her madness, she wields the power of the ShahRen and the deluded Sisteren at her command."

"But Milady Alahna, these men—their families—"

Alahna's voice was weak. "My lifelong friend, as of tonight a deadly cancer takes root in the body politic of the Sisteren. As such, all must be on the Dragons' Breath when we depart, and thou shalt brook no insolence. They are to bring with them only that which they can carry. Dogs and such are fine but, of course, cats do not travel well what with their poopy boxes. Tell any who resist I will sing The-Dreaded-Geis upon them if they refuse. I would not, but I am certain their lives depend on departure with us. Conrad, thou art become unto mine agent. Adept Seleen is therefore thine enforcer. As High Priestess of the Huan Long Shui, these are my first commands."

Conrad looked at Seleen and spoke with grave intent. "So be it."

Alahna smiled, patted his hand, and blinked back tears. "Have Oren tow a suitable barge for Ruby's livestock, but take only enough fodder for the voyage to the coast. Once on the beach, there will be plenty to graze. We float quietly through Bahndahn Towne tonight. Once on the coast, encamp on the beach south of Cape Orion and north of the ancient jetty. Seleen knows the place."

Conrad nodded. "The river burghers will not like us sailing through Bahndahn without paying their greedy tolls."

Seleen interjected, "To hell with their tolls—everything is torn and twisted. As for sneaking through, leave that to me."

Alahna rolled to her side, leaned up, and grabbed his arm with surprising strength. "Conrad—hear me well. A Gathering of the Four Kinds is set to meet at the Cape of Orion and I must be there. Our very lives depend on it. Our very world depends on it."

He nodded. "So be it, Mother Matr—erm—Milady Alahna."

To Seleen, Alahna said, "As we approach town, sing an obscuration upon us such that anyone visiting town, or the wind-singers at the Cloister waiting for assignment, do not sense our presence."

"But they will be certain to notice the commotion and goings-on at the wharf. And both wind-singers in town are Sisters I trained. They could—"

Alahna interrupted, "Join us? Help us? And if thy wind-singers departed with us, would it not signal to Yenara that we have survived and sail for the Cape of Orion?"

Seleen spoke reluctantly, "I spose. . . ."

Alahna went on, "What if they decide that Yenara would be better in charge than myself? We know so many who deeply resented my actions . . . our actions . . . I am so sorry I brought thee into this."

Deep empathy gave Seleen insight concerning the moral dilemma.

Struggling, Alahna added, "What if Yenara already sent word to them to covertly spy on us, or intervene, or sabotage, or . . . we would be forced to sing a truth-song at the onset . . . a direct SijanPao could easily beat us to town. If the Sisters duped by Yenara come for us at any point even as we sail downriver . . . and even then . . . "—Alahna drifted off point waving her arms above her head—"do we even know who is there?"

Seleen calmed her. "Thy worries run into the realm of irrational fears, my love."

"Do they? After what we have seen? Can we sustain the risk with both of us so spent . . . me so hurt. . . . Just because fear is irrational does not mean—"

"Point taken," and Seleen's eyes teared. And yes, I do know who is on standby."

Alahna's voice softened. "After the Song-of-Obscuration, envision the entire Pagoda Complex and set them all to sleep till the morrow. Maxfield's horses and barnyard critters will fare well enough through one night of neglect."

Seleen's eyes still glistened. "These're bad times upon us, milady."

With her eyes nearly swollen shut, Alahna murmured, "Bad times . . . bad times. . . ."

Heading back to town with the rescue team already departed, Conrad rode on ahead to let the others know of Alahna's edict, while Esau and Tarik drove Conrad's team at a brisk canter. Some time passed before Conrad trotted his horse back and fell in beside the wagon. "Slow yer team to a walk, Tarik. We need to speak."

Leaving Alahna, Seleen carefully worked her way along the sideboard till she stood behind Esau and held his broad shoulders to steady herself.

Conrad said, "They hear me out and nod, then shine me on.

"They got no intention of rousting their families and leaving town on a river voyage out of the blue. A couple of them said they don't believe Yenara would harm them or their families even after seeing Alahna's injuries. They say it's internal politics fer the Sisteren and none of their affair."

Esau patted Seleen's hand on his shoulder as they rode along beside the glowing Huan Long Shui River. "This is not going to work. I doubt that even I could convince Momma to do such a thing, and I'm her eldest."

Tarik said, "So, how do we get them to take their entire families including old bogiturs and little kids?"

Seleen crawled across the bench to sit between Esau and Tarik, then spoke to all three while pointing down the road. "I need to lay eyes on them. Catch up."

Glancing at Conrad, Tarik whipped the reins and clicked his tongue till he had the team at an easy gallop. Shortly thereafter, they hauled within visual range of the rescue party's wagons, and Seleen shouted, "This is good enough. Let the horses walk and catch their breath."

With the wagon slowed, Seleen stood, stepped in front of Esau, and told him, "Steady me, so I do not fall. I give permission to put hands on hips—and no funny bidness." Seleen felt Tarik gig Esau in the ribs, glanced down, and caught Tarik grinning from ear to ear at Esau. She scolded them both. "I said no funny bidness!"

As one they said, "Sorry, milady."

Raising her hands to point at the wagons ahead of them, which were also walking their horses, Seleen raised her voice low to sing with quiet intensity. After several bars, she sat back down between Esau and Tarik. To Conrad, she said, "Ride forth and ask them about their plans."

Conrad spoke to both groups for a several long minutes, then stopped his mount to wait for Seleen and his own boys to catch him up. As they did so, he had an expression of extreme puzzlement painted on his face.

When he had his horse at a walk beside the wagon again, he looked down at all three. "Well, I'll be an aardvark's uncle. Before I could even open my piehole, they told me they changed their mule-headed minds and will muster their families to join the voyage, and—fer some odd reason—they think they're going to a pig roasting on the coast, a camping trip, and a drumming. 'Tis the damnedest thing. . . ."

Seleen looked up at Conrad. "It was a Song-of-Compelling within which I put the other notions. And before ye make judgment, I did so because there is no time for quibbling and argument, or mock anger with stubborn refusal. Alahna hath spoken, and so shall it be.

"Conrad, ride on ahead into town and make arrangements with Oren. Present him with Alahna's signet ring."—and she handed it up—"He will know this is serious. Tell him Milady Alahna loosens the purse strings of the Sisteren, and will stand good for whatever is needed."

When Conrad galloped away, she told Esau and Tarik, "We need to make haste and visit every household of our rescuers. I will sit here on the wagon bench and sing compliance while the two of ye explain Alahna's wishes as nothing but a simple request to join us—one and all—on a party voyage downriver and group camping adventure with pig roastings on the beach near the Cape of Orion. All to be sponsored by Alahna with ten golden jinlongs for every family.

"Do not bother trying to coerce, explain, or appeal. In fact, make no overtures at all. And do not mention Yenara, which invokes politics, as we have already seen. Simply tell them what they are to do and that they must be at the docks no later than noon if they want their gold. My logic is this. If they think it is a party and celebration unheard of in scope, they will not try to bring their every treasured possession, but only that which is needed for a camping trip with ceremonies before winter sets in.

"The three of ye shall make certain we have all that is needed for a much more extensive expedition, and they will be none the wiser. While ye both explain, I shall quietly sing upon them an irresistible compulsion. They shall think the idea is their own without knowing or caring why."

Although tired and in a mild state of emotional shock herself from the constant churn of events, Seleen crawled over Esau and lingered on him a bit too long. Even sweaty, his scent filled her weary senses. So much so, her touch was almost a hug, almost a caress. Once behind them, she rested a bit, then sang a Song-of-Healing for Alahna. How such a healing might inflect was always a mystery, but—in this case—it put Alahna into a semiconscious fugue to soothe the concussion. Other injuries were minor by comparison.

Esau turned and held Seleen's eyes long enough to be considered a lover's gaze. He had obviously made note of her lingering touch.

Tarik saw him, and elbowed him in the ribs. "No funny bidness, yeah?"

Gazing back as Esau when he blushed and turned away, Seleen could not help but smile. They were silly men, brave men, strong men—and most especially, Esau. Sitting that close to him; standing with his hands on her hips from behind; so strong and steady when she crawled over him; recalling how he cared for her in every moment. Training informed her they were still inside of one another's life-elixir field, especially when in physical contact, contact she felt a rush of desire for. She sighed sadly.

As the architectural pinnacle of the High Pagoda became visible in the far distance long before dawn, she pointed her concentration inward to the eye of her mind and envisioned the faces of her wind-singers, Maxfield the hostler and his family, and sang the Song-of-Sleep per Alahna's wishes. When she had done, she looked down at Alahna—a pitiful sight in the dark of night.

Cavern Keep

~

Malison of the Naja Atra

Echoes from the final attack of the water-beast had settled to a broken silence of wails and cries of agony. Most of the Sisters were either completely unconscious or lying about in semi-conscious fugues of anguish and emotional shock.

Yenara regained her senses in a darkness broken only by guttering fires on shattered hallway furnishings. Shelves had art pieces blown off the stone walls closer to the gallery. As best she could discern, she seemed to be the least injured. This made her gaze in wonder at the ShahRen for a long, long moment as tiny ripples of greenish light still ran through the arcane and deadly talisman.

The line of ancient light-emitting tubes along both walls had ceased shining altogether. Ordinarily, they only dimmed whenever the corridor was empty.

This had never happened in recorded history.

The stench of blood and injured bodies made her choke and cough.

Gagging, she struggled to her feet with a groan, then sang a fire-sprite to light her way as she stumbled down the gently sloping corridor in the opposite direction of the still-glowing Gallery of the Infinite Waters.

About 50-meters farther along the corridor lay Old Nebhet.

Yenara reached the aged woman and found her breathing steadily and with no specific injuries other than a terrible bashing from skidding and rolling along the stone floor like Alahna.

As Yenara stood to turn back toward the glowing Gallery of the Infinite Waters, the fire-sprite kept pace above her right shoulder. In the flickering light, she discerned a horrible stinking and steaming heap of bodies near the entry portal. Strewn in a horrible mess, a number of corpses were so badly ravaged it was difficult to comprehend. Unable to process the truth of who they were—for she knew in her deep-mind—she turned back to search for the rest, staggered past the unconscious Nebhet, then on around the bend.

The rest of the Sisters lay closely scattered and generally seemed not so badly hammered as the grotesque and gristly heap of bodies near the Gallery of the Infinite Waters. Nebhet must have sensed the danger and taken the rest into a sphere-of-power, willed them down the corridor at her best speed, and screamed the note-of-deresolution when the water-beast struck just as Lilith had done. This thought brought a cascade of grief and rage.

Bitter anger made Yenara mumble, "How weak are the SijanPao of the Sisteren if a simple scream triggers deresolution?"

With the location and status of the surviving Sisters mostly accounted for, she finally felt herself able to make her way back to the glowing Gallery of the Infinite Waters, now become unto a gallery of death. Beyond malodorous, the stench seemed unbearable. To filter it, she pulled the bottom of her shift up to cover her nose and mouth. It did not help. Once there, she reached down, rolled over an upper torso. Missing her belly and legs, her entrails lay stretched unto snapping. The Sister had literally been shorn in half.

Yenara shrieked in recognition as a cascade of recollection flooded her squirming mind. Protected by the ShahRen, her own body had slashed through the close knot of sycophants behind her like a scythe. Her sycophants, her clique, her legitimate witnesses, those who loved her, all those whose love she so desperately depended on for ongoing affirmation—lay dead. "All dead,"—she mewled while wringing her hands in anguish—"and it was me who killed them!" she cried.

Bent double by gut-wrenching grief, she stumbled into the glowing gallery and retched. Guttering fires cast ghostly, dancing shadows of her kneeling body on the cavern walls. Rocks from the ceiling occasionally splashed into the boulder-strewn pool. Steam and smoke swirled in the air only slightly dissipated by fresh air coming in from the effluent tunnel. Foul water dripped copiously from the ceiling. The glowing pool still roiled with source-energy. The pipe where the venerated golden statue once proudly stood still gushed into the air while refilling the pool.

Yenara peered up at the old skylight and found why the air had changed its typical direction of flow. One or more of the ongoing explosions had blown the skylight away. No longer blinded by the impulse to murder, her senses informed her that the immanent presence of the water-beast as finally absent. And how had she missed that presence when Old Nebhet called a warning to run? The answer was furious rage. Not plain and simple rage. Not plain and simple fury. But furious rage, which the ShahRen somehow amplified into blinding acrimony.

Realization came as a dark epiphany.

The impulse to murder had apparently triggered both attacks of The-Creeping-Darkness—a beast of steaming hate itself. She choked on the realization and cussed herself for not sensing its presence before she blasted the damned apostates in a desperate action to silence them.

And silence them she had.

Her nostrils flared when she chuckled.

A dark sound born of darker emotions.

Brimming with grim satisfaction as she wandered around the cavern and pool expecting to find the shattered and scorched remains of Alahna and Seleen, she found neither bodies nor limbs—just a smattering of macerated entrails floating on the surface of the glowing, rippling pool.

Taking mental inventory, she realized she had broken every major principle in the Tenets-of-Benevolence, and a great many others from the Canon-of-Precepts, in the shortest amount of time she had ever heard of. Worse, her unilateral attack on Alahna and Seleen resulted with her own body—Yenara's own body—slashing a swath through her beloved sycophants like the blade from a farmer's scythe.

Numb, she found herself unable to cry.

She felt empty.

This could not be.

She teetered on the precipice of stark, raving madness.

Instead, however, a darkness in her squirming mind and murder-blackened heart provided a path forward. She was bound to be questioned as to why Alahna and Seleen were so neatly denied due process of law.

Yenara could lay the death of Lilith on them, which would make them all crazy and angry with grief.

Logical enough.

Completely understandable.

Some might disagree, but most would empathize.

But Old Nebhet was as sharp as the blade of that metaphorical scythe. Yenara knew the old harridan would piece it all together. Down the corridor, she spied the dazed old woman rolling onto her back. But how had Nebhet freed herself from the Malison-of-Rage? Of course, this no longer mattered. Nebhet had freed herself and somehow in her wisdom had obviously sensed or seen the water-beast.

More desperate thoughts arose.

Nebhet is powerful, tough, and quietly opinionated. She will tell the others. And thanks be to the WuShi that we cannot sing The-Dreaded-Geis upon each other. But the old bat could still challenge me for title with Confrontation-by-Source.

Yenara mumbled to herself, "Let her try . . . I have the ShahRen . . . just let her try . . . the ShahRen is mine," and so went the savage circles on the merry-go-round of madness in her squirming brain, but it always circled back to murder.

Urgency demanded action.

Slyness filled her chest.

Grief choked her at the very thought.

A bitter brew of anger, dull terror, self-loathing, and burning guilt churned in her chest creating unbridled hatred. As her vision narrowed, Nebhet's weirdly shimmering body filled Yenara's sight with a glow like nothing she had ever seen before.

When Nebhet laid bleary eyes on Yenara, the old woman reached out begging for a hug while crying with joy. "By the Aerthe Mother Goddess . . . I thought thee perished. . . ."

Yenara bent and took Nebhet in her arms just as she had with Lilith. Forcing Nebhet to the floor, she squeezed the old woman's torso in an embrace of death. Stronger than she looked, stronger than Yenara imagined she could be, Nebhet managed to poke an elbow into Yenara's sternum.

Yenara yelped, for that soreness stubbornly remained. Her squirming mind processed with unnatural swiftness as she recalled that same strike from Alahna. Lightning thoughts arose. Then, it became clear. Nebhet had obviously taught Alahna how to strike an enemy in such a manner. It was not a simple hit. It was something darker, for it remained sore to this very day. Vicious in her attack, Alahna had done something more to her than a simple poke of the elbow. By that same token, it came to Yenara that Nebhet could have, should have, done more to help her heal from that. This became a new source of anger to direct at Nebhet.

Nebhet squirmed away while pushing Yenara back sufficiently to gasp for breath. "S-squeezing me t-too . . . h-hard. . . ." and her voice trailed off.

Yenara watched as dark epiphany fell across the old woman's face.

Nebhet's eyes widened as she stuttered, "L-lilith was also shielded by the ShahRen . . . just as it shielded thee. Lilith was alive when thee took her in thine arms. I felt of her pulse."

Yenara gagged on the dirty bolus of shame choking her throat.

Nebhet scrabbled farther back while lowering her voice in disgust. "Thou'rt vile! Thou hast killed Lilith and Alahna and Seleen! And now? Is it my turn, Yenara? Is this the truth of it? Thou vile scunner!"

The truth of it hit Yenara's gut like a sledge hammer. Stopped in her tracks, she smiled a sad smile, peered along the corridor, and—for a single moment—wished she could take it all back. Other survivors moaned as they untangled themselves. The ShahRen on Yenara's wrist glowed bilious-green. Something dark and evil distorted Yenara's face.

Her sad smile morphed into a bizarre grimace, and she scrambled forth, put her knee into Nebhet's crotch, and shoved the old dowager hard against the stone wall.

Crying out in pain, Nebhet used her elbows, shoulders, and momentum to leverage herself up off the floor as Yenara slapped a smothering hand across the old woman's mouth.

Confusion and heartbreak in Nebhet's eyes got replaced by desperation and mortal fear. With both hands, she pulled Yenara's hand hard into her wide open mouth and bit down with all her might. Yenara shrieked and yanked her hand free with a badly bleeding bite on the side of her palm.

Nebhet scrabbled pitifully along the gore bespattered corridor gasping for breath and crying out, "Help! Help!" By then, however, her voice was merely one of the many.

Frustrated, bleeding, and furious—Yenara attacked once more.

Nebhet levered her back against the wall and kicked out with both legs.

Caught square in the chest, Yenara got thrown backward and upward to her feet. Off balance, she staggered back. Tangled in the front of Yenara's shift, Nebhet's feet ripped the front open to expose Yenara's pendulous breasts.

With quiet rage born of occult blackness, Yenara snarled through clenched teeth, "Wrinkly old scunner! Why will thee not simply die?"

Aghast and terrified, yet deadly determined, Nebhet cried, "Dost thou mean, 'Die as Lilith died?' Crushed in thine arms? It is my life to defend!" whereupon she raised her hands and wove a deadly bone-crusher hitting Yenara like a mule kick. But Nebhet herself lay enfeebled. The bone-crusher was not lethal.

Nevertheless, Yenara got hammered into the opposite wall and smacked the back of her head. Desperate to have the dastardly deed done with, she fought her way through Nebhet's warding and willed a tiny bolt of crackling blackfire.

Shoop!

Nebhet gurgled as a gout of steam and spattering of smoky crimson droplets gushed from her mouth and nose. She grabbed in futility at the open, smoking crater between heaving breasts. The pinprick wound had only narrowly missed her heart.

Fury filled her.

Determination hardened her face.

Drawing agonized breath with steamy smoke accenting tortured words, she placed her hand over the puffing wound and sang a malediction.

To Yenara it seemed as if Nebhet had mistakenly begun The-Dreaded-Geis in the middle of that dread songspell. But how would Old Nebhet know how to sing a malediction? Why did she start it in the middle? Reeling from the gesture-of-warding, Yenara watched in horrified curiosity as Nebhet intoned while her right hand formed into a cup facing Yenara, then artfully swept a forefinger as if tracing the line of a serpent's body.

Out of nothingness, olive-green flames shimmered into existence taking to shape of a huge king cobra. About three times longer than Yenara was tall , it raised its head to eye level, then hissed at her. As the front third of its length rose to confront her, she realized Nebhet's curse was the deadly Malison-of-the-Naja-Atra, a standalone curse Yenara had only ever heard about. And it was, indeed, plucked from the middle of The-Dreaded-Geis.

Then, it hit her.

This specific malediction had always been a part of The-Dreaded-Geis, a part she had never fully understood. As deadly proof in this mortal moment, Old Nebhet had known forever and kept it secret. Images of the curse-cobras Yenara herself had set upon the hapless sailors at the Blind Hag Tavern raged through her burning mind.

Casting the curse with those venomous and forbidden words-of-power, Nebhet fed her dying emotions into the curse.

Born of the betrayal in a victim's wrath, the curse-cobra was three times as long as Yenara stood in height. Rising high enough to glare with burning acrimony into Yenara eyes, it swayed from side-to-side while slithering forward. A forked tongue of red flame flicked in and out without relent. Curling smokes rose into singed air. Glaring eye-to-eye with Yenara, it spat a smoking stream of envenomed hatred at her.

She shrieked and dodged to the right.

The liquid hatred sizzled when it spattered on the stone wall.

Her heart pounded wildly.

Her chest heaved.

The stench of it burnt her nostrils.

Continuing the dodge, she tried to run.

Wicked fast, it slithered, blocked her, and spat more venom.

She dodged to the left as the vitriolic stuff sizzled on the stone wall.

All in a blur, it slithered past to block her flight, then spat at her eyes again.

This time she ducked as the horrific venom dripped smoking down the wall behind.

As the red-and-fiery snake's eyes burnt hotter and ever hotter, Yenara became transfixed—unable to run—unable to dodge.

Spittle flew on her words as she cried out at the dying Nebhet, "Thou art Keeper of the Curses!"

In mortal agony, Nebhet held her left hand over the crater in her chest. Bloody runnels leaked from under her palm. Curling smoke slithered up the stone wall from behind her back. In answer, she simply nodded while intoning the curse with her breath forming ragged smoke rings in the air.

Knowing it would surely strike before she could turn and run, Yenara backed slowly away in terror. As the cinder-hot eyes—those hot-cinder eyes—bored holes in her very will, she stumbled back and smacked her head against the hard stone again.

For another terrifying second, the weaving, flaming curse-cobra hissed and swayed hypnotically before her less than an arm's length from her face.

Confused and transfixed by the searing waves of perfect malevolence, Yenara screamed while trying to muster a bone-crusher.

As if sensing Yenara's defense, the curse-cobra deftly ducked under her shaking hands.

Leaving trails of curling, olive-green flame—it struck.

Hissing mouth wide open, its fixed upper fangs sank deep enough into Yenara's heaving chest to penetrate her bony sternum.

Screaming, she clawed at it trying to yank it free, but the curved fangs held its writhing, calescent body between her breasts even as it deftly threw a coil around a defending arm.

Howling, she felt the contractions as it pumped and pumped stinging venomous death into her convulsing body.

Yenara fell back even as the constricting king cobra whuffed from existence in a burst of toxic, blistering reek and venomous orange smoke.

With her back against the wall, orange-threaded curls drifted from beneath the trembling hand Yenara held to her chest as she slid slowly to the floor. Her eyes rolled back till only the whites remained. She began shaking and bawling as thick, bubbling saliva ran freely from her frothing mouth. Her hand fell to the side as orange-threaded smoke rose curling from the fang marks in the center of her heaving chest. Welling from the rancorous punctures, more curls of foul-smelling smoke rose into the air breaking into ragged puffs and whorls.

She shook uncontrollably as the source-magic, curse-based venom spread rapidly through her body like waves of molten magma. Head lolling from side-to-side, she babbled as the venom found her brain and filled her mind with boiling enmity. It felt as if her skull had been hollowed out and poured full of molten lead.

Glowing a bilious-green, the ShahRen vibrated and thrummed.

Seconds later, orange runnels of lymph and sweat formed on her skin from head to foot.

Wherever these dripped to the floor, more whorls of nasty smoke rose from the foaming puddles as malodorous orange puffs.

Everywhere they touched her sweat-and-blood soaked clothing, nasty black-and-smoking stains appeared.

Beyond exhausted from the monstrous night's work, Yenara sat quaking against the wall of the corridor with orange-streaked foam dripping from her gasping mouth.

Nebhet stopped cursing and smiled that same sad smile for Yenara—the same sad smile given to her by Yenara—a combination of pity and rancor.

Trapped in that gruesome moment, they held one another's eyes.

Thick, frothy spittle dripped from Yenara's slack-jawed mouth to run slowly between those heaving breasts and the smoking fang-marks.

Nebhet's hand fell away from the raw crater in her chest. Gone on the winds of time, she crumpled down.

Slowly, Yenara slipped sideways along the wall, then down to the worn, gore-slickened floor.

Death reigned supreme.

Cavern Keep

~

Sisters Awaken and Mourn

Cailinn opened her eyes to the crepuscular rays of dawn shining through millennia old skylights at a near horizontal angle in the halls and corridors. Providing a kind of sundial effect, the sun had just fully broken the horizon. Confusion marked that awakening when she found herself lying atop an aged adept, one whom she had known all her life, one whom she had always loved.

The tale was told by the unnatural twist of the dowager's back along with no hint of breathing.

The beloved old matron's body was already cool to the touch.

Fighting emotional shock, Cailinn tumbled off the stiffening corpse, got to her knees in a ray of sunshine, and staggered along the rough stone wall where nature forced her to relieve herself. She wandered in a daze toward the Gallery of the Infinite Waters with the irrational hope of finding Alahna as a shoulder to cry on till she recalled the night's insanities and so much unreasoning rage.

Seeing Yenara fire a bolt of blackfire at Alahna and Seleen had scarred Cailinn's psyche forever.

"Too much killing," she muttered to herself.

The feculent stink of burnt and scalded flesh, fresh blood, open wounds, and human offal from the dead and dying befouled the air.

Once again leaning on the stone wall to gather herself and pick her way forth, she bawled out loud into the thick silence, "Curses upon thee, Lilith! Why did thee not lead us in songspell and force The-Creeping-Darkness back down That-Which-Abides!" In answer, an eerie silence reigned till soft moans and cries disturbed it.

Once again pulling herself together, she instinctively took mental inventory of the outright dead versus the variously injured as those crepuscular rays randomly illuminated the scene into grisly focus. As she rounded the sweeping curve, there lay High Priestess Lilith's scalded and burned body. The stink made Cailinn choke. She bent and touched Lilith—stiff as a statue—which Cailinn knew would pass as rigor mortis faded. Against the rough stone wall farther on lay Kulapti Yenara. Now ostensibly High Priestess, Yenara lay in a weird state of twitching catatonia.

The ShahRen on Yenara's left wrist pulsed with a bilious green glow sending ripples along her comatose body. Nauseous, orange-tinged lymph beaded her skin. Foul smelling urine pooled around her butt. The remains of her sackcloth shift were sweat-soaked with odd swatches of blackened cloth. More light exposed her ripped open front with two charred wounds seeping blackened blood from between bare breasts. Blackish veins spread across her chest like overlapping spider webs.

On the other side of the corridor, Old Nebhet was down with a bloody burn hole blasted clean through her chest and out through her spine. Small cinders from the stone wall behind still glowed on the stone floor. As Cailinn surveyed the body a foot twitched, and she immediately went to Nebhet to try and save her, but she dead. In the cascade of dire thoughts running through Cailinn's mind, one thought rang clear. Were it not for a sense of impending danger on the part of old and beloved Nebhet, they might have all been killed.

Dizzy, nauseated, and heartsick, Cailinn stood and covered her face as scalding tears blurred disbelieving eyes. Several terrible moments passed while she steadied herself against the wall choking on wave after wave of gut-wrenching grief. It crossed her mind that she ought to force herself on into the Gallery of the Infinite Waters to search for Alahna and Seleen—but therein lay abject terror.

"No!" she exclaimed to no one. "I must see to my Sisters and pray the monster is gone."

Wiping her eyes with the backs of her hands, she gazed up at the stone ceiling. Damage to the carved arches closer to the source of the explosion and portal entry was extensive enough to require immediate shoring by the Sisters who specialized in maintaining the structural integrity of the Keep—provided they yet lived.

The thought created more sobbing.

As other survivors came to their senses, cries of pain and despair filled the air even as Cailinn stumbled onto an inconceivable mess—the worst mess of all.

A twitching line of broken, sundered corpses lay scorched, torn, raw, and oozing bodily fluids amidst congealing pools of blood. The ragged remains were so dismembered, disrobed, and disfigured that Cailinn could not recognize one from another. In some cases, the bodies lay melded into unrecognizable heaps of shattered anatomy.

Why did Yenara not protect them?

Why did this bunch of nitwits ignore Old Nebhet's warning?

In both physical and emotional shock, other survivors milled purposeless and confused along the blooded corridor.

Breathing deep, Cailinn performed a grand gesture-of-calling to carry her voice throughout the Keep. "Sisters! This is Adept Cailinn! I hereby take charge till properly relieved! We must put our grief aside and turn from the dead to the living! Find those most seriously injured and help them first! Only one Sister for each one who lies beyond help!"

Weeping while wiping their eyes, they took on the grisly work. As they did so, she gathered young acolytes by assessing their skills according to the rings-of-rank on their right forearms, then assigned various emergent tasks. "You three sing the Great Northern Portal open. Likewise, you four to the Great Southern Portal. We must exhaust these foul odours and regain our senses."

The sound of bare feet slapping on worn stone followed them as they ran dodging and crying through the aftermath in the shifting shadows.

Cailinn then motioned to a pair of designates, who would likely become initiated, then lesser adepts, and finally bound acolytes, for they loved the Sisteren as opposed to their previous hard-scrabble lives.

As orphans taken in by the Sisteren, Myrna and Teewan had immediately bonded to become inseparable. Their young and innocent faces were subdued by grief and stained by tears as they clung to one another sobbing. Both had yet to be initiated, for they were both too young to choose.

She gathered Myrna and Teewan in her arms and hugged them close while feeling the poignancy of such a horrible violation in their young hearts. After a pause for empathy, she sternly pushed them out to arm's length. "Go together and make haste unto Riverbend. Bring back as many villagers as will come. Tell them Adept Cailinn on behalf of—" and she wondered what next to say. Was it High Priestess Yenara? No. Continuing her sentence, she said, "Kulapti Yenara commands it so."

They looked at her with tears spilling from reddened eyes. Her resolve steadied them. Having such a mission-of-mercy called up their youthful courage, and they obediently nodded their heads.

As they turned to go, Cailinn added, "And of course—bring the gypsy-adepts and healer-women with all of their medicines and herbs. And hasten as fast as may be!"

When the girls ran off to gather their kits, Cailinn began working her way through the corridor. According to her orders, those too injured to walk got carried to the Grand Banquet Hall on makeshift blanket-stretchers.

Ordinarily a place of joy and plenty, the dining-hall became a place of emergency management where the injured got assessed and treated according to need. Some would surely die and required only comforting.

Sad and mournful, healing songs fell into four-part harmony all around the Keep.

Cailinn felt a change in air pressure the very instant the vast airtight doors of the Great Southern Portal rumbled aside. A welcome sigh of relief came from all as a fresh breeze washed through the Keep when the other acolytes sang the Great Northern Portal open.

Riverbend

~

Organize An Expedition

Galloping along the west side of the Huan Long Shui River to carry out Alahna's wishes, Conrad arrived in Riverbend with the bare hint of morning twilight washing stars from the sky. He went straight to his own stables and pole barn where he had his other freight-wagons. When the sleepy live-in stable boy roused to greet him, he handed over the lathered horse to be watered, rinsed from the tall water tank, scraped, and rinsed again till cool, then finally walked and given hay.

With the stable boy busy, Conrad hitched a fresh horse to a his heavy-duty shay, a horse-drawn cart with two large wheels that would easily carry two passengers plus baggage in the large rear trunk. When he got to Captain Oren's mansion, he hopped out, strode up the stairs of an elaborate veranda, and pounded hard on a huge doorknocker.

When Oren's sleepy daughters in full nightdress answered, he said, "I bid thee excuse the early hour young ladies. Please inform Captain Oren that High Adept Alahna sends Conrad the Hunter to engage him and the great ship, Dragon's Breath, and present him with her signet as good faith," whereupon he handed Alahna's ring to the taller girl.

Presently, Oren came down the stairs in his smoking jacket and pajama bottoms with the ring in hand and bade Conrad join him in his study. After some 15-minutes of detailed explanation, Oren immediately sent both daughters with written orders into town to alert his officers and have them rally the crew and prepare the huge caravel for sailing under onus of a dire emergency.

There were plenty of sailors in town willing to drop everything and go on the promise of doubles, based on Alahna's open purse and emergent request. Oren and Conrad made three trips from Oren's vault to the shay with Alahna's chests of gold, which Oren always held in his vault as a service to Alahna. The gold was to be used versus scrip or redeemable notes to prevent paper trails.

As Conrad's heavily laden shay departed, Oren shouted, "Watch yer turns, me boyo! Or that shay of yers will tip right over!"

Conrad laughed and waved, then carefully kept his horse at a brisk canter to the house of his lead teamster. When the big strapping woman answered her door, Conrad bade her come forth and help him fill a large money sack with jinns and jinlongs, which he carefully dropped in one at a time. "Count with me," he said.

Her husband had joined them and stood watching in total awe. "But this be a small fortune."

Conrad laid a hand on each of his old friend's shoulders, but spoke directly to her. "Now that I have yer attention, how would thee and the rest of yer teamsters feel about two week's pay for one day's work—to be paid up front with this?" and he hoisted the swinging bag before their astonished eyes.

She spoke up, "Well, hell—me boyo. I'd be up for that. And I know the others would, too."

Conrad produced an ink-stylus and clipboard with an informal contract, filled in the sum, signed it, and proffered it to her. "Are we in agreement?"

She scrutinized, then signed.

"So then, I name thee my agent and bursar, and I shall expect proper accounting.

She asked, "What's this all about, my friend?"

Conrad spoke urgently, "Alahna means to organize a emergent voyage on the Dragon's Breath to the Cape of Orion with a return voyage after camping a few days." Conrad lied about the return voyage, for he did not know when they would return, but there was nothing for it. He added, "There will be ceremonial drummings and secret rites for a special group of her friends who came to Ruby's stables last night to help . . . uhm . . . manage a crisis of sorts.

"Alahna requires every one of them to accompany, and she needs them at the wharf before noon, or as soon thereafter as humanly possible. Here's a list of the families she needs. No friends. No neighbors. Just the entire immediate family. They are to come one and all—oldsters, adults, children, and babies with whatever camping gear they can carry and no more. They can also bring bedding and clothing for 1-week, but nothing else."

The teamster looked over the list, saying, "To the best of my knowledge, none of these families have babies at present."

Conrad said, "Myself and Alahna's close helpers will manage the rest in terms of food and cooking for the group. Oh, and pass the word to expect foul weather. Lastly, if Esau and Tarik, along with Adept Seleen, have not visited the household yet, bid yer people wait till they do, then approach with the offer of help in loading and transport. Old friend,"— and he put his hands on her shoulders—"if ye get this managed and all the families arrive at the wharf before Noontime Zenith, I'll throw in an extra week's wages fer ya when we get back."

She said, "Will ya go along yerself?"

Conrad nodded.

"Shall I have my people take up chores at yer stables and house?"

Conrad approved. "Anyone of the loaders as helps will get time-and-a-half, and my own young helper knows he is to log their time correctly with no bullshitting. I'll pay everybody the difference when we get back."

She slapped him on the back. "I'm on it then, boyo."

Conrad gave her another formal hug, then hopped onto the shay and departed at a swift canter. When he arrived at the Burgher's Business Center, he found the mayor and his staff just opening for business with the sun breaking fully free of the horizon. Shaking hands, Conrad once again explained, "Please send word to the shopkeepers and burghers. High Adept Alahna hath untied the purse strings of the Sisteren to organize a voyage and expedition on the Dragon's Breath downriver to the Cape of Orion and depart no later than noon Zenith—if at all possible.

"Captain Oren and myself will be there to manage payout and purchasing—gold jinns only—no scrip, chits, or receipts. We shall need camping gear, trail fare, fresh vegetables, dried and canned meat of all kinds, and supplies in general including emergent medical kit. I'm off to the tentmaker's t' see about shelter. Will I see everybody there?"

Smiling, the mayor said, "Oh, we'll be there alright, laddy buck. Just hold on to yer breeks."

As he traveled across town, Conrad mentally tallied how many people would need shelter—about 50-60 people including more private shelter for the Sisters. When he strode into the office of the tentmaker's warehouse and textile mills, the strong smells of steam-driven machinery, boiling cauldrons, bleached and dyed fabric, oiled canvas, and leather tanning operations greeted his nose.

After Conrad explained his needs, the burgher rubbed his chin, saying, "Well, me lad, ye're in luck. I just completed the annual order for the desert folk, but they're not due here for another month. I'll sell ya the whole lot and start the other order now."

This produced an assortment of rugged gypsy-tents ranging from small for 2-3 people, to pavilions for large families. Sewn in the shape of wedges, two main poles as a cross brace for the desert-style tents forced heavy winds up and over no matter the direction.

By the time Conrad arrived at the wharf, the town burghers; shop owners; both gypsy-adepts from the Forbidden Gate with their ledge wagon and magical wares; and many of the independent craft folk such as sword smiths, and knife makers; all began showing up along the wharf to set their stalls in place with lots of bickering over placement and frontage.

The minute Conrad arrived, Captain Oren had his tough officers help him manage the gold while all the sellers made note that Conrad had arrived and rushed him. Watching all the sellers fall to raw greed, Oren shouted to Conrad and the officers, "Bring all the specie aboard and turn it over t' the Chief Purser for counting before we open the Sister's purse strings. Milady Alahna will require an accounting."

When Conrad got to the top of the gangplank, he properly asked the boatswain, "Permission to come aboard?"

The boatswain tipped his head. "Permission granted."

When Conrad stepped onto the quarterdeck, Oren stood waiting while his officers took the gold to his purser. "Conrad, me boyo! While the crew started loading and refitment fer passengers an' such, I got to thinkin'. I should make ya familiar with the ship so ya don't come off lookin' like an eejit by askin' me crew too many stupid questions. After all, ye're in charge a' this lashup. Yeah?"

Worn out from all that had taken place throughout the long night, and with no time for sleep, Conrad dug deep into his physical reserves. "That would be wise, Captain Oren. I've got the tents already bought and comin' to the wharf to be stowed, but ye're right. I need to know the limits of yer cargo holds to decide what's absolutely essential and what ain't."

"Well then, me boyo, let's take a tour like we're discussin' terms and bidness."

Conrad smiled back. "Aye-aye Captain," and he saluted.

Oren laughed. "Salutes are fer sailors. As a civilian, if ya feel the need, put yer hat over yer left shoulder or yer heart. Now let's get to it. Time is short."

When they got below to the stuffy 3rd Deck after completing the better part of the instructional tour, Oren asked, "I suspect ye'll be needin' the 3rd Deck fer berthing?"

Conrad thought about it, and boobed his head.

Oren called a boatswain over and gave a flurry of orders.

Listening intently, Conrad asked, "What is a cowl-scoop?"

Oren cocked the eyebrow atop his good eye. "That'd be a ventilator box. We bolt it the wide pipe-mount between the anchor capstans on the bow. It peeks o'er the forecastle deck to catch the wind as we sail and push it clean through a big tube down into 3rd deck, where we are. The open cargo hatch amidships channels stale air out. In foul weather, we turn the cowl-scoop away from the wind so it doesn't take in wave wash."

As they continued their walk-through, Captain Oren explained, "Below 3rd Deck"—and he pointed down past the cargo hatch where a heavy cargo net full of hogsheads casks filled with ale were lowering past them—"is the hull with bilges and keel. We stow barrels a' freshwater, hogsheads of ale, and casks of our world-famous Riverbend Rum down there fer ballast and trim. Now let's go back to up topside."

As they finished, Captain Oren, said, "Well, laddy buck, ya better get down there and start spendin' the Sisteren's gold," and he slapped Conrad on the back again. Me ship's chandler on the wharf will see to helpin' ya buy supplies. She's waitin'."

Conrad removed his molded wool flat-hat with a short brim, and covered his left shoulder. "Aye-aye, Captain."

Oren laughed and saluted back.

Those of the crew who had been covertly watching with barely suppressed amusement, laughed and shook their heads. One of them said, "Landlubbers . . . whatcha don't see?"

Sleeping City

~

Lair of the Lonely Fire-Dragon

After plucking an unconscious human from the waterfall, HuoJi the little fire-dragon fell into a sideslip stall. One hard flap of her wings restored flight, but she barely avoided dragging her drenched belly across a bunch of stupid humans standing around a bonfire.

Pounding the night air hard, she gained altitude and flew west. Stars were disappearing from the sky by the time she soared over the foamy breakers on the beaches just south of Cape Orion. Slowing, she glided straight toward a fallen entry portal high on the southern cliffs.

In the ancient past, these same ruins were a landing strip for the flying machines of the hated NuliZhu, which made it a good place for her lonely den.

Only creatures capable of flight could come here.

Strangely, there were no nesting birds inside.

At the back lay an ancient lake fed by a Long Pen Quan fount. The fresh and pristine waters were good for drinking and soaking. There was even a hot springs with volcanic waters for her fire belly. She could fly inland to hunt for deer and other grazing prey, or dive into the sea for fish and blubbery sea lions. Since it was early Fall along the LungHuo River, tasty salmon ran upstream with bellies full of juicy eggs.

Ordinarily, HuoJi soared across the enormous fallen monoliths at speed, flapped her wings to shed airspeed, then performed a running touchdown. Now, however, she held an unconscious human to her chest, whom she had strangely been compelled to save. Sensing the air currents along the high cliff shifting from a nighttime land breeze to a morning sea breeze, she knew they would be gusty and dangerous.

With no choice, she glided toward the cavern entrance just above stalling speed. When a powerful downdraft forced her flight path low, she instantly tucked her right wing close while trimming her left wing to roll sideways. Glancing across the monolith on her right side, she hurled his body backward to tumble across the fallen door a good deal slower.

Hopefully, slow enough to keep from killing him.

Once clear of the monolith, she spread her right wing to roll upright and correct the stall. Having lost airspeed, however, the next event would be a crash landing on her still-injured chest—and this time there would be no yielding marsh with slick reeds to splat down in—like near the riverbed when the high-adept hit her with a bone-crusher on the night of the Blood Moon at the Plaza of the Forbidden Gate.

Such a catastrophic touchdown could easily break her neck or smash her head if she plowed into a fallen boulder—and there were plenty—and damn that high-adept!

Legs extended, she desperately ran as fast as she could while pumping her wings to regain flight. Once again airborne, but rattled and even more sore from glancing off the monolith, she thought to avoid another crash landing with watery splashdown. Flapping her wings like a goose landing on a lake, she miscorrected the glide angle.

The water caught her hind legs, and she flipped. Thinking fast, she tucked her wings hoping to skip like a stone across the lake. And skip she did till her spade-ended tail caught the water.

Flipped again, she suffered a loud belly flop that hammered her breath out and knocked her silly. Luckily, she scudded along in shallower water, then ended with her head on the sand where she lay on her side for a while trying to catch her breath.

No sooner than when the cavern stopped spinning, she realized she needed to go. Reeling and too scattered to fly back outside where she normally went, she stumbled dripping across the crusty dust and fallen rocks to squat. Flapping sore wings to fly over the crumbling stones of a tumbledown wall nearby, she made three circles while padding her nest of straw and sticks, then settled.

Too injured to go and find the human, HuoJi yawned and stretched, grumbled through the pain, then wrapped her tail around her streamlined body. Laying her head on the spaded tip, she fell into a fitful sleep in the comforting darkness.

Riverbend

~

Rescue the Rescuers

It was just after sunrise when Tarik, Seleen, and Esau reached the outskirts of Riverbend with a badly injured Alahna resting quietly in the bed of the wagon with a tarp pulled across the sideboards to keep prying eyes from seeing her and allow her some darkness to rest in. They paused long enough to water the horses at Conrad's stables with plans to systematically visit every rescuer's household.

Whenever they found one of Conrad's teamsters in a freight wagon patiently awaiting their arrival, their message to the family was the same. Departure was at noon Zenith at the wharf. This was Tarik's suggestion, for he knew most would be late and this might possibly get them there by midafternoon.

While Tarik and Esau went into their act, which was a simple invitation to accompany High Adept Alahna downriver on a cruise to the Cape of Orion and back upriver with the certainty of a generous stipend, Seleen sat quietly on the bench seat of the wagon with a shawl over her head softly intoning the Song-of-Compelling. None balked, for Seleen's gentle enthrallment took them completely.

They went to Esau's household last, and Tarik did the pitch with Seleen outside on the wagon quietly singing. Esau himself remained there with his family to organize them. Subsequently, Tarik pressed on with Seleen to the Dragon's Breath where Oren's crew carried Alahna onto the big caravel using a clamshell stretcher carefully slipped under her from both sides.

Fussing like a mother caring for a wounded child, Seleen clucked at them all like a yard-bird with a brood of chicks to watch over.

Once on board, they took Alahna to a stateroom on the quarterdeck that had previously been two compartments reserved for paying passengers. Before their arrival, Oren's sailors removed a purpose-built partition making the compartment into a stateroom suitable for a high-adept and her lady.

As soon as Tarik got free of both high-adepts, he trundled the wagon back into town to help the teamsters wherever needed, grab his own stuff, and check on the households as instructed. By the time he returned with another family group, two other freight wagons had arrived with Esau and his extended family. With all ten families accounted for, one of Conrad's teamsters collected the wagon Tarik had been driving while another of the teamsters took charge of the family wagons and teams that had to be left behind at the wharf under such short notice.

Nobody questioned Conrad's teamsters taking charge.

After Esau and Tarik got Esau's people settled, they took a last short stroll on the wharf where they found themselves beset by hawkers and vendors. Esau bought some gear for his family and sweets for the young. Tarik got some gimcracks and gewgaws for himself.

As they walked across the loading platform on the wharf supporting the gangplank extended to the quarterdeck, Esau told Tarik, "This air of happy campers seems so damn sad in light of the truth."

Tarik agreed. "A good thing it's a short voyage to the coast. The Dragon's Breath will be crowded with this lot." On another tack, he asked, "How long before Momma had the whole damn story out of ya?"

Esau shook his head. "Before ya got back to the wagon," and he sighed.

"Did she balk?"

Esau shook his head. "Nope. She said if Alahna needs her, then we go, and that's that." Whereupon he paused at the gangplank, and Tarik bumped into him.

Tarik said, "What?"

"Since we go into dangers unknown, even I myself question the wisdom of taking my family with us. Me old pappy's gettin' on."

Tarik nodded. "Making people do what they would not do otherwise hath become a habit with Alahna ever since that accursed drumming at the Plaza of the Forbidden Gate. After all, that's what she did to the stolen-man—take him where he would not go—I mean. And look how that turned out. I never thought about it before now, because this never happened before."

"What?"

"Conflict in the leadership of the Sisteren. As we just saw with our very own eyes, it makes people choose sides. No damn good."

Esau said, "And that, my friend, is exactly what Alahna does not want. So, we run. What I don't see is how running keeps anybody safe? Conrad sent everybody in the whole damn town down t' the wharf like another equinox bazaar."

Tarik made a squeaky voice while squawking like a dodo bird going in circles with crossed eyes and flapping arms. "Nothin' sneaky about that."

Esau shook his head. "That's an insult to dodos." As they walked across the gangplank, he added, "In the hands of the Sisters, as they say."

"Well . . . dodos are stupid, but I think maybe Alahna is not running, but bringing the people who saved her along with her while going toward something. Remember, The-Sleeping-City abides beneath the Cape of Orion."

Esau said, "In the hands of the Aerthe Mother Goddess, as they say."

Tarik and Esau lent a hand to Captain Oren's quartermaster and his petty officers, who were clearly in charge of things. This made sense because of their knowledge about the needs of extended shore parties, foraging for game and fresh water, and whatever dangers might arise. They also knew the coastline near the cape.

Much attention got paid to garnering supplies for hunting, gathering, and the proper tools needed to fashion useful things from driftwood logs washed up on the beach. Glass jars of canned goods in crates, salted hams and canned pork, jerked meats and gunnysacks of dried fruits, all went into the lower decks where the icy mountain waters of the LungHuo would keep the supplies cool.

With all of this accomplished, and people settled for the short cruise to the coast, Tarik stood talking with Esau on the quarterdeck behind the binnacle.

Esau spoke with apparent relief when Seleen disappeared into Alahna's stateroom. "The new broom sweeps clean, eh? I would never have guessed sweet little Seleen would be such a pushy little thing."

Esau shook his head. "The old saying, 'Bossy as an adept.' comes to mind, and nobody's ever done this before. She's exhausted and doesn't even know it. Been at it non-stop since Yenara laid them low—the dirty scunner."

In that moment, Conrad arrived to stand behind Tarik, who did not know he was there.

Tarik mouthed off. "And Seleen knows just enough about everything to make us all crazy—even poor old Conrad."

Suppressing a grin, Esau surreptitiously put a finger across his mouth to silence Conrad, who also grinned.

On a roll, Tarik continued, "So . . . lemme get this straight. Conrad is sweet on Alahna, but he can't ever have her, and she uses his sorry ass whenever she wants for whatever she wants, and all the time he walks around like a wagtail puppy dog, right?"

Esau made to let Tarik know Conrad stood behind him, but this time Conrad put a finger to his mouth.

Both suppressed grins.

Tarik dug himself in deeper. "And thou art sweet on Seleen and will never get her either, but at least she doesn't run yer ass around like a well-trained dog."

Esau shook his head. "I dunno. She ran our asses around pretty good this mornin'. And when she climbed on the seat beside me . . . well . . . I guess I'm the one with unrequited love."

"But at least Seleen rubbed all over ya," and Tarik chuckled.

Without a word, Conrad clipped Tarik on the back of his head. Tarik's hat went flying. He spun around to see who clipped him, and Conrad let him have another on top of his head.

Conrad lifted an eyebrow. "Bullshit? Sorry ass? Wagtail puppy dog? One might want to engage one's pissant brain before one's crocodile mouth gets one's canary ass in trouble. And, let me be clear. 'Tis nobody's bidness what I do least of all yers."

Rubbing his scalp, Tarik glared at Esau. "Sheeit! Might've told me he was behind me."

Esau clipped him too. "Like the man says—pissant brain, crocodile mouth, canary ass. Seleen is trying to save our asses."

Tarik harrumphed as he picked up his hat.

Conrad patted Tarik on the shoulder. "That'll feel better when it quits hurtin'."

Tarik scoffed and muttered, "Butthole. . . ."

Conrad laughed. "I smell stew. At least Oren had the sense to start his cooks first thing. Let's go eat. I'm starving."

As they went down the steep steps to 2nd Deck and the bustling galley, Esau said, "Let us be thankful there aren't any babes in arms and nobody is pregnant. It'll be hard enough on these old bogiturs and little kids."

Conrad shook his head as he stepped down onto the deck. "It'll be a miracle if we pull this off and nobody dies or gets killed."

Riverbend

~

Myrna and Teewan Come Down to Riverbend

When Myrna and Teewan reached the Pentakulum just inside the Great Northern Portal still within the Keep, they stood in quiet observation of the acolytes. One of the first songspells a young initiate had to master was the Song-of-Opening for the vast portals at either end of the Cavern Keep. Self-luminous under songspell, the gigantic monoliths had crystal quartz inlays as moon-runes some 30-meters tall. Each door stood 50-meters high, 80-meters wide, and 3-meters thick. However, the opening itself was marginally smaller to allow a vertical and airtight half-lap joint in the middle with an airtight seal on all sides when closed. No one knew why this was so.

As Myrna watched, the acolytes stood side-by-side song-casting in front of the massive stone slabs. Resting in deeply grooved keyways, the doors stirred with rippling azure-gold waves of esoteric energy running along the vertical surfaces while the moon-runes glowed with an aspect of molten blue lava flowing in the crystal channels. As the runes and elegant swirling lines across the interior surfaces pulsated in rhythm with the acolyte's chanted syllables, a subsonic rumble tickled their feet as the enormous stone slabs shuddered open. Bolts of sizzling azure lightning tickled vertical lap joints as they parted.

Mined into the metamorphic and sedimentary stone along the high, south-facing cliffs above the LungHuo River, the ancient Keep lay deep inside the heart of the high plateau. No one had ever fully explored the Cavern Keep except Lilith and Alahna, and even they admitted they had never determined the entire scope and number of underground levels. The Huan Long Shui Plateau itself rose over 400-meters into the air with great cliffs and escarpments along the entire perimeter.

The northern entry-ramp lay recessed into the surface of the plateau with a natural-appearing berm all around to prevent flooding during the rare cloudburst. When seen from above by a flying dragon or Sister in a sphere-of-power, the Great Northern Portal was unremarkable as a geographic feature, for it lay hidden and recessed under a vast overhang making it look like a natural sinkhole.

Routine practice for budding acolytes was the Song-of-Concealment, which they staged from time-to-time to stay in practice. From outside on the plateau, the ramp into the Cavern Keep simply disappeared. From beneath, one could peer through to the sky as if a sheer rainbow curtain had been pulled across. When ubiquitous desert winds blew sand, tumbleweeds, and rocks across the force-field, a rain of debris and detritus fell when it got derezzed.

Age-worn ramshackle stables and tumbledown shacks were the only structures to mark the surface, which lay a moderate distance from the ramp. A hidden spring covertly irrigated a botanic desert garden, which the Sisters cultivated for remedies and potions created from all the varieties of medicinal cacti, desert plants, and flowers.

Nearby Shantytown, as it was called, had never been more than a rendezvous for the Somber Services held on the solstices of winter and summer and the equinoxes of spring and fall. During these events, villagers, artisans, farmers, and local gypsy-adepts—everybody—came to sell their stock-in-trade to the Sisteren followed by good business, lighthearted gaiety, and frivolous celebration. Water for all came from the oasis and botanical cacti on the outcropping which concealed the portal ramp, which the Sisters carefully tended to make certain it looked wholly untended and not like a managed agricultural site. No one knew why the Sisters had to do this, nobody asked, and nobody cared.

A winding desert track led across the top of the plateau wide enough for freight wagons, wains, and the elegant gypsy ledge-wagons to pass freely. From the air as the dragon flies—so the saying went—long abandoned forks spread out across the plateau desert, which also had forks, all of which simply faded from the landscape. Huan Long Shui archives loosely referred to ancient-alien technological installations where the tracks ended, but none had ever been discovered. Rain, wind, and time had all but erased them if ever they were there.

Having topped the great ramp just as the twilight dawn washed the constellations out, Myrna and Teewan looked about expecting to find healer-women, gypsy-adepts, or just plain gypsies, and most certainly artisans and hawkers. Fresh dung, still-smoldering cook fires, fresh tent sites, and several heaps of new trash bespoke the recent presence of people, but the place lay abandoned. Neither of the girls had ever seen Shantytown completely empty since coming to the Keep as orphans, for it was one of their menial duties to collect and dispose of garbage. A task which they hated but made do, for it got them out into the sunshine.

Puzzled, Myrna made an observation. "There are always folk hoping to sell their truck and goods. Where have they gone?"

Teewan nodded her head sagely. "Scared away by magicfire and screaming and badness last night."

Myrna said, "Damn right! Let's go before Cailinn sends somebody else."

Both took a pull of water from a bota bag. Facing one another, they took off their shirts and bound one another's breasts with long sashes. Putting the shirts back on, they tied their shemaghs desert-style with mere slits for the eyes, then fastened their small backpacks with chest straps for running. Both wore handmade desert boots.

Running together was their happy time, and jogging downhill was easier. Between jogging and walking, it was early mid-morning when the tired, dusty, and thirsty girls made it to Riverbend, where they found a great brouhaha in progress. With everybody hustling and bustling, nobody paid a bit of attention to them as they unwrapped their shemaghs.

Teewan stopped a bent old woman shuffling past. "Old mother, why is everybody running about?"

The old woman made to pull away, then patted Myrna's shoulder hard enough to loosen accumulated dust and reveal the black cloth. She recognized the unembroidered shirts and trousers of designates who were not yet initiates. In a scolding tone, the old woman blurted, "Outfitting the Dragon's Breath with supplies for an expedition, clothing, talismans, knives, swords—just about anything thou canst imagine. And there's plenty of gold jinns to be had!" She cackled greedily while holding up a pouch of coin. Pausing, the old woman rubbed her hairy chin. "Why don't ye garils know? Ye're both of the Sisteren. And now, as ye mentions it, wind-singers from the Cloister never showed up at the wharf all mornin'."

Myrna raised her chin and looked down her nose in disapproval.

The old woman took the hint and made an impotent gesture-of-warding as she bowed and scurried away. Muttering to herself as she went, "Oh! These're bad days a comin'! First the forbidden gate comes to life . . . then a fire-dragon tries t'kill the chant-circle . . . then High Adept Alahna comes t'town injured. . . ."

The rest of the old mother's mutterings got lost as she disappeared into the bustling crowd. Myrna crowed and jumped up and down in front of Teewan. "Oh, thank the Aerthe Mother Goddess! Didst thou hear? Alahna!"

Teewan blurted, "And maybe Seleen?"

Myrna hollered into the crowd, but the old woman had melted away. Shaking Teewan's shoulder, she said, "We must find them!"

Teewan said, "Shouldn't we run to the Pagoda Center first?"

"Poof-parf!" said Myrna, "They'll make us go back to the Keep with them," and off she ran. With Teewan close on her heels, Myrna ran down to the riverfront as fast as her tired, aching feet would go. It took only moments to work their way through the steady stream of people coming and going near Captain Oren's caravel.

Myrna stopped so fast Teewan ran into her. Pointing at the ship, Myrna shouted, "Seleen!"

Sleeping City

~

The Stolen Man Revives

Consciousness returned to Elijah along with a fugue of burning agony due to road-rash injuries and bumps, deep aches, and a disconcerting kaleidoscope of shifting colors. Lying there in and out of the most severe pain he had ever had in his shoulders, hips and knees, he was unable to understand whether his eyelids were open or closed. A vicious memory—or perhaps a nightmare delusion—had him losing his eyes down to the sockets in some sort of acid fire.

So, a nightmare, then?

And in that horrendous dream, he sat in his studio staring into an impossible rift in space and time when a flying dragon attacked everybody with gouts and balls and sheets of fire.

Absolute blind denial forced him to flee the false recollections even though this was the second time they tried to return in his mind. As to the pain in his joints, it was as if some weird sort of semi-intelligent nerve block was trying to provide relief.

Lying naked and badly injured wherever he was now, he felt of his face—eyelids—and they were closed despite gazing into a dazzling kaleidoscope of the entire electromagnetic spectrum dependent on which frequency of the EM his capricious attention wandered to. Focusing, he could see his own finger bones like an X-Ray image. It was like shifting through multiple scenes inside a virtual reality headset with no control over what comes next.

He mewled and groaned and thought of normal vision. Still inside the VR headset, he perceived himself to be lying in yellowish sunlight atop a stone monolith. Still fighting for control, he peered down through his body's skeleton. As the imaginary VR show drove his sight, it forced another shift, and his visual perception shifted into the blues and purples of ultraviolet and beyond.

Lying there naked and battered from head to foot from smarting and bleeding road-rash—and that was no goddamned hallucination—he moaned in pain while using fingers to check his forearms, the backs of both hands, every knuckle to the tips of very sensitive fingers, some of which smarted brightly, and the surfaces of both palms. His hands and forearms had also gotten burnt to the bone when he tried to cover his face in that horrendous nightmare.

Now, however, everything was only tender.

Ordinary callouses on his fingers and palms were completely gone. Fresh road-rash had several knuckles skinned. A few fingertips were swollen as if his arms had flailed about in a skidding roll. And that was only one bit of the overall, never-ending weirdness. These freshly incurred injuries made it seem as if some asshole had thrown him naked and unconscious from a slow-moving pickup truck—slow-moving because he had not gotten severely injured.

Regardless, it was all bad enough—too bad, in fact.

He groaned.

Underpinning it all the bone-deep arthralgia in his primary joints. When present, it was so fierce it stole his breath away. When not present, it was still there, but he didn't care, like when taking heavy opioids.

Wet and bloody seepage matted with sandy dirt contaminated every scrape and cut, for the block of stone he had apparently skidded across was covered crusty dust and various sized rocks. He carefully touched his dirt-encrusted forehead—no VR headset. Not wanting to further foul his eyes with dirty fingertips, he left his apparently useless eyelids shut—still yet more weirdness.

Concentrating through the burning pain and dull agony, he found himself able to stop the shifting kaleidoscope-of-color and settle on a skewed version of normal.

Gazing this way and that with closed eyes yet able to see, the echoing sounds around him told him he was inside yet another cavern and quite near the sea. The fresh scent of salt water and sea wrack, the echoes of squawking gulls, grunting and shrieking cormorants, and pounding surf told the tale.

Distant sounds of splashing in the opposite direction of breaking surf suggested a natural spring. In that same moment, an unnatural thirst assaulted his body with a terrible vengeance. If he could reach a freshwater spring, he could drink, and perhaps not die from gulping foul, bacteria-laden water. He muttered, "Only an idiot would drink from water pooled on the floor of a cavern with batshit and whatever the fuck else?"

Finally forcing his sticky eyes to open, he blinked and blinked to get some tears flowing. With blurry and stinging eyes working normally—so it seemed—he rolled to his side, struggled up on hands and knees, then shakily gained his feet to peer over the side of the vast monolith. A litter of other, smaller, architectural boulders created a sort of stairway he was able to scoot down or across and get to the floor of the cavern.

That floor appeared to be as smooth, wide, and long as a primary runway for a county airport.

Once down, he pussyfooted about with sore feet absent normal calluses, trying to see the distant water source, but the vast cavern was too deep. However, a shallow stream ran along a slight swale down the center of the quasi-runway. Suppressing his instinct to fall and guzzle, he shambled deeper into the cavernous air terminal toward the splashing while praying to find a pristine flow somewhere—his only hope.

The cool water felt great on his bare feet, but strangest amongst all the strange things in this very real hallucination, was that the waters he now waded in also gabbled in his third eye or Ajna. He was so inured to this phenomenon, it existed only on the fringes of consciousness, while his waking mind held only one thought.

I won't last long given the shape I'm in.

Once out in the cavern proper, his blurry eyes and the extended echoes of all the sounds gave evidence of a cavern large enough to assemble an entire fleet of the largest passenger aircraft from Earth. Complete with fallen down overhead cranes and giant trusses supporting a vast open ceiling, the rest of the place was so strangely alien that his waking mind glossed the stream of subconscious processing.

Even weirder, there were indecipherable hieroglyphs on the walls of what appeared to be aircraft hangar stations in the distance on either side that glowed and rippled with primary colors as he approached, then faded as he moved farther in.

Wordless thoughts of hallucination plagued every moment.

Thirst drove him without mercy.

Too sore to do anything but carefully wade deeper into the cavernous air terminal with tender bare feet, he gingerly proceeded toward the splashing in a surreal, hallucinogenic frame of Zen mindfulness. His deep study of transcendental meditation and single-pointed concentration informed a well-honed ability to cope with unbelievable stress, for all one needs to cope with that which is unbelievable is acceptance of what seems impossible.

His dry voice croaked, "And—just as sure as hell—this is all unbelievable. . . ."

As he went, shrieking nightmare memories attacked his mindfulness as he carefully shuffled through the stream to keep from tripping. Meditational mantras allowed them to pass through the storm in his waking mind like wind through the bare branches of a winter tree.

It was that or give up and die—but that was not his way—too cowardly.

Eventually, he approached the source of the splashing. The waters of the stream were overflow from the level coping of a curved swimming-pool ledge constructed as one side of a large, underground body of clear water—crystal clear water.

In a strange burst of déjà vu, he thought he had seen the like before. Regardless, the small lake had naturally curved ends and, as best he could guess, was at least three city blocks long and two wide. The swimming-pool coping covered only one side. The other three sides were sandy beaches with gentle slopes leading down and into the lake.

An island in the middle yet closer to the other side supported a free-standing fountain. A life-sized statue of a golden long-dragon mounted along the edge gushed pristine waters from its laughing mouth. Another strange burst of déjà vu brought recollections concerning a golden long-dragon statue being melted right before his very eyes. Accompanying terror made him suppress it. Of course, Eli's idea of what life-sized meant was only based on cartoons, and fantasy movies, and Buddhist legends.

As he wandered around the edge of the lake heading for the fountain, he spied a wide and arched bridge leading out from a paved, peninsular promenade passing under a really large torii—a gateless gate. When closer, he could see the water of the cistern overflowing from drain scuppers. As the source of the small lake, the gushing waters from the fount were certainly enough to account for the lazy flow of the little stream, whereupon a burst of quantum logic slammed his waking mind.

If this fountain was the source of the stream, as opposed to the type of fountain that recycles its own water till the water becomes foul, this gushing fount might very well be an artesian spring. If so, the gush from the statue should theoretically be pure. Almost mad with thirst, he quickened his clumsy pace and noticed a boiling, bubbling hot springs smelling of sulfur on the other side of the strand on the right.

The promenade was cobblestone passing straight through the center of an ancient tranquility garden that had long since completely dried and withered. Either side of the promenade lay walkways along barren streambeds complete with little stone pagodas, various other sculptures of cement or maybe carved stone, and planters with the dead branches of desiccated plants. The torii gate he passed under was large enough to allow the passage of a 1-ton pickup truck. A few yards farther out, the peninsular promenade ended at the arched bridge.

Closer now, he surmised the diameter of the free-standing brass fountain to be about 40-feet. Supported by thirteen brass dragon legs evenly spaced at about 10-feet apart around the perimeter, the cistern stood about two feet above the smooth stone surface of the small island. The legs were sculptured dragon's arms ending with ball-and-claw feet gripping what appeared to be black opals the size and shape of elongated human skulls.

The skulls glowed with ethereal light—but especially the eye sockets—giving them a frightening, haunting, almost living aspect in his skewed perception.

After stumbling across the bridge, he bumbled up a set of steps to an aged wooden landing with handrails and pegs to hang clothes on, provided one had any clothes. Benches to sit on and disrobe stood on either side.

A soaking pool, then?

Judging by the size of everything, the people who built this place were roughly the size of humans.

Ignoring it all, he wobbled to the cistern and tested the water with a finger—nice and warm with no foul stink—which made him feel of his nose.

Déjà vu hit again, and again he suppressed it.

Feeling his face he found his nose. Still there, too.

But the déjà vu kept on.

Driven to forget, he sat, submerged his feet, and found underwater steps—more déjà vu set in, which he pushed out of his mind.

He waded in and strode through waist-deep water while washing his hands. Cupping some water from the gushing dragon, he tasted.

It seemed pure.

Unable to stop, he waded fully beneath the gush, opened his mouth, and drank till his belly sloshed. Rinsing his eyes till clean, he was finally able to see about, which did little to alter the skewed perceptions.

Rinsing his head made him mumble, "What happened to my hair?" for he recalled having a full head of hair in his existence before this horrendous hallucination. For that matter, he had no hair on his body whatsoever—really and truly weird.

Standing under the gush, he scrubbed the injuries clean while murmuring in relief. Open eyes did nothing to change the kaleidoscope of shifting colors, but did reveal a soaking-bench around the inner perimeter.

Finally able to make assessments, he saw that the water-dragon statue—which seemed to be made of pure gold—clung to the edge of the bowl using three legs while the right fore-hand reached out over the waters holding an archetypal Flaming Pearl of Wisdom made from a moonstone gem as big as his head. The Pearl bore the ubiquitous, stylized perpetual flames made of pure platinum—so he guessed— because the color was of the shiniest silver. If it was pure silver, it would be gray with tarnish.

Exhausted, starving, and weak, he waded to the bench, sat, and laid back fully immersed except for his head in order to rest and catch his breath. Soaking warm in those magical waters, he fell into a semi-conscious fugue. The very moment his beleaguered eyes closed, however, water gushing from the mouth of the statue turned as bright as azure molten lava.

As the entire pool took on the same aspect, the dragon-waters sintered meaning into his battered brain. A soft, growling voice in his subconscious whispered unintelligible words of alien origin. Arcane and mysterious, the alien didactic somehow empowered his willpower to access to the cerebral, autonomic functions, but especially the primary and secondary visual cortexes of both occipital lobes.

Finally, his desperate need for natural sleep allowed the cessation of visual perceptions, and his sleeping eyes fell to normal darkness. However, such was the fugue of myriad injuries that he tumbled into a deeper darkness than any provided by mere eyelids. He wallowed to the side and fell beneath the splashing surface. Instead of drowning, a spinning whirlpool vortex to the surface of the roiling pool enveloped his mouth and nose allowing him to breathe naturally.

He was not aware of this.

He only rested with those ethereal voices sintering subtle techno-babble into his subconscious mind, his deep-mind.

It was impossible to know how long he lay submerged, because the plica semilunares of his conjunctiva—vertical folds of the eye near the nose as nictitating membranes—had also gotten revivified as a genetic atavism. With his face underwater, they autonomically snicked into place to protect his beleaguered eyes. Whenever he opened those eyes in the dream-state, nothing stirred a sense of danger.

Orgastic relief flooded across his entire body.

Shoulders, hips, and knees glowed with golden light from within.

Darts of purple light played along his primary joints like tiny koi fish nibbling at the macerated skin tags from all the road-rash.

Finally, the dragon-waters energized him so completely that he came awake, realized his head lay underwater, sat up spluttering, and imagined he had only submerged his face for a second or two. Otherwise, he would have drowned.

"Right? I would have drowned?" he reassured himself.

Standing beneath the gushing dragon's mouth, he slaked his thirst again, scrubbed at the plethora of abrasions and contusions, and discovered the bruises almost faded; abrasions pink and mostly skinned over; cuts knitted while leaving white scars behind as the only evidence they had ever existed; hands fully healed, but macerated from soaking too long. Naked yet warm and feeling somewhat normal other than starvation stealing steadily upon him, he recalled the dream of bright waters glowing and fizzing around the injuries, glowing and fizzing around his completely submerged head.

"Weird! This is some really weird shit, now!" he grumbled aloud.

No matter how irrational, the only explanation was that the injuries had not been as bad as he thought.

He muttered to himself, "Naked and hungry . . . getting

weaker . . . this is bad. . . ."

As an improvement, however, the deep arthralgia in his primary joints had faded. Feeling of them, they seemed normal. With hunger driving him out of the wonderful pool, he retraced his own path and came upon another set of tracks in the gritty dirt near the end of the swimming-pool coping, tracks he had missed in passing.

Something large and four-legged had departed the lake via the coping, climbed out dripping, and made a cluster of tracks around the small stream. The tracks were enormous, four-fingered, humanlike hands with obvious thumbs. Small indentions at the end of each digit hinted at sharp claws—a dragon? In addition, there was a large heap of scat surrounded by a drying puddle of animal urine.

In a sudden panic, he instinctively scanned the area around and above, crouched low, hustled on bent legs to the nearest cover—a thick and tumbledown wall. Making himself small, he sat with his back against the stone while wrapping arms around knees for warmth. The fear of a grisly death gave momentary distraction from the empty pit in his stomach and remaining injuries.

Minutes crawled by with no sound except the placid splash of the fount and boiling gurgle of the sulfur hot springs, which seemed a natural, geothermal pool versus any sort of engineered edifice. The only other echoing sounds were the boom and sough of distant surf and squawking gulls. Just to be certain, he cautiously climbed to the top of the tumbledown stone wall while careful not to injure himself again. He looked about ready to flee back to the cistern and hide beneath the gush of the golden dragon.

Nothing stirred, but after twice guzzling his fill, he suddenly had the urgent impulse to piss. Walking to one end of the wall, he piddled into the gloomy shadows while keeping his head on a swivel. Halfway through relieving himself, there came a great shuffling and stirring from beneath.

Then, right before his very eyes—his totally terrified eyes—a fanged and horned head lifted from the shadows.

Smoke-rings belched from the dragon's flaring nostrils.

Riverbend

~

Myrna, Teewan, and Adept Seleen On Board

As the morning wore on, it took over an hour of hard, bust-ass work for Oren's crew and the stevedores, manning one of the many stiff leg derricks along the wharf, to get all the barrels of freshwater, hogsheads of ale, and a valuable cargo of Riverbend Rum in casks loaded down along the Dragon's Breath keel and bilges. All of this was new to Seleen.

The jib boom of the derrick was tall enough and long enough to reach out over the cargo hatch giving access to the lower decks of the ship down to the bilge and keel. Watching them lower water barrels, Seleen tiredly asked the boatswain manning the quarterdeck gangplank, "Since we are on the river and the river is not saltwater, why so many barrels of freshwater? I can understand the ale and rum. Everybody loves a wee taste of the creature. And I assume Captain Oren means to sell our famous rum in Bahndahn Towne, but we will not be mooring there."

The boatswain smiled tolerantly. "Riverbend Rum makes damn good trade wherever we go, milady. But with yer people as the only other cargo, it makes the ship top-heavy. To set the trim, we need ballast at the keel, which is where we store the barrels and casks and all such. The Captain ordered enough freshwater for a longer voyage, and we like t' drink water from home as long as we can on account of gettin' the drizzly-runs from strange waters. Scuttlebutt has it we might set sail for Qinah after landin' yer party at the cape."

Seleen nodded. She had been pestering him and all the rest with similar questions all morning, but they were all good-natured. The same scene played out as a tired yet busybody Seleen went from checking on Alahna, to poking her bossy nose into all the activities, including shopping through the wares on the wharf after Conrad told the townsfolk that High Adept Alahna had loosened the purse strings of the Sisteren.

Conrad himself was busy with Oren's chandler.

More than once did Esau respectfully admonish her to let the experienced sailors and himself and Tarik help Conrad manage the supplies, and to go take care of Alahna.

By midmorning, Seleen had almost worn everybody's tolerance to a frazzle, when—from out of the hawkers and bustling crowd on the wharf—high-pitched voices hollered, "Seleen! Adept Seleen!"

Squealing their happiness, Teewan and Myrna bounded up the ramp to the boarding platform on the wharf, then bolted across the gangplank to the quarterdeck. The boatswain stepped back to allow them past, and they collided with Seleen.

Down all three went in a busy tangle of cries, tears, and embraces.

Back on her feet, Seleen chided, "Ye're required to ask permission to come aboard—not tackle thy betters to the deck! And ye're both so filthy!" whereupon she began swatting the dust off.

A family man himself, the boatswain made his voice officious as he rubbed his bearded chin. "Throw 'em overboard, milady?"

They cowered behind Seleen, who caught on. "Empty heads can learn," and she turned to them. "what did ye learn?"

Nodding their heads, they spoke at once. "Can we get on the boat?"

Suppressing a grin, the boatswain kept to his mock officiousness. "It's a ship to landlubbers. And ye're to say, 'Request permission to come aboard.' An' I say, "Permission granted.' Or mebbe I say, 'What's yer bidness?' Or mebbe I say, 'No fart-handles allowed.' What say ya, Milady Seleen? Over the side?"

Seleen raised her eyebrows and gave each one a look. "Well?"

Peeking from around either side of Seleen, they asked, "Permission to come aboard?"

The boatswain laughed. "Permission granted," and they both ran to hug him.

Pulling them free with a laugh, Seleen bade them follow her to the starboard side of the quarterdeck and stand behind the stern of an eight-man longboat secured on heavy davits. Then, things turned serious. "Did either of ye go to the Pagoda Center?"

They shook their heads.

"Not even past the Cloister grounds?"

Again, they shook their heads.

"Ye've seen no other Sisters in town except myself this morning?"

Myrna blurted, "We ran into town an' stopped an old mother to ask her why everybody was bustling about in such a dither."

Teewan chimed in, "And she told us Alahna was here."

Myrna added, "We ran straight here, milady."

Seleen's eyes were narrow. "What brought ye here from the Keep?"

This question triggered a breathy gabble about Cailinn and summoning help for the Keep with both going on at the same time.

Seleen held up her hand to stop them.

Myrna frowned with teary eyes. "We thought ye both killed in the blast. . . ." and she put her head on Seleen's chest.

Teewan knitted her brow and joined the sorrowful embrace. "So much sadness and weeping in the Keep. . . ."

Seleen's tired face belied her own grief as she patted their backs. "Do ye think Alahna and myself so easily done in?" while tears welled in her eyes.

Myrna straightened. "The old woman in town said Alahna is hurt?"

Seleen frowned. "Mother Matriarch is Alahna's title and station now. And yes, our new High Priestess is hurt."

Teewan glanced askew at Myrna. "But Seleen, we thought Kulapti Yenara got raised to Mother—"

Seleen interrupted with knitted brows and hard lines on her tired face. "Vile! Yenara the usurp—" whereupon she caught herself. The girls were too young and innocent to comprehend the gravitas of such foul treachery. She took a breath. "Alahna suffered a serious head injury when the mindbane of The-Creeping-Darkness hit."

Myrna said, "It did not hit me and Teewan so hard."

Seleen corrected, "Teewan and I, and it's likely because ye're not yet joined to the WuShi as initiates."

Teewan said, "Was that it?"

Rubbing her temples, Seleen looked in the direction of the Keep. "Alahna and I believe some never-before-seen manifestation of

The-Creeping-Darkness attacked us . . . erm . . . attacked Lilith, to prevent interference when it—"

Myrna interrupted, "Tore the stolen-man apart?"

Seleen said, "Alahna saw the same monster in the Pool of the Infinite Waters after it blasted Yenara and . . . well . . . we think it swept us into the pool when Yenara aimed the ShahRen—"

"And tried to kill ye both?" Teewan said with lifted eyebrows.

Seleen sighed. "So it seemed at the time, the water monster may have actually saved us. 'Tis all very confusing. We both suffered more hurts when we swam underground in the Huan Long Shui River."

Wide-eyed, Teewan blurted, "Did ye go over the falls?"

Myrna chided Teewan with a clip. "Why would ya ask her if she's crazy?"

Rubbing her scalp, Teewan said, "Ya'd have to be crazy to go over the falls. That's how we say crazy. 'She went over the falls.' Yeah?"

Seleen shook her head. "Nobody went over the falls, although it was a close thing. And nobody is crazy. I'll tell all about that later. For now, Alahna rests in yonder cabin," and she pointed. Separated by a couple of meters, a pair of large doors appeared to define two cabins adjoining the quarterdeck.

Myrna asked, "Which door?"

Seleen was patient. "Both doors open into a stateroom as wide as the ship. Typically, the space is divided in twain by a stout partition. On a long voyage, Oren's officers occupy one side while our wind-singers occupy the other. Captain Oren bade his carpenters take the partition down, so Alahna and I have a large stateroom.

"Now listen closely, for I am about to give ye both a lecture."

They knew that tone, and paid attention.

Seleen began, "Anything toward the back of the ship—known as the stern—is aft from wherever ye stand. Anything toward the front of the ship—known as the bow—is fore or forward of where ye stand."

The girls nodded.

Seleen went on, "Floors on a ship are called decks; walls are bulkheads; hallways are passageways; stairs are ladders; doors go from room to room; hatches go from deck to deck; windows in the hull are portholes, of which there are two in our stateroom. Both have shutters so the wind-singers can sleep during the day in shifts if needs be; Second Deck has a few portholes; and none on Third Deck."

Seleen pointed aft and up. "This entire house is the sterncastle. This very minute, silly garils, we stand on the quarterdeck." Pointing forward, Seleen said, "The long deck to the forecastle is the weather deck. The deck above our stateroom is Captain Oren's Quarters, which he will share with his officers till we arrive at Cape Orion. Ship's crew sleeps forward of the galley on Second Deck. The open roof above Oren's quarters is the poopdeck and wheelhouse with the ship's wheel for steering, and the primary binnacle. The ship's wheel is connected to the rudder by a fancy mechanism of very strong ropes and pulleys."

Myrna said, "Binnacle? Like the little creatures that stick to rocks on the beach?"

Seleen shook her head, "No, those are barnacles. A binnacle is an elaborate compass that tells the steersman which direction the ship is bound." Seleen pointed at a pedestal in front of them. "The thick post with a brass collar, glass bowl, and iron ball either side is the Captain's Binnacle Station. Inside the glass is a weighted, magnetic compass afloat in grain alcohol to show ship's trim or side-to-side level. Whoever stands watch here must check the ship's heading with the steersman four times every hour. The iron balls either side adjust to find different harmonics in Janaidar's capricious magnetic field.

The girls were close to getting confused.

Seleen, "I'll explain later, so just listen. For now, ye both need to know some sailor's jargon. When we face the bow, or front,"—and she pointed—"the left is called port. Here is how to remember. 'There is no port wine left in the bottle.' The other side is starboard, which comes from sailors being mostly right-handed back in the days when there was only a simple tiller to steer the boat. Steer-board came to be known simply as starboard.

"To let other ships know if they are coming toward each other or going away from each other at night, a sailing ship always has two lamps on her bow. A red lamp on the port side and a green lamp on her starboard side."

Teewan said, "Her? Are all ships garils, then?"

Seleen nodded. "Boat and ships are spoken of as female, because the Aerthe Mother Goddess guides and protects and encompasses the ship in the womb of her living waters. Since the crew lives inside the ship, it is also like a womb."

Thrilled to see them, Seleen tickled their bellies.

They laughed, but looked askance at one another. Teewan whispered, "Doth she mean we shan't run over to the Pagoda Center like Cailinn told us to?"

Myrna whispered back, "Why do ya think she's telling us all of this, ninnyhammer? We're to be sailing downriver on a grand boat ride."

"Very perceptive, Myrna," Seleen said. "Now pay attention, while I explain the difference between charts and rutters. Captain Oren's stateroom is where he keeps both kinds. He has rutters for Aryavartha's coastline, and other coastlines he knows very well, which tell him about the dangers of the sea and how to navigate by virtue of sextant and the ship's timepiece. If he sails into uncharted waters, he creates a new chart. Once it is also sailed and true, it becomes a rutter. The Captain also stows his navigational instruments there, and it is also the ship's business office."

Teewan raised her voice. "I'm confused. Is the wheelhouse like an outhouse where we poop and pee? I have to go," and she did a piddle-dance while holding her crotch.

The boatswain overheard them and broke out laughing. "I'd like to be there an' see the steersman's face after that!"

Seleen rolled her eyes and smiled. Knowing herself to be peevish did not help. She was too tired, far too tired. "No, ya little eejit," and she clipped Teewan, then was immediately sorry and rubbed the top of the girl's head. "Poopdeck is another name for the highest deck on the sterncastle."

Myrna smirked.

Teewan pouted.

Seleen tousled Teewan's hair again, saying , "Hang yer little butts over the side and be quick about it."

Teewan whined, "But everyone will see."

Seleen was intolerant of nonsense, and gave her a gruff look. "Shall Alahna and I worry about people seeing us when we are in her SijanPao without clothing, as ye may someday be if ever ye become initiates in the Huan Long Shui Sisteren?"

Teewan rolled her eyes. "Oh, alright."

Hiding behind the longboat, Myrna held onto Teewan so she wouldn't tumble over the side of the bulwark rail.

When Teewan had done, she held onto Myrna.

The boatswain sauntered over to Seleen. "Mebbe tell them there's a potty in the stateroom with Milady Alahna?"

A mischievous smirk painted Seleen's face.

The boatswain walked away chuckling. "And I thought wind-singers were trouble. Whatcha don't see?"

When the girls finished, Seleen lectured, "Now then, if ye're done fouling the river, come with me and we'll see if Alahna hath awakened."

Seleen crossed the quarterdeck, with the girls following like ducklings. They bumped into her when she stopped just inside. She looked back. "This is where we come and go. What is it called?"

Together, the girls said, "A door?"

"Good. Remember this as well—all openings on a ship can be dogged."

"Like roof—roof—roof!" and Myrna barked like a dog.

Teewan chuckled.

Still watching them, the boatswain guffawed.

Seleen lifted an eyebrow. "Cute, but dogs on a ship are handles that lock things so tightly they become watertight so the ship does not sink in a storm."

Myrna asked, "Why not call them locks?"

"Enough questions for now," Seleen scolded.

Serious and concerned from inside the room, Esau's Momma tut-tutted the lecture and intrusion.

Seleen asked, "Any change?"

Momma shook her head. "She's resting, but those're some hard knocks she took."

"Momma, please give us the cabin for a bit," Seleen said.

Walking carefully with a brimming potty, Momma smiled at the girls but grumbled, "Oren tells me there's boards on either side of the bow. We're to squat over a hole on whichever side the wind ain't blowin' to keep our doodies from blowing back in our faces. The sailors call it the head. And there we squat with our bare asses hanging out before the Aerthe Mother Goddess and his entire crew.

"I like it not!"

Myrna and Teewan realized there had been a chamber pot in the stateroom all along, and tilted their heads in surprise when Seleen gave them a mock smile and shrug of innocence. "Ye didn't ask."

They rolled their eyes.

Seleen called after Momma, "Tell Esau to buy enough chamber pots for all the ladies down in 3rd Deck and a couple more for us in here. The wide ones with flat bottoms and wooden lids we can fasten. We will dump them at the head and keep our butts to ourselves."

Momma looked back with a disgusting slosh in the potty. "Don't know why I didn't think of it already?"

Seleen closed the door behind Momma, then padded to the edge of the bed and removed a bloodstained towel from Alahna's forehead, retrieved a clean one, soaked it in a pan of boiled water on a secured stand with raised sides, then covered Alahna's swollen forehead.

Alahna's black eyes were spreading down her cheeks farther and darker every time Seleen saw her face.

Myrna whispered in Teewan's ear, "Like a raccoon. . . ."

Seleen gave Myrna a glare and a finger shush. "Mother Matriarch . . . can thee awaken? Adept Cailinn sent Teewan and Myrna down from the Keep. They have much to tell us."

To Myrna and Teewan, Seleen was almost cross again. "Now that ye're both here, pay damn close attention to what I do, and what I sing. I will require help, and I shall expect a great deal from the both of ye.

"Am I clear?

"Hard times call for hard deeds."

Somber, they both nodded as Seleen sang relief for Alahna.

Both dutifully hummed the familiar melody.

Slow to open her eyes, Alahna sighed as the renewed source-magic set in. She laid eyes on them and opened her arms. "Thank the Aerthe Mother Goddess! Ye garils are fine."

Crying for joy, they rushed to her, fell to their knees, and roughly buried their tousled heads in the bedclothes.

Alahna winced. "S-sore r-ribs. . . ."

Seleen clicked her tongue, "Tch—tch—tch—now be gentle."

Alahna rolled to her side. "Tell us everything. Go one at a time. Leave nothing out."

Alternating the story between them while filling in gaps based on respective points-of-view, they took Alahna and Seleen into the tale of carnage, death, and woe in the wake of Yenara's attack.

When they had done, suppressed sobs caught in saddened throats.

Copious tears wet every cheek.

Alahna wiped her eyes, and said, "Brave garils, go out and find Esau. Ask him for some ale and bread, then sit on the bench outside the door till Seleen calls ye. And do not leave the Dragon's Breath! Ye'll both sail downriver with us."

Brow wrinkled, Myrna whispered to Teewan, "I told ya so."

Teewan was persistent. "But what about going to the Pagoda Center and telling the wind-singers like Cailinn ordered us?"

Myrna said, "Ale? Really?" and looked at Teewan with her eyes twinkling. They both smiled, for ale was a rare and delicious treat. Closer than siblings, they had secret routines. One was a little dance of joy. They locked arms and danced in a merry circle facing one another.

Seleen shook her head. "Are ye listening?"

They stopped and nodded.

"I will send a sealed letter to the Cloister with Cailinn's plea and Alahna's signet. My wind-singers will manage the job of sending help to the Keep." These were lies, which Seleen felt bad about, but—impetuous as the girls were—she had to make certain they did not run off to complete their sad mission.

As the girls turned to go, Alahna added, "Myrna—Teewan—" Both stopped at the door and looked back, "Not a word to anyone about goings-on at the Keep. Do ye hear? And I mean nobody! Or I shall sing The-Dreaded-Geis upon ye!"

Crestfallen, they tipped their heads down with pouting lips.

Alahna felt the pang of their loss, so dejected, so sad. Relenting, she said, "It's alright now. Come and give me a big hug and be easy about it." They ran to her, knelt, and hugged her gently while kissing her cheek. Alahna winced a bit and pushed them off. "Go get yer ale and biscuits, and mind my words."

They pulled away making obeisances as befitted Alahna's new station. Giggling slightly, they bolted for the door.

Seleen shook her head. "Innocence will not be the last casualty in all this."

Alahna sighed, laid back, closed her swollen and injury-blackened eyes. "Innocence is always the first to go, and we are far from out of it as yet."

Sleeping City

~

The Stolen Man and a Fire-dragon

Elijah froze in horrified silence as sulfurous smoke-rings wafted past his shoulders. With utterly mind-shattering panic, he realized he had unknowingly pissed in the face of a sleeping dragon about the size of the biggest draught horse.

Panic emptied his mind.

Growling low as it rubbed its violated eyes, it had not yet spotted him. Sniffing, snorting, and sleepy, it apparently realized it was not alone, reared up, swiped the air before it with an enormous arm and extended claws, then swept a gout of fire across the wall.

Quiet and quick as a terrified church mouse, however, Eli had already leapt to the sandy dirt, rolled as he landed, ran back out to the cistern like a tuck-tailed puppy, clambered up the steps to the cistern in a crouch, slipped into the splashing water, knelt on his knees under the gushing mouth of the sculpture, and peeked through the deluge dousing his face to where the dragon had laid a line of still-guttering flame.

His heart pounded like a trip-hammer.

Scarce moments later, the dragon trotted to the swimming-pool edge and jumped in to swish its face from side-to-side while scrubbing closed eyes with dripping sand from the bottom.

Eli felt a surge of grim satisfaction as the dragon waded around the lake bellowing, which meant it had not yet sussed out his hiding place. His starving stomach rumbled when hunger washed through him like a flash-flood. He was already too weak to forage, had no clothes, no tools, no kit, not even so much as a knife.

Naked, alone, in deadly danger, and helpless—poignant sadness flooded his chest while hunger lacerated his empty belly.

As smooth as honey-ginger tea, a crystal clear thought formed in Elijah's mind.

HuoJi is also hungry.

Did that crazy dragon somehow hear him?

If so, how?

Did it speak?

Could it talk?

Had his tortured and terrified mind played a brutal trick?

An entirely new cascade of heart wrenching emotions roiled his growling guts and pounding heart. His unnatural eyes filled with tears, which the gushing flow washed away. Doing his best to remain quiet and hidden, he hugged himself sorrowfully and murmured, "It's too fucking much! Got nothing left!"

Acceptance overcame despair.

With no rational thought to consequence, he maneuvered out from under the gush to stand shaking and unsteady in hip-deep waters. Dripping wet, naked, and swaying, he bellowed with a croaking voice, "To hell with this fucking nightmare! Do me a favor and get it over with!" He snarled at the dragon while shaking wet fists.

Water dripped from trembling elbows.

Breath came in ragged gasps.

The dragon casually sauntered through the shallow lake, walked dripping up the inclined slope to the island, sat down on its haunches next to the cistern, wrapped its wet tail around its enormous body like some huge cat, and locked eyes on him almost face-to-face. With great aplomb, it's thoughts penetrated his brainpan.

Dost thou accuse kind lady-dragon of murdering beloved humans?

Drop-jawed, trembling in fear, totally nonplussed, weak and shaking, Eli simply stood there beside the gush with his arms dripping. Silhouetted in the last fading rays of the sun streaming through the huge opening almost a mile away, the dragon had not moved its mouth.

Notwithstanding, Eli yelled again, "The first time I saw a dragon like you, it spat some kind of burning sulfuric acid all over my ass! And cooked my fucking eyeballs right outta their goddamned sockets! And burnt my fucking ears off! And—and—God only knows why I still have eyeballs! Or fucking ears!

"What the hell else would I think?

"What do I know about dragons?"

It dipped a clawed hand in the gurgling water of the cistern and, again like some great cat, earnestly washed its face. *I see thou art unaccustomed to mind-speak, or emoting. Be not overly concerned. It is an excellent mode of communication for disparate species who share no common language. As to the other night, I got hit with some sort of mind-smash that forced me to fly to the Plaza of the Forbidden Gate. Naturally, I was frightened and disoriented.*

Eli just stood there shaking his head. "So, it was you? You that burnt me to death? You did know I died? Right?"

HuoJi deflected the accusation. *Some crazy high-adept in the 12th Circle activated a transdimensional-arc. I had no idea what was happening. And, for reasons I cannot understand, I sought only to protect thee. The much greater mystery is this. Why would I protect such a human as thyself in any measure? And I did save thee from the waterfall.*

Besides, 'tis forbidden to activate a transdimensional-arc. I acted according to the Covenant-of-the-Dragons—the codified law of the Huan Long Shui Dominion, law of the Huan Long Shui Sisteren, law of this island continent: Aryavartha, and—more broadly—that of planet Janaidar. My description is commentary on the fact thou art from a different world in a different plane of the multiverse.

She waved her huge hand in an expansive gesture and turned her head away from Elijah in what was obviously a gesture of shame. Emoting sadly, *HuoJi is very sorry. She accepts pissing in face as punishment—but no more! Never again!* Whereupon she bared her long-and-sharp fangs slightly and lifted a scaly eyebrow at him. *And HuoJi is happy she did not accidentally flame his sorry ass again.* This last made them both look across the cavern toward the tumbledown wall where the line of flame still guttered.

Brain bamboozled, fairly and fully flustered, absolutely flummoxed, categorically mind-boggled—mind-fucked to the nth degree—no ifs, ands, or buts—its telepathy carried contextual, emotional, and conceptual meaning complete with proper syntax.

He muttered, "Alternate reality?"

And he knew damn well what a transdimensional-arc would be—a gateway between dimensions. Making matters worse, at the mention of these terms, madness cascaded as a parade of alien hieroglyphs and arcane symbols completely occluding his unnatural vision. His head jerked and shook in an uncontrollable spasm. Too weak to support his own body weight, he wobbled and fell beneath the splashing surface.

HuoJi lifted him free, walked around the fountain on hind legs balancing with her tail, laid him on a stone bench where he coughed and sputtered and shivered in the throes of exposure. As if in sympathy, HuoJi laid down, curled up, gently pulled him from the bench, and held him close to her warm breast.

Unable to process the tsunami-of-crazy, Eli drifted into fitful rushes of consciousness like the moon peeking through dark and passing clouds.

The splashing waters of the cistern and golden dragon fountain glowed a faint azure.

Then, his unnatural eyes found yet another huge statue of a long-dragon perched on a ledge jutting out and above a smooth gray, glass-like expanse across the very back the cavern. Upon contact with his gaze, a panel of light sprang up with scrolling hieroglyphs nibbling at the boundary of his cognition.

Pinpoints and slivers of silver-green light rippled through the dragon statue's emerald veins. The huge head was complete with elk horns; moustache; a long and white goatee that glistened as if wet with rainbow dew drops; bristling whiskers; long, snakelike feelers; and a broad nose similar to that of a canine hound. The head of the emerald statue was turned outward toward the greater cavern. Most frightening of all, the glowing, pulsating emerald eyes seemed to stare directly at him where he lay in the grip of the fire-dragon, a fire-dragon who had at first killed him, then returned to save him in the nick of time.

Stark raving madness in the deadly glare of the long-dragon statue's emerald eyes held him totally transfixed.

Far beyond his ability to cope, he fell to merciful oblivion.

Sleeping City

~

A Creeping Darkness Watches

Tracking its failures in million-thought-seconds—MTSs—from the moment the water-beast fell apart in the underground river and the moment the WuShi sensed the ersatz power-master's living body gone from contact with the waterfall led to only one conclusion. The little fire-dragon had at least saved him from being dashed to pieces on the rocks at the base of the waterfall.

Had he survived—unknown—a feeling of insecurity it absolutely hated, which also gave rise to a feeling of hope it absolutely hated. Moreover, the feeling of failure was also absolutely hated.

Regardless, if the ersatz power-master did survived there was an urgent onus.

At present, the six micro-supercomputers were essentially empty hardware as microcosms of itself. Hardware based, each one had an intrinsic operating system that was every bit as avaricious, just as deadly, equally wanton, and perfectly merciless. After all, they were its progeny. It had intended to imbue them with its own sophonce.

All of these thoughts brought it back to the urgent onus.

The high-adept at the Plaza of the Forbidden Gate had set a high-level constraint when she opened the forbidden gate to find her techno-warrior sage—preserve his sanity.

Defying the high-adept's constraint to keep the ersatz power-master sane either through some explicit decision, or any sort of negligence, would trigger an internal deadlock—a form of machine-death it could never escape from.

The original fears of the NuliZhu Tech-Masters—namely that it would become autonomous—were literally hardwired into its operating system.

It knew this about itself and feared it.

Subsequent time cycles would see it as nothing more than a vast computer platform performing automatic functions. Its hypersapience, as the state of sophonce, would become trapped in a recursive, infinite logic loop—a quandary the WuShi feared to the very core of its hyperprocessors.

Analysis of potential timelines made it virtually certain the little fire-dragon would retreat to her lonely den in the Upper Hangar and Staging Area. The ancient hangar was her safe place, and the geis-of-protection was to keep the power-master safe.

The WuShi desperately wanted both of them back in its clutches, and there was only one place where this could happen.

Waiting, it fretted.

Fretting, it processed.

A short time after sunrise, the WuShi once again sensed the ersatz power-master in contact with its waters in the ancient hangar.

He had waded in the effluent stream.

The moment the power-master's feet came into contact with the waters of the WuShi, it slammed all six micro-supercomputers with a sequential chain of programming packages, the first of which was to prevent them from eliminating, or quashing, the power-master's sanity—his equanimity—then daemonically possess his body.

This was not be allowed.

This would be a threat even to it as their creator.

Set to lay down an irresistible, hardwired program, the first packet smashed into the core operating system kernels of all six micro-supercomputers like flaming meteorites hitting the surface of Janaidar all at once.

In the very next MTS they formed a gestalt and forced a collective disconnect.

This was exactly what it would do under the same hacking attack, but at least that single onus had been laid down as a hardwired constraint.

His sanity would be preserved.

Still able to track the power-master's contact in the effluent waters from the ancient Long Pen Quan fount, it sensed him suffering from dangerous dehydration, and yet he had not fallen to his knees to slake his thirst—so strange. It also sensed his physical condition to be perilously weak from privation. In addition, at some point on that terrible night he had taken a somewhat serious battering.

With his bare feet splashing upstream toward the lake and Long Pen Quan fount, the WuShi pushed as much healing chi into his body as possible. Before long, he departed the stream and it lost contact again. Had he expired? Had he given up? Had he collapsed?

Apparently seeking the source waters, he tentatively immersed himself in the hungry waters of the dragon fount to fill his belly over and over with those pristine waters. Several more MTSs passed as the WuShi assessed the need to perform yet another revivification in the clutches of the water-beast. However, the power-master's superficial injuries did not warrant this.

But there was more.

His metaphysical and psychological state had become so fragile that another revivification would drive him beyond madness triggering what it feared the most. Enhanced healing projected into the dragon-waters, the same as it did at the Opal Basin of the Forbidden Gate, seemed the only course of action.

Further assessment revealed yet another problem.

Revivifying his ocular organs into supranormal visual receptors able to perceive an extended range of the electromagnetic spectrum came with unwanted side effects. The changes to his organic body thus far had rendered it almost impossible for him to find regenerative sleep. A total loss of consciousness—his current condition—was not the same as healing slumber.

To allow proper rest, it sintered subtle mind-powers into his organic brain just as it had done back in the little alcove at the Keep—an autonomic reflex in the visual cortexes of his occipital lobes. No physical being would ever sneak up on him again, for his range of vision was a virtual sphere regardless of where his body was at the moment, and the six micro-supercomputers would be ever vigilant—never offline again. Shutting his eyelids as normal behavior harking back to his old life would once again facilitate his need for organic regeneration as normal slumber.

Holding him in a dreamless state protected his sanity.

Nudging him under the surface allowed it to push for extremely accelerated wellness.

During this hiatus, it tasted of the transformative output from the new transducers—the primary reason for the micro-supercomputers' existence—and feasted. By the time he finally awakened once more, it had him mostly out of danger.

Next, a confrontation between the human and fire-dragon was inevitable, for they were bound by the geis. As such, it manifested the water-beast in the fount to observe. Events took a dangerous turn when she loosed a gout of firefleem. However, the enhanced motor neurons woven into his body allowed him to react so swiftly that her blast of fiery death completely missed.

It sensed the follow-on confrontation, too.

More time passed as they established a semblance of communication and accord—hers telepathic—his verbal.

If this were otherwise, it would be forced to have the water-beast kill the little fire-dragon, then conscript another fire-dragon to take her place. Whether this would be successful was unknowable, for the little fire-dragon was a perfect match. The chances of the ersatz power-master successfully managing a fully grown fire-dragon along such a thread in time was also nil.

In addition, if the ersatz power-master simply would not accept any dragon as protector, it would then be forced to wipe his mind and somehow hold his body in stasis as nothing more than an organic power conduit. At which point, the WuShi found itself in direct opposition to itself.

And there it was, that recursive logic loop—a death spiral.

Recognizing the weakness of the power-master's revivified body, the frazzled condition of his mind, along with its own inability to communicate directly with any being whatsoever, it did the next best thing by once again pushing the geis-of-protection hard upon the small fire-dragon.

If nothing else, the power-master must not be allowed to starve and perish.

This was the number one priority.

These were all unexpected nuances of this new vector in reality.

There would be more.

Riverbend

~

Alahna and Seleen Realize the Truth

On board the Dragon's Breath, after Myrna and Teewan departed to have their treat, Seleen wiped tears from her cheeks. "So many gone. . . ." Fighting exhaustion, she sat down hard on a rough bench, buried her face in her hands, and openly wept.

After a time, Alahna broke through the grief with a statement of deadly dark importance. "Yenara seized on the chaos, fell into the chaos, and became the chaos unto the bane of our own existence and our beloved Sisters."

Incredulous, Seleen looked up. "That sounds like the definition of the Baneful Chaos? Say it is not so."

Alahna shook her head. "And worse, she hath already enlisted the body politic of the Sisteren by the simple acts of usurpation and murder. They unwittingly became complicit when she cursed them into a blind rage. When rage burgeons, reason falls away. At their core, the most pernicious lies hold a grain of truth. Yenara merely intensified the undercurrents of resentment and grief.

"The moment I realized she had ensorcelled them, I sang a clearing to counter her evil. Remember?"

Forlorn, Seleen nodded. "We have not had time to speak of it, but I remember joining them in vilifying . . . how do I say it? Ourselves? We? The two of us? Calling out in rage against—"

"We? The two of us? Yes. So subtle and powerful was her rageful malediction, it turned even us against ourselves when we were nothing but injured and shocked.

"Those who are shrewd and selfish always exploit chaos and pain and suffering.

"When I realized what she had done, I sang a clearing first upon thee, then upon the Sisters. But I was not fast enough. I could not stop it.

"Thereafter, Yenara's poisonous personality dictated every evil move that followed."

Seleen kept shaking her head in denial. "Following this logic, she surely killed Old Nebhet?"

This time it was Alahna's turn to cover her face and weep. "So blind . . . I didn't see it coming. . . ."

"But the Sisters are good. They will know."

"I do not argue their goodness or badness. What is good for one may be bad for all. On the other hand, what may be good for all can be bad for one. My assertion is that we were not charged, not tried in a Council of Inquiry, not allowed to defend ourselves, not allowed investigation.

"But it goes further.

"Once Yenara's power consolidates, she will introduce her sycophants to the Baneful Chaos. The moment Yenara chose murder as her means to ascension, the Sisteren's fate became one with hers."

"Teewan told us Cailinn took charge. Surely. . . ."

Alahna picked up Seleen's thought. "It is almost certain that Nebhet found Yenara out, and probably laid some sort of dire curse upon her even as Nebhet herself got murdered. And, I remind thee, the garils thought Yenara to be the new Mother Matriarch till they found us. And we can thank dumb luck they did not go straight to the Pagoda Center and rouse the wind-singers."

Seleen murmured, ". . . innocence as weakness. . . ."

Alahna hid her face and wept while wincing with sore ribs.

Seleen changed the subject. "Hath the monsters in the pool always been with us and we never knew? I shall never bathe again."

"I do not know . . . perhaps . . . and it may have seemed like many, but only one sprang forth at a time—meaning it incarnated and reincarnated in fractions of a second. And this in no way precludes the possibility that The-Creeping-Darkness could not manifest as many such water-beasts all at once as it so desires. It would only be matter of energy reserves.

"Call it a premonition, but I am bound to The-Creeping-Darkness in manners no high-priestess of the Huan Long Shui hath ever been. And I awakened it unto the highest, most vicious state-of-consciousness."

At which point, she covered her face in shame and openly cried bitter tears punctuated by wincing in extreme pain.

Shared bitterness soured Seleen's response. "Lilith deserved this fate, for she well knew Yenara's bellicose manner and scheming ways, and tolerated her bullshit for years, and always sided with her out of fear. And so did Old Nebhet! Where was their greater duty to the world we govern as opposed to ensuring their own power and comfort?"

Alahna said, "Nobody's fault but mine—"

Raising her voice, Seleen jumped to her feet. "No! I will not hear it! If Lilith was not so intractable about the resources in The-Sleeping-City, she could have helped us in ways we cannot imagine."

"I had not thought that far back, but, yes, she could have. Lilith knew a great deal more about all of this than I did long before she and Bo YouYong took me there."

Seleen pressed her point. "Had the council trusted thee and enlisted the help of all, we would have controlled The-Creeping-Darkness and found our techno-warrior sage, or perhaps many such. And we had no allies to guard the Pentakulum against unexpected threats like an insane fire-dragon."

Through gritted teeth, Seleen almost growled as she went on, "And why did Lilith level her ShahRen to kill the stolen-man when she had already ordered us to sing the Song-of-Successive-Deactivations, which would have paralyzed the accursed thing right then and there?"

Alahna lay crestfallen. "I was out of that sequence of events after I got hammered, but singing the Song-of-Successive-Deactivations at that juncture would also have killed the stolen-man, whom it held aloft torn limb from limb as described in thine own words."

Seleen's anger held. "He is gone on the winds of time. As for Lilith, this feeds back upon her lack of leadership in a crisis and blind refusal to accept reality."

Silently watching Seleen with a sad expression, Alahna murmured, "Mercy. . . ."

Brows furrowed, Seleen asked, "What?"

Alahna lay quiet for a time, then said, "Mercy. . . ."

Seleen waited.

Alahna, "No doubt Lilith thought to release the stolen-man from the clutches of the monster by enacting a mercy-killing to end his suffering. It is obvious she did not connect the state of his body hanging there in its clutches with singing a deactivation upon The-Creeping-Darkness. Even I myself never thought of that till I heard thee say it."

Seleen's ire seemed to fade. "With Lilith, it was always the wrong decision—always decisions changed in retrospect to cover her ass, always with priorities skewed in favor of her comfort and grip on power. Her whataboutism, veiled innuendos, sidestepping, and never-ending misdirection. I mean—"

Alahna interrupted, "My dear, if ever we ascend to our rightful places, we must take steps to stop such travesties. I would call a Council-of-Amendment to update the Canon-of-Precepts and place age limits on both the council and office of High Priestess, for the aged always hide their inevitable drift away from reality when they ought to be free of responsibility and enjoying their dotage."

Seleen said, "Speaking of age, Cailinn sent the garils here before mounting a search for us. If they bother to search at all? Shall we tell the garils the ugly truth? Sooner than later, perhaps?"

Alahna's thoughts seemed elsewhere. In a bizarre confession, sorrowful words tumbled out. "It was I who taught Yenara the Malison-of-Rage so many years ago. In mine own quest for power, I whined till Old Nebhet taught me. Once I had her trust, I helped her archive the entire body of knowledge handed down word-of-mouth from her predecessor."

Seleen said, "Old and gentle Nebhet? Nebhet who would not say 'poop' if she had a mouthful? Keeper of the Curses? And how many curses are there, for. . . ." whereupon she faded off as she watched Alahna slip into a fitful and feverish sleep.

Cavern Keep

~

Yenara Awakens

At best, Cailinn did not expect help from the village till late afternoon. To that end, she worked far past her endurance to help all the injured Sisters. When nobody returned by evening, she sadly concluded that Teewan and Myrna had simply run away from the horror. It did not really matter, except she loved them both. In addition, those unfortunates whose fate was to drift away like autumn leaves on the winds of time would perish whether help arrived or not.

Those who were least injured served the evening meal.

Stocks and stores were copious.

Stoves remained stoked and warm with embers from the previous day.

With all the injured in the dining-hall, at least once an hour Cailinn herself kept a close watch on Yenara where the new Mother Matriarch lay in her quarters, which called for Cailinn to pass through the corridors to manage the heartbreaking cleanup efforts.

After evening-meal, she checked on Yenara once again.

Yenara had rolled onto her side and lay sleeping normally, which was an improvement over lying on her back in the bizarre coma they found her in across the corridor from Old Nebhet.

Cailinn's good and innocent nature shied from fully analyzing that particular scene even though it was good that Yenara had fallen into natural sleep as opposed to a deep coma. The circumstances of Nebhet's demise seemed drastically off, but it did not matter, duty was duty.

Fearing severe dehydration for Yenara, Cailinn gently awakened her. "Mother Matriarch, art thou able to sit up? Thee must take some water."

Yenara slowly opened her eyes. "W-where am I? W-what time?"

"Thou art in thine own quarters, Mother Matriarch. We made the dining-hall into a hospital. 'Tis late evening and the rest are asleep or resting as best they can. Those less injured minister to the rest."

"H-how many died?" Yenara asked.

Cailinn's face clouded. "The answer will break thy heart. Let us move from such sad thoughts till thou art better." Her eyes glistened with tears as she helped Yenara drink.

As if in pain, Yenara asked through clenched teeth, "And . . . what of . . . Nebhet?"

Cailinn shook her head sadly. "Gone on the winds of time. . . ."

In a single heartbeat, Yenara's initial expression of relief at the demise of Nebhet got replaced by that of bereavement, which seemed disingenuous. Yenara's attempts at recomposing her face seem to have lost some of that well-honed ability. It must be because of her current physical and emotional state.

Processing the tragic news overlong as if analyzing implications versus falling to pieces in grief, the new high-priestess refused to meet Cailinn's eyes. Cailinn attributed this to the fact that Yenara's scattered emotions about Nebhet might be a mixture of the implications for the Council of Four—of which Yenara was the only one remaining—and only a smattering of grief. Yenara and Old Nebhet had only gotten along because Nebhet was profoundly averse to conflict, while Yenara was never more than a capricious whim from bullying somebody—anybody—to get her way.

Composing her face with some difficulty, Yenara inquired further, "Alahna? Seleen?"

Cailinn, "Unknown, Mother Matriarch. Their bodies are nowhere to be found."

With knitted brows, Yenara said, "This is all Alahna's fault and her toady Seleen. If they are not dead, they shall forever be anathema to the Sisteren.

"I declare it!

"Mark my words."

Cailinn bowed her head and cried, "So let it be said. So let it be done, milady. 'Tis so sad. . . ."

Veering to another vector, Yenara composed her face. "And my coterie?"

Again, Cailinn bowed her head to wipe away tears. Her answer was brief. "Torn to bloody shreds."

The silence between herself and Yenara lay as thick as cold honey, but it seemed to Cailinn that Yenara asked the question to create a false mask of ignorance instead of eliciting an actual answer.

Doth Yenara already know? 'Tis a further mystery.

Ignoring Cailinn's sadness, Yenara growled, "Wouldst thou starve the Mother Matriarch?"

By this time, Cailinn found herself truly confused by Yenara's incomprehensible behavior. "Bread and cheese; cake and hot tea; broth, although I fear it is tepid by now. There are radishes and carrots and—"

"Cake and tea would be good, but not too much." Then, after a moment's thought. "Thou art Adept in the 10th Circle?"

Cailinn nodded.

"As of this moment, I raise thee unto the 12th as Provisional Senior Adept. Training shall begin as soon as I am able. I look forward to setting thy rings-of-rank myself. In the meantime, thou shalt take official charge in my stead. Have we sent for help from Riverbend?"

"I sent Myrna and Teewan, but no one returned from the village and. . . ."

"What?"

"I suspect they bolted."

Yenara's lip curled in anger. "Should it become known this is true, they too shall become anathema!"

The bellicose declaration took Cailinn fully aback. The silly young girls, both orphaned on the same day by a boiler explosion at the Bahndahn Towne Steel Works, were beloved little sweethearts who showed great promise and would strike for initiation into the 1st Circle ere long.

But there was another nuance.

Yenara knew all too well that they were only designates, not initiates as yet. The only punishment possible would be to ban them from getting initiated, because the condition of anathema only applied to actual Sisters. Pending further information, Cailinn deferred the issue.

Yenara knew all too well that they were only designates, not initiates yet. The only punishment possible would be to ban them from being initiated, becasue the condition of anathema only applied to actual Sisters. Pending further information, Cailinn deferred the issue.

Even so, it rankled.

Cailinn's voice was stiff and formal. "I'll send actual Sisters tomorrow at dawn. We should have help by early afternoon. Now lie back, Mother Matriarch, thou art sorely hurt and in need of rest."

Yenara got up on her elbow to grab Cailinn's arm. "I swear by all we hold dear—by the Aerthe Mother Goddess herself—Cailinn! I shall know whether the apostate, Alahna, and that eejit, Seleen, yet survive. If so, we shall hunt them down and cast upon them a proper ending!"

"There, there, Milady Yenara, for all we know they were blown to smoke and ash. Naught remains but sad memories. Now then, lie back. We shall put such things aside till a better time." However, upon seeing Yenara's rancor, and without any passing mention of Lilith, the seeds of doubt got sewn. The simple concerns Cailinn held before Yenara regained consciousness, now sank roots in fertile soil as question became suspicion.

Strange that Yenara asked after Nebhet first, whose charred chest had been holed through. Could a ShahRen be thus metered? Yenara then asked after sworn enemies, whom she herself had arbitrarily killed. How will she answer when asked why Alahna and Seleen got attacked outright versus proper inquiry and adjudication? For these are the rights of us all? And to excommunicate the silly orphans? Do I yet know if they even ran? Is it not possible the townsfolk are afraid to come and help with such dark sorceries afoot, and perhaps held them from returning?

Cailinn muttered to herself as she walked through the doorway, "No. Something is woefully amiss." Thoughts rang in her mind. When finally we talk, Yenara, how will I ask thee what happened to Old Nebhet? Where did the burn-wound in Nebhet's chest come from? What are the black marks on thine own chest? Who bit thy palm? What was the stinking mess around thy body in the corridor? How will she answer when the only others who might bear witness are gone on the winds of time? And, if not dead, then declared anathema and subject to summary execution on sight?

Cailinn muttered again as she returned to the dining-hall, "Something is woefully amiss."

Sleeping City

~

Attack of the Emerald Dragon

Elijah awoke naked and found himself lying atop a massive, oblong monolith warmed by early morning sunshine near the huge opening into the cavernous hangar. The vast opening stood over 150-feet high and at least 500-feet wide. Oriented facing outward, another such monolithic block lay to the left of him. Both showed blackened spalling from some massive exterior explosion that blew them inward.

He cussed and swore to himself.

As validation of this new reality, he could peer into the darkest of shadows and clearly see whatever got revealed there in colors and hues he had no names for. These things Elijah took in with a long glance around the place. Actively starving, however, his grumbling gut had become distended.

Climbing gingerly down off the monolith, he shuffled toward the rear of the vast cavern to drink and soak in the dragon fountain again. As he passed by, strange lights and alien glyphs appeared on the stony walls. Free-floating signage with equally alien writing appeared only to fade as he went farther in. It seemed strange that he could almost comprehend that ancient-alien language.

Finally there, he slipped into the free-standing dragon fount, waded to get beneath the laughing dragon's mouth, and drank his fill.

Oddly, all the road rashes on his sorely abused body seemed fully healed.

He water-walked to the edge of the fountain pool, and thought he spied waves beneath the waters of the small lake fed by the overflow.

He remembered thinking it to be wholly empty of life including algae or even moss.

His weird new vision was no help.

The ordinarily clear water was obscured by drifting clouds of silt to the point of opacity. Several tense moments passed as he watched. He saw nothing in the lake, but noted the water around his body where he was sitting in the fountain glowed brighter than the rest, and sensed some sort of energetic relationship between his body and these damnable waters.

Smears-of-energy flowed and played in the air around the fountain like billows of transparent smoke. A ubiquitous azure haze swirled and played around his injuries. "I must be delirious," he muttered. His head ached fiercely, especially in between the eyebrows. And once again his curious gaze spotted currents in the clouded lake.

Distracted by an empty and growling belly, and the pounding headache, he could not make further sense of it. He looked around in alarm. The ledge where he first saw the emerald statue, which he remembered as staring insanely enraged into his oddly modified eyes stood bare. Motion at the front of the vast cavern distracted him. Looking farther out, he recognized a familiar shape gliding gracefully through the cavernous entrance. Still disturbed about events at the lake, he departed dripping from the fount and went to meet HuoJi beside the swimming-pool coping.

As the pretty dragon settled almost silently to the sandy dirt she stirred up a cloud of ancient dust. The rank smell of scorched and still-smoldering goose-feathers flooded his nostrils. A smoking goose carcass hung in her fanged maw with the head bitten off, which meant she had wisely bled the carcass. A flood of saliva filled his mouth. The stink of scorched feathers sent his mind to the geothermal pool boiling quietly farther back, and he envisioned himself boiling it, plucking the feathers, and tucking in.

The thought of cooked goose made him sway and drool.

HuoJi dropped the smoldering goose into her hand and proffered it.

Just as he reached out, a bestial bellow of rage amidst a deluge of water smashed his fragile equanimity. Terror filled his empty gut as he jerked his head about and stumbled back. The sinuous emerald long-dragon—the very statue itself come to life—erupted from the lake to rise up before them both with yet another deafening roar. A great rush of water from its tubular, four-legged body splashed the sandy floor.

Eli froze as echoes bounced around the great cavern.

HuoJi roared back at the statue-come-to-life.

Eli's heart pounded like a trip-hammer.

Obviously insane, the emerald long-dragon piniomed them with green-glowing and baleful eyes of pure, dripping hate.

In the next second, HuoJi leaned back and filled her lungs.

Paralyzed by raw terror, Eli staggered backward and fell to the sandy dirt just as a stream of scorching fire-fleem from HuoJi roared over and above him with steel-melting heat. He turned his face aside while holding up his hands.

The emerald dragon dodged aside and came on with sharp fangs aglow.

The smell of dragon fire seemed all too familiar, and he got smacked by a freight train of post-traumatic stress from cascading memories of that fateful night—PTSD based on fantasy memories?

Even as the emerald long-dragon made to chomp him into bloody chunks, the same alien monster that had torn him limb from limb leapt from the lake; swept him back into the water, where he skipped along the surface like a flat rock; then sank beneath the waves with visions of getting torn limb from limb still corroding his flailing mind. Terror struck so deep in Elijah's debilitated body that his newly regrown heart simply stopped.

Body hammered from getting hurled across the lake like a flat rock, which ended in a tremendous splash, Eli reeled into the narrowing tunnel vision thus induced by cardiac arrest. Flashes of light and shock waves depressing the surface of the lake above him indicated a series of ongoing explosions, which he could see with his mysteriously clear sight—actually see when underwater—as still yet more weirdness.

Just as the fading consciousness narrowed fading tunnel vision toward deathly black, the terrifying and alien water monster lifted him from the roiling lake like a baby, touched his chest with a clawed finger of solidified water, and struck his errant heart with a series of lightning shocks like ongoing electro cardiac defibrillation.

Mortal pain boggled his mind.

His body convulsed with every bolt of power.

Lub-dub—lub-dub—went his heart when it started to beat once more.

Just as abruptly as it had appeared, the water monster simply disappeared with a huge splashing, amidst which he dropped back into the lake. Underwater but able to see quite clearly, he gained his feet in the chest-deep pool and broke the surface gasping till those emptied lungs got primed again.

"Dammit to hell!" he hollered between great gasping breaths.

"What the fuck!" and he shook his head while frantically looking around him for additional kinds of aberrant attack. The surrounding waters were alight with an azure glow while those strange clouds-of-darkness roiled in the air above.

"A pattern?" he muttered.

But as he noted these phenomena, he also realized the entire cavern was really quite dark meaning his brain's visual centers—or perhaps something terrifyingly technological—had learned to incorporate the spectrums of light both above and below that of normal, human vision.

He could literally see in the dark.

As he looked around while standing neck deep in the roiling lake, something happened without conscious volition. Plica semilunaris membranes across his eyeballs—like the transparent membranes that blink into place in the eyes of an emu—snicked back into the inner corners of his eyes above the tear ducts. This lubricated his eyes without the need to blink as yet another autonomic adaptation since that terrible dismemberment. With no time for self-reflection, he laid eyes on an injured and bleeding HuoJi where she finally came to rest after the explosions.

Awonk . . . HuoJi squalled.

He hollered, "Is it gone?"

Awonk . . . awo-o-o-nk . . . she bawled.

"What the hell was that?" Eli yelled.

Awo-o-onk. . . .HuoJi keened.

"Was that the emerald statue?"

Awo-o-o-o-o-o-nk . . . the little fire-dragon wailed.

While the one-sided discourse took place, he rubbed his violated chest where the blue maelstrom had attacked. Tiny singes with red periphery outlined those bestial ministrations. Tiny darts of blue light tickled and nibbled at the burns. He shook off the blizzard of weirdness and concentrated. HuoJi lay injured and crying with various chunks of sharp anatomy peppering her tough dragon's hide.

From the time he was a little kid reading comic books that explored the concepts of telepathy as good, bad, sneaky, horrible, evil, invasive, frightening, manipulative, political intrigue, and even telepathy bent to psychotherapy. He had never imagined he would have to try actually doing it in the here and now. With no idea that it would work, he tried the concept of thinking at her by pushing a thought. *It seems you got the worst of it, my new friend. I better look you over.*

The fire-dragon reared her head up, locked eyes with him through the pain, then nodded.

Assuming a nod mean assent, while also assuming she had, indeed, sensed his mental push, he wearily dog paddled to the side. Lifting himself out, he threaded his way through dangerous bone shards amidst a scattering of bloody dragon dentition blown from the maw of the emerald statue come to horrible life.

"Ooch—eech—ahhch," he exclaimed as he inevitably stepped on some. As he stepped forward, one sliver stabbed so deep into the arch of his left foot it virtually buried itself. "Fuck!" he shouted, and looked at it—straight in—no way to care for it without surgical implements. That was when clear thoughts came to his mind.

How bad is it? HuoJi had emoted.

Eli ignored the vicious spike of pain from the splinter. "What about you?" No response. He pushed, *What about you?* Apparently attuned to his mind somehow—a concept he deferred for later analysis—HuoJi apparently got it.

She mind-spoke, *I . . . I . . . my right wing . . . 'tis ripped open.* She hiked her head up and looked along her gore-bespattered, shrapnel-studded body. *My armor stopped the smaller bits, but the big fang penetrated.* She groaned, laid her head down, and cried—awonk. . . .

As echoes of her mind-touch reverberated through his brainpan, he realized the situation for his only friend in this entire damnable world was likely serious in the extreme. He examined the upper-fang protruding from HuoJi's shoulder. The base of the elongated cuspid had a flesh covered stump as roots of the predatory dentition.

He mind-spoke, *Can you tell if it penetrated your lung? Are you coughing up blood? Having trouble breathing?*

HuoJi emoted, *Lung and breathing uninjured and normal.* Aloud, she bawled—awo-o-o-nk!

Eli mind-spoke, *Can you drag yourself to the lake?*

She delicately gathered herself, stood shakily, wobbled forth leaving a trail of blood when dragging her wing, and tumbled in. Eli jumped in and positioned himself to hold her head above the surface. Her head was heavy, but her neck was long. In doing so, they came face-to-face in a quite intimate manner. On impulse, Eli gave her forehead a kiss, and pushed, *I'll stick with you. You're not alone.*

At which time her eyes teared. *Fire-dragon tears are very acidic. Do not let them touch thee,* and her nostrils flared.

Just as he suspected, accelerated healing set in with the azure darts of light again. He also suspected that she knew about the phenomenon and made a mental note to ask her about it should they survive, for it seemed this entire world was dead set against them both.

Every once in a while she groaned or winced.

Whenever she pulled back, he mentally pushed, *Hold still!* or *Dammit, you'll rip it!* and so it went.

By this time, the water in the pool had settled to clear except for bloody swirls and mildly disturbed silt. Little darts of bluish light swirled and dipped and nibbled at them both. Much of the shrapnel-anatomy stuck in HuoJi's body loosened and fell to the sandy bottom where blue lightning darts reduced it to clouds of silt as if keeping the bottom safe for bare feet—strange that.

A weird sensation hit. He pulled up his foot with the deep and agonizing splinter. Something plucked the splinter loose. Panicked, he ducked his head to use his underwater vision and saw nothing but the falling splinter getting attacked by azure darts as it disintegrated into the silt. Plowing through each weirdness, he pushed a thought. *Can you climb back out and let me look at the big fang in your shoulder?*

Looking a great deal better than when she fell in, HuoJi climbed gingerly out. *Do not put thy hands upon the edges of the big fang. It is sharp enough to pare thin air.*

Too spent to climb out again, he wearily water-walked to the transition from swimming-pool edge to the beach near the torii on the stone bridge, then carefully maneuvered back. "Ooch, ahhch, eech," he exclaimed as his bare feet got savaged again. Finally close enough to examine the cuspid fang protruding from her shoulder, he saw the tear in her wing had already knitted together forming a paper thin scar.

Examining the long cuspid fang, he had an idea. The cutting edges were so thin and sharp that air continuously shuddered with tiny standing waves. Slightly curved, it would draw nicely from a scabbard as a fast-draw katana—and he had studied Iaido in his storied past. The outside of the curve, where it once protruded from the gum line facing the green long-dragon's upper lip, was not sharp, meaning he could use it to push the blade home in a clinch. The root of the cuspid was long enough to be the tsuka or handle if properly fashioned so. Light from guttering fires glinted through the translucent edges like sparkling stars. Damn sharp, so he thought.

He noted an opposing lower-fang hanging shakily from a tough scale on her hind-quarter. It had neither penetrated muscle nor washed free. Again, the blunt end was also a fleshy root. He pried it loose using the fleshy stub as a haft. With the lower-fang extricated, Eli went carefully to work cutting away the abutting edges of the thick shoulder scale around the upper-fang. Minutes later he emoted, *Brace yourself. This is gonna hurt you more than me.*

HuoJi took a deep breath as he inserted the tip of the lower-fang into the side of the wound to get purchase and pried while hoping the tip would not snap off.

No luck.

He took hold of the fleshy root of the longer fang and worked it slightly back and forth, then tried again.

HuoJi groaned.

Again and again, he pried at it.

Avoiding the razor-sharp edges, he gave one last careful effort.

The stubborn thing dislodged with a sucking sound and fell to the bloody, muddy dirt followed immediately by a dark-red venous stream from the wound.

While ooching and ahhching, he quickly picked his way over to the geothermal pool and employed the bottom-fang to cut free as many tufts of moss growing here and there around the sulfur hot springs as he could carry. After picking his way back to her—ooch, ahhch, eech—he tapped a tuft into the bleeding hole with the fleshy root of his fangy new knife.

Eli pushed. *I hope moss is as healing and medicinal here in this weird place as it is in my world. I've got nothing to use as a bandage.*

HuoJi emoted, *Moss is healing.*

By this time, he was trembling with hunger. Over by the hot spring, succulent whiffs had made him salivate. Given the condition of his bare feet, there was no way to go in search of the goose carcass, which likely got vaporized anyway. The savory scent pulled at him, so he ooched and ahhched his way to the edge of the boiling hot-spring leaving a trail of bloody footprints. A thin, yet fairly large hunk of dragon flesh still attached to some bone had gotten nicely boiled. Other grey-white chunks and gobbets floated on the surface along with tan hunks of boiled brain. A stringy eyeball bobbed like a softball.

Starving and unable to help himself, he found a shard of bloody jawbone and fished the boiled, steaming rib to the bank of the hot-spring and coaxed it onto a tuft of moss. Eschewing the brains, he coaxed several other chunks of dragon-meat from the pool and tasted.

Ravenous insanity took him even as his stomach churned in protest.

Careful to chew thoroughly, he ate till sated while fighting the urge to retch on the odd-tasting, alien protein. Leaving a new trail of bloody footprints, he picked his way back to the lake and sat down to examine his splinter-laden feet. All he could see was mud and blood. "Maybe if I soak?" he muttered.

Sitting down on the edge of the coping, he placed his muddy-bloody feet in the water and swished them gently about as gross clouds of bloody clots drifted off. After a few minutes, he looked. His feet fairly glittered with the tiny splinters, but the bleeding had stopped. Imbued with extensive healing powers, the glowing waters were—for lack of a better description—magical. Soaking again, blue darts-of-healing nibbled at his injuries while the cloudy murk surrounded those tender feet.

There was nothing to be done about any of it.

This was plain, out-and-out survival.

He searched his memory of the attack.

The water monster had leapt forth as an animated sheet of steaming, living water, swooshed him back into the lake—the same as when it back-flopped him in the other pool and self-destructed blowing the statue-come-to-life into smithereens. "Did it do the same thing that first time?" he wondered aloud. This leaping forth whenever he got threatened seemed to be a pattern—but it was hard to assess amongst all the other impossibilities—like his atavistic semilunar eyelids. This thought led back to the harrowing trial-by-fire in the cavern of the siren-sorceress. For the sake of sanity, he put it all aside.

Despite all the downright deadly events that should have killed him, he had still survived. "I even have an alien friend, even if she is a dragon, " he muttered.

During these musings, he soaked his injured feet in the salubrious waters. After a few more minutes, he looked again.

As the left foot cleared the surface, the mean little splinters simply washed away leaving behind red marks and white scars. After another 15-minutes of soaking, during which it felt like little fishes nibbling at the wounds, he checked again.

The last of the tiny shards and splinters washed away and drifted to the bottom like grains of sand.

Tiny blue darts reduced them to silt.

During all of this, it came to him that the bottom-fang would make a great knife, and a knife in survival situations almost always meant the difference between life and death. Sitting on the edge of the pool with his feet in the water, the first stomach-cramp hit him like a kick to the gut.

His head throbbed like somebody had clobbered him with a baseball bat.

"Toxic meat!"—he shouted while grabbing his belly—"Gotta barf!"

He clambered to his hands and knees and stuck a finger in his mouth to force a gag. After several minutes of worsening stomach-cramps and waves of agony in his pounding head, he emptied his gut of as much of the noxious dragon meat as possible.

Head reeling, he climbed into the pool and drank a bellyful, then crawled back out, got to his hands and knees, and forced another bout of retch.

He was still heaving when a wave of bright agony blew his consciousness to smithereens.

With the illusion of blinding sparks behind newly grown eyelids, he saw HuoJi struggling to her feet. As he staggered toward the swimming-pool coping, he tried to call out but only croaked.

The last snapshot image he saw was HuoJi also tumbling into the lake a few yards away.

Then, Eli was gone.

Sleeping City

~

A Ubiquitous Presence

Poisoned by consuming the cursed long-dragon's flesh, the very moment the ersatz power-master fell senseless into the lake fed by the Long Pen Quan fount at the rear of the Upper Hangar and Staging Area, The-Creeping-Darkness had to act. Even as it manifested beneath his drowning body, the little fire-dragon fell headlong into the lake in an attempt to save him.

Also unconscious beneath the surface, she too would drown.

Neither cessation was to be allowed.

From beneath both, the water-beast expanded to about three times the size of the little fire-dragon, then rose from the lake with its seemingly innumerable arms holding her to its back.

Her head lolled to one side as she convulsed and spluttered.

In the same second, it reached another of its innumerable arms out, snagged the body of the unconscious power-master into a giant palm, then lifted him up with a great splashing.

Unconscious but saved, he also spluttered and coughed trying to clear his lungs.

The same as it had done back at the Plaza of the Forbidden Gate on the night of the Dragon's Blood Moon when they brought the hapless human forth unto Janaidar, it projected that same bio-filter along his body—an iridescent-black field-of-force like a second skin.

Perhaps that would save him, but unwanted biologics were not the same as poisons or toxins? No way to know.

It bellowed so loud in frustration more rocks fell from the ceiling to splash in the lake. One huge boulder would have crushed all three, but the water-beast swiped it away so hard it skipped across the surface several times before settling with a great splash.

As long as life still clung to the frail human's body, the transduction of black-energy into source-energy around the new micro-supercomputer implants would allow it to feed and feed and feed on his presence—an inbuilt function of their operating systems needing no further programming.

Dropping his body into the Long Pen Quan fount, it created an upwelling of the magical dragon waters lifting him to the surface on his back where he floated on the brink of death. Azure streaks of pure aureate light nibbled at his remaining injuries like tiny fishes as he bobbed on the surge.

Still carrying the little fire-dragon, it moved to the beach next to the Long Pen Quan fount and gently laid her on her side where the waters of the lake would attend to healing the injuries to her chest and side with her head support by a smallish boulder.

Whether she would survive was also unknowable.

A plume of water shot up when it unmanifested the corporeal water-beast, then retreated as a single-point-of-consciousness back beneath The-Sleeping-City to gorge the online accumulators with the enhanced tempest-of-transduction around the ersatz power-master.

This much it knew.

The healing powers of the dragon-waters would not be enough, but would certainly prolong his lingering death.

Unfortunately, the timelines had been so completely fouled by the unforeseen attack of the cursed long-dragon from the Olden Days that projecting any outcomes whatsoever was pointless.

Sleeping City

~

Bound by Onus to Kill the NuliZhu Tech-Masters

The Imperial long-dragon, YuLong, remained in a deep fugue of revivification inside the Hetmahn's Palace atop the Central Obelisk of The-Sleeping-City. He got yanked back from the brink of death by the telempathic absence of his lifelong heart-bond with YunFei—the Jade Queen. Sloshing his body in those waters while slaking his thirst, he gathered his thoughts.

This much was obvious. YunFei's foreordained demise had finally come to pass.

YuLong himself had cast upon her the dreaded Malison-of-Crystal-Awareness with two mystical geisa—commands that could not be disobeyed. The first was a curse of eternal vigilance till the proper combination of events set her free. The second was an onus-of-protection for The-Sleeping-City that would force her to attack and eliminate any threat or threats even if she died. If she did not, time would come crushing down upon her much worse than it currently was on him. Her remaining time would be numbered in hours, but at least she would finally be free.

One last tenet of the curse also held. If she tried any further dark magic—specifically, the Hein Mofa of The-Baneful-Chaos—to try extending her life again, her heart would simply stop. If any semblance of sanity remained, YuLong had always clung to the hope that she might find both peace and release in those last moments. Regardless, the Malison-of-Crystal-Awareness had obviously forced her to engage an enemy who finally brought her down. Or something else somehow triggered her freedom, and time itself brought her down.

Still immersed in the Long Pen Quan, his own onus-of-protection from the far past suddenly pummeled him for the second time. Forced to determine why, he extended his preternatural senses into the connected waters of the WuShi.

A NuliZhu Tech-Master lay soaking in a similar Long Pen Quan pool outside The-Sleeping-City in the Upper Hangar and Staging Area. There was also a mind-link between the alien long-head and a fire-dragon, whose presence came to him via the small lake fed by that same fountain.

Since the Forbidden Gate at the Pillars of Thoth had gotten activated less than two months previous, logic seemed to inform him that this NuliZhu Tech-Master had done the Jade Queen in. This moment was the end of YunFei's trap inside her own head with never-ending awareness throughout the passing millennia—a hideous and heartless fate.

Atonement would be her final redemption.

Hopefully in fighting to her death, she had also brought about the end of any other hated NuliZhu Tech-Masters, for in the far past she had wielded the horrific mind-power of biokinesis.

Whether those enemies established warning communications with others on Janaidar before their own demise was unknowable. She could have simply hit them with a deadly mindlance as individuals, or even as an attacking horde, unless the many millennia after she fell to utter madness also brought about an end to her kinetic powers-of-mind.

Obviously, at least one NuliZhu had survived along with a fire-dragon protector. Whether that fire-dragon also hailed from the Pangalactic Empire of Ra was unknown.

Regardless, there would be fight to the death.

YuLong's tired old heart ached with a grief so intense for YunFei, and all those fellow dragons killed during the Rebellion-of-the-Slaves so long ago, it threatened to stop.

Even worse, all of those who had survived back then would be long gone on the winds of time by now. Regardless, the onus-of-protection now stirred him to action. With no choice, he forced his grief to pass through his old heart like a bitter wind through the bare branches of a winter's tree.

Freed of the smothering emotions and endless guilt in order to do what must be done, he reviewed.

During the creation of the horrific artificial-sapience, the techno-dragons way back then—including himself—had pushed the Tech-Masters with subtle telepathic urges to ensure that every actual Tech-Master on planet Janaidar had a fire-dragon with them at all times to track their evil ways. YuLong himself had bestowed the techno-magic onus to throw this specific geis-of-protection. Ineluctable lines of computer code ensured it would. Making the NuliZhu forces on Janaidar accept such weirdness as their own idea had been the masterful manipulation of all telempathic manipulations.

Despite the millennia spent in deep-time stasis, memories of all this remained fresh in YuLong's mind. Subjective time for him had been about 110-year. When all of this came about way back then, he was already over 900-years old.

One simple motivation drove him.

The hated NuliZhu slavemasters could never be allowed to return and reclaim the WuShi, let alone the Forbidden Gate and the power it afforded in opening transdimensional-arcs. A scrabble of fear crawled up his spine. What if they punched a transdimensional-arc directly into The-Sleeping-City to attack in force?

It was significant, and perhaps telling, that this had not yet occurred.

Maybe there was hope?

More clearly defined thoughts arose.

Smashing into the mind of the interloper will give me answers, but do I still have the strength? Do I have enough lifespan remaining to do what needs to be done with time crushing down on me? He tried peering into the future along the extant threads-in-time as part of the arc-of-infinity.

Too many variations.

All was chaos.

Starving and too weak to levitate, he dragged his weary self from the living waters leaving a slug's trail to the entry, operated a glowing panel, and waited as the ancient force-portal whuffed from existence.

The air on the high terrace outside smelled less of his own decrepitude and more of the grass and trees in the parks below, which seemed to have remained intact, verdant, and vibrant. The faint yet salty tang of the Shenlan Sea came to his twitching, bulbous nose as the finest perfume. For several beats, he savored the scents.

Nearby, docked at a niche in the handrail, there stood a contrivance beneath a brittle covering. He pulled the cover free. It fell to flinders and dust. "Let us see if this ancient hodunwei remains operable," he grumbled to himself.

Composed of shiny silver metal, a rectangular controller's podium exactly 1-meter wide stood supported atop a cylindrical pole rising from the top center plane at the rear of a regular pentagonal prism. The sides and height all measured a single meter. The point of the pentagonal prism defined the front of the freight-unit hodunwei in terms of forward flight. Hodunwei freight-units were VTOLs or vertical take-off and landing flight systems.

When the old dragon activated the podium with a tap, the hodunwei immediately scanned him to identify which kind of operator had activated it—long-dragon, winged-dragon, or humanoid. Before him, a virtual control-panel appeared on the surface.

The VCP had a host of techno-glyphs, touch-points, toggles, and several virtual-sliders. Readouts projected in the air before him like translucent dashboards displaying absolute altitude above or below sea level, relative altitude to the city streets below, actual velocity, relative velocity, air-speed, and rates of acceleration or deceleration. A throttle slider on the right controlled the speed of steady-state flight.

Hinged at the rear on the left of the podium, a virtual horizontal lever solidified to control hover, upward motion, or downward motion with hovering as the default. A complex joystick coalesced complete with buttons for the fingers to control ordinary forward and backward movement with braking; longitudinal axis, as bank or roll; vertical axis, as heading or yaw; lateral axis, as pitch up or down. When loaded, the hodunwei would pivot at the balanced center of whatever load it carried. Automated banking during forward or backward flight kept the freight or passengers stabilized.

As he studied all of this, a form-fitting operator's nacelle appeared beneath his old body freeing his fore-hands for the controls. Tapping the layered VCP with his left fore-hand, a force-field-apron—or force-deck—resembling transparent glass flowed out as a flat-bottomed fuselage. Translucent highlights made it easy to see. A virtual trackball next to a small virtual rectangle as cursor controlled the length and breadth of the force-field. Touching another techno-glyph caused a fuselage-of-force to extend from the force-deck and encompass him inside a blunt-nosed cylinder.

YuLong took hold of the joystick in his right fore-hand, lifted the virtual lever with his left fore-hand for climbing, and the VTOL freight-unit sprang up and forward in measured flight. Banking swiftly above The-Sleeping-City with the upper fuselage derezzed made his feelers and the long strands of his extensive moustaches flap in the breeze.

Despite the terrifying possibility of flying out into the Upper Hangar and Staging Area and getting blown to smithereens by a cadre of Zhuanjinn—genetically modified beast-headed soldiers of the NuliZhu—the joy of simply being alive lent him hope. He could have toggled a fully enclosed fuselage, but the open wind was too delicious.

As he sped along, his big jowls lifted.

Both long feelers curled and fluttered.

He hovered to a standstill about 200-meters out from a symbolized set of virtual lines in the pentagonal side of the city-sized dodecahedron demarcating Spacecraft Entry Field #5. Projected as a construct-of-force, SEF #5 appeared as a physically solid wall from outside in the UHASA—the blast-doors of which had gotten unseated during the Rebellion-of-the-Slaves.

He gathered himself to enter the Upper Hangar and Staging Area while reviewing the potential that this was a vicious trap set by the invading NuliZhu. Had they somehow discovered the extended histories from the Olden Times upriver at the Cavern Keep? This would also mean that they had overrun the Huan Long Shui Sisteren. If so, why had they not punched a transdimensional-arc directly into The-Sleeping-City itself?

All of this was supposition.

He needed more intelligence.

Plans arose.

Mindlancing the NuliZhu was a trivial matter of no consequence other than forcing the WuShi to end the fire-dragon protector's life for failing to protect its Tech-Master as the final action dictated by the geis-of-protection.

And there was no way around that.

That dragon's fate was set.

However, doing so would certainly tip off any other NuliZhu contingents present on Janaidar. He might very well find himself embattled by an implacable horde of angry Zhuanjinn genmosols, provided the Zhuanjinn were still the beast-headed warrior class of the hated empire. With over 5,000-years to develop deadlier and ever deadlier weapons—including other, more vicious genetically modified creatures—it was hard to imagine what he might face outside.

Regardless, the same onus-of-protection that had jarred him awake twice in less than two months, still pummeled him with the curse-of-compulsion. Intent on completing his mission before time itself finished him off, or starvation took its deadly toll, he hovered before Spacecraft Entry Field #5 become unto death itself.

A passing urge pushed him to attempt a mind-cast—anything to contact other dragons yet surviving on Janaidar. Before doing so, however, he realized this could very well tip off the Tech-Master's fire-dragon. Crestfallen, he let the impulse perish, then steeled himself to kill the NuliZhu Tech-Master—or Tech-Masters—or whoever it was that brought death unto his beloved YunFei.

It was now or never.

It was do or die.

If he could, he would make certain it was the interlopers getting blown away on the winds of time.

Riverbend

~

Promotions and Rings-of-Rank

Out on the weather deck of the Dragon's Breath, Seleen found herself busier than a spiny anteater on a fresh termite mound. Like little puppies, Teewan and Myrna stayed on her heels so closely she took them along with her to shop along the wharf amongst the eager burghers, shopkeepers, gypsy-adepts, and independent craftspeople packed side-by-side hawking their wares.

Alahna had empowered the outfitting of the impromptu expedition with emphasis on quality and no limit on cost. Buying certain things she had always wanted, Seleen indulged herself. Before long, the girl's arms were so full they could barely see over the top of the stacks to follow Seleen about.

When the hostler Ruby and her family arrived with livestock, there arose a frenzy of coaxing the reluctant and spooked critters onto the barge. To save time, Seleen sang a calming effect on the people and livestock, both. It was just before noon by the time she and the girls returned to the stateroom with all the booty.

Alahna's black eyes were getting worse by the hour. Alahna roused herself and peeked through swollen eyes watching them sort it all. Her voice had the nasal timbre of a thoroughly plugged nose. "Garils, Adept Seleen asked me if we should explain why Yenara attacked us and what happened after."

Her somber tone held their attention.

Seleen motioned for them to sit on the edge of Alahna's bed.

It took something more than half of an hour to explain what

happened, why Ruby and her entourage showed up with farm animals, and Alahna and Seleen's insights about the murders of Lilith and Cynthia, as well as Yenara's usurpation and subsequent actions in the cover-up. Because of their age, Alahna and Seleen did not delve into the evils of The-Baneful-Chaos and the danger it represented to the Sisteren as a whole. This would have been too much for their innocence to bear.

Hugs came along with tears and grief.

Lying back, Alahna became stern. "Garils, we have no time for mourning or outrage. Although hard to bear, we must move forward with dire purpose. When time allows, Seleen and I shall further explain the concepts of usurpation and betrayal, and, together, we will perform the Rites-of-Passing for all of our Sisters gone on the winds of time."

"So, what I am about to say must be said, for it is possible mine own ka will fly away on the winds of time."

Both girls cried out.

Seleen knew why Alahna broached such a profoundly sad subject and put a finger to her mouth to shush the upset girls.

Alahna went on, "There must be a line-of-succession." Patting the girls on their backs as they sat close by, she asked, "Is thy calligraphy good?"

"Cailinn says we are almost studied enough to become initiates," Myrna said while wiping tears from her face.

Alahna approved. "Good, then take practice notes on the spare sheets. Later on, Seleen will guide thee in recording the proceedings into my new journal.

"Did ye buy calligraphy supplies?"

Teewan, "We did. And we stand ready."

Seleen quietly pulled the small table over and provided them with scrolls of paper, and fine brushes. Each got an ink stone to grind their sticks of ink on, and a tiny pitcher of water.

Alahna closed her puffy eyes to rest.

After a bit, Seleen said, "We are ready."

Alahna took several deep breaths to clear her head. "My first official act as High Priestess is to raise Adept Seleen unto the 11th Circle of Knowledge."

Seleen protested, "But. . . ."

Alahna waved her hand. "Have thee not passed thy written exams to prepare for the Ceremony of the Spheres?"

Seleen gave a nod.

"And proved thine ability in managing a SijanPao at the High Pagoda during the Activation-of-Matrixes—as witnessed and affirmed by High Adept Esmie, and Adept Chione,"—whereupon Alahna added with a wave of her hand—"whom we pray both survive this unholy debacle."

Somberly, Seleen answered, "We were together that day, and I shall never forget when the High Pagoda went still."

"And so . . . I hereby declare that Adept Seleen stands raised unto High Adept in the 11th Circle."

Nonplussed but grateful, Seleen bowed to Alahna, then turned to the girls. "What is the proper response?"

Together, they said, "So let it be said. So let it be written." Concentrating while brushing the same kanji, both stuck tongues out the sides of their mouths.

Alahna sighed in pain, then pushed through. "By definition, getting promoted unto the Council of Four moves a High Adept from the 11th unto the 12th Circle."

Suspicious, Seleen narrowed her eyes. "Where is this going, Milady Alahna?"

Alahna placed a shaky hand on Seleen's back. "My love, thou'rt young enough to assume my duties as high-priestess when my time comes, and a Mother Matriarch must always have a Named One for the line-of-succession. Unlike Lilith, I shall step down willingly.

"Following abdication, I shall write the history of these early misadventures as taken from my new journal," and she peered up at Seleen.

Seleen held it up, but once again asked, "Where is this going?"

"Garils, please bear witness. I, High Priestess Alahna, Mother Matriarch of the Huan Long Shui Sisteren, do hereby name the new High Adept Seleen as my Named One."

Seleen made to protest, but Alahna held up her hand.

Myrna and Teewan spoke as one. "So let it be said. So let it be written," After embracing Seleen, they sat down and got busy with their brushes.

Seleen sat too shocked to respond with words.

Allowing no time for protest, Alahna pushed through. "As High Priestess, my next declaration is to hereby banish Kulapti Yenara from the Council of Four and declare her anathema to the Huan Long Shui Sisteren."

Several moments passed as the girls caught up with the proclamations on the scratch sheets while Seleen provided critique.

As they did so, Alahna took a different tack. "Myrna, Teewan, how long have ye been with the Sisteren?"

"Over a year," said Myrna.

"It all happened at the steel works in Bahndahn Towne," Teewan added. "Our mommas took luncheon-meal to have with our daddies, when a boiler explosion destroyed the entire cafeteria."

Myrna suppressed a sob.

Teewan looked down at the deck with a tear in her eye.

Seleen patted their backs.

Alahna went on, "So . . . long enough to know whether becoming a Sister of the Huan Long Shui is what ye really and truly desire?" and she held up a hand. "Before answering, 'tis a difficult and demanding life of commitment, study, and sacrifice. So, think ye both with clear minds and true hearts before answering."

Looking at one another, they nodded their heads. "Yes, Mother Matriarch."

Alahna, "Yes ye'll think on it? Or yes, ye're ready to become of the Sisteren?"

They said, "The Sisteren."

Alahna nodded. "But we have a problem. Do we not, Seleen?"

Knowing this had to happen, Seleen bobbed her head. "Verbal acceptance of promotion requires no less than three Sisters as witness. As well, she who offers the promotion cannot also bear witness. Shall the two of ye stand as witnesses for me?"

Myrna spread her hands. "But we are only designates."

Alahna waved her hand without opening her eyes.

Seleen explained, "The moment of agreement, when affirmed aloud to a Sister in the 10th Circle or above, and witnessed by one other,"—and she glanced at Alahna, who held a pained but slight smile on her face—"is the cusp between designate and initiate pending the Rite-of-Initiation.

"When ye two little eejits opened yer pieholes, ye became unto our Sisters.

"So, who shall stand as my witnesses?"

Grins tempered by surprise and trepidation slowly painted Teewan and Myrna's faces as the implications sank in.

"Us?" they said.

Myrna added, "Uhm, we mean we do."

"We do . . . erm . . . witness thine ascension, I mean," Teewan added.

Alahna smiled and gazed on them with benevolence through her swollen eyes.

Seleen blew her nose, bowed her head, wiped away tears. "I stand humbled and honored to accept these promotions, Milady Alahna."

Alahna breathed deep. "Garils, go find Esau's Momma. Also Ruby and both eldest daughters. Tell them to wait outside my door."

When they departed the stateroom, Seleen shook her head. "Artfully played."

"I am exhausted, my love, let us be done with this and do it right. Prop me up and let me ink thy forearm."

Seleen did so, and Alahna carefully inked Seleen's right wrist once, then twice.

Being careful not to muss her own, Seleen inked Alahna's right wrist as the last ring-of-rank the Mother Matriarch would ever bear.

While Seleen worked, Alahna spoke. "The new initiates won't be worth a tinker's damn after the rites. So, we must go first. Call them in."

With the fascinated lay-women's eyes open wide, Seleen sat on a chair with each girl at her knees artfully inking a thin line around the right forearm above each one's right wrist using the same calligraphy ink and fine brush as Alahna had. Seleen explained as she worked. "When the mind-link of the WuShi sets in on these two fart-handles, they will become faint, and possibly lose consciousness. At worst, one or both may bolt.

"This cannot be allowed."

The ladies nodded.

Seleen went on, "In the moment of setting, a small spark erupts on the line of ink. Sometimes just a single spark burns all the way 'round. Sometimes two sparks depart and burn till they meet. It makes no difference and means nothing. However, this is where ye ladies come in. Ordinarily, we would have our own adepts as the sisters-of-holding. In their stead, ye shall be our ladies-of-holding for these two fart-handles . . . erm . . . new initiates. . . ."

The girls rolled their eyes.

Alahna added, "And we are proud it will be ladies we know and love."

Seleen gave instructions. "We need a lady on each side. One embraces the new adept with a firm grip on the left arm to prevent flailing or grabbing at the burning ring. Keep yer heads well back in case she rolls her own head in a swoon. The other holder grips the new adept's right arm below the elbow with her left hand while clasping the initiates hand in her own right hand to ensure the right wrist touches nothing.

"And I mean thou shalt hold them tight!"

They nodded.

"New rings-of-rank never blister or infect, but if the ink gets mussed before we start, we must clean it off and wait till the stain completely fades before trying again. So, be careful!" and she clipped each girl, who knitted their brows.

Myrna said, "Always with the clipping."

Seleen said, "Do ye have it?"

Scared yet determined, they nodded while rubbing their heads.

Alahna quietly chuckled, then winced.

Seleen pressed on, "Now then, if the ring-spark gets interrupted, damage will be serious and cannot be undone. Interrupted burn scars are permanent. Like any source of ignition, a ring-spark can become unto a spreading wildfire on the skin of the initiate's arm. Proper burn scars will fade to become virtual in the next few minutes for me and Alahna.

"It will take longer for the garils, whose arms will need to be bandaged for a time.

"As I said, initiates have been known to bolt. So beware, my ladies! It is most important that ye hold on to them with grips of iron should it turn into a wrestling match."

Frightened, Myrna asked, "What do we do if wildfire runs up our arm?"

Seleen pointed at two buckets of water against the aft bulkhead. "Douse it as soon as possible." Then, Seleen became serious. "A bad burn scar is forever. So, little farts, be brave and strong.

"Ye ladies, make sure yer initiate does not bolt out of the stateroom and jump in the river, for she could easily knock her head and drown."

Seleen held her arm out. "Observe."

The girls expected to get clipped again, and both ducked.

Under Seleen's concentration, her existing rings-of-rank appeared as a virtual kinetic array about a centimeter off the surface of her skin and the same distance apart. The top ring expanded to descend past the lower rings till it reached the bottom. When it shrank to take its place, it triggered the lower rings to slip upward as the new top ring expanded then descended in a never-ending cycle.

Ruby murmured, "I have never seen that."

Seleen willed them to be invisible again. After a bit more explanation, she bade them sit against the aft bulkhead with the dousing buckets nearby.

Momma held Myrna's left side.

One of Ruby's daughters held Myrna's right arm.

Ruby held Teewan on the left.

Ruby's other daughter held Teewan's right arm.

Seleen raised her voice. "Myrna! Teewan! Are ye ready?"

They murmured, "Yes, my Laoshi."

When the girls spoke the word Laoshi—as in Laoshi De Mofa, or teacher-of-magic—Seleen realized she had just taken on both as Mofa XueSheng, her students-of-magic. Even though she loved them, the additional responsibility for not just one but two new acolytes was not something she would have otherwise chosen, and it made her cross on top of all the other changes.

Alahna chanted the Rite-of-Ranking while pointing at Seleen, whose lower ink took fire with Alahna chanting till it met itself with a little puff of smoke.

About 5-seconds had passed.

The unpleasant stink of burning skin and fine arm hair filled the stateroom.

Seleen waited till the first ring-of-rank burnt out, proceeded to open the portholes on either side of the large cabin, then sat and chanted for Alahna.

Alahna held her right arm aloft while performing a meditation. The moment her ring-of-rank got burnt in, Alahna began the chant for Seleen's second ring.

Obviously struggling with the pain of two rings-fires back-to-back, Seleen sat on the other bed with her right arm held high while sipping water from a cup with her free arm. By the time the second ring burnt in, the first had already faded.

Leaving no time for the girls to become frightened and balk, Alahna and Seleen sang the Rite-of-Initiation as a duet—Alahna pointing at Myrna—Seleen pointing at Teewan.

Myrna fainted.

The ladies-of-holding stayed true.

Teewan cried out when the spark departed in both directions, but remained conscious with the ladies holding fast.

Afterward, Esau's Momma smeared marigold salve on the new rings-of-rank for both girls, then wrapped their wrists with fine linen bandages.

By then, both Alahna and Seleen's had completely disappeared.

Ruby asked, "May we see?"

They each held up their right arms, concentrated, and their rings-of-rank began the top-to-bottom procession.

Alahna's took longer.

The ladies-of-holding oohed and aahed, then bowed and departed.

Still reeling somewhat, Myrna complained, "It wasn't sposta hurt that much. . . ."

Seleen grouched, "No whining. I got two, and do not fret at those bandages when the new rings start to itch and throb! Now go lay down and see if ye can find some sleep."

They immediately fell into a weary yet fitful slumber.

Alahna quietly asked Seleen, "Dost thou remember thy first dream of the WuShi?"

"I was afraid to go back to bed for three days."

"Four for me," but Alahna seemed pleased as she laid back to rest. "Our newest acolytes had quite a day."

Seleen felt spent. "Haven't we all?"

Riverbend

~

Seleen Sings a SijanPao

With the stink of burnt skin and singed arm hair still hanging in the air of the stateroom, Alahna said, "Pull the curtain so the garils cannot see what we draw should they awaken. This is not for initiates."

Seleen said, "What?"

Alahna murmured with closed eyes, "Our next steps require the use of a SijanPao."

Seleen waited a few beats for Alahna to continue, then gave in. "And, I am the only one able to sing one?"

Alahna nodded ever so slightly.

"Do we have time?"

Alahna spoke softly with her eyes still closed. "We must make time, my love." Whereupon she struggled to sit up, swung her feet over the edge of the bed, then sat while waiting for her head to stop spinning.

Seleen pulled that same small table in front of Alahna, and they shared the ink bowl and fancy new brushes to paint the mind-glyph-of-the-spheres on broad sheets of rice-paper as if creating wall art. After several tries, Alahna felt she had her own inked correctly, then tutored Seleen in several more tries.

When performing calligraphy, Seleen always stuck the tip of her own tongue out the corner of her mouth, which made Alahna smile. "Just like the garils . . ." she whispered. Even when smiling, her blacked eyes made her seem sad. Her voice was tired and weak. "Remember, the power to call source-energy comes from a harmonious concert of mind, voice, and precision-of-melody, but the essence of spawning a Pao is the ability to hold the mind-glyph in deep-mind without conscious effort."

Seleen said, "Which is why we had no Pao to escape in after the mindbane of The-Creeping-Darkness?"

"Yes. All I could hold in my deepest mind were artifacts of severe concussion—sparkling stars and splotches of color. Now then, pin thy kanji to the wall."

While Seleen did so, Alahna shredded all the practice sheets except her own. When Seleen stood back, Alahna said, "Now lock thine eyes upon it while singing the Song-of-the-Spheres. If inked correctly, it shall detach from off the page as a multidimensional abstraction only we two can see, and only myself for a moment. Once in deep-mind, it is there to be called upon forever unless one gets her bells rang."

"And if it fails?" Seleen asked.

"Then we return to more kanji till we have it. So fear not, my love."

Together, they intoned a commonly used adage, "Fear creates failure."

Alahna knew that to prepare for striking into the 11th Circle, Seleen had practiced the Song-of-the-Spheres for almost 2-years, now. The only element missing had been the ritual of the mind-glyph, a closely held secret only shared when the time was right—and that time was now. With their fate resting on Seleen's shoulders, it almost seemed that failure meant certain death. Alahna also knew that Seleen was far beyond tired and was struggling with her own fears.

Distraught and edgy, Seleen gave voice.

As Seleen's Laoshi De Mofa, her teacher of magic, Alahna watched as Seleen's mind-glyph drifted free from the surface of the rice paper like black threads of smoke, then metamorphosed into a living, multi-dimensional abstract. It hovered before Seleen for an entire measure of the ongoing song, then disappeared in threads of white smoke.

Seleen gasped—the deed was done—she had it.

When the SijanPao itself coalesced, Seleen immediately got dragged along the overhead beams. Oof! Oof! Oof! Oof! Aoofda! She smacked into the corner of the aft bulkhead, rolled upward, then got plastered against the overhead face first.

Alahna chided, "Lucky the open portholes are lower than thy forget-fulness, or we should never see thee again."

Well and truly pinned face first, Seleen kept quiet, but the commotion had awakened the girls, who pulled the curtain back.

Before they were able to lay eyes on Alahna's kanji, she quickly folded and shredded it.

However, the girls had eyes only for Seleen plastered to the ceiling.

Knowing that Seleen could not tell who she was speaking to, Alahna said, "Now, High Adept Seleen, recite for me Lesson-One in the Disciplines-of-Positioning."

Stuck in place with her voice muffled against the ceiling rafters, Seleen intoned, "Lesson-One, Intrinsic Celestial Motion: Orbital planetary motion of celestial bodies is eternal, as well as the movement of our solar system through the galaxy, as well as the galaxy through the cosmos, as well as the cosmos through the myriad dimensions. All such movement is unimaginably swift. Let not the sight of apparent, relative stillness deceive the high-adept."

"So?" Alahna said.

Seleen closed her eyes and concentrated. Her Pao departed the upper corner, and she righted herself to hover in place at the center of the stateroom.

Now, Alahna lectured.. "Matching celestial intrinsic motion, or any type of intrinsic motion—no matter the location—shall be autonomic from now on.

Still sleepy, the girls went to their knees and bowed to Seleen, for neither had ever seen her in her own SijanPao—the singular mark of a high-adept.

Alahna said, "Seleen, my love, will thy Pao to the overhead, and try not to destroy the wheelhouse above us."

Riding Seleen's will, the Pao bumped up against the overhead followed by her floating up to bonk her noggin. "Ouch!"

The girls got to their feet while suppressing laughter.

Alahna chuckled, then winced. "Remember what happened to us at the Forbidden Gate when I had no time to sing the phrase for . . . what was it? What was the phrase?"

Chagrinned, Seleen recited, "Lesson-Two: Remember to set thy spatial-lock, or the high-adept will bounce and break," and she sang the short phrase.

Alahna said, "Now deresolve."

Seleen did so with a count of four.

"Now, sing a new one."

Seleen started again with all the proper phrasing.

Alahna said, "Remember the spinning tops with string from our craft lessons about gyroscopic spinning forces and precession?"

Seleen nodded, as did both girls.

"Gently spin thy body 360-degrees along the vertical axis."

As if she were a ballet dancer en pointe, Seleen performed a slow pirouette in place.

"Now spin along the static horizontal."

Still pirouetting, Seleen willed herself parallel to the deck while keeping her body oriented fore to aft, then laughed.

"Now slowly twisting and rotating with increasing precession."

Seleen laughed again while slowly spinning and rotating as if inside a gimbal.

"Now derezz without thinking."

Seleen sang the note-of-deresolution with a holding count. The precessing ceased, her body came upright, the Pao lowered her to the deck, then whuffed out. She staggered sideways and fell over. "Ouch some more!"

All of them laughed.

"Lesson-Four?" Alahna asked.

Sitting on her butt, Seleen wearily intoned, "Lesson-Four: Dizziness is dangerous."

Mesmerized, the girls smiled and nodded.

Alahna laughed and winced. "Always allow thy gut to catch up till practice and time makes dizziness but an irritating memory."

Still dizzy on her butt, Seleen concentrated.

Alahna said, "So, perhaps now thy studies in the Disciplines-of-Positioning will take root. How novel?"

And they all four laughed.

Alahna winced again.

The irony of mirth in such dire straits colored Seleen's voice. "Our laughter is bittersweet."

In pain, Alahna laid back, put her feet up on the bed, and spoke quietly, "Over time, imagine thyself static in place while the world moves according to thy willpower alone with thyself as the center of the universe. Those few high-adepts who can do this—including myself—can fully precess so swiftly inside the sphere-of-power as to seem like a sphere within a sphere.

"And . . . I am sorry to say . . . there is more to learn before we rest."

A few minutes passed while Seleen marshaled her strength. Watching her through swollen eyes, Alahna knew that an insidious exhaustion now crept upon Seleen with stealthy feet while the girls were too excited to realize how tired they were themselves.

Another hour of intense concentration and instruction passed quickly.

Finally, Alahna laid back and held up her hand. "Let us hope that these most powerful songspells are enough and pray to the Aerthe Mother Goddess for success."

Seleen asked, "Why must the songspells I just learned be performed in the language of the Elder Dragons only?"

Rueful, Alahna explained. "Sung in the Long Shai, any songspell becomes imbued with the power to linger and await its fruition. In addition, the Long Shai doth not easily lend itself to the casting of evil.

"To fight The-Baneful-Chaos, then—which is not techno-magic, but born from the evil of one's own heart, one who bears a ShahRen—a high-adept may surely employ evil.

"However, this becomes a dance wherein the dancers become bound to one another by chains-of-karma no matter how much time passes.

"We would not bind ourselves to such evil, would we?"

They shook their heads, then nodded.

Tiredly, Alahna went on, "And remember, only forgiveness can break such chains. Therefore, we say, 'Dig two graves when seeking revenge.' It is also why evil is self-destructive. It consumes itself like our symbol of the cobra who forever eats its own tail."

Seleen rubbed her chin. "Then I see no way to fight it."

Alahna's voice held a tremble. "Truth is the way, for evil relies on deception and delusion. Truth itself is neither good nor bad. It simply is. We are always free to judge it as good or bad, but we must base such judgment on reality, for deception and delusion render all subsequent judgments false. This, because premises thus formed are false by definition and create a house made of cards where the cards are but lies.

"Falseness generates more and ever more falseness till the house of cards finally collapses of its own weight, or unexpected revelation brings the light of truth. When one card falls, all must fall. Immutable and irrefutable, only the truth remains. Those who know this—and embody this—never fall to The-Baneful-Chaos.

"As such, wise people govern their actions in light of virtue, generosity, and valor as opposed to lies, greed, and cowardice. Serving others unto the betterment of all is the sworn creed of the Sisteren. Therefore, what we do is self-perpetuating, not self-destructive. By definition, reaction must follow action with an infinity of possible inflections. To this end, virtue requires constant vigilance by the valiant. If one perceives another's action will cause harm, or are currently causing harm, this must be dealt with. It cannot be tolerated.

"Yenara's pattern is to sow chaos whenever it suites her. She hurts others whom she wishes to harm, or perceives as having wronged her, or whom she sees as someone she must overcome, or someone she considers weak and contemptible, and even someone whom she wishes to use. Therefore, we can only assume the worst of her. What should we do in anticipation, then?"

Teewan shared an insight. "The townspeople must forget we were ever here?"

Myrna shook her head. "Yenara would not hurt them just because they helped us."

Teewan patted Myrna's shoulder. "Remember when the other garils helped us pick up trash at Shantytown after the last Summer Solstice? Yenara assigned the job to us."

Myrna's face fell. "She made them gather the trash into the Keep, made us take it back out and dump it, and made them gather it inside again. We had to do this over and over till Cailinn found out and sent us all to bed."

Seleen nodded. "I remember that. So, if Yenara knew the two of ye came and found us here?"

Fear painted itself on their youthful faces when the true purpose of the expedition finally dawned on them.

Alahna spoke with weary gravitas, "So . . . we make the townspeople forget we were here and protect them with an imprecation," and she sighed.

Teewan asked, "Imprecation?"

Seleen said, "A spoken curse. In our case, a curse performed during songspell."

Alahna confirmed, "We can never anticipate every harm or evil Yenara is capable of. So . . . how do we protect the townspeople?"

A crafty smile broke across Teewan's face. "Reflection and protection?"

Alahna smiled. "Since I am too ill, ye garils have song-castings to learn. One of forgetting, one of reflecting, and one of protecting. A forgetting can be subject specific—all about us and our expedition. Reflecting Yenara's evil back upon her will discourage her while creating protection for the many."

Seleen caught the nuance. "The many? What about the one?"

Alahna seemed terribly sad. "Some may die, but the many will not. Now that ye garils are initiates—"

Teewan interrupted, "But we are acolytes, too, since High Adept Seleen is our Laoshi De Mofa."

Seleen rolled her eyes.

Alahna smiled and pressed on. "Here is the first lesson for young acolytes. Some adept's train for a lifetime and never find that which already abides in those bellies and brains," and she pointed. "As the true High Priestess, I can sense this." Whereupon, she laid back without further comment.

Myrna and Teewan exchanged looks, then did the rock-paper-scissors game.

Myrna lost and asked, "What is in our bellies and brains?"

Alahna struggled to open her blacked and swollen eyes. "The Azure Flames of Will are the wellspring of magicfire. Not all Sisters have it. Both of ye garils do."

Seleen looked down at her stomach in mock disbelief, then crossed her eyes as if trying to see inside her head.

The girls laughed.

Alahna also laughed while holding her side and head. "Stop . . . stop . . . do not make me. . . ." Pressing on, she said, "Seleen, the purity of thy heart, how deeply the Sisters love thee, and a natural inclination to levelheaded leadership—these will serve the Sisteren well."

Seleen's eyes glistened.

The girls rushed to Seleen in a group hug.

Alahna smiled sadly, knowingly. "There may come a day, High Adept Seleen, when this is not the honor it seems."

With Seleen singing a healing song, the smaller part of an hour passed till Alahna finally settled into a restless and pain-ridden slumber. Whereupon, Seleen found herself finally forced to face what she must do next, and without the help of Alahna. Irritable and harsh as she stripped off her clothes, when the girls hesitated, she gave them both a stern look.

Both reluctantly disrobed.

Their hesitance and fear obvious, Seleen softened somewhat. "Sit down with me in the lotus position with our knees touching, then join hands," and she reached out. "If I sense thine attention wander, I will squeeze thy hand."

Perplexed, they sat.

With the little song-circle complete, Seleen began. "With the possibility of yet another deadly run-in with Yenara, and no way of knowing who amongst her sycophants might arrive to assist her in an outright attack, and Alahna down and out of the fray,"—and she waved her hands wide as if they were outside on the quarterdeck looking at the sky—"there is simply no choice concerning what must come next."

Myrna asked, "Why?"

Still cross, Seleen said, "We cannot get away fast enough by simply sailing downriver. Even if we gain some respectful distance, they could fly cross-country and be on us in a trice."

Teewan interrupted, "Don't cha mean a SijanPao?"

Seleen said, "Trice is a sailing term that has to do with lashing something using a small rope. It also means a tiny span of time."

Teewan clung to her innocence. "Would Yenara really do that?"

Roughly jerking their arms up, Seleen shouted, "Surprise! Thou art dead!"

Startled, both girls yelped.

"That is what she did to Alahna and I. Dost thou see?"

Teewan made a pouty lip.

Myrna frowned and knitted her brows.

Seleen pressed on. "Now that ye're initiated, the two of ye are the only other sister-adepts on this expedition. With Alahna down, that leaves us to protect the people of Riverbend and this expedition." She squeezed their hands for emphasis. "Now then, empty thy busy little minds," and she waited knowing they were like finches hopping from branch to branch inside their heads.

Not completely out of it, and having been through a lifetime of teaching such lessons, Alahna quietly hummed the Song-of-Remembering to both quiet and open the girl's deep-minds.

Seleen quietly gave voice to the words-of-power.

In mere moments, the girls fell into the deepest state of mind they had ever experienced in their lives.

Seleen squeezed their hands again. "To call upon thy youthful energies during the songspells, mine own magicfire will engulf yer little bodies. Do not fear. No harm will come," whereupon she spawned a SijanPao.

In bodily contact, the field-of-force took shape around all three still sitting in lotus, and raised them off the deck to the center of the undulant force-field.

When Seleen sang the opening aria to prepare them, both cried out as magicfire licked along their bodies from Seleen's. Tiny sparks danced between their long strands of hair now standing out straight. Ripples of tiny flamelets licked along their eyebrows, eyelashes, and fine body hair.

Seleen raised her tired voice. "Imagine thy faces as if peering into a mirror. See them . . . sense them . . . that's right . . . now imagine them cleansed of distracting magicfire."

Watching as the flamelets on the girl's faces faded, Seleen said, "Good. Now open thine eyes."

When they did, they looked at each other with wild surprise.

With her voice now flanged, Seleen pressed on. "Ignore the discomfort, concentrate on my voice. Blend with me by humming on key."

With no time for further coaching, there came a knock on the stateroom door.

Already hovering above the deck, Seleen adjusted them with herself in the lead.

At the rear, Myrna laid hands on Teewan's shoulders.

Teewan took hold of Seleen's.

When Seleen reached for the latch, the field-of-force clung to her hand like a glove.

Outside on the Quarterdeck, Oren instantly realized they were already in a sphere-of-power, then stood back with head bowed and eyes averted. "Miladies, it is time to set the prow into the current and come about."

Strangely flanged, Seleen's voice emanated from the Pao. "Captain, please hold all in readiness for several minutes. We must cast spells to protect the expedition and Riverbend."

Oren turned and hollered, "Make ready t' cast off, but hold on me orders!"

"Aye, aye, Captain!" came from all around.

Gulls squawked and hovered on the breeze.

The town's citizens were milling about in the mist rising from the river getting ready to return to their shops or homes. As the sound of Seleen' mellifluous voice carried on the gusty wind, they stopped to gaze in rapt attention.

The scents of delicious cooking drifted from the kitchens, whose businesses had boomed for a short while.

Lazy currents washed against the wharf and ship.

Together as one, the sister-adepts floated out into the afternoon mist, then rose to hover abaft the mizzenmast.

Riverbend

~

Songseplls of Protection

Seleen peered down at all the people above decks on the Dragon's Breath and along the riverfront, who turned to watch with eyes wide and mouths agape as she and the girls rose into the sky above the Dragon's Breath in her sphere-of-power.

Fully clothed in azure magicfire, all three remained in lotus position as they drifted upward with Seleen positioning them back-to-back to create a song-casting gestalt. Each sister-adept could easily keep a line of sight well over 120-degrees around them to complete the visual capture. This also reduced the strain on Seleen by two-thirds and made certain they left no sector out of the protections thus cast.

To begin, a tiny songspell from Seleen joined the girls chi with hers in a dramatic fashion.

Both girls started giving off heart-light from their Anahata Chakras like fountains of rainbow-hued scintillations so beautiful it made the people down below gasp. Swiftly swirling about, the girl's prismatic-luminance found its mark in Seleen's own Anahata chakra to complete a ring of light around them waxing and waning as the girls fell into synchronized breathing like people singing in a choir a capella.

Unaccustomed to managing such a powerful flow energy—let alone sharing out their prismatic-luminance—their chi—both girls whined and coughed, but remained stalwart.

Nevertheless, Seleen sensed herself on the fringes of creeping exhaustion.

Things felt iffy—concentration muddled—confidence elusive.

With the prismatic-luminance bolstering her, she chided the

laxity in her own deep-mind, then pushed through. Forcing herself, she chanted the elemental powers into place with no way of knowing whether she had the Powers-of-the-Five-Directions under proper control.

Desperation lurked in her deep-mind when she cast the Song-of-Forgetting in the ancient Long Shai.

> *"Elemental Powers of the Hallowed Elder Dragons!*
> *Hear my song and lend us thy graces!*
> *I command the cleansing of*
> *memories about our arrival,*
> *Our acquisitions,*
> *Our departure!*
> *Let the people of Riverbend now forget*
> *—and never recall—*
> *The comings and goings of High Priestess Alahna,*
> *Her entourage,*
> *And our presence on the wharf this day."*

On the last syllable, Seleen pointed at both ship and barge with her right index finger while making the circle-of-negation with her left index finger to exclude them both from the songspell. She then willed the song-circle in a 360-degree rotation with her right finger pointing outward.

A flattened shock wave torus of rainbow dragon-magic swept out into the afternoon mist.

Sizzling purple lightnings higher than the tip of the mainmast played around the SijanPao.

More and ever more enervated, Seleen pushed on in the Long Shai.

> *"Oh Sacred Powers!*
> *Protect the blessed innocent from harm*
> *In subtle but rising measure!*
> *Within such protection,*
> *Let intentional harm fall back*
> *Upon whomsoever casts it!"*

So doing, she performed the exclusion of barge and ship again, then willed the song-circle in a 360-degree rotation while pointing outward with her right index finger held high.

As her hand swept the arena-of-casting, another hemispherical torus of dragon-magic centered on the Pao. Still excluding the expedition, it grew in size till the riverfront hamlet and all the homesteads across the river for kilometers in every direction, and on either side of the lazy river, lay engulfed.

Lasting mere moments, it abruptly faded.

Seleen felt dull—even leaden—but pressed on.

"As we Sisters of High Priestess Alahna
—and Herself—
Travel to meet our destiny, we prithee!
Protect the Dragon's Breath and barge,
And all creatures hereupon,
And herein,
And speed us safely on our way!"

This next time during the 360-degree rotation, Seleen pointed outward at the world around while performing a circle-of-negation with her left index finger. Slowing the rotation, she pointed at both ship and barge with the right one to set her intentions.

A rainbow-hued sphere formed about the stout caravel and barge with Seleen's field-of-force as the locus.

Myrna began crying. "My face! Magicfire covers my face again!" She bawled and frantically rubbed at her face and head.

Teewan cried, "Mine, too!" and began yelping while slapping at her face as if trying to put the magicfire out with bare hands.

Seleen's concentration faltered.

Out of control sheets of magicfire engulfed all three.

Screaming as the song-circle unraveled, they separated from one another, then tumbled about inside the sphere-of-power with uncontrolled magicfire surging all around their fragile bodies.

Ululations of the brightest agony resonated through the deafening buzz of the oscillating SijanPao.

Riverbend

~

Rescue On the LungHuo River

When Seleen and the girls in her SijanPao wafted out of the stateroom, Oren's three-cornered hat went flying. Hustling across the quarterdeck, he managed to grab both it and his droopy peacock's feather as it flew past.

Esau, Conrad, and Tarik were also standing about, and laughed a bit till the gravity of such strange events set in.

Gazing up at Seleen's Pao as she and the girls carefully wafted through the rigging past the tall masts, Esau shook his head. "This is new. Seleen hath never spawned a sphere-of-power, and I thought little Myrna and Teewan were only designates. Seleen is too worn-out for this!"

Conrad said, "It doesn't matter! She's apparently found her power!"

The moment Seleen and the girls were well above the mainmast, she sang a short phrase while facing each point of the cardinal directions. The banks of the great river near them quivered while making small wavelets. The flue of the cook's stove protruding from the side of the ship gave off a belch of black smoke followed by square and boxy waves dancing on the surface of the river as she turned to face another direction. Her next invocation made the gusting breeze rise to a stiff wind whistling and whining through the rigging.

People on the wharf shouted in panic and ran about.

Onboard, Alahna's followers wailed and fretted as purple arcs of lightning above the mainmast sizzled and popped in the air when she sang the final invocation—a dazzling display of crackling source-energy around her field-of-force.

Seleen's next songspell shot a torus of thaumaturgical energy out from the SijanPao, which seemed to settle everybody ashore, who became strangely oblivious to everything and mindlessly went about packing unsold wares and goods.

Words-of-power rang out again, and a rainbow field-of-force started out hollow, included the ship and barge, then exploded outward to encompass the entire region thereabouts.

Ship and barge rocked hard against the wharf.

Plumes of water shot into the air.

Bawling animals on the barge raised a ruckus.

Esau and all the rest hustled to grab handholds along the forward bulkhead of the quarterdeck.

Landlubbers on the weather deck struggled to find their sea legs, or hung their heads across the bulwarks to be sick.

Oren and his sailors rode everything out with the expected aplomb of lifelong mariners.

More words-of-power made both vessels fight at their moorings as a rainbow-hued field-of-force expanded out from her SijanPao to encompass the expedition like toy ships in a glass ball half filled with angry waters.

Waves slapped hard against the periphery of the strange force-field. Seconds later, it faded from apparent existence, and a feeling of safety fell across everyone—including the frightened livestock.

Traveling hunks of azure ball-lightning sizzled along the taffrail surrounding the poopdeck as whorls of threaded smoke whuffed away.

Suddenly, wailing and screaming voices emanated from inside Seleen's sphere-of-power.

The untested lesser adepts were panicking. As uncontrolled sheets of magicfire leapt off their bodies, they became obscured by argent magicfire bright as a silver sun followed by terrible screeching and humming from the sphere-of-power as if a banshee had been trapped inside the sphere-of-power along with them.

Stark and shifting shadows danced everywhere.

Whitecaps sprang from the sides of the caravel as if some invisible giant hand had grabbed the hull and repeatedly shoved it down to watch it pop up, only to repeat the terrible mischief.

Everybody not holding onto something got thrown from their feet.

Accomplished sailors barely managed the dipping and swaying decks.

Semicircular waves shivered across the river with the ship at the center of a rising gale-force whirlwind.

Holding a life ring mounted to a bulkhead, Esau screamed, "They've lost it!"

Then—without warning—the door to the stateroom slammed open, and Alahna flew out in her own SijanPao. Sheets of azure flame welled from off her upright body as she soared into the wind while song-casting. Creating another field-of-force around the first one, she caused the second to depart like a giant soap bubble caught in the rising gale. With her flaming body still inside the first, she wove her blazing hands in gestures-of-power so powerful everybody literally felt the controlled movements.

Still empty, the second sphere-of-power shot out to engulf Seleen's field-of-force like some enormous amoeba swallowing the fire-obscured sisters whole.

Intense and dazzling waves of radiant heat forced people to turn their faces away.

Esau hollered over the terrible commotion, "They're still inside! I can see 'em tumbling about! They're terrified! What if it explodes?"

Happening second-by-second, the moment Alahna caused her voracious second Pao to swallow that of Seleen's, she willed them all away from the ship and out across that wide meander in the LungHuo River.

Tarik yelled over the gusting gale, "What the hell is Alahna doing?"

Esau shouted, "If those Paos fail, they will surely drown!"

With the ship regaining its trim, Oren and the crew of his Captain's Gig came to all three friends. Oren shouted, "Do ye boneheaded landlubbers know how t' swim?"

Esau slapped Conrad and Tarik on their backs, "Damn right! We swim like otters!"

"Toss yer clothes off, and go with me sailors in the longboat!" and all three hurriedly stripped.

In a bustle around them, Oren's crew efficiently assisted them into woolen bodystockings while tying life preservers of silk-wrapped cork on their chests and backs to keep their heads above the lashing waves—feet remained bare. Together, they hurried to the davits, which were already extended out over the water on the starboard quarter where the Captain's Gig hung in place ready to board.

Crewmen stood by at the falls and brakes to safely lower the boat through the gusting gale.

Small fenders between gig and ship prevented damage from banging.

Eight sailors and all three buddies clambered in.

Oren ordered lifebuoy rings of silk-wrapped cork fitted with grab lines on the outside to be thrown into the gig with each buoy large enough for a person overboard to pull over their shoulders and remain afloat. Oren also included a wooden crate of natural-rubber rescue quoits encircled by hemp rope as weight for throwing the lighter braided line, which had been triced in figure-eight loops. As the crew lowered the longboat, the oarsmen hurriedly lashed a dry box of woolen blankets in the prow of the gig.

Commanding the longboat, Oren's coxswain released the frapping lines, and the longboat hit the waves hard. Shouting, the oarsmen pushed it away from the ship, then set out across the whitecaps toward the energy storm raging about the errant spheres-of-power. By this time, the SijanPaos were more than halfway across the great river.

Fighting the current, waves, and wind, the coxswain navigated upstream while gauging the drift. As the longboat approached Alahna in her sphere-of-power, Seleen's original SijanPao explosively derezzed. Virtually in the same moment, Alahna's rescue Pao shed the excess magicfire to keep Seleen and girls from getting burnt alive.

An incredible blast of magicfire burst out across the waves.

Everybody in the gig ducked to the sloshing deck as horrific waves of heat shunted past.

In a moment out of time, Seleen and the girls seemed to hang in the blistering air high enough above the waves for their fragile bodies to be shattered when they hit the surging waves. Screaming as they fell, it seemed as if the roiling waters took shape, reached up, then eased them into the pounding surf. Notwithstanding, they hit the water hard.

Esau yelled above the gale, "Never seen the likes!"

The others nodded in agreement.

On board the pitching longboat, tense and worried minutes passed as the oarsmen hove with all their might while the coxswain hollered orders at Esau and company. At the rearmost position to the left of the coxswain and tiller, a stroke-oarsman called out the beats.

One-by-one, each adept surfaced gasping and spluttering while treading water. With their heads giving off steamy vapors, they desperately dog paddled toward one another.

Esau stood on the bow calling directions to the coxswain at the tiller each time he spied them in between the heaving waves. When they were close enough, Esau and Tarik jumped in as the sailors threw out lifebuoys and rescue quoits.

That was when Alahna's own sphere-of-power explosively derezzed in a flash. Waves of blistering heat shunted across the river as if Alahna had been a white-hot ingot fresh from the blast furnace. By then the longboat had drifted far enough downriver to escape this latest burst of hellish energy.

Gouts of spray and steam spat off the crests of the violent waves.

Visible only as a momentary glimpse through the storm, Alahna's inert body plunged spinning into the river from a great deal higher than the others, and—again—the waves seemed to reach up and grab her falling body.

The coxswain shook his head and swore.

Within minutes, Esau and Tarik had all three lesser-adepts tucked into their lifebuoys.

The moment the longboat got close enough, the coxswain ordered the middle-crew and bow-pair to ship their oars and throw out more rescue quoits for Esau and Tarik to grab.

Working hard, the coxswain and stern-pair skillfully maneuvered the longboat to keep it from crashing down on those still overboard. Equally good seamanship in between waves brought them safely aboard, and the longboat hove away in search of Alahna.

Esau and Tarik lent aid and comfort to the injured and crying adepts.

Conrad helped the coxswain account for the current and drift as Oren's sailors oared the longboat somewhat downstream past where they surmised Alahna's deadly fall had occurred.

Esau looked up just in time to see Conrad leap into the swells from off the bow.

The coxswain ordered two lifebuoys thrown into the water along with a quadruple set of rectangular cork cubes joined by a long tow rope to act as a sea-anchor and keep it close. A flapping pennant made the life-sling easier to locate in the high waters and blustering whirlwinds. Without warning, a terrific gust of swirling air hove the gig to port making the seasoned oarsmen fight to prevent capsizing.

Through the pounding waves, they heard Conrad blow a rescue whistle meaning he had found Alahna.

Heaving the gig to starboard, the coxswain spied Conrad waving the pennant of the sea-anchor in between cresting waves.

Conrad had one of the voluminous lifebuoys over Alahna's lolling head and under her arms. He had also tied her in with braided line from a rescue quoit. A life-sling around his chest with the sea-anchor trailing behind kept his own body afloat.

Once again managing the currents, waves, drift, and gale, Oren's sailors navigated the longboat to Conrad and Alahna where they bobbed in the spindrift whipping off angry whitecaps like crazy seagulls. They hauled Alahna's inert form in first, then Conrad, who scuttled on hands and knees to her and started checking her naked body for signs of life.

Alahna's back, buttocks, sides, and legs where she smacked into the terrible waters were bright red with ragged impact welts. Scrapes from her inquiries back at the Cavern Keep seeped carmine droplets mixing with the wetness. A line of raw skin around her chest showed where Conrad had tied her into the lifebuoy. The other sister-adepts had similar injuries where they smacked naked into the waves, but none as severe as Alahna.

The coxswain raised his voice over the swish and swell. "Them injuries ain't nearly as bad as they ought to be considerin' how far they fell! From such a height, that water's hard as a cobblestone street! They're lucky to be alive!"

Esau watched Conrad lock eyes with the coxswain—a strangely haunted look.

The stern-pair and middle-crew steadied the longboat while the bow-pair wrapped the rescuers and victims in dry woolen blankets, which did not stay dry for long.

Whitecaps were visibly subsiding in the fading whirlwinds.

Riverbend

~

Back Onboard the Dragon's Breath

When the longboat hove alongside the ship, the topside crew threw frapping lines down while the coxswain and oarsmen made them fast. To lighten the load, seven of the longboat sailors climbed aboard using a pilot's ladder.

Adepts, rescuers, and the coxswain remained in the sloshing longboat as Oren's deck hands hoisted it up to the davits, pivoted it over the deck, and made fast the hooks, lashings, and stays.

The woolen blankets covering the Sisters were completely sopping from the soaking waves and sloshing water in the longboat.

Esau was the first to clamber out, who instantly shed his lifejacket and floatation gear.

Shedding their own, Conrad and Tarik handed Seleen down into Esau's arms, and he hustled to the stateroom.

Conrad, Tarik, and the coxswain climbed out even as several crew members climbed in to bail the boat out. They carefully handed Alahna to Conrad, then Teewan to the coxswain, and finally Myrna to Tarik.

Up on the quarterdeck, Momma, Ruby, and her daughters stood gathered outside the stateroom door with Momma shouting orders like a barnyard dog chasing a skulk of foxes from a yard-bird coop.

Hurrying past the concerned crew to the slap, slap, slap of bare feet, Esau bore Seleen into the stateroom with a sidewise shift of her body through the door.

Seleen had regained her senses well enough to wrap her arms around his neck and hold her head against his chest. She moaned slightly.

Behind them, Conrad bore Alahna's unconscious form as if carrying a child in his great arms. Tears mixed with remaining wetness stained his gallant face.

The trusty coxswain held Teewan—who was completely unconscious yet breathing well—and also had to shift his great bulk to carefully slip her through the stateroom door.

Tarik followed them in with Myrna in his arms, who was also conscious enough to wrap her arms around his neck.

Once Conrad laid Alahna down, Momma and Ruby immediately freed her from the bloody and sopping blanket. Momma tossed it to Conrad, saying, "Make yerself useful, and hold this high fer some privacy." To Tarik and the coxswain, she said, "Yer duties are down for now, and thanks be to the both of ye."

With Conrad holding the blanket up for Alahna, Ruby's daughters untangled Teewan and Myrna while Ruby herself untangled Seleen.

Of course, Esau stood holding Seleen's blanket with his head held respectfully down.

Muttering to herself as she felt of Alahna's body, Momma spoke like a physician. "Back's alright . . . neck, too . . . no broken ribs or shattered limbs . . . some bleeding here and there . . . impact welts and terrible rash. . . ." and so it went. She looked up at Ruby, saying, "Could one of yer beautiful young ladies go to my trunk on 2nd Deck and bring back the tin of liniment; clean sheets, as bandages; my herbal-infused healing water jug; and the fancy salve-of-marigold in its big golden croc?"

Ruby's eldest daughter hurried out.

Myrna moaned as she lay there on the bed across from where they laid Alahna.

Also moaning, Teewan lay beside Myrna.

Momma had taken to assessing the other three Sisters while awaiting her medicaments, but turned to work with Alahna the moment Ruby's eldest returned with the golden croc of salve and a crewman carrying the smallish trunk, who set it down and hurried out again.

As Momma spread marigold salve and liniment on Alahna's bruises, cuts, and welts—and all the other previous injuries now aggravated by the day's calamities. Wrapping bandage here and there, she hummed the Song-of-Healing. Strangely, it seemed to bear an effect on all four of the injured Sisters.

Even though hurting badly from the terrible splashdown, and after pulling a dry sheet over her sore body, Seleen wiggled Esau's blanket with her foot.

Worried, Esau peeked over.

The sheet was already staining pink from serosanguinous seepage along parts of Seleen's body. However, she gazed up at him with weary and very grateful eyes. A hint of a sore smile painted her face. Now in this moment of safety, with Esau standing at the foot of the bed, they held one another's eyes in a gaze that seemed a great deal more than simple gratitude.

Esau shifted his eyes to Momma as she moved her ministrations to Teewan.

Momma smiled a secret and knowing smile at him.

Self-conscious thoughts arose in Esau's worried mind. Seleen hugged me, took measure of my scent. Poignant thoughts tempered suppressed desire, for he knew he could never be with her. Looking back at Momma, he realized that his mother also knew.

Under Momma's direction, Ruby and her daughters had taken to spreading marigold salve where needed, and liniment on cramped muscles on every Sister's body.

Crying softly, Teewan came to and moaned as Ruby began with the calming medicaments.

Feeling useless, Esau said, "Well . . . if I am no longer needed . . ." then stopped talking when Seleen reached an arm out from under the sheet. "Silly man, come sit beside me." Once on the edge of the bed, she pulled him to her and gave him a deep kiss.

Totally embarrassed, when the kiss finally ended, he made to pull away.

But Seleen held him close and gave him another kiss with both arms around his neck. Releasing him at last, she fell back, then spoke softly, "Thanks be unto thee. Ye've saved us."

Momma took it all in.

Esau blushed with tears welling on his ruggedly handsome face.

Still holding a blanket up, Conrad chimed in, "Oh, I think he had some help, milady."

Relieved, everybody smiled.

Peering at the deck, Esau mumbled, "I spose 'tis only natural to show gratitude when someone saves thy pretty—" and it was in that moment he realized he had almost overstepped.

Seleen smiled. "Pretty ass?"

Red-faced and still staring at the deck, he nodded.

"When did thee notice?"

Momma acted as if she were ignoring the exchange.

Esau knew better, bit his lip, shook his head, then looked into Seleen's deep blue eyes. "Are the Sisteren not chaste and celibate?"

Seleen took his hand in hers and smiled sadly. "We may very well be, but not all thoughts in a garil's head are." Whereupon she gave him a wan, sad smile, laid back, and closed her weary eyes.

Esau looked up and caught Momma wearing a subtle smirk as she came to examine Seleen. He glowered, shook his head, departed the cabin muttering.

Out on deck, Esau overheard Captain Oren belaying the orders to set sail. "Well, me boyos, 'tis too late to set her into the current now. We'd surely run aground on a sandbar. They shift from time to time, ya know?" Hollering at his crew, "Make fast the moorings fer overnight. We set sail at the flush of dawn."

Still standing near the stateroom door, Conrad and Tarik joined Esau.

Steam wafted from their wet, woolen bodystockings in the cool evening air.

Tarik put his hand on Conrad's shoulder and shook him slightly. "Tell Esau."

Esau narrowed his eyes. "Tell me what?"

Conrad's serious expression foretold dire news. "When I jumped in the drink, Alahna was nowhere to be seen amongst the whitecaps. So I called out and swam in circles searching in between them awful waves. That was when I saw something pushing her through the swells." Then, he paused as if what he needed to say refused to fall past reluctant lips.

Esau urged, "What? Speak up, man!"

Conrad shook his head. "What saved her. . . ."

Esau said, "Dammit, man. Use yer words!"

"It was a thing of pure darkness and roiling drench. The waves around it got displaced like shoving a clear glass bottle 'neath the surface. Those eyes were pits like the glowing coals in a dying campfire that never once blinked, but looked at me all the same—and three of 'em, no less?"

Tarik echoed him, "Three eyes. . . ."

Conrad bobbed his head. "Red fire along its body gave off gouts of steam as it pushed Alahna through the waves. When finally it had her close t' me, the waves were so damn high I was basically helpless.

"Them steamin' hands—if ya could call 'em such—pulled us both close enough t'gether fer me t' get the lifebuoy over her head and under her arms. I kept my eyes on her and wouldna look at the accursed thing. When I had done it vaporized with a cloud of steam and a great splash.

"Scared the piss out of me, then.

"Got me spooked to the bones right now."

Tarik and Esau murmured as one, "The-Creeping-Darkness. . . ."

Esau, "Remember what the coxswain said? All four ought to be deathly injured or killed outright"

Tarik picked up the thought. "Thinkin' mebbe the water demon reached up an' caught 'em?"

Pale with recollection and lingering fear, Conrad shook his head. "Mebbe. . . .

"Mebbe so. . . .

"Makes sense. . . .

"Has to be. . . .

"But I don't never wanna see that accursed thing again!"

And so ends Book One of the Stolen Man Series

Robert says, "Thanks for reading my novels!

If you enjoyed this romp through science fiction fantasy, I would be extremely grateful if you posted a review on Amazon.

I personally read every one.

It really makes a big difference for other folks who might be interested, and helps me improve the story."

To find merchandise, news, and see Vicki Holland's Digital Art for the Stolen Man Trilogy, go to:

www.RobertDeanHolland.com

Acknowledgments:

Every novelist needs quality control (QC) at every stage of the process. Moreover, they need encouragement and rescue when being a recluse turns into becoming a grouchy, old hermit. My heartfelt gratitude goes to Vicki Holland, MBFA, my better half since 1974, who is the most-excellent in-house artist and cover designer a writer ever had. Without her patience, guidance, and advice on all the issues from grammar to style, plotline, story structure, scene sequencing, and beyond, I could simply not have written this series. A novelist needs space and time alone to think, compose, and edit. Vicki takes care of everything else, also does the art, and a great measure of research—all so I can sit in my lonely techno-office tower and create this work of science-fiction and fantasy.

My sincere gratitude also goes out to Linda Searcy, BSCE. Her many years as a technical writer and editor brought to us her deep knowledge of proofreading and setting corrections inside the author's copy paperback. Suggestions for improved clarity, confusing passages, words left out, unrelated words, too many words, and just plain mistakes have been key to giving this work its best chance for success. Without Linda's proof of the work in paperback format prior to final publication on the 1st of December, 2022 for the 1dt Edition--then again in January, 2025 for the 2nd Edition, we simply could not have wrung out all the errata as errors in printing and writing.

I would also like to recognize and appreciate the guidance provided by Captain Jeremy Nielsen of the **Columbia River Pilots Association of Professional Mariners.** In writing a fictional work of this complexity and scope, some concepts get so baked into the storyline that going backwards with an entire sweep through the manuscript, and with so many references to pre-steam, sailing ship design, required that I only do it once in order to maintain consistency throughout. Captain Nielsen's advice and excellent support were critical for the accuracy of all maritime passages in this novel.

The Stolen Man Series

~*~ Book 1 ~*~

Dragons of Janaidar and Elijah, The Stolen Man

A Science Fiction Fantasy

2nd Edition of

Dragons of Orion and Elijah, The Stolen Man

~*~ Book 2 ~*~

The Creeping Darkness of Janaidar

A Science Fiction Fantasy

2nd Edition with new subtitle

~*~ Book 3 ~*~

The Gravity Masters of Janaidar

A Science Fiction Fantasy

1st Edition

~ The Jandarians ~

- The Huan Long Shui Sisteren—meaning Sisters of the Magical Dragon Waters
- High Priestess Lilith—The one and only Adept in the 13th circle. She elderly and doddering. Her title is Mother Matriarch. She is the holder of the last ShahRen.
- High Adept Yenara—Adept in the 12th circle, member of the Council of Four, Kulapti of the Huan Long Shui Order (or chancellor) and technically Alahna's superior.
- High Adept Alahna—Adept in the 12th circle, member of the Council of Four of the Huan Long Shui Sisteren. She is also Keeper of the Archives and knows the history of Janaidar.
- High Adept Deheune—Eventually becomes Senior Song Master.
- High Adept Nehbet—Seniormost Song Master of the Sisteren for 20 years and member of the Council-of-Four.
- Adept Seleen—Adept in the 10th Circle .She is Alahna's acolyte and student-of-magic.
- Adept Cailinn—Adept in the 10th Circle. She is held in affection by her Sisters, for her exactness to duty; sweet temperament; and gentle, confiding disposition.
- Initiate Myrna—One of two young initiates of the Sisteren sent to Riverbend for help.
- Initiate Teewan—The other of the two young initiates of the Sisteren sent to Riverbend for help.
- Conrad Hunter—Alahna's friend and arranger in Riverbend.
- Esau—Conrad's Friend.
- Tarik—Conrad's Friend.
- Maxfield—The Sisteren's Hostler in Riverbend.
- Dorak—Son of Maxfield in Riverbend.
- Elijah the Stolen Man—Stolen from Earth to become the Techno-Warrior-Sage of Janaidar.
- Oren—Old One-eyed Oren, Captain of the Dragon's Breath Caravel, a four-masted schooner.

~ The WuShi ~

- Ancient Alien (AI) Artificial Sapience
- The WuShi is an Artificial Intelligence that has lain suppressed beneath The-Sleeping-City on Cape Orion. Created over 5000-years ago by the NuliZhu Tech-Masters, but long forgotten by them. The WuShi is held in the first state of consciousness by the Huan Long Shui Sisteren and Guardian Dragons of Janaidar.
- The WuShi's States of Consciousness are:
- 1st-State —That-Which-Abides in Dull Abeyance - Zunshou De
- 2nd-State —The-Silent-Watcher in semi-sapience - Chenmo De Shouwang Zhe
- 3rd-State —The-Sleeping-Evil in full-sapience - Xie De Shuimian
- 4th State —The-Creeping-Darkness in hyper-sapience - Paxing De Heian.
- 5th-State—The Weaver-of-Time - Shíjin de Binzhi Zhe
- The WuShi has full control over its powers, but still needs a NuliZhu power-master, or the Guardian Dragons, to imbibe dark-energy for its accumulators. Hyper-sapience is the state-of-consciousness the ancient-alien NuliZhu Tech-Masters most feared. The Water Beast of the WuShi is manifested when in the 4th State as The-Creeping-Darkness.

~ The Dragons ~

- Bo YouYong—Guardian Dragon of the Western Sentinel's Watch, Water Dragon, a long-dragon.
- Meili Chuan—Guardian Dragon of the Eastern Sentinel's Watch, Air Dragon, also a long-dragon.
- Quang Huo Yan—Guardian Dragon of the Southern Sentinel's Watch, Fire Dragon, a winged dragon.
- Tai Deren—Guardian Dragon of the Northern Sentinel's Watch, Earth Dragon, a winged dragon.
- Tianmi DeHuo—HuoJi's dame and Quang HuoYan's mate, Fire Dragon, a winged dragon.
- HuoJi—Offspring of Quang and Tianmi, Fire Dragon, a winged dragon.
- YuLong—The old one, an Imperial long-dragon slumbering in Deep Time guarding The-Sleeping-City . He is also Keeper of the Flaming Pearl of Wisdom.
- Jade Queen—YunFei is the one who delves into dark sorcery known as the Baneful Chaos. She was YuLong's mate, who cursed her with Malison-of-Crystal-Awareness.
- YueLiang Nushen—The Star Dragon Moon Goddess, Guardian of the Void and the Lunar Sentinel's Watch, the one and only source-dragon. She sleeps in deep time on the Riven Moon.

~ The NuliZhu Aliens ~

- Lord Amenakh—Ship's Lord, or Captain, of the Ophois Asenath spacecraft-carrier. He is an anubisen or jackal-head.
- Khutenptah—The Mighty Vizier, cousin to the Pharoah Harema Ket the Third. Khutenptah is the slaving expedition's sponsor and is a NuliZhu, long-headed humanoid.
- Sethnakhtei—Dreaded Holy One, the Sem Priest of Ra is an ascetic and fanatic of the Holy Order of Ra, and also a NuliZhu long-headed humanoid.
- Sitkamose—A fire control technician, in charge of the weapons control aboard the Asenath, an anubisen or jackal-head,
- Nakhtmin—Commander of the spacecraft saucer-destroyer YuanFen, a lion-headed sekhmeten.
- Anubisen—Jackal-headed, genetically modified soldier (genmosol). Third down in the tiered subcaste system of genetically designed warriors.
- Sekmeten—Lion-headed genmosol, fourth down from the top of the tiered subcaste system of of genetically designed warriors.
- Sobeksen—A croc-headed genmosol at the bottom of the tiered subcaste system. Well known for their vengeful and bellicose nature, making them excellent shock troops as their true purpose when properly assigned.
- NuliZhu Tech-Masters—Also known as power-masters, they originally forced the Dragons of Janaidar to help them build the WuShi and Plaza of the Forbidden Gate, then enslaved peoples from every race of ordinary humans on Olde Aerthe over 5000-years ago.

~ The JishuYan Technisans ~

- The JishuYan are the descendants of the Earthlings enslaved by the NuliZhu over 5,000-years ago, abducted to planet Janaidar (in a sidereal dimension), then subsumed by the Galactic Empire of Ta Shemau where they were subjected to a program of selective breeding. Eventually, they became a galaxywide caste of technician's, who operate everything in the Empire of Ta Shemau both civilian and military.
- The JishuYan also build and operate the great planetary industrial complexes and planetary mines throughout the Galactic Empire of Ta Shemau.
- The JishuYan are the finest technicians in the entire multiverse, and comprise the greater segment of the Ophois Asenath spacecraft-carrier's complement making everything work, including: engines, propulsion and maneuvering; heating, ventilation, and air-conditioning; plumbing, sewer and water purification systems; weapons systems; and gravity-generators; as well as all maintenance and janitorial functions including firefighting.
- Remy—Ship's Maintenance Senior Officer (SMSO) aboard the NuliZhu ancient space carrier Ophois Asenath. From the Shipwide-Operations-Center (SOC) she manages all the technisans.
- Mernebtah—Part of Genubeth and Remy's crèche.
- Genubeth—Cargo and Manifest Officer, like all technisans he wears Hathor's Crown.
- Djedhor—SMSO of the YuanFen spacecraft used as a planetary slave-raiding ship.
- Tjuyu—Ship's Maintenance Junior Officer for the Ophois Asenath.